CU00919448

HAWKS MC: VOLUME #1
Ballarat Charter

HOLDING OUT
CLIMBING OUT
FINDING OUT

Hawks MC: Ballarat Charter: Volume One
Copyright © 2017 by Lila Rose

Holding Out © 2014 by Lila Rose
Climbing Out © 2014 by Lila Rose
Finding Out © 2014 by Lila Rose

Editing: Hot Tree Editing
Interior Design: Rogena Mitchell-Jones

All rights reserved. No part of this eBook or book may be used or reproduced in any written, electronic, recording, or photocopying without the permission from the author as allowed under the terms and conditions under which it was purchased or as strictly permitted by applicable copyright law. Any unauthorized distribution, circulation or use of this text may be a direct infringement of the author's rights, and those responsible may be liable in law accordingly. Thank you for respecting the work of this author.

Hawks MC: Ballarat Charter: Volume One is a work of fiction. All names, characters, events and places found in this book are either from the author's imagination or used fictitiously. Any similarity to actual events, locations, organizations, or persons live or dead is entirely coincidental and not intended by the author.

Second Edition 2019
ISBN: 978-0648481621

HOLDING OUT

BALLARAT CHARTER

LILA ROSE

Holding Out Copyright © 2015 by Lila Rose

Hawks MC: Ballarat Charter: Book 1

Editing: Hot Tree Editing
Interior Design: Rogena Mitchell-Jones

All rights reserved. No part of this paperback may be used or reproduced in any written, electronic, recorded, or photocopied format without the permission from the author as allowed under the terms and conditions with which it was purchased or as strictly permitted by applicable copyright law. Any unauthorised distribution, circulation or use of this text may be a direct infringement of the author's rights, and those responsible may be liable in law accordingly. Thank you for respecting the work of this author.

Holding Out is a work of fiction. All names, characters, events and places found in this book are either from the author's imagination or used fictitiously. Any similarity to persons live or dead, actual events, locations, or organizations is entirely coincidental and not intended by the author.

Fourth Edition 2019
ISBN: 978-0648481607

CHAPTER ONE

WITH A BLOODY NOSE AND LEGS, a split lip and wild tremor going through my body, I picked up the phone and called the one person I knew would help me. "Hey, wench, you never call from the house phone... what's wrong?" My best friend's voice had started out happy, then suddenly taken on the edge of panic.

"I-I, Dee, I need your help," I whispered and looked over my shoulder to my passed-out husband on the bed.

On the bed where he had just beaten and raped me.

Yes, we were married; still, no meant no. Cries of pain meant something was wrong. Screaming meant that the one who caused it should stop.

But he didn't.

My husband invaded my body and mind, ruining me in so many ways. I wanted him to pay for what he did. I wanted him to hurt.

But I was scared, and I only saw one way out of it all.

To run.

"I'm coming, Zara," Deanna uttered into the phone and then hung up.

Knowing my husband was so high and drunk that he wouldn't wake, even if the house exploded around him, I started to pack.

Deanna must have heard the urgency in my voice; the journey that would usually take half an hour only took her fifteen minutes. My husband knew nothing of Deanna, and I was glad I'd kept it that way. He hated me having friends; he hated me doing a lot of things, and stupidly I had listened to him at the start. Because back then he was different, he showed me the world and told me that he and I were going to shine through it all.

It took him a year to change, to become his true self, a man I would never have married if I had known how cruel he was. He liked things his way or no way at all.

Deanna came running into the bedroom; I had given her a key months ago, worried something like this would happen. She looked from me to the bed.

"That motherfucker." Her hand went behind her and when she pulled it back around it held a gun.

"No," I cried, my hand going around her wrist as she pointed it at David.

Deanna turned her hard gaze to me. "Look at what he did to you, hun. He—"

"Please, Dee. Please understand I don't want his death on my conscience. He will be more hurt and pissed if we let him be and he wakes finding me gone. I need to get out of here, honey. I need to find a place where he can't find me."

"I want to hurt him, Zara. I want to gut the fucking pig." Tears filled her eyes as she noticed the blood running down my thighs from under my short nightie.

A sob tore through me. "I want to make him pay in the worst way…and me leaving, escaping him when he thought I couldn't and wouldn't, will be my revenge. Please, please, hun."

"Jesus," she snapped, shaking off my hold on her arm and reaching for my cases. "Are you okay to walk?"

"Y-yes." I sent her a pathetic smile and started for the door.

I wouldn't look back. David was now a part of my past, and he deserved nothing from me from that day on. No thought, no tears...nothing.

Deanna was my guiding light. She had been since I met her at the library in our book group. From that night on she was more so. She took me from that house to hers; there she helped me clean up and after we started to make plans.

From her computer I emailed my parents, telling them I was now out from under David's thumb, but I needed time to make sure things would be safe for all of us. I couldn't and wouldn't risk my parents' or brother's lives going back to them. So I moved, with Deanna, to another state. It was there I found out David had left me with last parting gift...I was pregnant. And I would say gift, because when Maya was born my heart couldn't think of her as anything but special. She was my new world and I would do anything to keep her safe.

SIX YEARS LATER

I was enjoying the walk home in the afternoon sun. My boss had an assignment and she kindly gave me the rest of the day off. Maya, my six-year-old, was attending the school sleepover for her grade. So I picked myself up some chocolate, a DVD, a bottle of wine, and Chinese takeout for dinner. Even better, my best friend, Deanna was coming over later to help me make the most of my relaxing night in.

I rounded the corner to my street and froze. My annoying, but hot neighbour was standing out the front of my other neighbour's house talking to the Campbells' nineteen-year-old daughter, Karen. I hung my head, ready to stride past, humming a tune along the way to cover their voices. Still, her high cackle broke through, as irritating as always. I was close to freedom and just past them, deafening myself with my out-of-tune hum when someone grabbed my arm and spun me back around.

"Kitten," Talon said.

My eyes closed of their own accord to cherish the sound. It happened every time I heard his deep grumble of a voice.

"Uh, what? Oh, Talon?" I blushed and bit my bottom lip.

He laughed. "I asked where Maya was."

"Oh, um, she's at school. Her class is having a sleepover," I informed him. Though I didn't know why.

"Right. So...." he began but stopped to look into my shopping bags. "We're watching 27 Dresses, eating Chinese, and drinking wine. Sounds like a plan. What time do you want me to come over? I could bring dessert." He grinned mischievously.

I looked around him to Karen. She huffed something and stomped off. I then turned my gaze back to the hunk with his messy, needs-a-cut black hair and dark brown eyes.

I'd never forgotten the day I moved onto the street and into my three-bedroom weatherboard home two years ago and learned that I was living across the road from the local biker compound, with their head honcho right next door to me. I had just moved with Maya out of Deanna's house after being there for four years. I was feeling frightened and overwhelmed, as well as a little inebriated after having a few welcome-to-the-new-house drinks with Deanna. Deanna left and I was in bed, but Maya kept waking up from the loud music being played next door. After she drifted back to sleep for the third time, I went—armed with the confidence of the alcohol —next door, dressed in my pink nightie with a kitten on the front and combat boots. I banged on the door. A short, hairy guy opened it and raised his eyebrows at me.

"Who is the freaking owner of this place?" I demanded.

"Yo, boss," the man called over his shoulder.

And I swear my heart stopped when Talon walked his broad, muscular form my way dressed in jeans and a white tee with a leather vest hanging open over it. Everything but him faded into the background.

"Whadup, cupcake?" He leaned against the doorframe and crossed his arms over his chest.

My eyes closed. Until I remembered, I was there for a reason, and that reason was more important than Mr Hotness.

Upon opening them, I went straight into a glare that could scare most young children. His mouth twitched. "I just moved in next door. I thought 'wow, what a nice place to start anew! That was until your bloody stupid music started blasting on a freakin' Monday night. I have a daughter who is starting her new school tomorrow." I stepped up closer. "Turn down the music. *Now*," I hissed.

"Wow, boss, you have a fuckin' wildcat living next door," someone said from behind him. Manly chuckles began. I ignored the others and kept my glare on bossman.

"More like a wild kitten." He smiled, looking down at my nightie. "Don't worry, kitten. I'll turn down the music. But, it'll cost you."

I blanched and stepped back, all confidence gone. "Wh…what?"

The men laughed louder.

"Just one kiss, babe."

"Talon!" A woman growled from somewhere behind the laughing crowd.

"You're a… pig," I said and walked away. Not long after that, the music was turned down.

From that day on, no matter how many times I tried to dodge Talon Marcus, I still managed to bump into him and make a fool of myself—something that he greatly enjoyed. I could tell from his small teasing smirks or laughter at my expense because he knew what he did to me and my libido. He enjoyed playing games with me… and okay, sometimes I even enjoyed them, deep, deep down. Because every time something happened, he made me feel desired.

However, feeling *that* scared me, and in turn, caused me to become a chicken, so to avoid the man who invaded my dreams I spent a lot of time with my daughter at Deanna's.

An example of why I had to steer clear of such hotness was what happened four days ago. Maya was at Deanna's while I quickly ran home to do a few errands and clean the house without my daughter making more of a mess. I had just gotten out of my car when Talon magically appeared out of nowhere.

"Kitten." He smiled.

Upon opening my eyes, I squeaked, "Talon," and tried to walk around him. He wouldn't have it of course and stepped in front of me.

"What are you doin' tonight?" he asked, and I watched as his hands slowly rose to tuck my long wavy hair behind my shoulder. My eyes stayed glued to his hand as his fingers gently ran down my arm to my hand. There his fingers wrapped around mine and tugged.

"Kitten," he chuckled.

Shaking my head, I looked up and glared at the bad, bad biker man.

God, he loved playing with me.

Still, even though my body loved to be played with, I was no longer that woman.

The woman who risked.

And it was a guess, but I was sure it was a good guess that Talon Marcus, president of the Hawks Motorcycle Club, was one huge risk to my heart.

"I'm,"—I licked my dry lips, my eyes widening when his beautiful eyes watched my tongue—"I'm busy, um, it was, ah, really nice to see you, Talon, but I have to go," I blurted, and then to my… disgrace, practically ran to my front door with his deep chuckle following me.

As soon as I was inside my door, I closed it quickly and leaned against it, my breathing erratic. In the last six months I had frequently seen Talon popping up out of nowhere wanting to talk to me, to ask me what my plans were, and every time I acted like a freaked-out teen whose boy crush had just spoken to her.

No matter how my body wanted to jump his bones and get jiggy with him, my mind stayed strong and reminded myself that a relationship came with too much trouble.

At least that was what I kept telling myself.

"Zara?"

I blinked back into the now and answered, "I—ah. No, I don't think. I mean, I'm not good company, and I have a friend coming over—"

"That's fine, just means we'll have to be quick." He winked.

Rolling my eyes, I walked off, but not before he slapped me on the behind and then strode past me laughing.

I grumbled under my breath all the way up the steps, ignoring the other bikers across the road at the compound laughing, yet again, at me.

Two hours later, I'd had a bath and gotten into my pink-with-black-kittens flannel PJs. Deanna texted an hour ago saying, *Hey, twat head. Not sure if I can make it. I'll let you know.*

So I sat down at my small, four-seater wooden table by the kitchen's large bay windows to eat my reheated Chinese. I had always found that Chinese tasted better when reheated.

Only then the doorbell sang. *Maybe Deanna made it after all.* I walked through my small lounge, which was furnished with a floral couch and one chair. A television sat on a long black unit against the wall, and a wooden chest acted as a coffee table in the centre. Nothing matched and that was the way I liked it. I'd saved and bought all of it myself, so I loved every piece of furniture in my house. I smiled before opening the front door.

"Kitten," Talon said as he looked at me from top to bottom. With a grin, he moved fast, because the next thing I knew, he was kissing me. My eyes sprang wide when his hot mouth touched mine.

"Talon," I mumbled around his lips, trying to shove him back.

Unfortunately, well, not really, but still, yes unfortunately, when I spoke it gave Talon's tongue the chance to sneak in. As soon as it hit mine, I melted on a moan of abso-freakin'-lute pleasure. My abdomen clenched and my nether region quivered. I wrapped my arms around his neck and gave back as good as I was getting. In return, I received a groan. He picked me up, stepped inside, and kicked the front door closed behind him.

Holy crap, Talon's kissing me. ME. God, he is good. Wait, why is he kissing me? ME?

"Hot damn. I need some popcorn for this," I heard my best friend say.

I pulled away. My arms dropped to my sides, and he let me take a step back. Both of us were breathing hard. I took another step back, looked over Talon's shoulder, and found Deanna, smiling hugely, standing in the doorway with her hand still on the doorknob.

"Girl, you said he was fine, but you didn't say he was fucking F.I.N.E."

Talon raised his eyebrows at me and turned to face Deanna, in all his tight jeans and white tee glory.

"I-I've never said anything," I muttered.

"Hey, Talon. I'm Deanna, Zara's best mate. I've been waiting for a glance of you for two fucking years. Oh, and I'm the one who will whip out some whoop-ass on you if you fuck her over, biker dude or not," she said in a pleasant tone, and then smiled sweetly.

Talon surprisingly didn't laugh. He looked her over and looked back at me. I knew what was running through his mind. Deanna and I were complete opposites. I was on the short side, had curves and lightly tanned skin from my Mexican background. I was sure Talon had the same sort of mix in his blood, only his skin was a little more like cocoa with a dollop of milk.

I had long, wavy, dark brown hair, and dark, forest-green eyes. Deanna was tall, thin, and was lucky enough to have been bestowed with a great rack. She had blonde hair, sky-blue eyes, and freckles on her nose to make her look that much cuter. She also had a big case of attitude. Though, it was all a front, of course. We'd both been through our own personal hell. We were just lucky to have found each other at the end.

"Nice to meet you, Deanna, and you have nothing to worry about," Talon replied.

What does that mean?

Deanna glared at him for a moment and then smiled. I felt, for a second, a pang of jealousy. Her smile had been the end of many men over the years, and right now, in her black pants and hugging tee that read 'watch 'em bounce' she looked great.

"I better not. Alrighty, wait till I get some popcorn and you two can continue what you were doing." She clapped her hands together.

"Uh, no. We can't. That—nuh-uh,"—I shook my head—"shouldn't have happened." My mind was in a whirl of thoughts.

Talon turned to me and said calmly, "It's been a hell of a long time coming."

"Wh-what?" I shook my head again.

"Come on, Zara, give the shmuck a chance. Then at least if it doesn't work out, I get to kick his bad-boy biker arse. A cute one at that; right again, lovey." She nodded at me.

I glared at my *ex*-best friend. "I have never said anything about his behind. Deanna, a word in the kitchen." I gestured with my head. Then I looked at Talon. "Uh, maybe you should go."

"I think I'll stay, kitten." He grinned and made his way to the couch. He sat down and propped his feet up on my chest—the wooden one—and turned on the TV.

I pulled the smiling Deanna down the hall, into my bedroom, and closed the door. Then I frantically got changed into jeans and a tee. Talon had already seen me in my PJs once, and that was once too many.

I spun to Deanna, put my hands on my hips, and glowered at her as she sat on my bed grinning.

"Oh, don't start. You need to live a little, girl. And I think biker boy can help you along the way."

"Deanna," I hissed. "I see nothing but danger with him around; and for God's sake, I am nowhere near his type. Look at me," I said, waving my hands up and down my body.

"And?" Deanna asked while looking at me like I was a loon.

"I have hips, I have a pudding belly, and I have dark brown hair. Not blonde and skinny, like he's always with, and have seen leave his place, and... Jesus, what the hell am I explaining myself for? There's danger all around him. Danger, Deanna. I can't go back to that. You'd have a better chance with him. Not that I want one."

She ignored my last statement. "You sound like that fucked-up robot off... shit, what's that show you like?"

"*Lost in Space.*"

"That's it." She took a deep breath. "Zee, hun, you don't know that. Sure he's a badarse, but he ain't nothing like that other jerk-off. Nothing."

I threw my hands up in the air. "*You* don't know that. I have to think of Maya. She's my number-one priority."

"What about you, though? When will you let yourself be happy?"

"I'll wait till Maya's twenty. Then I can think about myself," I said, and crossed my arms over my chest.

"I bet—" Deanna was cut off by a knock on the front door.

I looked at Deanna and raised my eyebrows. I didn't know why, maybe I thought she magically knew who was at the front door. She shrugged, and then we both heard Talon growl, "Who the fuck are you?"

We bolted from my bedroom and ran down the hall. Coming into the living room, I focused on who was at the front door.

Oh, hell.

"Um, hi, Michael." I waved over Talon's shoulder because he hadn't moved from the doorway. He still held the door with one hand, as if he were ready to shut it on Maya's teacher from last year's face.

"Hi, Zara." Michael smiled.

"What are you doing here?" I asked, and tried to open the door wider to get it from Talon's grip. But he wouldn't budge, so I gave up.

Michael produced a bunch of wildflowers from behind his back. "I saw these and thought of you."

"She doesn't want them," Talon said.

"Talon!" I scolded.

"And who are you?" Michael asked.

"Her man."

I coughed and sputtered. "Ah, no you're not."

"Hot damn," I heard in the background from Deanna.

"Yes. I am." He turned to me, his form blocking my view of outside and Michael.

I put my hands on my hips. "Since when?" I glared.

"Kitten." He smiled. "Since I stuck my tongue down your throat and you curled your body around mine, moaning for more."

I was sure my eyes popped out of my head and walked off, then skipped with my heart down the path.

"Hot-double-damn!" Deanna laughed. "You'll have to give her a minute. Sorry, Mike. I think you're about ten seconds too late."

Talon shut the door in his face, which broke me out of my trance.

"Goddamn it, Talon. That was rude. And I am not your woman!" I opened the door and stomped down the front steps after a retreating Michael.

"Michael, I'm so sorry about that Neanderthal. That was very sweet of you to bring me flowers." Though, I didn't understand why since I'd told him "no" fifty times already when he'd asked me out.

"Don't ever do it again," Talon warned from the front porch.

I glared up at him. He winked and smiled down at me.

"I can see I've come at the wrong time. Maybe I should come back?" Michael asked.

"Uh…" was my response.

"No," came from Talon.

"I wouldn't bother," from Deanna.

I turned to them and sliced across my neck with my finger. Really, I was prepared to kill the both of them.

Spinning back to Michael, I smiled. "I'm sorry, Michael, but right now, at this time, I'm not ready for anything—"

A scoff came from Talon.

I continued, "The thought was very sweet, and I think you're a great guy—" God, I hated doing this; I always felt bad. Especially with a guy who was still holding flowers for me. "And you never know, maybe in the future—"

"Try never," Talon growled.

"Ever." Deanna giggled.

I winced. What was with the running commentary from the loco-train people? "Sorry, Michael."

"That's okay, Zara. I'll come back in a couple of weeks, see how things are."

I stopped myself from rolling my eyes. *Is that the future?*

"You come back, I'll kill you." Talon started moving from the front porch toward us. I quickly ushered Michael out the front gate and closed it.

"Everything okay, boss?" Griz asked. Griz was short for Grizzly, his biker nickname because he was built like a bear, in a cuddly sort of way. Not that he had a belly; he didn't. He was just tall, with very wide shoulders, arms, and legs. Griz was stalking across the street toward us. Two others, whom I hadn't met, were standing on the other side of the road, legs apart, arms folded across their chests, looking menacing. I'd only met Griz because he helped me one day when I was attacking my lawn mower with a sledgehammer when it wouldn't start. He'd jogged across with an amused expression and asked, "Can I help, lady?" I let him, of course, or I'd be in jail right now for murder. I would have found a gun somehow.

I saw Michael studying Griz who was in his full motorcycle ensemble, including his black leather vest with a Hawks patch sewn onto it, their club's name.

"Y-y-you're a member of Hawks," Michael stuttered.

Griz stopped beside Michael and stared down at him. "Yeah, what of it?" he snapped.

"N-nothing." Michael turned back to Talon. "He, he called you 'boss.'"

Talon grinned his wicked grin and I grabbed the fence for support as Talon said, "Heard that, did ya?"

"Um." He looked to the ground. "Zara, I don't think I'll be back. Bye." He quickly marched off to his car. I was surprised his car didn't fly off, squealing down the road.

Deanna burst out laughing and walked toward us.

I sighed and ignored Talon's presence beside me. Instead, I turned my attention to Griz. "Hi, Griz. How's things?" He looked from me to Talon and then back.

"Great, Wildcat, and you?" He smirked. Wildcat had become my nickname from all the bikers since that first night. For some strange reason, no one else was allowed to call me kitten except Talon.

"Fine." I rolled my eyes and watched as the other two bikers disappeared into the compound.

"Now that's what I call entertaining. Girl, I gotta come to your house more often." Deanna grinned.

"Deanna, I think from now on I'm going to be a regular visitor at *your* place." *Just like I have been.*

"Kitten—" Talon began with a tone of warning.

"Pfft. Don't you 'kitten' me," I said with my back to him. He slipped his arms around my waist and pulled me close against his front. I held off a sigh of pleasure and tried to move away. It was impossible. I looked over my shoulder at him and bit my tongue to hold the moan. He looked gorgeous, even though his eyes told me he was annoyed. Still, they were laced with a little bit of lust as well.

Griz laughed but covered it with a cough when Talon glared at him.

"Oh, girly, we need to celebrate this. Let's get drunk," Deanna said. "Lord knows I need it."

I doubted I was supposed to hear that. I looked over at her and knew she was hiding something from me, but what was the mystery?

"And what are we celebrating exactly?"

"You and Talon gettin' it on." She gave me the *duh* look.

I went to move again but didn't get anywhere. "Uh, no. There is no Talon and Zara."

"Uh-huh." She smiled and looked at us from top to bottom. Okay, so to some it could seem different. Because I may have relaxed against Talon's warm, hot weight and my arms may be... okay, were resting on top of his, which were still wrapped around my waist.

Holy crap, I'm in Talon's arms.

He moved an arm from around me and swept my hair aside, then kissed my neck, which involuntarily arched so he could have better access.

Holy cow, Talon's kissing my neck. In front of people.

That didn't help my side of things. I nudged his head away with my own, and with some force, wiggled my way from his—wanted... so much needed...No!—unwanted and unneeded comfort.

I made my escape to Deanna's side.

Oh, my God, is my breathing heavy again? Yes, yes it is. Damn him and his sinful body.

"You"—I pointed my finger at him and glared—"stay over there. This"—I gestured between the two of us—"can't happen."

Deanna scoffed. Griz laughed.

"Kitten, I know you want me. Your body doesn't lie. It's only a matter of time before I'll be in your pants..." He trailed off as Griz's phone rang.

Griz flipped it open. "Yo? Yep." He closed it and looked at Talon. "Business, boss. Later, ladies."

"Bye, Griz." I smiled. It wasn't his fault his boss was a chauvinist arse-hat.

"See ya, hot stuff," Deanna purred, causing Griz to look over his shoulder, confused. He didn't understand that Deanna was attracted to older men, and Griz was definitely older. Deanna and I both sat at twenty-six. My guess, Talon was mid-to-late thirties, and Griz, with his long, muddy-brown-with-grey hair, and hard-aged eyes seemed to be hitting early forties.

"Kitten, I have to go. But if you two are having drinks, why don't you come by the compound later. I'll have a couple with you." With that, he grabbed my chin, kissed me hard and quickly, before my knee had the chance to hit his groin, and left.

Of course, I watched his fine arse walk away, and I was sure he knew it.

"Yeah, you keep fighting that, hun." Deanna laughed and walked into the house.

CHAPTER TWO

I FOLLOWED Deanna back inside and reheated my Chinese, again.

Who did he think he was informing people he was 'my man'? Yeah, right! And why would he want me? He wasn't making sense.

This has been a long time coming. My arse it had. I couldn't recall how many times I'd avoided him for that reason alone. I was not some conquer-and-move-on type of girl if that was what he thought. And that was exactly what he'd want. I'd lost count of how many women I'd seen leave his place in the early hours of the morning. All blonde, I might add.

Though… it had been a while since the last one. Still, that didn't matter. The man was a tart when it came to women.

Urrh! I just wanted to scream.

"You're thinking too hard. Here, drink this," Deanna said and placed a glass of wine in front of me.

I turned a glare on her as she sat across the table from me and continued to roll her food around her plate.

I tipped my head to the side to study her. She'd never played with her food before. Usually, she'd have it gone in a second. And she never put on weight. *Bitch.*

"Stop lookin' at me like that. I will not fuck you, no matter how much you beg."

I snorted. God, I loved her. She was the only one who'd kept me somewhat sane through my two years of hell with David. I prayed every day he wouldn't know where to start looking to find me. I hadn't seen him in almost six years. So, my guess was we were just too good at disappearing a state away to the small town of Ballarat, where Deanna's other house was, or something had delayed his search for me. His business always did come first.

Still, I knew he would be looking for me eventually, because he didn't like to let go of possessions, and I was one. I'd hate to think where I would be, what I'd have put Maya through if I were still there. Deanna meant more to me than she could ever know. Which was why I was worried about her now.

"Tell me what's going on."

"Nothin'," she clipped and took a sip of her wine. A second later, she drained the rest of her glass. One problem with Deanna was that she was as stubborn as a mule. If she weren't ready to talk about what was obviously on her mind, she wouldn't, leaving me to be the stress-head that I was and fret about it.

"Let's talk about Talon." She grinned.

"Let's not and have a drink instead," I said, and then drained my glass.

"I'll drink to that." She moved from the table to grab the bottle of wine but turned back around. "We're gonna need more than this. Where's your stash, woman?"

It was my turn to grin. She knew me too well. "The bourbon is in the laundry room, top cupboard." I needed something on those nights when I was about ready to hog-tie my brat of a child to her bed. Which I was sure every parrrenttt felt at one point in time or more.

A COUPLE OF HOURS LATER, I was feeling fabulous. We were dancing around the living room to Pink's "Fun House." Nothing was bothering me, and I could see that Deanna was having just as much fun as I was.

Then Deanna dumped her skinny behind on the couch, grabbed the remote, and turned down the tunes. At first, I was going to complain, but then I realised I was the verge of peeing myself.

"If you could be any superhero, who would you choose?" I called from the bathroom down the hall.

"What the fuck did you just say?"

Okay, so maybe it didn't come out like I thought it had. It could have sounded something like, "You be suuperaro what you chooose?"

"Ya heard me," I said while washing my hands.

"I think it's cut-off time, cocksucker."

I met Deanna in the kitchen, where she handed me a glass of water, and I drank every drop.

"I'd be Batgirl."

"Hah, knew'd ya heard. Me be..."

"Wonder Wanker."

I sprayed my second glass of water all over the floor, choked on my laughter, and gasped for air.

As I cleared my throat, a thought popped into my head, so I had to share it. "Oh, oh, I have one for Talon. Perfect Pecker Man." We both cracked up. Not that I'd seen his pecker, but I was sure it would be perfect.

Two more glasses of water later, and many more made-up hero names, I still felt a little foggy, but at least my speech had improved. Well, I thought it had.

"Man, I'm so glad I came over here tonight," Deanna said. Then there was a knock at the front door.

"You've still got time to take it back. Who the heck is that?"

"How many times do I have to tell you I can't see through things?" Deanna teased as she followed me to the front door.

Deanna started bouncing from one foot to the other. I asked, "Do you have to pee? Or are you having one of those spontaneous orgasms you keep telling me about that I don't believe in?"

"No, no. None of that, and it is true, jealous whore, happened a couple of times anyway. But I just have a thought on who it'd be. Come on, open the fucker. I need some excitement."

I had a feeling too, but I hoped it wasn't. Me, plus drinks, plus Talon equalled something that should not be mixed.

Unlocking the door and swinging it open, I realised I should have hoped a little harder. Talon stood there looking spunky in dark jeans, a black tee, and motorcycle boots. His hair looked wet from a recent shower, and I wondered if I could blow-dry it for him with my mouth. My traitorous heart leaped, my body tingled, and…what the frig? How'd my underwear get wet already? Wait, had I peed myself? I looked down at the floor. Nope, wasn't wet.

That meant only one thing. "I need to get laid or break out my Gold Finger on maximum speed."

Deanna burst out laughing, and Talon seemed smug. I looked at them both, confused. *Oh, hell no.* I did not just say that aloud. See! Drinks, Talon, and me. It was a no-go!

"I could be of some help, kitten. In either way," he purred.

Or was that me purring?

I closed my eyes. My head fell forward, and I shook it from side to side. I was ready to die.

Deanna was going to be of no assistance; she was rolling around on the floor still laughing, so I asked, "Did you come over for a reason, Talon?"

"You're supposed to be at the compound, drinking."

I glanced up with my head cocked to the side. "What?"

He stepped closer. "Drinking. Compound. Now."

Straightening up, I glared and informed him, "No."

He took one step closer again, so he was flush against me. "What?"

"Did. I. Stutter?"

Something flared in his eyes, while something flared in my womb. Trouble was a-comin'. Talon bent his upper body level with my belly, and then he leaned in so I was flopped over his shoulder.

"Go, PP Man," Deanna shouted. She got up from the floor and followed Talon like a trained horny dog, out the front door and down the path. Thankfully, she had enough sense to shut the door behind us.

"Shut up." I glared at Deanna. "Talon... Talon put me down, now!" I ordered.

We'd made it to the gate when I heard new movement. Talon placed on my feet and pushed me behind him.

"Who the fuck are you?" he growled, and then looked over his shoulder. "Don't tell me you have another admirer."

"Um."

"Um? How fuckin' many do you have?"

"Um."

"Jesus Christ." His attention went back to the new arrival. "Again, who the fuck are you?"

"Zara?"

I gasped. I hadn't heard that voice in many years. "Mattie?" I looked over Talon's shoulder to see my now twenty-year-old brother, Matthew Alexander.

"Mattie," I cried, and flung myself at him. He wrapped me up in his arms and held on tightly. Though, it wasn't tight enough, because the next thing I knew, I was pulled away.

I glanced up and around to see Talon's fierce glare at my brother. I patted his hand at my waist. "It's fine; he's my brother."

"What's he doin' here? I haven't seen him before."

That was true. I looked back at my brother, and that was when I really took in what was in front of me. Instead of the free, fun-loving brother I was used to seeing in my mind, I saw a dirty, tired, worried and sad one. How had he found me? I left my family behind to keep them safe.

I stepped back farther into Talon's arms. "What's happened?" His face saddened in a way I didn't think was possible. "No, no. Don't tell me. I can't...no."

"They're dead, Zee."

"No!" If it weren't for Talon holding me, I would have crumpled to the ground. Deanna came to my side and grabbed my hand.

It couldn't be true. I'd only just finished planning a trip to meet my parents in Melbourne. They were to meet Maya for the first time. They were excited; I could see how much through the emails I'd sent them and Skyping with them.

I was excited.

Oh, God.

"It was a car accident. They say it was a freak accident."

My body shook; I felt cold and empty, I looked through my teary eyes. "Y-you don't believe that."

He shook his head.

Shit! It was him. I just knew it. It was David.

Snapping my emotions off, I stood tall. I had to go. Get away. Maya needed to be safe. She was what was most important.

Everything else could wait. My pain and heartache could wait... it had to wait. I needed Maya safe.

"Zee?" Deanna whispered. She knew what I was thinking.

I pushed away from Talon and started back to my house. I spun around to see the three of them following me. My gaze flicked across Talon on the phone and Deanna's worried look, until I settled on my brother.

Clearing my throat, I asked, "Were you followed?" He was unsure; I could see it. "Fuck, Mattie, were you followed?"

"I don't know." He looked at the ground. "I don't think so. I was careful, Zee."

Fuck! I couldn't risk it. I couldn't.

"Kitten."

Even when everything inside of me screamed to cry, to mourn for my beautiful parents, I didn't. I wanted to, I so wanted to, but I didn't. Stomping up the front steps, I flung the door open. I went to the kitchen and grabbed garbage bags, walked to the living room, and started bagging some of Maya's toys from her bin in the corner while wiping away the tears still falling; they just wouldn't listen to me when I said stop.

"Kitten?"

"I have to go," I uttered. "I have to get out of here. Shit, Maya's at school for her sleepover. That's all right; I'll get her. Mattie, you'll come with me. I can't lose you too—" I broke off on a sob. "How did you find me, Mattie?" I glanced over my shoulder to see him staring at me in shock and pain.

He shook his head. "You told mum the address." My eyes widened. Mattie went on, "No, she never wrote it down as you instructed. But she ended up telling me in case anything... happened to them."

There was a knock at the door. I screamed and dove for the couch. "Get down, get down," I whisper-yelled to Deanna and Mattie.

"Kitten, it's for me," Talon said and answered the door to Griz and three other bikers. They walked in, stopped, and closed the door. They took in what surrounded them and then focused on Talon, waiting. For what, I wasn't sure.

"I have to go," I whispered. I wanted to get up, pack the rest of my stuff, and flee into the night. But something held me there; my mind was reeling with unwanted thoughts. I was scared. So scared and hurting. My chest wouldn't stop aching.

"My parents are dead."

Mattie and Deanna moved toward me. I saw tears in Deanna's eyes. She never got teary. She was tough. Before they could get to me though, Talon moved in their way and knelt in front of me.

"Kitten. I'm sorry."

"Don't say that," I snapped. "You never met them. You could have, maybe one day... but now... I have to go. I have to move before *he* finds me." With a shaky hand, I reached out to his face and ran the back of my fingers over his unshaven cheek. "I'll miss you. I think. No, I will. We won't get to… you know. I think I would have enjoyed it." God, what was I saying?

Soft laughter started behind me.

Talon smiled. God, he was hot. "There's no thinkin' there, kitten. I'll rock your world."

"Maybe so. But not now, because I have to go." More tears fell from my eyes. My heart clenched tightly. "They're gone, Talon."

"I know, sweetheart."

"I have to go."

"You aren't fucking moving," Deanna shouted.

Suddenly, I found myself standing with my hands on my hips, facing her. Deanna stood in the same position on the other side of the couch. Anger fuelled my words. Anger was better than pain. "I have to. You know this, Deanna. You, of all people, know this," I yelled.

"Blah fuckin' blah. You ain't movin'. If he comes, we'll take care of it. I'm sick of you being scared." She pointed at me. "I hate seeing you always checkin' your doors, always looking over your shoulder. You will never move on and root hot pecker boy there and live your fuckin' life so you can be happy." She took a deep breath. "I'm sick of our past shit catching up," she said.

"Screw you!" I screamed, but blanched, my hand going over my mouth. I had never screamed like that. I had never spoken like that to Deanna. I was losing it. But my apology was lost because next Deanna jumped over the couch and tackled me to the floor.

"Holy shit," I heard Mattie say.

While we rolled around, I kept trying to make my point, all sanity went when Deanna pulled my hair. "He'll come. He'll come and kill everyone I love. He'll take Maya and me away. We'll suffer for the rest of our lives."

"Not gonna fuckin' happen," Deanna hissed.

"Griz," Talon growled. Then I was lifted up and held against a muscular chest, as was Deanna, only she was struggling against Griz's grip on her. She didn't have a chance; and because she was pissed, she was missing out on the feel of Griz against her, which would probably piss her off even more.

"I will not let him hurt you. I'll kill him first," she said. "You know I will."

"I can't risk it, Deanna." I cried. "I'm more worried what he'll do to you, to Maya, Mattie and—" I looked over my shoulder at Talon, who seemed angry about something. "I won't let any harm come to any of you; and if *I* can stop that by leaving, I will do it."

"The fuck you will," she sneered.

"Yeah? I get it, Deanna. I get you're some tough bitch. You think you can take him, but I won't let you. I need you around. I care about you too much."

"Care on this." She gave me the finger.

"Screw. You. Again." I glared. God, were we acting like juvenile girls. Shame burned low in my belly, letting fear override any rational thoughts.

Deanna said nothing, but I saw in her eyes the same fear. We were *it* for each other, had been for so long. She didn't want to lose me like I didn't her.

"Holy fuck, boss! They're both wildcats," one guy said from near the door.

"Enough!" Talon snapped, and something in his tone made Deanna and me pause our argument. "Both of you shut the fuck up."

"Eat—" Deanna was about to swear until Griz placed his hand over her mouth and whispered something in her ear. Her eyes widened; he took his hand away and stepped back.

I turned in Talon's arms and glowered at him. "Don't you dare tell me to shut up."

"I will if you're an idiot."

I didn't like being called an idiot. It was too close to home. I had been an idiot staying with David. So, feeling fired with anger, I went to punch Talon; he dodged it and grabbed me around the waist, blocking my arms at my sides.

"Do that again, and there will be consequences."

"Yeah, like what?"

He moved his lips to my ear and whispered, "My tongue in your mouth; my hand down your pants in front of everyone, and still, you'll enjoy it."

I gulped. How was I contemplating what he said when only seconds ago I'd been upset, scared, angry, and annoyed.

He pulled back and looked down at my face. What he saw made him smile. "Yeah, just what I thought." He pointed to the couch. "Now sit the fuck down, both of you, and start explaining."

My brain must have shut down, I sat and listened to him without saying anything back.

CHAPTER THREE

Damn him and his hot bossy words.

Was he right? Had this—us—been a long time coming? All those morning glances, teasing words and flaming wild wet dreams.

I guess it had. But the thing was—it was too late. Now I had to leave, to stay safe and keep others protected.

Which, at the end of it all, could be good for me, as it'd also keep my heart in one piece.

I wanted to hurl, to chuck my guts up. I wanted to cry, scream, and have sex.

Wait, what?

Could anyone make sense of that? Because I couldn't.

My heart and stomach clenched.

Oh, God...my parents.

Maya.

Deanna.

Mattie.

Smoking hot Talon

I placed my head in my hands and shook it. What was wrong with me? Why was I also thinking of Talon when my heart felt as though it'd been torn from my body with thoughts of my parents?

Maybe I was losing my ever-loving mind. I was no longer sane. Yes, that had to be it. Well, it was either that, or I was dreaming. If so, what a stuffed-up dream!

"Kitten."

Nope. Not dreaming.

I peeked out of one eye, which brought me face to face with Talon's jean-clad perfect pecker.

Shit!

"You—" I sat up straight and pointed at him. "—you need to leave. You're a distraction, and I need to have a breakdown where I'll ugly cry, scream, and throw things." Or collapse in a heap and feel nothing but utter devastation.

Deanna snorted beside me. I'd forgotten she was there and that I had other company in the form of hot bikers.

"Kitten," Talon said again, with more of a growl.

Deanna sighed loudly and said, "Oh, for fuck's sake! Leave her alone. She's had some big shocks in such a small amount of time, and her pea brain is trying to handle it. Also, it doesn't help you standing there all manly, but whining at her like an old woman."

I loved Deanna!

So I told her just that. "I love you, Deanna."

She smiled. "Yeah, yeah. I'm all roses and chocolates and vibrators about you too, hun."

"Fuckin' hell. It's like talking to two deranged children." Talon glared at the both of us, causing laughter from the group near the front door.

"Hey," I snapped, a little late, even though I thought the same most times when Deanna and I got together.

"At least they're good-looking," one of the strippers commented —*bikers, Zara, bikers.*

I really must meet them all one day. Hold up—one day could never come. I sighed loudly to myself; at least I could be hospitable now.

I stood from the couch and faced them. "Sorry, guys. I should have asked this ages ago. Would anyone like a drink? Or, oh, what about a cookie? Everyone loves cookies. I can get more chairs too. I hate seeing people standing when I've been sitting my lard-arse down."

No one said anything; their gazes stayed fixed on Talon.

"We're fine."

I looked at Griz.

"Thanks," he added.

"Huh, I wouldn't have minded a cookie," the youngest and closest one uttered.

Well, at least I could make my brother more comfortable. I felt bad he'd been witness to all the craziness.

I turned to Mattie, who was sitting in a kitchen chair near the doorway, looking very confused, a little shocked, and a lot worried. "Mattie, what can I get you? You must be hungry? When was the last time you ate? I know, I can go set up the spare room bed."

Because it seems I won't be allowed to leave tonight.

Right! That was it. I stomped my foot because Mattie hadn't once looked at me; his gaze also fixed on Talon.

I spun back around to Talon. "You suck!" With my hands on my hips, I glared at him. My maturity had obviously left the building. Then again, I was sometimes a little different in the head than most.

He looked at the roof and sighed deeply. Probably praying for patience to deal with me. *Well, suffer in your tighty-whitey jocks, Talon.*

There was a knock at the door. A squeak escaped me and I went to dive for the couch, but a hand reached out and pulled me to a rock-solid body. Talon wrapped his arms around me and nodded to...

"Pick, open it," Talon ordered.

Pick, with the shaved head, goatee, and pale blue eyes nodded and turned to open the door.

I breathed a sigh of relief and unclenched my hands from Talon's black tee when I spotted Blue, the only other member I knew of Talon's men. He'd been kind enough to help me unload my car one day after I'd been crazy shopping with Deanna. He was the only other one I found it hard to not stare at. Anyone with a humming passage would cream their pants if Blue came at them with his big muscles, skintight shirts, black leather pants, and biker boots. To top the look off, he had longish blond hair, light green eyes, and a smile that made my panties want to fall off and follow him everywhere.

"What's doin', Blue?" Talon asked.

"Cody." That one word made Talon stiffen and suck in a breath.

A child around twelve with scruffy black hair and deep blue eyes popped his head around Blue and gave a wave. "Dad."

What. The. Heck?

"What's goin' on, Cody?"

"Mum's busy, so I came here. Not here, but to the compound, and Blue brought me here," he said in a whisper. He seemed really shy, averting his eyes from Talon to the floor and back again.

"Shit!" Talon spat.

"Hey." I slapped him on the stomach. "No swearing around kids. Hi, Cody." I waved, smiled and stepped around Talon. "I'm Zara. I live here with my six-year-old daughter, Maya. Only she's not home at the moment, but at her school for a sleepover."

Blue gently guided him farther into the house with a hand around the back of his neck, and then shut the door.

"Can I get you anything, sweetheart? Would you like a cookie? A drink—"

"A chair," Talon muttered. I glared over my shoulder at him as he smirked back. "We've been through this, kitten. No one wants anything."

I watched Cody's expression change from puzzled to shock in a second when Talon called me kitten.

"Shush, Talon. Stop being so dang bossy."

He laughed, wrapped his hand around my neck, and brought me nose-to-nose with him. "You know you like it," he growled.

I pushed at his chest. "Whatever." I sighed and rolled my eyes. *Yeah, all right. I kinda like it.*

"We have shit to talk about, kitten—"

"Damn, I mean dang it, Talon. Stop swearing."

"I've heard worse." That whisper came from Cody. It was then I realised Talon and I were having our conversation still with our noses touching. I whacked his hands away and turned back to Cody.

But then quickly spun back to Talon, and on my own growl, I said, "Yeah, mister. We do have things to talk about, and one would be why the frig I'm just finding out now you have a son."

Talon laughed and then whispered, "There are a lot of things we don't know about each other, kitten. I look forward to finding out *each* detail." He scanned my body from top to bottom.

I shook my head and felt the need to shake my soaking panties, but resisted and faced Cody once again.

Distractions were always good. It was what I needed right then. Something to keep my mind chugging along on a different lane. A lane where my world wasn't ending, where my parents were still alive, still happy.

"Now, where was I?" I asked. "Oh, yes. You may have heard worse, Cody, and if you hang out with Deanna for five seconds, I'm sure you'll learn way more than any child should." Laughter filled the room. "But the point is, sweetheart, in this house, there is no swearing from anyone!"

Well, when children are around, that is.

"Okay, ma'am."

Deanna burst out laughing.

"Cody, you can call me Zee. All my friends do."

He gave me a half smile and then stared at the floor.

Talon came to my side, one arm placed around my shoulders, and he leaned in and kissed my temple. "That'll do," he whispered, which sent shivers down my spine. And with the hand that left my shoulders, he patted my behind and walked to his son, replacing Blue's hand with his own.

"Kitten, I'll be back. Griz, stay here. Boys, with me, now." And with so many wonderful words—*not*—he walked to the front door, opened it, and left with all the boys but Griz.

"Bye, Cody. It was nice meeting you," I yelled before Blue winked at me and closed the door after him.

"Well, I'll be damned. What a fucked-up night," Deanna said as she stood from the couch and stretched. I caught Griz taking it all in, but when he saw me looking, he went into the kitchen.

"Come on, Mattie," Deanna said. "We'll sort out your bed in the spare room. And, Zee…" She came at me. I tensed, but she hugged me instead. "Get the fuck into bed, hun. You look awful. I'll be in soon."

I nodded against her shoulder. She knew me. She knew I wanted to crash and burn. I needed my breakdown, and she was giving me the opportunity for it. Before I did though, I walked over to a quiet Mattie and pulled him against me.

"I'm sorry. So, so sorry that it took this to bring us together again. I love you, Mattie, and I'm glad you're here."

"So am I, sis, and they would be too. They'd be happy, darl', to know you're being taken care of. Even if they are a bit full on."

I laughed on a sob, kissed his cheek, and walked off to my room.

With the door closed, and without undressing, I fell to my bed and cried my soul out. I let it all free from its dark deep place within me. I let the pain out, the deep grief of no longer having my crazy but loving parents on this earth. The loss I felt was overpowering. It hurt in so many places: my head, body, spirit, but most of all my heart. It ached in a way I didn't think I could get over, but I knew I had to because of my precious little girl. And my parents would know that, they would understand why I was giving myself just that night to mourn the loss of them. Come tomorrow, I had many things to do; first of all was to get Maya to safety.

SOMETIME LATER, I was still in shattered pieces when I heard the door open. I didn't bother looking up. I knew it would be Deanna. I heard shoes hit the floor, harder than Deanna would treat her precious pumps, but thought nothing of it until a solid, hard warmth hit my back. Unless Deanna had morphed into a male, it definitely wasn't her.

"Jesus, kitten. I'm sorry, Zara. I should have been back sooner." Talon's breath ran across my neck, and then he kissed it.

His sweetness made me want to cry harder. "D-don't. I can't handle you being n-nice. Be an arse, please."

He chuckled and pulled my back flush against his front. "All right, kitten. Wanna fuck?"

I snorted and wiped away my fallen tears. "Dick."

"Wench."

I sighed and snuggled in closer. "I'm scared, Talon." So very scared and hurt.

"I know. But, as words spoken from Deanna, you ain't fuckin' leavin'," he growled. "We'll get through this."

And that was what also scared me—the 'we'll' part. He'd placed himself in there with me. Was I ready for that? Hell no.

But as sleep started to take me, I felt protected.

"Keep your perfect pecker to yourself."

I heard another rumble of laughter before I drifted off.

CHAPTER FOUR

I DID NOT WANT to get up and face the day. Could it be possible that no one would notice my absence? Doubtful. I still had to get to work, pick Maya up, and fly the coop without any problems. Just the thought made me groan. I knew it wasn't going to be easy. Problems were bound to come my way.

Problem one, the most important one: the fact I had to bury the loss of my parents for now while I skipped town and got my daughter and brother to safety. My heart didn't want that. It still wanted to roll over and cry.

Problem two: whenever I closed my eyes, all I pictured was Talon in my bed. I turned my head to see that spot now empty. It was probably for the best. I wouldn't have been able to control myself as I had through the night. When I woke, and he was holding me tightly against him, other than feeling like I was being smothered, it felt nice. Then I realised where one of his hands was. Cupping my sex. Of course, I had to wriggle a little, only I shouldn't have because it sent a pulse of lust throughout my body and I so wanted to do it again. My first thought was maybe he wouldn't notice if I accidentally got *off* from his hand. I wiggled again, holding back my moan, and that was when his shiver-worthy voice rumbled at the back of my neck.

"If you do that again, you'll see how perfect my pecker is."

I froze and damned him into a coma so I could continue with his hand. Unfortunately, it didn't work; so then I contemplated the thought of just using him for the night, to forget, and because I wouldn't be around much longer.

"Stop fucking thinkin'. The noise your brain makes is keeping me awake."

I settled back with a loud sigh, just to annoy him. Fine, if he was going to be an arse, I was going to keep my wet tunnel away from him.

Double fine, if he was going to be an arse about it and not move his hand, I was going to ignore it and sleep.

And I did.

Eventually.

Problem three: the voice I heard rise down the end of the hall in the kitchen. Who Deanna was yelling at, I had yet to figure out. I could only hope it wasn't my brother. I was sure Deanna's foul mouth could just about scare Satan himself.

Problem four: my bladder was screaming at me to get out of bed and deal with it.

I got up, peed, had a shower, and dressed in jeans, a red sweater, socks, and with my hair still damp, I walked out of my room.

On the way down the hall, I paused to listen in on the conversation being held in the kitchen.

"You fuckin' mean she doesn't work for that law firm anymore?" Talon asked.

Deanna snorted and said, "Turn up your hearing aid, old man, and listen carefully. No, she doesn't work there no more."

"Where she at now?"

"At some PI place not far from here."

"Hell. Please don't tell me *We put the P in PI*?" he asked with disgust in his voice.

"Yeah, I think that's it. Like I said, she hasn't been there long, two weeks tops."

"Fuck!"

I heard a bark of laughter that didn't sound anything like Talon or Deanna, so I guessed Griz was still here.

What was the big problem with where I worked?

I found Violet, Chuck, and Warden great people to work with. It wasn't like I was doing any of the PI work. I was their secretary and that was it.

"Griz," Talon barked. *Ha, I'm right.* Griz's laughter died.

"Come on, boss. It'd have to be a co-winky-dink."

"I doubt it."

"A fuckin' what?" Deanna asked with a smile. I could hear it in her voice.

I peeked around the corner to see Griz stiffen and glare at her, and then he said, "A coincidence."

"Yeah, uh-huh." She raised one eyebrow.

For the first time, I turned my gaze to Talon, and I wished I hadn't.

He was leaning against the sink in jeans and—yes ladies, that was it! I got a full view of his stunning, bare...um, let's say feet. His chest wasn't that bad either. But what topped it off, what made me feel the need to fan my private area, again, was the tribal tattoo that covered his left shoulder, and then another tattoo on his right set of ribs of a fierce-looking dragon. Maybe I could haul him by the hair of his head to bed and have my wicked way with him.

Distractions were good.

No. That wasn't an option.

I had hoped to wake with no one to deal with, so then I'd have the chance to make a clean getaway. Of course, that would have been after I called work and explained that soon there'd be a madman after me, so I wouldn't be able to work there any longer because I'd be running for my life. Then I'd ask them if they wanted me to drop off some coffee and donuts on the way.

But no, yet another plan foiled.

Stupid, caring people.

Sighing, I stepped out from around the corner. "Morning all," I chirped and looked out the kitchen windows. "Oh, poop. It's drizzling outside." *Damn it, my stuff is going to get wet when transferring it from the house to the car.*

"Can't be helped," I added. "So, what's everyone doing today?" I asked while pouring myself a freshly brewed cup of coffee from the maker besides the sink.

"Either you did her last night and did her good, or she's high," Deanna said.

I wish. I could go for a bit of both.

"Deanna, hun. Whatever do you mean?" I turned to look at her.

"*Zee*, sweet chops, I know you."

"Huh? What's that got to do with anything? A-a-a-anyway, thanks for staying last night, but, uh, y'all better get going. Isn't there work to get to? And I got to get ready for mine. So, uh, thanks."

"And there we have our answer," Deanna said smugly, leaning back in her chair.

"What?" Talon asked. I still hadn't looked at him; my eyes stayed on Deanna or the floor.

"She wants us gone so she has the chance to run and hide with her head up her arse."

I stiffened, my cup half raised to my lips. Stuff Deanna and her knowing me too well.

Talon's head fell back, and he let out a deep rumble of laughter, sending goosebumps all over my body.

He shook his head and then looked at me...no, I should've said glared at me. Hoo boy.

He pushed away from the sink and slowly, sensually, moved toward me. He took my cup from my hands and placed it on the bench behind me. Which gave me a chance to draw in a good whiff of him, causing my body to respond.

My hands went to his chest; his went to my waist. I looked up at him.

"Let's get one thing straight right now, kitten." I nodded. "I won't have you runnin'. This is your fuckin' place; nothing is runnin' you off. I won't fuckin' let it. You get me, woman?" This time I shook my head. He sighed. "Even though my dick ain't been in you—yet—I still classed you mine once my mouth touched yours. You have my protection, kitten. My boys' protection. Nothin' is gonna fuckin' happen to you, Maya, or Hell Mouth there."

"Thanks," Deanna grinned.

Wow! What was I supposed to say to that? Was he like this for all his hoochie mamas? Not that I was his HM. We hadn't even slept together.

Still, no matter how his words made me feel, the urge to run and hide was stronger than anything else. Not only for my sake, but for Maya's, and to keep those who wanted to protect me safe.

"No."

His eyebrows rose. "What?" he said with a growl.

"I can't let you do that. I won't have any harm come to you and your boys because of me, and you can't ask that of them either. Promise, I'm really not that good of a lay."

He leaned his forehead against mine. "For fuck's sake, kitten." I could hear the smile in his voice.

"Too damned considerate," Deanna grumbled.

Griz stood abruptly. We all watched him leave the room and heard the front door slam seconds later.

"What's his problem?" Deanna asked.

"Nothin'," Talon said. He kissed me quickly—way too quickly if you asked me—stepped back, and said, "We got shit to talk about. Finish your coffee, babe, and then both of you get your arses in the living room." With that, he stalked out, down the hall, and no doubt into my room to use my en suite.

"I'm upset with you, bitch," Deanna said, crossing her arms over her chest.

"Yeah, well, I'm upset with you too, whore." I glared. "Why did you have to tell them what I was going to do?"

"'Cause I see the way PP man looks at you, and I knew he'd put a stop to your fucked-up plan." She got up from the table and came over. Deanna gently took my face between both her hands, holding my gaze with the strength of her own. "I can't lose you, woman. I'd be in a fuckin' mental home if it weren't for you. I need you to listen to me. You need to stay and fight. You have people willing to fight at your side with you, or for you for that fuckin' matter. Don't run. Please, please, don't run."

Tears formed in her eyes. I had never seen Deanna like this in all the years I'd known her.

I grabbed her in a tight hug, fighting my own tears. "Honey, you know that's not me. I can't have people fight my battles."

"We want to. If that's what'll keep you and Maya here, we will."

"I know *you* do. I know. And Talon, maybe. God only knows why. But Talon's boys?" I shook my head on her shoulder. "You know what dickface was like; if one of Talon's boys got hurt, or worse, because of me, I couldn't live with myself."

"Lounge, now," Talon's gruff voice ordered.

We pulled apart, wiping our faces, and saw Talon leaning against the doorframe. He had wet hair and wore jeans and a black tee. How long had he been there? I wasn't sure. But God almighty, he looked good enough to eat.

"I hate you," Deanna said to me before she left the room.

"And I hate you, too." I smiled at her back as I followed her into the lounge. Finally, I knew she understood.

We both sat on my couch. Talon grabbed a kitchen chair, dragging it in to sit opposite us across the wooden chest. The front door opened, scaring the crap out of me, nearly causing me to jump in Deanna's lap. Griz stomped back in, but it didn't stop there; about ten other bikers walked in behind him. They made themselves comfortable standing or sitting where they could, while Deanna and I stared with slack jaws.

What's going on?

"Man, I wish to fuck I had a shower now before this," Deanna grunted. I giggled. I would have felt the same way if I was still in the clothes I had on yesterday, and the massive bed hair she had going on. Still, she looked beautiful. The nut sucker.

"Kitten. Start explaining." It wasn't a question. It was an order.

"What? Now?"

He rolled his eyes. "Yes, now."

I looked around the room, wondering why Talon wanted me to tell my sob story in front of so many badarse bikers.

"*Kitten,*" Talon growled.

"All right, all right. You are damned bossy. Has anyone ever told you that?"

"All the time," he said. His boys laughed.

"Yeah, well, it'll only work on me so many times; in the end, you'll have no chance to get in my knickers." My hand flew to my mouth. I really just said that in front of people.

He smirked. The guys laughed again.

"I'm willing to think otherwise." He grinned, then it disappeared. "We don't have all day, babe. Some of us have to work."

I sat up straighter. "Speaking of which, I've got to call my boss. She'll be wondering where I am."

"Already done," Deanna said. I turned to her in time to see her shrug. "I said you wouldn't be in. She asked why. I told her to mind her own fuckin' business."

My hand went to my mouth again. "You didn't."

"She did," Griz said.

"Jesus, Deanna—" I started to tell her off good and proper, but there was a knock on the door.

"Better not be another fuckin' suitor," Talon said through clenched teeth.

Pick was the closest to the door and opened it. I saw Warden's tall form over everyone's heads. "I'm after Zara," Warden barked.

"Who the fuck are you?" Pick asked.

43

Talon stood, his fists clenched at his sides. I could read the look he was giving me: 'not another fuckin' one.'

"None of your damned business." Warden took a step forward and leaned down to get in Pick's face.

I stood quickly and waved over everyone. "Hey, Warden. Over here." Out the corner of my mouth, I whispered to Talon, "I work with him."

Warden stalked through the many bikers, came right up to me, and pulled me into a tight hug. I patted his back and then waved Talon off when I saw him approach.

"Get ya fuckin' hands off her," Talon growled.

Warden, being Warden, fazed by nothing because he was big enough to take on all of them, simply ignored Talon. He pulled back from the hug and gently grabbed my face between his palms, then said, "Looks like we made it here in time."

"We?"

"Violet's parking the car. She saw all the bikers comin' in and she told me to get my arse in here. Lucky I did. Now, what the hell's going on?"

"Shit!" Talon hissed. "You need to back the fuck up, or we're gonna have problems."

Warden stiffened. He removed his hands, turned, and placed me directly behind him. He was trying to protect me. *That's so sweet? My co-worker likes me and we haven't even been working together long.*

The front door swung open, and in it stood Violet in a fighting stance, holding a gun to the room. She kinda looked funny, not that I would tell her that. She's tiny, not only short, but she's slim, with long black hair, which was always in a ponytail, and dark green eyes.

However she looked, I still knew not to mess with her. Honestly, it wouldn't surprise me if she shot someone and thought nothing of it.

"Who do I have to shoot first?"

See.

"Vi," Talon said in a low voice. On hearing it, Violet stiffened. Her eyes found him through the mountain of bikers—one that I wouldn't mind climbing—and she straightened.

"Brother." She sneered her contempt.

What was that? Did I hear right? I think I went deaf there for a second and my mind made up its own word. I stuck my finger in my ear and wiggled it.

My hand dropped when Violet walked into the room, kicked the door closed, holstered her gun, and strutted her way over to stand next to Warden.

"Really, Talon. I didn't expect you here. Zara's not your type—"

"That's what I said," I added.

"She's too good for you."

"Well, I don't know about that." I shrugged.

"What the fuck're you doing here?" Deanna asked from *still* sitting on the couch.

By all means, Deanna, don't get up. There's going to be one hell of a fight. All. Because. Of. Me. But just sit back and enjoy the show, Deanna. Want some popcorn?

"Well, Barbie, I knew something was up when you and your foul mouth called. I know Zara isn't one to not call herself. So I had to pop in and find out what was going on."

"And you thought it had something to do with me, right?" Talon glared.

"Couldn't be too careful. Imagine my surprise when Zara walked into my office one day asking for a job, and I just happened to see her address on her résumé. I knew it was fate. It was up to me to keep an eye on her—from the likes of you. But look-see here, you've already got your claws into her. Now tell me what's going on?"

"Violet—" I started.

"Kitten," Talon warned. I looked over to him; he shook his head and held his hand outstretched. "Come 'ere."

Damn, it was a test. Like those ones people put on dogs when one master stood on one side of the room and the other on the opposite side and they both called the dog to see which one was the favourite master. Actually, you know what? That was a bad example. I was not the dog in this scenario.

But I did feel I had to choose, and my gut, head, and heart only had one answer.

I stepped around Warden and made my way to Talon. I placed my hand in his; he pulled me tightly against his side with a smirk on his lips.

I punched him in the side. "Don't go all alpha on me and be a smart-arse. Violet, Warden, you may have different opinions of Talon, but he isn't all that bad. And now just finding out you're his sister, I'm sure you've got some stories to tell me." I leaned forward and whispered, "I look forward to hearing them and getting some dirt on him.

"And sure he's as bossy as a shithead sometimes, but you've got to look at his good side as well. Okay, it may be hard to find, and you have to really squint to see it, but it's there, and I kinda like it."

The room burst out laughing. Talon gripped my waist, so I looked up at him. He was smiling as he ran his knuckles down my cheek and then proceeded to kiss me in front of everyone. There were some hoots and hollers.

He took his lips away from mine, and I think I complained a bit, but then he whispered, "You'll pay for that shithead comment, kitten. And next time, do not say this crap in front of my boys. I'm a badarse motherfucker."

He straightened and announced to the room. "Let's get this shit sorted."

"We're staying," Violet said.

Talon gave her a chin lift and continued, "Kitten, sit down and start explaining." Talon's phone rang. He answered it, and whatever he heard on the other end made his smile turn upside down because next he growled deeply, "Bring the fucker in."

CHAPTER FIVE

A FEW SECONDS LATER, the front door opened and the young cookie-liking biker walked in, closely followed by Blue. I was shocked to see Blue restraining a reluctant dark and handsome stranger.

"Blue?" I asked. Talon pulled me closer, both his arms wrapped around my waist.

Deanna stood up from the couch. "What's going on *now*? I don't mind the entertainment, but it's startin' to get a bit much." She turned her concerned eyes to me. I shook my head. This was as surprising to me as it was to her.

"Who the fuck are you and why are you hounding around this house?" Talon asked the shocked-looking guy.

Said guy gasped. "Holy Mother Mary, I've hit the payload. No fucking wonder he deserted me to come here. The bastard. Where is he? I'm going to cut off his penis."

Blue shoved the guy hard, and he stumbled forward. It was obvious to everyone he wasn't a danger. Besides, if he did—which I doubted—try anything, the house was already full of mean-looking people who'd take him down. But it was also a sense that he wouldn't have the heart to hurt anyone.

He straightened, fixed his clothes on his lean body, turned to

Blue, and glared. "Well, really. I like a bit of roughness, but only in bed, honey."

Blue snapped, "Fuck off."

I giggled. I couldn't help it. Blue turned a fierce glare on me, but my giggle also brought the attention of our guest.

"Well, spank me. You must be Zara." He smiled.

My eyes widened. Talon stepped in front of me and said, "You do not speak to her or look at her until you tell me who the fuck you are."

"Don't get your knickers in a bunch, love muffin." He looked over Talon's shoulder to me. "He is lickably-'licious, sweetheart."

"I think I love this guy," Deanna said.

He faced Deanna. "Thanks, doll, aren't you gorgeous too. I'm sure the feeling will be mutual."

"Fuck." Talon made a beeline for the guy, who started backing up quickly.

"Whoa, hold up, Hercules. I'm just making friends here."

"Tell me who the fuck you are or my fist—"

"Julian?" The room turned to see a startled Mattie.

Talon stopped his pursuit and stalked back to me. His arms wound around my middle again.

"Hell, I think I just soiled myself." Julian sighed.

"What are you doing here?" Mattie asked.

"Who is he?" Talon glared at Mattie.

"A... a friend."

"Seriously, dickface? You forgot the *boy* in front of that friend. Or is it because you've found your sister and a house full of Chippendales that I'm suddenly a memory?"

Mattie, with an outstretched hand, said, "No, no. It's nothing like that."

"Whatever." Julian harrumphed, crossed his arms over his chest, and ignored my brother's gaze.

"Oh, this is exciting." I smiled, wiggled my way out of Talon's hold, and walked over to Julian. "It's so nice to meet you." I hugged him. "Mattie only got here last night. I had a little breakdown, but I'm sure if that hadn't happened, he would have told me all about you."

"Well, aren't you just beautiful? Thank you, precious, and I'm so sorry for your loss. I understand Mattie wanting to find you and tell you himself, but to leave me behind? Nope." He shook his head. "That just doesn't jive with me." He leaned in and whispered, "I think he was worried how you'd take to him being gay." He stood straighter and smiled. "But you're handling it just fine and dandy. Now tell me, cupcake, how in God's name have you got a house full of orgasmic men?"

I grinned and pointed to Talon. "That one thinks he has some claim on me because he stuck his tongue in my mouth yesterday. He's their head honcho."

"Fuck me." Talon looked at the ceiling.

"I'll take you up on that, Iron Man," Julian said with a flutter of his eyelashes.

"Julian!" Mattie snapped. "Sorry! He's sorry. He didn't mean it."

"Christ, enough. What the hell am I thinkin'?" Talon asked.

I put my hands on my hips and glared at him. "I certainly don't know. But I can easily fix that and leave."

"Say or think that one more time, I'll take you to bed and fuck some sense into you."

Julian squeaked beside me. "He sounds serious."

I looked at Julian and rolled my eyes. "He probably is."

"Everyone shut it. We need this shit sorted."

"He's real bossy too," I said to Julian.

"*Kitten*," Talon growled.

"All right, jeepers." I grabbed Julian's hand and led him over to the couch. The silently watching Violet and Warden moved to stand near Talon, across from us.

Julian sat between Deanna and me, and Mattie breathed deeply and plopped himself on the edge of the couch.

"Hey, I'm Julian." He held his hand out to Deanna.

"Deanna." She gave him a chin lift.

"What's going down here?" Julian asked.

"Her PP man is waiting for an explanation on her past, and why she fuckin' wants to up and leave ever since Mattie found her."

Julian raised his hand, yelling, "Oh, oh. I know why. 'Cause her crazy ex, right?"

Deanna nodded and went on. "So now, the idiot keeps getting the thought in her pea brain head that it's best to just up and run to keep her and Maya safe as well as everyone else here."

I glared. "You don't get it. No one does. If he finds me, someone will end up getting hurt. I'm—"

"Woman." Everyone looked at Griz when he barked that one word. The other bikers who had been playing with their phones or quietly talking amongst themselves fell silent and stood straighter as if waiting for their cue. "That's why I left earlier. You may have a hard time coming to terms that you're Talon's woman, but once he claimed you, you became a part of Hawks. We take care of our own, and now, that means you. So don't fuck around with thinkin' and worrying 'bout us. We live for this shit. We'll protect you no matter what shit you dribble. Ain't that right, boys?"

A chorus of 'Fuck yeah', 'Damn straight', and wolf calls echoed through my tiny house, which brought tears to my eyes.

I held up one hand. "But—"

Griz interrupted and said, "Shut ya gob and go with it; nothing you say will change anything. Now get the fuck back to work."

I realised he wasn't talking to me when the bikers started to disappear out the front door. Only a few stayed: Griz, Blue, and Pick.

"Kitten, it's finally fuckin' time to sort this shit."

Me, being my stubborn self, shook my head. I thought if he didn't have the information, he couldn't go off half-cocked and get him and his boys hurt.

"Okay, if you ain't talkin', I will," Deanna yelled.

"Don't. You. Dare," I snapped.

Violet cleared her throat. "If she doesn't, I will. You need to stay safe. And against all my better judgment, I think my brother can do that."

"How do you know her shit?" Deanna snapped.

Vi wrinkled her nose, raising her upper lip. "Barbie, I'm a PI. Of course I did a check on her."

"You suck, just like your brother." I crossed my arms over my chest and slouched down in the couch acting a like a child, but I seriously didn't want my story retold, it was had enough living it, so hearing it wasn't up on my top choices of things to do that day.

"Just for that comment, I'll tell your whole frigging history."

"Violet!" I snapped.

"Nope." She shook her head.

"Someone just fuckin' start talkin'." Talon sighed. "Give me the info I need to keep my woman safe."

Vi took a breath and began, "Zara Edgingway was actually born Zara Alexander. She accidentally told me her last name when she came in, and I realised it was different from the one on her résumé. Zara grew up in Manly, NSW with her parents and her brother Matthew. She graduated high school. But then she met David Goodwill when she was working at Starbucks. He charmed her into believing he was a good, caring guy. They married young, but—"

I couldn't look at anyone. David had suckered me into his fairy tale, and now my whole life was being aired like some leather-fetish grandma.

"—unbeknownst to Zara, David Goodwill dealt with the mob on the side of his club business. He's also dabbled in drugs, selling women, and guns. He's one evil motherfucker."

Holy cow... I knew he was bad, but not like that.

"Why'd you leave him, Zara?"

Oh, that hurt. Not kitten, but Zara. I couldn't tell him the real reason. I was already Zara. If he really knew the truth, the filth, what would I become then? Nothing. So I shook my head and lied, "I found out what he did."

"Zee," Deanna uttered. I caught her gaze with my own pleading eyes. She sat back and said nothing.

Something shattered. I gasped and looked up to see that Talon had thrown a vase to the ground, one that had been near the television. "Don't fuckin' lie to me!"

"Talon," Blue barked.

"I'm not, and don't throw my stuff around," I said with my head held high.

"Two years I've waited for you to come to me. I've been waiting and watching, Zara. I know you. I know when you're angry, when you're sad, upset, worried, happy, horny, and fuckin' lyin'. Tell me the truth. Why did you leave him?"

My bottom lip trembled. Goddamn him for saying that shit to me. The arse wasn't allowed to say nice stuff. I was going to have to ban it from the house.

Though, this could work. If I told him, he'd move on. Let me go. It would hurt, but it'd be for the best.

And besides, nothing could hurt more at that moment than still feeling the loss of my parents.

Standing, I glared at him, my fists clenched at my sides, and yelled, "You honestly want to know? I'd had enough of his beatings. Something had changed in him. He never hurt me until two months before I left. But what topped it off, what had me call Deanna in the middle of the night and escape, was when he came home drunk, beat me, and *then* raped me!" I pounded my chest.

Talon's hands were clenched; he was breathing deeply through his nose. My eyes widened as, what felt like, a mountain of rage filled the room. Griz quickly started issuing orders.

"Fuck! Deanna, take Zara to her room. Gay guys, PIs, go with them." Blue and Griz ran across the room and grabbed Talon's arms. "Go now," he growled.

Vi, Warden, and Mattie were already heading down the hall. Deanna grabbed my hand, Julian took the other one and dragged me along with them. We'd gotten my door shut before a roar of fury filled the house. "I'm gonna fucking kill that motherfucker! Let. Me. Go."

The boys must have let go because the next thing we heard were things being thrown around.

"Talon, get the fuck outside," Blue yelled.

We listened to the front door being snapped open, hitting the wall.

"Clean this shit. We'll calm him," Griz said to someone.

Moments later, the rumble of Harleys started and took off down the street.

"Well, honey, I think I can honestly say I have never seen this much action in all my life. I love it here. Mattie, we're moving." Julian smiled from where he sat next to me on the bed.

"That was fuckin'… wow. I have never seen a man that… super angry before. Hot or what?" Deanna gleamed with excitement. She was sitting on the other side of me.

Deanna and I both knew we'd seen others that angry before. However, this was a different situation. We knew that no harm would come from said super-angry person. It was actually funny how un-scared I was, especially with what my past had detailed. In fact, I was anything but scared. What I felt was nauseous and sad that I had upset Talon in any way.

"So hot I think I came in my pants. Sorry, honey," Julian said. Mattie smiled and nodded in agreement, then patted Julian's leg.

"Hot-frigging-headed. He's always been like that," Vi said, shaking her head. She and Warden were standing in front of the door.

"Maybe… maybe he'll leave me alone now," I uttered.

"Oh, here the fuck we go. Where is that mushed-up brain of yours leading you?" Deanna asked.

"Now he knows."

"What, Zara?" Mattie asked.

"He knows I'm not good for him. I'm filthy."

"Fuck," Warden hissed, opened the door and left.

"Too much girl talk for him, I'm guessing." Julian smiled. "And Zara, my potato pie, from what I just witnessed and heard, Talon is far from done with you. You ain't filthy, girl. That pubic-hair-flossing ex of yours is as good as dead. You are much loved here, woman, and if it ain't you or Deanna or Talon doing the killing, you're going to have many others stepping forward to fulfil that job. That fucktard should never have laid a harmful hand on you. He's gonna pay, pop tart. No matter what you say. And Talon will be at your side through all this hell to come. Everyone can see the hard-on he has for you."

CHAPTER SIX

"ALL RIGHT, while my brother goes off to cool his jets, I need infor-mation. First, why are you so interested in running off half-baked? Which will probably get you into more trouble than before," Violet asked, looking almost as angry as Talon had.

"Someone could have followed Mattie. I need to get out of here before they show up, or the dickhead gets here himself," I said.

"Not that she's sure Mattie was followed. If anything, they would have followed Julian," Deanna said. "Fuck," she uttered when she saw my wide eyes of worry.

"You're safer here than anywhere else in the world. Talon will go to great lengths to keep you that way. As you can see and have heard a million times, Zara, it's not only him. I'm sure Barbie would as well. Then you have the guys and me."

I rolled my eyes. "That right there is why I have to go."

"You're scared. That's all it is. You're not thinking."

I bounced down to the end of the bed; there was a lot of jiggling going on, which must have looked like a treat. But I was pissed. I got up and in Violet's face.

"Of course I'm scared," I hissed. "If a man like that was after you, wouldn't you be? And I am thinking as straight as Talon in a gay bar."

Julian chuckled behind me. "I'd like to see that."

"Oh, no, no, in a gay strip club," Deanna added.

"Shh, you guys," Mattie ordered.

Vi glared and said, "No. You. Aren't. If you were, you'd know that this, staying here with us all, was the right choice. Not only the right choice for you but for Maya. Think, Zara. If you're out there on your own, running for your life, what are you going to tell Maya? How are you going to keep her safe? You'll be by yourself."

I teetered back. "I...I don't know."

"I understand the urge to run. I do. But it won't help. It's time to trust the people around you, to lean on them for help when they're so willing to do just that. No matter what may come of the situation."

I flopped back on the bed. Damn, she was right.

All I wanted was to run, to keep everyone safe, but I hadn't been thinking clearly. Maya was the highest priority, and it hadn't dawned on me that she'd need more than just me to keep her protected from her cuckoo father. Even if the thought of having others involved in my stuffed-up situation still sent me into panic mode and wanting to sit in the corner sucking my thumb, I needed to stop, take a breath, and think.

I sat up straight and turned to Mattie. "You have to leave before things get ugly."

"*If*," Deanna said.

Mattie smiled. "We're family, and I've only just gotten you back in my life—"

Julian interrupted, "Oh, my Gawd, I'm gonna cry. This is one of those Hallmark moments." He sniffed.

Mattie rolled his eyes. "And I've had my fair share of ugly in my life, so I'm kind of used to it."

"You better not be referring to me, sac sucker."

Deanna laughed. "I love that one, sac sucker. I'm going to have to use it."

"Make sure to use it on a straight guy. Lordy, that would be funny."

Deanna turned to me. "So, you're staying?"

"Yeah."

"You're a fucking miracle worker, but I still don't like you." Deanna glared at Violet.

"And you think I care." She turned her bored gaze to Julian. "I have a question for you, though. How'd you know Mattie was here?"

"I overheard the convo' he had with his mum about where his sister lived. I memorised the address as well."

"And you didn't tell me because…" Mattie's wild eyes told me he was a little annoyed by the fact Julian hadn't said anything.

"Oh, I knew one day you'd sneak off without telling me, on a mission to get to her, and not tell her where you preferred your dick to lay every night. Of course, I knew if I showed up, she'd love me, and in the end wouldn't judge you. Which is how it all worked out."

"Still, you should have informed me," Mattie mumbled.

"Your ex doesn't know anything about Maya, right?" Vi asked me as she moved away from the door.

"No, he doesn't," I said.

"That there is great news. Honestly, it's been this long, he's either given up or is too stupid to figure out where you are."

My door suddenly swung open, revealing Warden; his eyes met Violet's. "Done a sweep. Nothin' out there. Your bro already has men on the lookout." His eyes then fell on me. "Got his number from that wanker out there—"

"Fuck you," Pick yelled from the front room.

"Rang your man; told him what you said—"

"Warden!" I yelled.

"On ya, dude." Deanna laughed.

"Goodness," Julian breathed.

"Shit," Mattie uttered.

"He's on his way back." Just as he said that we heard the sexy rumble of the Harleys. My heart rate skyrocketed, and I was ready to run and hide in my closet. But for some reason, I thought the people in the room would have told him where I was.

Quickly scooting back down to the end of the bed where Deanna and Julian were sitting, I placed myself in the middle. We all listened to the front door being opened, heavy footsteps coming down the hall, and then Warden moved away from the doorway as Talon filled it. I gulped and gripped Julian and Deanna's hands. Deanna snorted, shook off my hand, and rolled from the bed.

"That's it. You are no longer my best friend. Let it be known I am now taking interviews to fill her spot," I told the group.

She rolled her eyes at me. "Whatever."

"Oh, oh. I'll take you up on that. I want a girl bestie, and I'll stand by your side, snookums." Julian squeezed my hand. I grinned at him. Talon growled low in his throat. "O-o-or not. Later, gator." Julian moved quickly from the bed, gave me an apologetic smile, and said to Mattie, "Come on, hun, I think Thor wants alone time."

My arms went up in the air. "What the hell?" I cried, and let my arms fall back down.

The bedroom door closed. Talon stood leaning against it, watching me. I wondered if I started whistling and looking around the room, would he get the hint I wasn't ready for any type of conversation? Or it could just make him unhappier because he looked very...annoyed. Probably option two, so I refrained from whistling.

"So," I drew out.

"Tell me what your mate said wasn't true?"

"Depends on what he told you." I went for a sweet smile and raised eyebrows.

He glared. "That you'd fuckin' think I'd leave you because of what had happened to you?"

Crap.

"Uh, maybe. But really, let's look at this." I tapped my chin. "There isn't anything to leave because we aren't together."

He stiffened. I gulped and sat straighter.

"Now isn't the time for fuckin' games. I take a hike to cool my anger because I just found out my *woman*," he clipped, "had been beaten and raped by her ex, and then some dick calls and informs me *my* woman is in her room looking scared shitless and wondering if her *man* would think she's filth." He took a step closer.

"What do I have to do to prove this is happening between us? I want this, and I know you want this, no matter what crap you spew." He closed his eyes and took a deep breath. Upon opening them, he said, "You need me to claim your body now, is that it? If I have my dick in you, will you get that this is happening between us?" With one swoop, he removed his tee and threw it to the floor.

I tried to back up to the headboard of my bed. Waving my arms out in from of me, I perved, drooled, and yelled, "Whoa, hold up there. W-what are you doing?" *Oh, my God, I've died and gone to bad-boy heaven.*

A thought of David advancing on me like Talon was flashed through my mind.

A normal person may have been petrified in this type of situation. But I wasn't. *I* had also watched and listened to Talon for many years. I knew he talked rough, and his actions screamed scary badarse biker, but I also knew he treated women with care. No matter what he said, what he implied or had done, he would never hurt me physically or mentally.

"Proving to you that I want you. That no matter what your past was, I'd still want your hot body. You fuckin' drive me insane, kitten. I'd let no one else get away with it, do that to me. No one, kitten, but you." He was at the end of the bed now. My eyes nearly popped out of my head when he popped the button on his jeans.

My heart pounded against my chest. Every word, rude or not, *warmed* me throughout.

Still, I stuttered through my nerves, "W-wait. Holy hell—uh, wait. Put your tee on for a sec—" I covered my eyes with a hand.

"Holy shit, he's got his top off," Julian gasped from behind my bedroom door.

"Fuck, that guy moves fast," Deanna said.

"What are you two doing?" Mattie fake-whispered. The door rattled.

"I just want to see," Julian whined.

"See?" I moved my hand and pointed to the door. "We have an audience."

"Everyone better fuck off before I kill them all."

"I think he's serious," Julian said.

"We're not waiting around to find out," Mattie said.

"Fuck it," Deanna complained.

Talon knelt on the end of the bed. The sight of him, of his muscles flexing, sent a zing to the right spot.

Still, I said, "Whoa, whoa, whoa. Hold up there, slugger. I can't perform now thinking of them out there."

What was wrong with me? Why was I stopping this? *Scared.* Not of him though, of me, of falling into what he had me feeling already.

"It's fine, kitten. I'll do all the work. This time."

"Wait! What's the time?" I looked over to my alarm clock on my bedside table. "Oh, look-see, it's two. I have to pick Maya up from school soon. We'll, uh, have to get back to this another time." I nodded.

"We'll be quick." He gave me a small smile and a wink.

"No. I—uh, have a headache," I said, rubbing at my forehead.

"I'll make it better." He smirked, grabbed my ankles, and pulled me so I was flat on my back.

"Hang on. Goddamn it, Talon. Wait." I crossed my arms over my chest and glared at him as he spread my willing legs, *the hussy traitors,* and moved to kneel in between them. "I just realised I'm still shitty with you."

"You'll get over it." His hands went to each side of my waist.

"Talon. We need to talk," I said with a heavy breath as he made his way up my body until he was leaning over me. His strong arms blocked my head in, with his crotch resting against mine and my drenched panties. I closed my eyes and prayed for some resistance. It was so flipping hard! The resistance and *him*.

Yum.

I opened my eyes. God, he was gorgeous.

"You have a son?"

He closed his own eyes and cursed. "Really, you want to do this now, kitten?"

"Yep," I whispered.

No! my naughty bits screamed.

He thrust his hardness into the right spot. "Oh, hell," I moaned and wished my clothes and his would vanish.

"Just tell me one thing before I give in to *you*," he whispered.

"Um. Okay." I nodded.

"You want this, between you and me?"

Shit.

"Uh...Oh." He thrust against me again.

Damn it, clothes, be gone!

"Tell me, kitten," he said and kissed my temple. "Tell me," he ordered and kissed my nose.

Dear God.

"Oh, all right." I sighed. He smiled a smile of pure satisfaction, the prick, and then rolled to my side, bringing me flush against him.

"What do you want to know about Cody?"

Okay, clothes, you can stay. "Everything," I uttered. *Like, who in the heck is his mum, and are you still seeing her?*

"He's a smart kid, quiet, but I think he'll grow outta that soon. His mum and I don't have the best relationship. We used to. We were wild together."

A pang of jealousy hit me.

He picked up a strand of my hair and tugged it gently, then scoffed and said, "Then she turned into a bitch. She had friends and family who saw themselves as better than anyone else and eventually taught her I was scum. After Cody was born, she left; said she didn't want him growin' up around me and the way I lived. Funny thing though, she used to live this way as well and loved it. So now she's livin' the high, fancy fucked life with her new man."

I shouldn't have asked. To me, it sounded as though he still had feelings for her. It hurt.

Resting my hands on my stomach, I cleared my throat. "Uh, what did Cody mean last night that she was busy?"

"They had some friends over. Cody hates it. They always want him locked in his fuckin' room. I'm sure he came over just to piss her off. Can't say I blame him."

Poor Cody.

"It seemed, to me, he'd like to stay with you."

He went up onto one elbow and looked down at me. "And I'd have him, but she won't have it. I've tried. I fought her, been through the courts. They always take one fuckin' look at me and say 'hell no.'" He took my hand in his, fingers entwined.

Staring down at them for a moment, I couldn't help but notice how much I liked seeing it. I enjoyed the way his thumb ran over my own while he waited for me to speak again. What I didn't like was the smirk he had on his face when I looked up at him, because he knew I liked his hand in mine. "Um, are you still getting weekends with him?"

His smirk turned into a smile as he nodded. "Every second. This one comin'."

"Good. I'd like to get to know him."

Something flared in his eyes as he looked at me. I liked what I saw, but I couldn't trust it. He still loved his ex. The mother of his child.

"He and I would fuckin' love that. Now—" He looked over his shoulder at the clock. "We still got time to fool around, kitten."

"Uh, no."

He arched one brow. *Am I the only loser who can't do that?* "Kitten," he whispered.

"This, uh, shouldn't happen between us."

"Christ. What is going on now? You'd just said you're—"

"Wait. That wasn't me talking; that was... ah, my... um, fandola."

Both brows raised that time. "Your fuckin' what?"

"You know. My"—with my eyes, I gestured to my privates —"down there."

He smiled and then burst out laughing. "Fuck me. You can't even say pussy, vagina, cu—"

I jumped him, placing my hand over his mouth, which brought me to lie across him. His arms tightened around my waist. "No. That word is not to be used in this house." I glared.

He grinned behind my hand, his eyes turning warm.

"And anyway, we can't have anything between us when you still love your ex."

Shit, shit, shit. I shouldn't have said that. His eyes turned hard and scary. I thanked the high heavens when his phone chose that moment to ring. He sat up, and I landed back on the bed.

"What?" he hissed. "Right." He hung up and turned toward me, leaning down so our noses just touched.

Damn it, I should have taken that time to bolt for the door.

"I don't know where you got that fucked-up idea in your head, but it had better be gone when I get back."

"Um."

"No. No 'um,' I do not still love that bitch. If I did, I wouldn't be pursuing you so I could have your nice piece of arse in my bed. I don't play games, kitten. Now, kiss me."

"Huh?"

"Kiss me, kitten. I've gotta go deal with shit."

"Uh, I have to go get Maya."

"I know that. So fuckin' hurry up and kiss me and I'll see you tonight for dinner."

"What?"

"Dinner, I assume you eat it. I'll be over 'bout six."

"But Maya will be here."

"I also know that, babe. She's gotta get used to the idea of us two, may as well start tonight, and then she can meet Cody when I get him tomorrow after school."

"But—"

"Fuck it. You're takin' too long." Then he kissed me, a toe-curling, panty-dripping, tongue-bathing kiss. He pulled back and leaned his forehead against mine. "I reckon you'll be worth it. See ya tonight, kitten." And then he left.

What in the hell just happened?

CHAPTER SEVEN

I HAD no time to process anything. As soon as Talon left, my door swung open and in piled Deanna, Mattie, and Julian, holding a platter of crackers, cheese, and dips.

While we ate, I told them what went down.

"Oh, my fuckin' God," Deanna said when I got to the part about him coming back for tea, and Maya, and Cody, and every—freaking out—thing.

"I know, I know." I sighed and paced the room while munching on some crackers. "He thinks it's time to play family. I haven't even slept with the guy. What happens if he's no good, or he thinks I'm no good and runs a—"

"Shut the fuck up," Deanna said in her most mild-mannered way from where she sat on my bed.

I'm really starting to get sick of people telling me to shut up.

"You are both gonna rock each other's world; no doubt about that shit. And I reckon he's right. If he don't step up and get the kids involved, you'll run a fuckin' mile, scared outta your brain again."

Oh, that was low and cunning, and how come I never thought of it that way?

"I think, hun, what this chica meant when she said 'oh, my

Gawd,' was regarding you thinkin' Captain America still loves his ex." Julian smiled from the bed.

"Oh."

"Yeah, oh—" Deanna began. I held up my hand.

"Before you start telling me what an idiot I am, can we leave it, 'cause I have to go get Maya?"

"You know I would have said more than idiot, but I shall delay my knocking some sense into your dumb-witted brain until later. Let's scat, people. We have a devil child to pick up."

I rolled my eyes. Maya wasn't a devil child. She was just born thirty and smarter than Deanna most times.

"Hey, where'd Vi and Warden get to anyway?" I asked as I exited my room.

"Some PI crap. Said they'd catch you sometime. Oh, and don't come in to work tomorrow since it's Friday. Start back Monday," Deanna informed me.

I turned to face her once we were in the lounge room. "That's nice of her. But I need to keep my mind occupied, and work will do that."

"I'm sure Gladiator will keep you busy enough tomorrow." Julian grinned and then looked to Mattie and back to me, saying, "Hey, nut crackers, how 'bout you two go, and we'll make a start on dinner." Julian did some weird gesture with his eyes.

It took me a second to figure out what he meant. But then it clicked: Mattie was nervous about meeting Maya for the first time.

I smiled and nodded my understanding. Actually, I was excited to bring Maya home to meet her uncle. She'd seen photos of him from when he was younger, but I didn't have any recent ones. I wondered if she would recognise him.

A pang of hurt hit me.

How was I going to explain to my six-year-old that she'd never get to meet her grandparents? I knew it would be harder for me to tell her than it would be for her to hear.

Oh, God.

Before I was allowed to wallow in worry and sorrow, Deanna pulled me toward the door and reminded me of yet another situation to worry about.

"Don't forget Zee's human vibrator will be joining us tonight."

Spotting Maya in a crowd was easier than getting Deanna not to swear. Honestly, many things were a lot easier than stopping Deanna from cussing. Maya came bounding our way with a big smile on her face and her long, dark, curly locks tied in a ponytail on top of her head.

I looked behind me at our tail. Talon had obviously asked Pick to follow us wherever we had to go. He was standing a few paces away, leaning against a car, waiting and watching. All Deanna wanted to do was go to the drug store and pick up some condoms, tampons, and pads, then call out to Pick and ask him if they were all okay. Thankfully, we didn't have time.

"Hi, Momma. Aunty Deanna. Guess what we learned today?" Maya grinned as she reached us and handed me her backpack to carry.

"Let me guess, that all boys have cooties?" Deanna asked. I smacked the back of her head.

"No-o-o."

"Your two times tables?" I asked as we made our way home with Maya skipping beside us and Pick following. I didn't understand why he wasn't just walking with us. On the way to school I tried to ask him, but before I even had a chance to take a step toward him, he barked out a 'no' and 'keep walking.'

Maya turned to me so I could see her eye roll. "Ma, I learned that in prep. You're never gonna guess, so I'll tell you. Do you know what lots of geese are called?"

"No, baby, I don't."

"A gaggle."

"Wow," Deanna said dully.

"What about asses?" Maya asked.

Deanna laughed; I hid mine with a cough. "I think you mean donkeys."

"That's what Mrs Faith said, too. But Donny said they're also called asses, and 'cause she's a teacher she can't lie, so I asked if that was true and she said yes. So do you know what a group of them are?"

"Men," Deanna muttered.

I shook my head at her and said to Maya, "No, I don't have a clue."

"A pace."

"That's interesting stuff, Maya. I'm glad you learned something today."

"Me too. So what's for dinner, Mum?"

Was every child on the face of the planet programmed to ask that question after school? I think they were.

"Not sure just yet. But I have a surprise for you," I said as we walked up the front steps to the porch.

"Oh, what, what?"

I opened the front door. There was some noise coming from the kitchen, and then Mattie and Julian came running around the corner, excitement, and concern in their eyes.

I gave Maya time to dissect the newcomers. She looked from one to the other, and then at me with a smile upon her sweet face.

"That's my uncle, right?" She pointed to Mattie, who was grinning from ear to ear. Julian's hand went to his mouth, tears welling in his eyes.

"Yes, sweetie. That's my brother, Mattie, your uncle. And with him is Julian, Mattie's partner."

Mattie's shocked eyes rose to mine. He was worried about me telling Maya he was gay, but I already knew it wouldn't faze her.

"Cool," she said, and walked over to Mattie. He bent to hug her, but she reached out first and placed her hand upon his cheek. "You got Mum's eyes. That's how I knew." Her smile grew. "Hi, Uncle

Mattie." She wrapped her arms around his neck and hugged him tightly.

I pulled my lips into a tight line to hold back my own emotions.

"Well, ain't this ducking grand," Deanna said beside me. "I hate emotional sh...stuff." I watched her wipe away a tear and laughed. "Flock off, you." She glared at me.

We both looked back to Maya as she stood in front of Julian. "Can I call you my uncle, too?"

Julian looked at the ceiling and back down at Maya. "Oh, sweet honey dew, of course you can." They hugged.

I WAS LEANING against the kitchen bench, watching Julian and Deanna sitting at the table arguing about some answers for Maya's homework. Maya sat with them, doing a good job of ignoring them both and continuing her way through it. Not that there was a lot anyway; some reading and spelling words. She was only six, for goodness' sake. Mattie was busy next to me, finishing off the casserole for tea that he'd prepared earlier.

Seeing this made me feel happy, yet sad. I loved to watch people; I was a watcher from way back, and what I was seeing was that I finally had a house full of family that I loved.

Only I was never going to see my parents again, and that hurt.

A hand fell on top of mine on the bench. I looked down; it was Mattie's, and I glanced up to his sad eyes, and I knew he knew what I had been thinking. It was his way of showing me things would be okay.

I could only hope.

"All right, people, clear the table," Mattie called. "And don't worry, Maya honey, I'll help you later, so you'll have all the right answers." He grinned. Maya sighed in relief and nodded at her uncle.

"School sucks anyway, kiddo," Deanna said. "You should just

quit, become an actress, and support your mum and me for the rest of our lives."

"Deanna," I warned.

"Don't listen to her, sugar plum. School is great. Learning is better, so then you can get a high-paying job and *then* support us all." Julian winked at Maya, who giggled in return. I rolled my eyes and thanked the high heaven that Maya knew they were talking nonsense.

The table had been cleared of schoolwork when the front door opened, and I froze with knives and forks in my hands. All of us turned to the kitchen doorway to see Talon in his godly form walk in.

"Talon!" Maya chirped.

While my woman bits chirped for him.

Maya ran at him. He lifted her up and twirled her around. Not something you'd see a hard-core biker do every day.

"Maya, you been good today?" he asked after he placed her feet back on the floor.

"I'm always good, Talon. Whatcha doin' here?"

Talon raised his eyes to me, questioning me in his silent way on what I'd told her. I chose to glance at a spot on the kitchen ceiling and bite my bottom lip.

Is that a growl coming from him? Shit.

"I came to have a word with your momma. Could you give us a minute?" We all knew that wasn't a question. He stalked over to me, grabbed the knives and forks out of my hands, placed them behind me, then took my wrist and pulled me from the room, down the hall, and into my bedroom.

Before he closed my door, we heard Maya squeal and announce to the people in the kitchen, "I hope he's going to kiss her. They're always lookin' at each other with yucky love eyes." They burst out laughing. Talon closed the door and faced me with a smirk.

"Talon—"

"No, kitten, even your daughter can see something has been

going on between us for a while now. All I want to know is what you're going to tell her?"

I waved my hands up and down, my eyes bugging out of my head—not a pretty look. "What am I supposed to tell her?"

"That you're my woman and I'm your man. That she'll be seein' a lot more of me around 'ere."

I sat on the edge of the bed and looked at the floor. This was it. I was going to have to be honest. "It's not that simple, Talon. I'm not one of your bimbos who you can screw over. I need stability for Maya and me. I need long term—"

"Seriously, Zara," he clipped. "If I thought you were just some bimbo to warm my fuckin' dick for the night, I wouldn't be here. Hell," he rumbled. In the next second, he was on his knees in front of me. With one finger under my chin, he raised my head. Our eyes met, and my heart skipped a beat.

I was about to have a heart attack.

I watched him lick his lips, and then those lips turned into a smirk because he knew I was watching them.

"I hate this talkin' shit. I want you as my woman. Long-fuckin'-term. I know we still got a lotta shit we need to learn 'bout one another, but that's the best part. For once in my life, I'll try to be patient, for you."

Oh, my flipping God.

Was Talon worth risking my heart being broken?

Especially now?

Did I trust him?

Shit. Heck. Dick—yes, Talon's.

"Okay," I whispered.

His eyes flared. He let out a breath, and he smiled a burn-your-eyes-out-'cause-it-was-so-hot smile. One I had never seen before on his lickable mouth.

Then, thank the high heavens, his mouth was on mine, demanding and sensual. I was all too willing to comply with whatever his needs were. My hands curled into his hair, pulling him

71

closer; his groan of approval made me smile. One of his hands traced from my hip up to my breast.

Shit, did he just press a magic nipple button to send a wave of lust down to my core?

Yep. I had magic nipples.

Holy Moses, that feels great.

Talon brought up his other hand to cradle the side of my face, and I wrapped my legs around his waist and moaned when I felt his large-oh-crap-will-it-fit penis rub against my centre.

A knock on the door broke through my horny fog. "Uh, guys," Mattie whispered. "Can you hold off on the sex right now? Tea's ready and we're hungry."

Talon leaned his forehead against mine and muttered some curse words. Then he said, "One fuckin' time we'll get to finish this. And honestly, I don't want people around, because if your pussy is as demanding as your mouth, I won't want to leave, or anyone to interrupt."

With that, he got up, adjusted himself, and walked out the door.

I could not believe he just said that. I did not have a demanding... fandola.

"Talon!" I yelled.

He stalked back to the room, grinned, kissed me hard, grabbed my hand, and started for the kitchen once again. Only this time, he was dragging me behind him.

We walked into the kitchen. Everyone was already seated around the small table. Two places were left, one for me and one for the Neanderthal. I watched Maya's eyes go from our faces to our joined hands, and then she smiled.

"Are you stayin' for dinner, Talon? My uncle made it." I could hear the pride in her voice.

"Yeah, I'm staying," Talon said, and sat down next to me at the table.

Somehow, when he said 'I'm staying', I was sure he meant more than just for tea.

CHAPTER EIGHT

Concentrating at dinner was hard. Talon sat next to me; sometimes he would rest one hand on the back of my chair, and other times he would play with the ends of my hair. All of it made my brain go ga-ga. Still, the conversation went on, and by the time we'd all finished, I felt full and content.

I turned to Maya. "I'm just going to help clean up, and then we'll do your reader before bed." I rose and took some plates to the sink.

Talon came up behind me, and with an arm around my waist, he whispered, "Can I help Maya with her reader?"

I went stiff and closed my eyes.

It had always been just me.

"Kitten," he uttered, "that mean somethin' to you?"

I nodded.

"Good." He kissed my cheek and turned to Maya. "Come on, squirt, you're readin' to me tonight."

"Yay," she sang, and bounced up and out to her room with Talon following.

I turned around from the sink and my eyes met Deanna's. She also knew it meant something *big* to me.

With a hushed voice, she said, "Well, thank fuck—"

"Deanna. Language," I snapped.

"Oh, give me a break. I can only go so long, and she can't hear me now." She grabbed the rest of the plates and brought them to the bench. "It's good to see, Zee. It's so good to see."

"I double that," Julian said from the table, where he sat next to a smiling Mattie. "I haven't known you long, sponge cake, but you deserve this. Him."

"He's right, Zee," Mattie added. "I can see you're scared, but let it happen. I think with Talon beside you, you'll both shine for that precious girl in there." He pointed in the direction of Maya's room.

I pulled my lips between my teeth and nodded.

"No need to be holding out anymore, bitch. What you have right there in that room is fuckin' worth holding on to," Deanna said. "Right, enough said. Let's get this shit cleaned and go veg out before I gotta hit the road."

That was yet another worry I had to voice. "I don't want you going home alone, Deanna."

"I don't want to hear this. I'm fine; I reckon you're worrying over nothing. And besides, it's not like he'd come after me. Hell, he doesn't know who I am."

"You don't know that. He could be watching. I think from now on you should move in here."

She rolled her eyes and became a little rougher with the dishes as she loaded them in the dishwasher.

"If you break even one plate, I'll have to hurt you. And don't go ignoring me, wench."

"I love the relationship they have," Julian said to Mattie.

"It's a little strange," Mattie added.

"But strange is beautiful." Julian smiled.

"Whatever, meat slappers." Deanna rolled her eyes. "Look, it's going to be fine. I'm going home, and that's the end of the story."

"No, you're not." We all looked at the doorway to see Griz standing there glaring at Deanna.

"Did anyone hear him come in?" I asked. They shook their heads. "Great lot we'd be if we were ninja attacked."

I watched Deanna face Griz with her hands on her hips, head held high. With her upper lip raised, she snapped, "Yes. I. Fuckin'. Am."

"You do all this tough-talking, and telling Wildcat there to keep herself safe by staying and trusting. Why don't you do the same?"

"Yeah!" I yelled and fist-pumped the air.

Deanna snarled at me to shut up, and then said to Griz, "Because he won't be after me, oh wise one." She raised one eyebrow.

"You can't be sure of that. If he's watching Wildcat, then he'll do anything to get at her; meaning, he won't have a second thought of taking out someone she cares about."

I gasped. "What about Maya at school? I'll have to keep her home."

"No, darlin', she's covered by the boys. Someone will always be there watchin', so you don't need to stress."

I nodded, though I still felt uneasy.

Griz turned a hard stare on Deanna. "You'll be staying at the compound. In my room."

She smirked and crossed her arms over her chest. "Well, hot stuff, if all you wanted was to get me into bed, all you had to was ask."

He straightened. "You'll be in my bed, on your own. You ain't my type, princess—too young and just a pain in the arse."

"Yeah, right, handsome, I bet every morning when you're in the shower you jerk your chain thinkin' of this arse." She slapped her butt.

Griz growled.

Julian giggled. "Did she honestly just say that?"

I sighed.

Mattie nodded while looking concerned.

"Jesus Christ." Griz shook his head. I thought he would have put her down or stalked off, but instead, he said, "That's right, sweetheart. I come every morning thinking of bangin' you so hard it'd work some of that pole outta your arse. As I'm sure you fiddle with your nub every day thinking of how hard and long I'd take you."

"Oh, boy, is it getting hot in here?" Julian asked, fanning himself.

I looked back at Deanna, surprised she was still silent and shocked to see a blush upon her cheeks.

"Fuck you," Deanna uttered.

He smirked. He knew he'd just won. "In your dreams, princess. Now, Pick will meet you out front when you're finished here. He'll show you to your room. You better not fuckin' fight him on this," he said, and then walked out of the house.

"Deanna?" I pressed.

"Shut the fuck up. I don't wanna hear it."

"He's a nice guy," I said.

She snorted. "Too old for me. What is he, fifty?"

"Forty," Talon said as he came into the room, up to me, and moved my body so he could stand behind me with his arms around my waist.

Holy heck did that feel special. It had been so long since I felt something for someone. I forgot all about the heart palpitations, the butterflies, and weak knees. I wanted to cherish it for a little longer, just standing there in his arms. However, I needed to change the subject before Deanna had a full-blown hissy fit, so I said, "Come on y'all, I need a Jensen Ackles fix. *Supernatural* is on soon."

Any woman who didn't find Jensen strip-worthy was insane in my books.

Deanna smiled at me. She knew I was taking the attention away from her and she appreciated it. Didn't mean I wouldn't drill her later on what all the sexual tension was with her and Griz. Not many men would go head-to-head with Deanna, and I think she'd finally met her match. I wanted to jump with glee.

Julian groaned. "Honey, I'll watch *Supernatural* and get freaked the fuck out, but only if you all watch *Burlesque* with me. I brought it from home."

We all moved from the kitchen to the lounge and found seats.

"Oh, I am so there. But we all gotta go say goodnight to Maya first."

Maya was more than happy to have everyone in her room showering her with hugs and kisses. We then all filed out to the living room. I sat between Deanna and Talon on the couch. Actually, I was more on Talon's side, leaning against his chest because he'd hooked an arm around my shoulders and pulled me against him.

To start off with, I'd been stiff; of course, I got over it when his luscious voice whispered in my ear to relax.

Mattie and Julian squeezed themselves into the lounge chair together, moaning about how fake *Supernatural* was; not that it stopped Julian from squealing and hiding his eyes with Mattie's hand on the more scary parts. Once *Supernatural* finished—pout— we started *Burlesque*. Another favourite on my movie list.

"You know, I'd turn gay for Christina Aguilera," I announced. I felt Talon chuckle beside me.

"Not if I got to her first." Deanna yawned.

I shoved her and said, "Dude, she'd have my shoes under her bed way before your stinky ones."

"Actually, I'd have to agree; she is hot. I think I'd even turn straight for her," Mattie said, receiving a look from Julian. We laughed.

It was a great movie. I had to rewind it three times to the part where she sang on stage for the first time. Just as it was finishing up there was a knock on the door; we all looked at each other while Talon stood and walked over to answer it.

"Boss," Pick said with a chin lift. His deep blue eyes looked stressed. He ran a hand over his buzz cut, and then scratched his cute goatee.

"S'up?" Talon asked.

Pick looked over Talon's shoulder; his gaze fell upon Deanna, and then went back to Talon. "Griz said to come grab her if I had to take off anywhere. I have to take off, boss."

"What's happenin'? I thought Griz was 'round tonight; he could have come himself."

"He thought so too." Pick leaned in closer. "She called."

Huh, what? Say again, or just speak the frig up. Who's she?

I glanced at Deanna and knew from her drawn brows she was wondering the same thing.

"Again? Fuck," Talon barked. "Where you gotta go?"

"Need to help my ma with somethin'. Griz didn't want to leave it to the recruits. The others are busy either workin', drinkin', or fuckin'. So I gotta take her over and lock her down before I leave."

Talon nodded. He turned to the room. "Hell Mouth, time to get your arse outta here."

"Does it bother anyone how bossy these pricks are?" Deanna asked the room.

"Yeah, a little bit," I answered because sometimes it was also downright *hot.*

"You know I can walk across the road on my own. I ain't no fuckin' child."

Pick sighed. "I was told if you pulled any shit, I was to haul you over there over my shoulder. Is that how you want it, woman?"

Deanna got up, grumbling and no doubt cursing under her breath the whole way to the front door. "See you losers tomorrow." She waved over her shoulder and Talon closed the door.

"Well," Mattie yawned, "I'm buggered. I'm going to hit the hay."

"I'll join you, honey," Julian said. "Leave these two love birds alone." Julian added a wink.

Why did I all of a sudden feel very nervous?

"Wait." I bounced up from the couch. "Ah, doesn't anyone want a hot chocolate? A coffee? A shot of something stronger?" *I know I could use one.*

"No thanks, sis," Mattie said. He and Julian both came over and kissed me on the cheek goodnight. And no matter how much I pleaded with my eyes, the dicks went off to their room.

I faced Talon. "Well, I guess it's time for bed."

He gave me a chin lift. "Right, I'll lock up."

That was easy. "Okay. I'll, ah, see you. Thanks, you know. Ah, night." Maybe I should have given him a kiss goodnight, but I was a chicken and bolted for my room while Talon locked up and went home.

I got ready for bed while pondering how easy it had been getting rid of Talon. I thought he would have grabbed me or said something like 'Kitten, what the fuck are you forgettin'?'

I slid under the covers and it dawned on me. I kind of had hoped he would've said or done something, and now I was disappointed that he hadn't made an effort. Maybe he was getting sick of me already?

My bedroom door opened and Talon walked in. I couldn't keep the smile off my face.

"You thought I was goin'," Talon said with a chuckle. "I am damn happy to see that smile on ya face from just knowing I'm still here." He pulled his tee off in one quick swoop.

The smile fell from my face and I sat up. "You, ah, can't stay here."

He sighed loudly. "And why the hell not?" he asked while removing his jeans, leaving him in black boxers.

Hallelujah! My magic nipples and fandola sang.

"Um, because of Maya."

"Jesus, kitten. I'm stayin'. Look, if it'll make you feel better, I'll move to the couch before she wakes up. But right now, I wanna sleep with my woman in my arms." He walked to the side of the bed, lifted the covers, which I was clinging to, and climbed in.

What could I say? He was willing to move to the couch so I wouldn't worry if Maya thought we were moving too fast.

Or was it that I thought we were moving too fast?

I didn't know; my brain felt scrambled. I still had so many things to worry about. Was David out there watching me? When was he going to strike? Was I just overreacting with...well, everything?

"You gonna sit up all night, babe?" he asked, his deep voice sending a shiver down my spine.

God, even my spine is happy he's here.

I looked over my shoulder. He had one arm behind his head and the other was outstretched for me to lie upon. My heart was already going wild, but it stepped up to an even more frenzied rhythm. And why did it sound like it was pumping to the beat of "Bad to the Bone"?

"Damn, kitten. Are you always this nervous?" He chuckled.

"No." I glared. "Only around you." *And when psychopaths are looking for me.*

"Good to know." He smiled and pulled me down so my head rested on his chest and his arm held me tightly around my waist. He kissed the top of my head and uttered again, "Good to know."

"Talon?"

"Yeah, babe?"

"Can I ask you something?"

"Only if it's quick. 'Cause the more you talk whispery, the more my dick gets hard, and I can't fuck ya with a house full."

I smiled. It was good to know I affected him like he did on me. I rolled into him more and bravely slid my hand from his stomach to his chest. His hand came down upon mine.

"Kitten, you keep being cute-like, I'm gonna have to take you. I've only got so much fuckin' restraint. Ask your question and let's get some shut-eye."

"Well." I cleared my throat and had to think real hard what my question was again because all that was on my mind was Talon taking me. "Um, I was wondering why you and Violet aren't close."

He started to trace circles on my hip. I wanted to purr.

"She didn't want me to get involved in our uncle's club. He came to us eight years ago and said he wanted to give me the chance to run Hawks if anything happened to him. I felt honoured. Violet felt disgusted. We both knew the club was running drugs and selling women." I couldn't help but stiffen. Talon felt it, but he continued, "Vi thought it'd lead me down the wrong path. It did for a while, and Vi hated that; in turn, she hated me, because by then she was on the other side of the law. I lost her trust, I lost her love, and her in total as a sister. Then my uncle passed away five years ago. I was in charge and encouraged my brothers to run a clean club. The club members look after each other; we own three Harley stores over Victoria and have a few strip clubs. Look, we no longer do any of that past shit, but it doesn't mean we don't help out. An ex-member left 'cause he still wanted to deal with hookers. Outta respect, we look out for his woman while they're on our territory. Babe, there's a lotta dicks out there who don't believe the club's clean, but I don't give a fuck. I'm happy, and my brothers are happy."

"So, ah, across the road is... um, just the compound?"

"Yeah. But at the side is a mechanical business and it's also where I manage *all* club businesses from. Never fuckin' thought I'd spend most my life on a phone or computer doin' that kinda shit. The only good part about it is that I've got many members to fall back on when I don't want'a deal with the crap. That's when I get to take off on my Harley, whenever I fuckin' please."

"Okay." I nodded. "So, nothing untoward happens over there? Like... um, those friends and their hookers rocking up?"

"Babe, none of us have to pay for pussy. And yeah, we fuckin' party hard, but that's it. My life is clean, kitten. If it wasn't, I wouldn't have involved you in it." With one quick movement, he was on top of me, studying my face for something. "You're too good for that kinda shit."

I blushed and nodded, my arms encircling his waist. "Do—" I stopped when he spread my legs with his knees. "Uh, do... do you think that you and Vi could make up?"

He kissed my neck. "Maybe one day," he said, and then his eyes met mine. "You surprise me, kitten. I like that about you. I tell you I was involved in shit and you take it in stride, thinking nothing of it."

I smiled at him. "Everyone has had shit in their lives, Talon.

What makes a person is if they can climb out of it before it hurts more people, and I believe you have. You've also succeeded at it."

He closed his eyes and rested his forehead against mine. "I gotta have a bit of you, babe. I can't fuckin' wait. You gotta be quiet, kitten. All right?"

Shit a doodle duck. Was I all right with him 'having a bit of me?' What did he *mean* by a bit of me? I didn't know, but my body did because my head nodded without my brain's acknowledgment.

CHAPTER NINE

TALON GRINNED WICKEDLY AT ME. He kissed me hard, but all too soon his lips left mine. I was about to complain when I felt them at my neck. I arched to give him better access. Licks, bites, and kisses he delivered upon my neck, and then slowly he moved to my collarbone. I let out a moan. He shushed me, but I felt his grin on my skin.

I was feeling overwhelmed like I was being touched for the first time. Maybe I had become a born-again virgin.

As his lips played, his hands roamed from my hips up under my t-shirt to my magic nipples and ultra-sensitive breasts. He tugged my tee up further; my slutty arms rose on their own and he threw my t-shirt to the floor.

Finally, he moved lower. I had been just about ready to strum my fingers on the bed while waiting for his mouth to be on my breasts. Now I didn't have to. Only he wasn't there long enough. He went to move on, but I wasn't ready for that yet; I pulled him by his hair and positioned his mouth back where I wanted it. He chuckled and bit down on my magic nipple, causing a moan to escape.

"Quiet, kitten," he growled.

"Seriously?" How was that even possible with a lover like him? I glared down at him as he stared back with his teeth clamped around my nipple. He bit. I shoved my fist in my mouth, smothering my moan.

Jesus, if he doesn't get a move on, I'm going to combust.

"Talon. Honey. If you don't get a move on, I'll come on my own."

He stopped his attention to my stomach and hips and looked up, smiling. "So eager."

"Well, when it's been six years—"

I didn't get to finish what I was going to rant about. He hissed, my shorts and underwear disappeared, and his mouth was feasting upon the most vital—right now, anyway—part of my body.

The shock of the invasion caused me to cry out. It wasn't long before his lips and tongue brought me to a climax.

"Fuck. You taste un-fuckin'-real."

Oh. My. God. I was mortified that I'd lasted seconds. I covered my eyes with my arm; I knew my face was burning bright red. Talon settled between my legs; his arms folded across my hips and I knew his head was rested on those arms, watching and waiting for me while my body and breath recovered, along with my dignity.

"Kitten," Talon said.

Holy shit. Did my stomach just wobble when he spoke? That was beyond mortifying. I wanted to die. He was so used to perfection, and yet here he had a woman who hadn't had sex in… forever, and only took a second to climax, while he stared at my cellulite.

I felt the bed shift. Talon climbed up my body and lay next to me, his arousal at my hip. He tugged my arm.

"No," I stated. "You, ah, better go to the couch now." *Wait.* That was kind of rude of me. No one had gone *down there* before, so shouldn't I be showing my appreciation? Maybe if I did I wouldn't be so embarrassed; he could have something wrong with him. Then we'd be even.

I was going to have to do this fast, so he didn't see my wobbly bits doing their own jig.

I pounced. My arm flew out, knocking him in the head. He swore; I mumbled a sorry as I spread his legs with my hands while he was in a daze. Before he got a good look at me moving, I rested between his legs with the sheet over me. I grabbed the waist of his boxers and pulled down; his erection sprang free.

Talon's hands lay over mine, stopping me. That was okay because I was still in shock from seeing a cock. *Gulp, so freaking big.* Or was it just the average size? From the experience I'd had in the past, I wasn't sure. But there was the possibility that if Talon and I had a chance to do the dirty, he would be impaling me on his hard pole.

"I like the way you're looking at me, kitten. And I love the fact that you just licked your lips. But why in the fuck did you pull a speed marathon to get down there? I didn't eat you just to have you return the favour."

"Um," I said to his perfect pecker. Damn him. Why did he look so fucking good? *The prick.* "It's not about returning the favour. I want to do this." His cock twitched with…glee? I realised then that it was true. I wanted to please him, and that thought also pleasured me.

Before he could say any more, I went deep. My whole mouth covered all of him, making my eyes water. *Huge.* I pulled up slowly and flicked my tongue side-to-side along the way.

"Fuck," Talon hissed, arching and fisting the sheets.

I loved seeing that reaction from him. That it was me causing him to do that. I swirled my tongue at the tip and gently bit. Talon growled. I smiled and went down once again, taking my sweet time.

"Kitten," he warned. He wanted faster; I wanted to go slower and memorise the way his body moved, the way his eyes closed when I reach the base of his cock, and started back up once again.

He fisted my hair tightly; I moaned. Our eyes met; desire pooled in both. With the pressure of his hand in my hair, Talon took control; his cock slid in and out of my mouth perfectly. I clenched my legs together; what I wanted was to let my fingers do their job and finish me off once again. My body was craving to be pumped like my mouth was. It was such a friggin' turn-on. Something I had never felt before and wanted to feel for the rest of my life.

"Hell, kitten." Talon closed his eyes and moaned. He was close; I could taste it.

He let go of my hair. I kept the pace going on my own, enjoying the rush of seeing him spread out and exposed.

"Fuck, I'm gonna come, babe," he groaned.

His first shot reached the back of my throat; I drank it down with the rest. Even after there was no more, I tightened my grip at the base and pulled up, squeezing the last drop out before licking it off.

I was about to wrap the sheet around me, but before I could, hands came under my arms, and I was pulled up to lie across Talon's naked body. My legs went around his waist, my arms to each side of him; I looked down, my hair spilling around my shoulders. I was shocked and happy to see that my own naked body wasn't making it hard for him to breathe.

He grinned up at me. "No one has ever sucked me that hard or taken it to the very last drop. That was fuckin' heaven, kitten."

A blush filled my cheeks, and I looked away. *Now I blush, what the hell?*

He laughed. "No need to go shy on me now, babe." He pulled me down and kissed me stupid. His expert mouth moved to my ear and he whisper-growled, "Don't ever fuckin' hide your body from me again. I love every inch; and eventually, I will have tasted every inch, going back for more and more until I die."

Oh. My. Fucking. God. Words like that were going to make it hard for me to not fall for this biker.

"Let's get some sleep before I have to fuckin' move." He rolled me to his side and tucked me close. One of his arms went around my shoulders as I rested my head on his chest. His other hand took one of mine and placed them on his stomach. I entwined one leg through his.

Again, he had me feeling safe, warm, and protected, even cared for. I wanted to cry.

Waking up feeling well rested was something out of the ordinary for me. I stretched as moments of last night played on repeat in my mind. I smiled and reached out to the side Talon occupied last night. He wasn't there. I giggled; he had moved after all. I had been so sedated I didn't feel him leave.

My bedroom door opened. I pulled the sheet around me tightly as Maya skipped into the bedroom and onto the bed.

"Morning, sweetheart," I said as she plopped down next to me.

"Mornin', Momma. I had a dream last night. Wanna know what it was about?"

"Sure." I rolled to my side and faced her as she looked up at the ceiling.

"Toby, from school, was being mean to Becka, so I kicked him in the balls."

I closed my eyes, only to open them when the room filled with deep laughter. Talon was standing in the doorway.

"That's good, kid. Even in your dreams, you gotta protect the ones you care for."

I rolled my eyes. Still, I couldn't help but smile at Talon. "But you have to remember that kicking a boy there can hurt them a lot."

"I know, Momma. So I'll only do it when they really annoy me."

Talon chuckled again. "Come on, kiddo. I'll make you breakfast; let your ma get up and ready."

She grinned and bounced down to the end of the bed, then stopped. She looked from Talon to me. "Momma?"

"Yes, baby?"

"Talon's your boyfriend now, right?"

I froze. That I wasn't expecting, so early in the freaking morning. What could I say though, after what happened last night? I looked up to Talon; he stared back with a worried expression. "Yes, Maya. He is my boyfriend."

"More than that, kitten." He smirked and turned to Maya to say, "I'm her man, baby girl."

"Cool." She beamed, and then her face was puzzled. "Then how come Talon was sleeping on the couch when I came out this mornin'? Shouldn't he be in here with you?"

Talon chuckled. I blanched.

"From now on, Maya, that's where I'll be," Talon said.

She shrugged and said, "Okay." Then bolted out of the room with Talon chuckling and following behind her.

I flopped to my back, placed the pillow Talon had used over my face and screamed. How was it possible that children were so care-free when it came to life-changing situations? Ones that would freak any adult out? Just like it had me when anything regarding Talon and me happened.

I was prepared to lie there for quite some time and debate on what to do next. Should I panic some more over the fact that my daughter wasn't fazed by the fact that I would now be having a man sleep in my bed? A bed that she jumped into nearly every morning to wake my zombie form up from? Or should I leave things as they were, and not bother freaking out about anything that just occurred?

All thoughts soon left me, because Talon's scent from the pillow distracted me, sending image after image of last night into my mind.

It was time for me to get up and have a cold shower.

I walked into the kitchen wearing a long, striped black-and-grey skirt with a black tee that read 'Get Low and Go'. My hair was still wet from the shower, so I left it down. No doubt, by midmorning I would have to put it up because it would turn out to be one big frizz bomb since I'd run out of my hair product that kept the curl at bay.

I snorted. Let's see how Talon handled that look; he could still run a mile.

Rounding the corner, I stopped dead. Maya was sitting at the table in her school uniform. Yeah, that was fine. Mattie and Julian were leaning against each other and the bench. Yeah, that was fine also. What had me going *o-kay* and made my eyes pop from my head was Talon, my badarse biker man, standing behind Maya and doing her hair in a ponytail, with a flipping ribbon to boot.

Talon's hard eyes turned to me. "Do not say a freakin' word," he growled.

My heart swelled. I wanted to run to him and maul him like a wild woman. Not only was he caring for me by caring for my daughter, but he was doing it in front of witnesses. To top it off, he actually listened to me and chose not to swear in front of Maya.

Shit. Tears were forming in my eyes.

Talon's eyes stayed on me as I saw them turn sweet. He knew it meant something to me, and just in case he didn't, I walked over to him and gently kissed him. My lips met his, and when I went to pull away, he pinned me back with his hand around my waist and deepened the kiss.

"Aw, yuck," Maya moaned.

I smiled against Talon's mouth. He chuckled. I stepped out of his reach and went to the coffee machine on the counter. Though I didn't miss the gentle shove Talon gave Maya, or the wide happy smile that was on her lips.

If this was how it was going to be, I could handle that.

"Mornin', guys," I said to the two grinning fools. I hipped Mattie out of the way of me reaching my morning coffee. "Get outta my way. If I don't have my fix in the next twenty seconds, all heck will break loose, and it's way worse than me PMSing." I took a sip and turned to Talon. "Let that be a warning to you."

"Got that, kitten." He smirked.

A knock sounded on the front door.

"Open up, duck heads, I *need* a good coffee," Deanna yelled. Mattie moved off to the front door.

"Momma, can I go play before school?"

"Have you had breakfast?"

"Yeah, Talon got it for me."

Wipe the tears off my heart.

"Teeth?"

She rolled her eyes. "Yes, Momma, Talon already told me to."

Forget wiping tears, let the flood begin.

"And I can see Talon has already done your hair. So yes, baby, you can play. We'll leave in ten."

"Okay." She got up from the table and ran out of the room, calling a quick hello to Deanna on the way past.

"Coffee, bitch, quick," Deanna ordered.

I got a cup ready and handed it to her as she sat down at the table. Talon walked over to me and placed me in front of him, his arms around my waist. It seemed to be his usual stance when I was concerned. Not that I minded at all. I sighed and relaxed into him. He grunted his approval of me not fighting him on the close comfort he was offering after taking care of my young. *And melting my heart into a big puddle of goo. The hairy ball sac.* Though, I couldn't help the smile creeping onto my lips.

"Yo, boss man," Deanna started after her first sip. "You gotta get better fuckin' coffee at the compound. It nearly choked the hell outta me." She shuddered from the memory.

"You got work today?" I asked Deanna.

"Yeah." She rolled her eyes.

"Who in their right mind hired someone with such a colourful vocabulary?" Julian asked. Mattie nodded in agreement as he leaned back in his seat and placed an arm around Julian's chair.

I giggled. "The library."

Talon chuckled behind me. "You have got to be shittin' me."

Deanna flipped him the middle finger and then swung it to Julian.

"Oh, don't give me that, caramel cake. I think it's a great job for you. All that silence." He snickered. "No wonder you swear like a trooper when you've been cooped up all day."

I cleared my throat. "Actually, she only works a thirteen-hour week."

Julian raised his eyebrows and turned to Deanna. "I guess all the colourfulness just comes naturally."

Deanna snorted. "That's right, sugarplum. Anyway, now that I've had my fill of all your shit, people, I better be off." She rose from the table, bringing her mug to the sink.

"Who's on you today?" Talon asked.

Huh? What does he mean?

Deanna sighed loudly. "I don't need no arsewipe babysitter."

Well, that explained that.

Talon's phone rang, and he answered with a gruff, "What? Yep, she is. That right. Okay." He flipped the phone closed and placed it back in his pocket. "Don't fuckin' move a muscle," he ordered.

I moved out of his arms and faced him with a glare. "Don't you talk to me like that; and I'm not moving, and keep down the tone. Maya's still in the house."

He smirked. "I wasn't talkin' to you, kitten." He nodded over my shoulder. I turned to see Deanna near the doorway, looking out into the lounge with a tense body.

"Deanna?" I asked.

Julian squealed. "Whoo-boy, something's going to go down. I so love this place. It's like having your own private movie. Wait, I need a snack while watching this."

"You just had breakfast," Mattie said, shaking his head.

"Come on—"

"Guys," I interrupted, and then spun back to Talon. "What's wrong?"

"That was Griz on the phone; he asked Hell Mouth to wait while he had a quick shower. He got out, and she'd disappeared."

Deanna turned back around, hands on her hips and a scowl on her face. "Oh, come the fuck on. I needed a coffee."

"You could have waited." Talon glared back at her. "Have some fuckin' respect, woman. Griz had a shit night; he doesn't wanna deal with your crap all day, but he is."

"Whatever." She shook her head and looked at me. "This is what you call friendship. Now I have to put up with a body-fuckin'-guard all day and night."

I gasped. She was right; I was a terrible friend. All my past poo now affected her life in more ways than she could handle. I know Deanna; she'd hate being crowded all the time.

"Don't start all your wah-wah crap." She rolled her eyes and walked over to me. Our gazes met. "You know I wouldn't have it any other way. I love ya guts."

I nodded. She smiled, and the front door banged open.

"Get your arse out here, woman, or you'll be late for work," Griz snarled.

"I'm coming!" Deanna yelled back. She sighed, hugged me, and made her way out. "See you losers later."

CHAPTER TEN

TALON and I walked Maya to school. We walked Maya—my daughter—to school. As in together. Both of us walking with Maya, to school. Like a real-life couple. It felt amazing. He held my hand. Maya held his other hand, and as we walked, we talked. More like Maya talked to Talon, and I walked along while trying not to bawl my eyes out, trip, or sing, "The hills are alive with the sound of music."

Once we got back to my place, he announced, "Kitten, I gotta take off for a while. Blue's coming over, but I'll be back later before you hav'ta get Maya from school. I'm gonna bring some of my shit with me to keep here; saves me travelling home every day."

I gulped. This was serious stuff. Still, I couldn't stop from saying, "Talon, you live right next door. It's not that hard."

He laughed. "Babe, I don't live there. I sometimes crash there when I've had too much. I live out on some land in Buninyong." He kissed me before I had a chance to think.

I went to my tippy toes and tightly wrapped my arms around his neck. He growled deeply, sending a shiver to my fandola. I loved it when he did that. Our tongues did the tango with the expertise of practiced partners.

"Ah, don't mind us."

I moved my head back enough to look over Talon's shoulder, panting, and saw Julian and Mattie standing in the kitchen doorway. I wanted to hiss and yell at them to flock off. But I was also grateful they turned up, or I'd be turning myself inside out to claw my way into Talon's pants.

"Fuck it. One day, kitten, one day, I'll have you, and then you won't be glad to be interrupted."

I looked into his amused crinkled eyes. "Well, I wasn't totally happy about it."

"I agree," Julian said. "She was giving us laser eyes."

"That's good to know." He smiled down at me, kissed my forehead, and moved off to the front door. "I'll pick up some takeout for dinner after I get Cody from his mother," he said over his shoulder.

"No need, Thor. Mattie and I are going shopping; we'll have enough to feed an army."

I raised my hand to get his attention. "Oh, um, what's Cody's favourite meal to eat?"

Talon's warm eyes turned to me. "Any kinda roast, kitten, just like his dad."

I looked over to Mattie and said, "Can you get me a leg of lamb?"

"Sure thing." He smiled.

"He'll love it, babe," Talon said. "I'll catch ya later."

Five seconds after Talon left, Blue walked in. Maybe I should lock that door one day, but now it seemed to be the traffic way for hot bikers.

"Hey, baby." Blue grinned and walked—no, more like stalked—over to me, and ran the back of his hand down the side of my cheek. My eyes widened as he nodded over my shoulder to Julian and Mattie.

"Alrighty, we're off down the street, hun," Julian said. "If you think of anything else, text me, *baby*." He wiggled his eyebrows up and down. Then he coughed under his breath, "Slut."

I gave him an eye roll. "Uh, wait. Um…" I turned to Blue. "Shouldn't we walk with them, to keep them covered?"

"Everything is set, baby. As soon as someone steps out of this house, another is upon them."

Wow. Talon wasn't taking any chances.

"We're going in Julian's car," Mattie said.

"Don't stress, you'll be covered," Blue said.

"Okay. Uh, guys, I'll see you soon." In other words, do not leave me alone long with Blue. Because seriously, what the heck was that about? Sure, Blue had flirted before, but he'd never made contact with me.

After the front door closed, I gulped. Now I was in a house alone with yet another hot biker, but he wasn't the one who was going to get the green-means-go sign into my panties.

"Blue—"

"No. Don't say anything. I just want you to know, before and *if* you and Talon take this further, I want my chance. I need you to know that Talon wasn't the only one watching you. What makes me different is that while I was watching, I wasn't doing anyone else. I think you're incredible, Zara. I want you in every way." He laid a kiss on my cheek and went over to the couch, sat down, and turned on the television.

Oh. My. God. What in the hell was that? No way, no flipping way. Blue wanted me? In every way?

Wait. What did he mean by while he was watching me, he wasn't doing anyone else? Did that mean Talon had?

Oh, who was I kidding? Of course he had. I witnessed myself his whoring-ness.

I shook my head to clear it. I didn't have time for this; I had enough on my mind. If I let that get to me, I'd be sitting in a corner rocking back and forth, sucking my thumb.

"I'm going to clean. Yeah, cleaning is good."

Blue looked around the house. "Everything seems clean to me, baby."

"No, no, it isn't." I walked over to the couch and pointed to the carpet. "Look, can you see the crumbs?"

He leaned over, smiled, and said, "Nope."

"They're there." I got to my hands and knees, shoving my head down nearly into the carpet. "See there? It's really crummy."

Blue laughed. "Sure, baby. Clean away."

I got up, harrumphed, and added, "I have to dust first."

By MID-AFTERNOON, I had dusted, cleaned the bathrooms and bedrooms, and vacuumed. Now, I was in the kitchen making Blue and myself sandwiches for a late lunch. I felt kind of terrible I hadn't offered him anything before that time, so to make it up to him, he was not only getting two sandwiches, but a piece of chocolate mud cake, a coffee, and a soft drink. I placed them all on a tray and took them into the lounge where his behind was still planted on the couch. Blue was now laughing at *Judge Judy* on TV.

"Wow, baby, maybe I should have confessed my devotion for you a long time ago if this is what I'm going to get."

I blushed and stuttered, "U-uh, no. I mean, I'm sorry for not…for being busy all morning and forgetting lunch. Um, no devotion needed here." I nodded and went back into the kitchen where my own lunch was waiting to be consumed.

I'd just sat down at the table when the phone rang. "Hello?" I answered.

"Why the frig have you not called me yet?" Deanna quietly hissed into the phone.

"Why would I call you at work?"

"Your brother and his partner popped in for a visit. They laughed at me 'cause I was as sweet as pie, no matter what they did; but then they informed me that Blue was all up in your face this morning. What happened?"

"Um, I can't talk right now."

"The fuck you can't…oh, I am so sorry, but I do not believe that is an option for you." I laughed. Someone must have walked into the library to cause Deanna to change her tune like that. On another hiss, she added, "Unless you want me to tell Maya about that time we smoked a joint when she was a baby and you ended up laughing so hard you cried 'cause you thought you had an ugly ape baby, you had better start talking."

That was a bit uncalled for. Not every baby was cute, and it just happened that Maya was one of them; didn't mean I loved her less.

"Jeesh, all right. Hang on a sec'." Taking my plate with me, I got up and walked out to the lounge, where Blue gave me a knowing smirk. "Uh, I gotta take this. Be back." And I quickly headed down the hall to my bedroom. "You ready?" I asked into the phone after sitting down near the pillows on my bed.

"What do you think? Hurry it up, woman, before I get a customer."

"Okay, the quick low down. Blue came in, walked up to me, ran his hand down my cheek and said 'morning, baby.' Mattie and Julian left. Then—oh, my God, Deanna, then he confessed that Talon wasn't the only one watching me for two years. So had he. And he wants me in every way."

"Holy David Hasselhoff!" Deanna yelled. "Sorry, sorry." I knew she was apologizing to people at the library. "Heck, Zee. What are you going to do?" she whispered.

"Nothing."

"What do you mean, nothing?"

"Deanna, hun, he isn't the one who gets my heart and loins racing when he walks into a room. Sure, he's great looking, but… my-my heart already knows who it wants. Even if that guy can be a bossy, alpha-male arse sometimes. He's all of those things and mine."

Silence on the other end. That was never good coming from Deanna.

"Deanna?"

"That's good, Zee. I'm glad for you. Look, I gotta go. See ya later, loser." She sounded deflated, or her boss had just caught her on the phone once again.

"Yeah, okay, I'll see you later." When we'd have a serious talk.

After we'd hung up, I dropped the phone to the bed; a second later it rang again. I answered it with a chirpy, "Hello."

Nothing but air on the other end.

"Hello?" I said again.

Zilch reply.

"Look, if this is one of those heavy-breathing idiots, go out and get a job."

Still nothing.

My bedroom door was flung open. Talon stood there, breathing hard. Two steps and he had the phone out of my hand and had ended the call.

"Hey!" I glared.

"Kitten." He closed his eyes and breathed deeply. Upon opening them, he pulled me from the bed and wrapped his arms around me, then whispered, "It was him."

I froze. Somehow, I knew who he meant, and it certainly wasn't a random pervert.

"No." I shook my head against his chest.

"I asked Violet to hook me up," he said, still whispering. "We have your lines covered; you call out, we know who you're calling. We can hear the conversation. Anyone who calls in and says nothing, we trace their number. He had the balls to use his own phone."

"Talon," I whispered.

"He won't get to you. I promise."

He was telling the truth, but I was still scared out of my mind.

"Let it roll off you, kitten. Don't let him win."

Again, all I could do was nod.

"What's goin' on?" A concerned Blue asked from the doorway.

"Nothin' to concern you, *brother*," Talon growled. He turned us both so we were facing Blue.

"I think it does, brother. I'm here to help, aren't I?"

"I think you're fuckin' here for other reasons, like hittin' on my woman."

My eyes widened. Blue looked at me. Did he think I said something?

"I-I never…"

"It's all right, baby." He smiled at me and turned a glare on Talon. "The phone call, right?" he asked.

Oh, crapola. Talon's words came rushing back to me. *We have your lines covered.* He had heard everything I'd said to Deanna.

"Yes," Talon snapped through clenched teeth. "But something you didn't hear, and that Zara would never share, 'cause she wouldn't wanna hurt you, was that you aren't the one who makes her heart race when you walk into a room. She already knows who she wants, and it ain't fuckin' you."

"Talon." I gasped because he was right. I would never have told Blue that.

"What, babe? At least I didn't mention anything about your loins." He chuckled. I buried my head in my hands and cringed.

"Well, congratu-fuckin'-lations."

I stood straight, my hand reached out to Blue.

"Blue—"

"It's all right, sweetheart."

"No, it ain't. Brothers don't do that shit to each other. A brother never goes after what's already another brother's. You knew I'd claimed Zara. What the fuck?"

"Come on, Talon. Look at her. She's one sweet piece in every way. Most bitches around our area only want one thing, a cock to lay on and get off. I'm sick of that crap. I want more, and I saw that in Zara. I knew I was too late; I could see it in her eyes the way she looks at you. But you can't hate me too much for trying."

"We'll fuckin' see. Right now, we got other stuff to deal with. Get back to the compound. I'm takin' *my* woman to get her kid."

"I get it, Talon, loud and clear."

"Blue—"

"Don't stress, baby. 'S'all good."

I nodded, looked at the floor, and without thinking—but feeling—I quietly said, "One day someone will come along, Blue, and you'll know she's it. She'll do something that will blow your mind, and then she'll be stuck there, and not a minute will go by that you won't think about her. But that isn't me, and I'm sorry."

"Fuck," he hissed. "See what I'm talkin' 'bout, brother? She's got class, balls—especially to stand up to you—and sweetness. A total package."

"I know that, brother," Talon said. "Why'd you think I stopped stuffin' around and grabbed her while I could? I'm just lucky enough she's willin' to grab me back."

I pulled my lips between my teeth so I wouldn't cry. This was a wonderful moment in my life.

It wouldn't be until much later that I remembered about the phone call.

CHAPTER ELEVEN

BLUE LEFT JUST as Mattie and Julian arrived home with their arms filled with groceries. It was lucky they had the help of Vic, another of Talon's guys, to carry it all in. Vic had short blond hair, blue eyes, and was tall and slim, though you could tell he'd still hold his own in a fight. Or if he couldn't, he'd probably scare a bloke with the permanent scowl he had going on. Though, I wasn't entirely sure that scowl was permanent; it could have been there because Mattie and Julian had tortured him all day, dragging him here and there.

"The sex shop was the funniest." Julian cackled, just before Talon and I walked out the front door to collect Maya from school. Talon found that hilarious, whereas I found it worrisome. Because if it weren't for me and my…situation, Vic wouldn't have been put in that spot in the first place.

Poor Vic, he'll end up hating me.

"Kitten," Talon said as I walked quietly beside him.

"Yeah?" I looked over at him.

"Wanna talk 'bout your loins and how they race for me?"

I blushed, pulled my hand free of his, and shoved him. "No, jerk. Want to talk about the fact that you didn't mention doing anything to my phone in the first place?"

"No. I'm glad I didn't. Or I wouldn't have found out what your heart already wanted…me."

"Yeah, right. I was actually talking about the postman. Hoo-wee, he gets me going."

Talon stopped and whipped me into his arms. "Don't. Don't joke about this, kitten. I may be teasin', but I'm so fuckin' full to the brim with…gratefulness to hear that come outta your mouth. You had me worried that I was the only one feeling this, but now I know I'm not, and it makes me happy for the first time in a hell of a long time."

"Talon—"

It was then, in the middle of the street, not far from Maya's school, that he kissed me. And it wasn't only lust riding the kissable train that time, but some feelings had jumped aboard as well.

It was magical.

WE STOOD out the front of Maya's class, receiving a lot of stares. Mainly because I had never shown up to collect Maya with a male before, and the way Talon hugged me to his front, it was undeniable that we weren't just friends.

That was when I saw Maya—who was usually the first one out—come out last with the teacher following her.

"Uh-oh," I said.

"Relax, babe. Can't be that bad. Maya's a good kid."

"Hmm." *We'll see about that.* He had never been with her down the street when she wasn't getting what she wanted. I swear she'd become possessed by the devil.

"Hi, Miss Edgingway," Mrs Faith said with a sigh.

"What's wrong?" I asked though she wasn't looking at me. Even when she greeted me, her eyes were on Talon. Did he have that effect on all ages? Because I was sure Mrs Faith was at least sixty.

"Um—"

And she'd never done that before; I didn't think 'um' was in her vocabulary.

She shook her head and focused back on me. "Do you mind if we have a word alone for a minute?"

"Sure. Maya, honey, why don't you go and show Talon the play area?"

"Okay, Momma." She pulled my sleeve so I was eye-to-eye with her. "Just remember it was real important I done what I done." With that, she spun away, grabbed Talon's hand, and skipped off while Talon walked beside her to the play equipment.

A moment later, I realised I wasn't the only one enjoying the view. Though, *I* wasn't staring at Talon's butt like Mrs Faith was. I was admiring how great it looked for Maya to have Talon beside her, as he looked down listening to something she was saying and then burst out laughing.

I cleared my throat. "Sooo," I started.

"Yes, I am sorry to tell you this, but we had an incident today that involved Maya. We don't condone violence at this school; and honestly, I was shocked that your daughter decided to use such force when she got angry at another student. I have had words with her, and I am sure you will as well. Please make sure that she will not head down that path again."

"What actually happened?"

"Maya hit another child in the stomach, quite hard actually. She didn't like something the other student had said to her. Of course, we both know that even if she doesn't like something, it should never come to violence to get her message across."

"Yes, of course. And I will be speaking to her about the matter this afternoon. I am terribly sorry for what has happened. But, um, can I ask what was said?"

"I think I will leave that up to Maya to inform you. Have a good weekend, Miss Edgingway."

"Yes. Uh, thank you, Mrs Faith."

She turned and scuttled off into her classroom. Old stuffy bat; I was sure it wasn't as bad as it sounded.

I sighed. Time to find out what my little monster had done. I walked around the corner and saw red. Talon was standing by the side of the play equipment watching Maya being a monkey, swinging from one bar to another. That was fine. What I didn't like was *what* was standing by Talon. Okay, maybe I shouldn't say what; it was a she. Stacey MacDonald. The sluttiest of all sluts. And okay, maybe I shouldn't say that, because I hardly knew the lady, but I'd heard enough about her. All the mothers talked about how much she flirted with all the fathers and male teachers at the school. And right now, she was running a hand down Talon's arm, and they were laughing at something she'd just said.

I stalked over, walked around her to Talon's other side, and wrapped my arms around his middle.

"Oh, Zara. Hi."

I grinned but glared. "Yeah, hi, Stacey." I turned my gaze to Talon and gentled my look. "You ready to go, honey?"

He smirked, his lips twitching. Was he seriously fighting not to laugh right now?

"Sure, kitten. Maya, we're goin'."

"Okay," Maya called. She knew she was about to get into trouble because usually, it would take me calling her at least five times before she listened.

Stacey cleared her throat. "Right, bye, Zara. Talon, I'll see you around some time."

WTF?

"Um, no. I don't think you will, Stacey. I plan on keeping Talon very busy for a *very* long time."

She rolled her eyes. "Sure, Zara."

I shook my head, grabbed Talon's hand in mine, and took Maya's hand within the other and left.

Stupid, slutty wench.

Talon leaned into me and whispered, "Do you wanna piss on me as well, kitten?" Then he chuckled.

"Not funny, Talon."

"What's not funny, Ma?"

"Nothing, honey. Now, any chance you want to tell me what happened today?"

She groaned. "I had to do it, Momma. Toby was being mean."

"Maya, what was Toby saying or doing that was so bad to receive a punch in the stomach?"

Talon chuckled. I elbowed him in the ribs and sent him my evil glare. He shut up, but a grin stayed upon his lips.

"It was my turn for news—"

"Yes." I nodded. "And you showed everyone that *Monster High* doll, right?"

"Yeah, but I also had way better news than that."

"And?" I prompted.

"I told the class I had a daddy now." I gasped. Talon's hand in mine grew tighter. "Toby said Talon wasn't my daddy, just someone my mum was dating. I thought he was not right. He was yelling that he was, and said I was silly for even thinkin' it. So I punched him."

Oh, dear.

Not knowing what to say, I decided to steer clear of that whole dad topic—leave it for when I had some inspirational answers, which always came after a bottle of scotch.

So I moved on to the lecture of not hurting anyone, even if they think they were right and were vocal about it. Maya then stomped off up the front steps after I took her hour of television privileges away for the night. In other words—her world had ended. Maya wasn't the only one I didn't want to talk to about the dad subject. As soon as I was in the front door, I headed for the kitchen where I could hear Mattie and Julian.

"All right, where are we at with dinner? Because a roast takes a while, and then there's all the other preparing to do with the vegetables."

"Did you smoke a joint while you were out?" Mattie asked. I was shocked that came out of his mouth; usually, he was more reserved.

To prove my shock, my eyes bulged, and my mouth dropped open. "No, I did not."

He turned to Julian and said, "Something happened on the way home."

Julian nodded. "Oh, definitely."

I didn't get to respond because Talon walked into the kitchen with his phone to his ear.

"Right," he barked. "Well, drop him at the compound." He ran a hand through his hair. "I'll be there. What time? That's none of your business. Well, I could just come and get him like it was fuckin' planned, woman." He sighed. "Christ, fine."

"Talon?" I asked. He was very agitated.

"Stupid bitch. I was supposed to go and grab Cody. But she's bringing him here."

I stiffened. "As in here, here?"

"Nah, kitten, across the road. I wouldn't wanna burden you with that slut. I'll be back soon. No one leaves the house. I'll have guys watching, but no one leaves. Got it?"

"Sure thang, Spiderman." Julian saluted. Mattie nodded.

Without thinking, my body went to Talon. I curled my arms around his waist and met his gaze. He was annoyed, and I wanted to make him better. "Sorry, she's made you mad, honey."

His eyes softened. "You doin' what you just did, and saying what you just said, made putting up with her a whole lot easier. 'Preciate it, kitten. Now kiss me."

And I did.

It started out slow, a touch of lips. But as soon as Talon's tongue touched my bottom lip, I dove, and it soon got hot and heavy.

"They should charge money for this. It's nearly like porn, but they're clothed," Julian commented.

I pulled away and smiled at Talon, his eyes showed he was amused, but his mouth frowned, and he grumbled, "One fuckin' day, kitten."

CHAPTER TWELVE

AN HOUR AND A HALF LATER, dinner was ready, but it was still keeping warm in the oven while we waited for Talon and Cody. Deanna had turned up and was sitting in front of the turned-off television with Maya, playing with her *Monster High* dolls. Mattie was at the table reading the paper while Julian sat beside him reading something on his iPad. I was checking the kitchen floor for any uneven ground as I walked back and forth over it.

That was when we all heard yelling out the front. I looked at the guys at the table as they looked at me. We bolted for the lounge.

"Maya, baby, come to your room and show me all your *Lalaloopsy* dolls," Mattie said.

"Sure, Uncle Mattie." Maya, none the wiser—at least I hoped not —ran off to her room with Mattie following.

Deanna, Julian, and I were just about to peek out the front curtain when we heard, "I should at least get the chance to meet your new whore before she plays house with *my* son."

"Bianca, just fuckin' leave. Hell, it's none of your business who I'm doin'."

Well, really. He hasn't even done me yet.

"Holy shit," Deanna said, grinning. I hadn't had a chance to speak to her…okay, I had a chance, but she ignored said chances to talk in private.

There was a knock at the front door. "Open up, bitch!"

"Mum," I heard Cody hiss in a whisper.

Oh. My. God. She was acting like this in front of her son. That was just…disgraceful.

I opened the door to witness Talon grab his ex by the arm and pull her roughly away from the door.

"Honey," I said with a buttery-sweet tone and a smile on my face. "Don't go doing that, I would love to meet…Bianca, wasn't it?"

Bianca looked at me from head to toe with a sneer on her face. She was beautiful. I could understand why Talon had married her. She had long blonde hair, light blue eyes, and a slim body that was wrapped up in designer gear.

I was sure I looked a treat, too. "Sorry, if I'd known I was receiving company, I would have spruced up a little. I've been cleaning all day."

"You clean your own house."

It wasn't a question, it was more of a disgusted statement.

Deanna stepped forward from behind the door. "No, woman, fairies fly outta her ass and they do it for her."

Cody laughed, but he quickly hid it behind a cough when his mum glared at him.

"Hey, Cody." I waved. He smiled. "Why don'cha come on in. Julian will take you to meet Maya."

"Bye, Mum," he whispered as he walked past her into the house, only to stop just inside when his mum spoke.

"Now hang on a second, bitch!" She turned to Talon. "I don't want him stayin' here with one of your pieces of pussy."

"My time with my boy, I do what I want. And if spending that time is with *my* woman, it's fuckin' what we'll do."

With hands on my hips, I said, "Talon, honey. Check your language in front of the kids."

Talon looked at me with a smile on his face. "Right, kitten."

Bianca gasped.

"Come on, little Thor. Let's leave these cats to hiss it out," Julian said, and with a gentle hand on Cody's shoulder, he ushered him forward and down the hall.

"You are fucking shitting me!" Bianca screeched.

I stepped out the door with Deanna behind me and closed it. I'd had enough. I turned to Bianca with a glare.

"I would appreciate it if you would be more civilised around my house. I do not condone bad language when my daughter is present. Now, I am not trying to replace you in any way when it concerns Cody. All I wanted was to meet and get to know *my* man's child. I'm sorry if that hurts you in some way, but if this *is* what Talon wants, then I will stand by him."

She looked from Talon to me. "You have got to be kidding me. This? That is what you're fucking choosing to screw? Some toffee fat bitch?"

"Watch what you fuckin' say, Bianca."

"Yeah, right, you won't do anything about it, 'cause you know you'd lose Cody."

Holy heck. She was really going to play that card with him?

"Now that's just uncalled for," I said.

She took a step toward me. "I don't give a fuck what you have to say or think, bitch."

Deanna started bouncing up and down on the balls of her feet beside me. "Oh, come on, come on. Let me at her. Talon? Zara? Please."

Bianca looked to Deanna. "And who the fuck are you?"

Deanna ignored the question and looked to Talon with pleading eyes. "Please."

Talon chuckled. "If it's okay with Zara, have at it, Hell Mouth."

Deanna begged me with her eyes. I would have loved to have said my piece, but I didn't want the children to overhear. I didn't want to cause Talon any more damage, and I thought if it didn't come from me, then the problem wouldn't escalate. Also, Deanna sure did have a way with words, and when she wanted to get a certain message across, she did, with a firework result.

And who was I to spoil her fun? I nodded at Deanna.

She beamed, stepped in front of me, and snarled in Bianca's face, "Don't you ever fuckin' come here giving shit to my sista and her man. I will fuckin' take you down, slut. I'm not a pulling hair, sissy fighta. I claw, bite, and give my all, and there is a lot. And if you even think of holding Cody against Talon, I will rip you and your life apart. You think you got money and you can do or say anything? Well, shit, woman, I got so much money I could use it as toilet paper. So, I have every chance to fuck you and your husband over. Now back the fuck up, woman, and leave. Let them have this. If you don't, I'll rain down on you faster than you can blink."

Bianca did indeed blink…and then again. She opened her mouth, shut it and then stuttered, "B-but—" She shook her head and stood straighter. "Hang on a sec, she just swore."

I shrugged and said, "Yeah, but she was quiet about it. The kids wouldn't have heard that."

"What-fucking-ever." She turned and went down the steps, then left.

"Honey, your ex is a…not a nice person," I said as we stared after her.

Deanna sighed. "Zee, she's a bitch."

"That she is, Hell Mouth, and so much more. But I think you just scared the fuck outta her. So, thanks," Talon said.

"Not a problem, bossman. I enjoyed it."

Talon took the steps two at a time and was in front of me, then I was in his arms. "Sorry 'bout that, kitten."

I wrapped my arms around his waist and grinned up at him. "Don't apologise for that thing, honey. I just hope we can salvage dinner."

"What did I ever do to deserve you?" Talon grinned.

"And me," Deanna said.

Talon chuckled. "Yeah, Hell Mouth, and fuckin' you. Let's go eat, babe."

DINNER WASN'T TOO BAD. The meat was still tender enough that we didn't have to carve it with a chainsaw. Maya adored Cody, and I think the feeling was mutual. Cody didn't say much while we ate, but he did smile, and of course laughed at Deanna and Julian a lot. Though, who wouldn't?

After checking with Cody first, we set up a bed in Maya's room; she was over the moon to have company. I hoped she didn't talk his ears off. Talon's only comment was that I needed a bigger house. I laughed and said I liked it the way it was. That was when he informed me that tomorrow we were staying at his house with the kids because at least there the walls were more soundproof and he could have his wicked way with me. I gulped.

It wasn't until Julian and Mattie had gone to bed, Deanna had left with Griz, complaining all the way, and Talon and I were in bed and asleep—after fooling around for a bit—that I woke in the middle of the night from a nightmare about *the* phone call. If Talon hadn't been there, it would have advanced into a full-blown panic attack.

"Like I said, kitten," Talon whispered, "we're going to my house tomorrow; not for the other reasons, but 'cause it's safer. I have an alarm system and cameras. We'll take everyone if we have to. I'll keep you safe, babe. Always."

"Okay, honey," I said. Because I knew that was true.

CHAPTER THIRTEEN

"Momma, Mum, Ma. Mummy, wake up."

I woke up wishing my daughter had a snooze button like my alarm clock. She didn't, of course, so I had to pry open my eyes and pay attention to her.

"Yes, Maya, my wonderful, pain-in-the-beehive daughter. What is so important to wake me up on a Saturday morning?"

"I'm hungry."

Seriously? Where was that duct tape when I needed it? I sat up slowly, looked next to me, and found the bed empty. Well, there went my morning nookie.

Wait. Where in the heck did that come from?

Why was I thinking about nookie in the first place with my daughter present?

That damn Talon.

"Maya, was that all you needed, hun?" Because last I knew, we had a house full of people who could have helped her out; and also, from the sound of it, they were *already* awake.

"No. I've got swimming, remember?" She smiled.

I glanced at the clock and hissed, "Snap." I threw the covers back;

thankfully, I was wearing my PJs, so I bounced off the bed and ordered, "Right, Maya, get dressed, get the bag from the laundry with a towel in it, and be ready. I'll throw some clothes on, and we'll get going. Okay?"

"Okay." She ran from the room, yelling, "We're late, we're late."

We weren't that late. Swimming started in ten minutes and we lived five minutes away by car from the centre. Okay, so maybe we were going to be a little late, but we had to go; my little-uncoordinated angel needed as many lessons as possible.

I dressed in black leggings, a tight long-sleeved black top under a looser fitting tee that read 'This ain't no milk store'. I slipped on a pair of combat boots and ran from my room to the kitchen where Talon and Cody already were.

"Gotta go, gotta go, people," I said, as I quickly filled a travel mug of coffee. I was about to walk out of the kitchen and yell at Maya to get her beehive out here when Talon called, "Kitten."

"Yes, honey?" I turned to face him. "Oh, sorry. Morning, Cody. I hope you've had breakfast. Hey, do you want to come with us? I'm sure Maya would love to show you how not to swim while trying to learn to swim."

Cody beamed and looked from me to Talon, so I moved my gaze to Talon also.

"Kitten, get your arse over here."

I sighed and rolled my eyes. "Talon, I don't have time for this. I need to go. Maya!" I yelled.

"Comin'!" she yelled back.

"Kitten." There was a tone of warning in his voice.

I sighed. "Yes, Talon?"

"Get your arse over here. Kiss me, and then you can go. I'll bring Cody with me in a moment; I gotta see to something at the compound."

"Oh, okay." I grinned, walked over to him, and gave him a quick peck on the mouth. Talon wasn't having any of that. As I went to pull away, he brought me closer and really kissed me, so thoroughly that my legs went wonky and my fandola sang "Let's Get it On." Then I remembered we had an audience.

I stepped away and glared at him. "Talon," I snapped. "None of that in front of Cody—"

"He don't mind."

"That's beside the point. I do not neck in front of our children."

His eyes went extra soft. What had I done or said to receive that response from him? I wasn't sure, but I knew I liked it.

Though, then I remembered. "And do not say the a-word again, mister," I said, jabbing him in the chest with my finger.

"Babe." He smiled. "Let's leave the cursing lesson till later when you're not going to be late."

I gasped, looked at the clock on the microwave, and yelled, "Maya, let's move it." I gave Talon a quick peck, Cody a hair ruffle, and over my shoulder, I said, "See you there."

Maya met me in the lounge. She said a quick goodbye and we left.

MAYA WAS in the pool room that was glassed off from the parents. I was in the sitting area watching through the glass, which I found was better for the children because they were able to concentrate on their teacher without having parents yelling orders. I also thought it was wonderful because it blocked out the noise of rowdy kids for half an hour. I was in the back row near the front door, so it was easier for me to keep an eye out for Talon and Cody while watching Maya.

I grimaced as Maya dove in—well, more belly-flopped in. I glanced over my shoulder once again to see some woman run out of the centre, when I spotted Cody walking through the door. I smiled and waved him over.

"Hey," I said as he sat down next to me.

"Hi," he whispered. Something was wrong.

"Um, Cody, are you okay?"

"Yeah."

Alrighty.

"Cody, where's your dad?"

He looked over his shoulder, and as he did, his top lip curled up in a look of disgust. "Coming," he said.

I looked behind me to see that Talon was coming in, but with him was a blonde-haired, blue-eyed, big-boobed bimbo. She was dressed in the tightest of tight jeans, where anyone could see her camel-toe and a tight white tee. I turned my attention front and centre and tried my best not to jump over the chair and rip her apart for touching my man. Unfortunately, they stopped too far behind us for me to be able to hear what they were saying.

"Who's that, buddy?" I asked Cody.

"Dunno. But don't worry, Zee. Dad likes you better." He looked at me with concerned eyes.

I smiled and patted his arm. "I know, bud."

Whoever she was, she had to go. It was making Cody uncomfortable and upset.

"Be back in a sec," I whispered to Cody. "Can you watch Maya for me?" I pointed her out. He didn't say anything, only nodded.

I got up, plastered a big smile on my face, and walked up to Talon and Pamela Anderson-wannabe.

Before she noticed me, I heard her whisper, "So, when are you gonna give me another chance to have that cock of yours?"

"Pam," Talon sighed. His eyes were on me as he added, "I already told you, I got a woman now—"

"I don't mind sharing. You know that." She smiled and leaned her tits into his arm.

I took a deep breath and stopped in front of them; she looked at me and glared. "Hi." I grinned. "I'm Zara Edgingway, Talon's woman. Can I ask that you refrain from rubbing up against *my* man? I don't like to see it, and his son doesn't like to see it. Actually,

I find it disgusting that you would even act in such a way in front of these people. Do you have a child here?"

"Yes," she hissed.

"You better run and be a good mother then, instead of coming on to a man who already said he's taken, and acting like some dog in heat."

She stalked off without another word.

I glared up at Talon with my hands on my hips and snapped, "I am seriously thinking of tattooing a sign on your forehead when you're asleep that says 'Property of Zara.'" Then I walked off, leaving Talon chuckling behind me.

After Maya finished, we stood outside in the warm midmorning, waiting while Talon and Cody had a great laugh about what I'd said to Talon earlier. Cody was laughing his pants off. I was a little annoyed, but also happy to see Cody smile and laugh with his father, even if it was at my expense. Maya was standing silently beside me, only because she was chomping down a lollipop that Talon had bought her after swimming.

"All right, let's get a-goin'. Babe, you gotta pack some stuff to take to my place."

"Are we stayin' at Talon's?" Maya asked.

"If that's okay with you." I smiled down at her.

"That'd be cool. Cody was telling me all about it and how big it was; and, Momma, they got a Xbox *and* a PlayStation. I wanna try those."

"I'm sure that would be fine."

My daughter is easily bought.

"We'll meet you back at the house," I said, then turned to walk off, only my arm was caught on something, and that something pulled. I was spun back around and wrapped up in tight arms.

"When're you gonna flippin' learn?" Talon growled.

"Uh," was my smart response.

"When one of us is leavin', kitten, I want your mouth. Now give it to me."

116

"And what did I say about necking in front of the kids?" I glared.

"They'll get used to it." He grinned and then proceeded to kiss me, and of course, once his mouth was on mine, my brain went blank and my body took over. Meaning, we were definitely necking in front of the kids.

He stopped the kiss, stepped back, smirked, and gave a chin lift to someone behind me. I turned to see one of Talon's biker brothers do the whole chin lift back. Only when I looked back at Talon, he was already on his way to his car with Cody.

"Ma, we going?"

"Yes, Maya."

We walked over to my car, a beat-up black Volkswagen Beetle, got in, and it was then that Maya informed me, "I like Talon for a daddy. He makes you smile a lot."

I bit my bottom lip, smiled at her and nodded. Pulling out of the car park, I noticed Talon's biker brother followed us all the way home. I should have noticed that morning that I had a tail, but I hadn't. Really, I should have been the one in the first place to have asked someone to follow or come with us in case anything happened. In case *he* had someone out there watching and waiting for the right moment to commence his payback, but I didn't think of it.

Why?

Because Talon makes me feel safe.

TALON and I walked in the front door at the same time, and at the looks on Julian, Mattie, and Deanna's faces, I wanted to walk right back out. Mattie quickly ushered Cody and Maya into Maya's room to play games. Then Griz walked out of the kitchen carrying a bunch of bright pink assorted flowers.

I looked at Talon. His body went solid beside me as his hand squeezed mine. "Did you buy me flowers?" I asked, though I already knew the answer, only I didn't want to admit it.

He shook his head.

I closed my eyes. "They're from him, aren't they?"

"There was a note, boss," Griz barked.

"Kitten, look at me."

I kept my eyes closed and shook my head. I didn't want to look at him. I didn't want to see the note, or the flowers, or the pity from anyone. I wanted to lock my family, friends, and myself away in an oblivious bubble and not think of anything.

"She's gonna blow," Deanna said.

And, in fact, she was right. I felt the pressure build, the stress and the heartache of not having enough time to mourn my parents, of having to deal with this prick again in my life. I was angry, pissed, annoyed and sexually frustrated.

I didn't realise I was still shaking my head until Talon captured it between his palms and tilted it. My eyes opened and saw he was just as furious as I was.

"You can't do this right now. I'd love to let you loose, but not now, and not here with the kids. Do not let this fucker win."

"I need something, Talon. I need to vent soon, honey, or I'm gonna go crazy."

"Girls' night!" Julian cried. I stepped out of Talon's hold and turned to him as he continued, "Or day, should I say. You need to vent, kidney bean; we'll do that in style. Drinking, massages, make-up, dancing, drinking, crying, screaming and drinking some more."

"I can't, Julian—"

Mattie emerged from the hallway saying, "No, it's a great idea. I can take care of the children. Zee, it would make you feel so much better."

"It's not right. Not now, I can't leave Maya and Cody alone. Not that they'd be alone... I just shouldn't."

"Babe, you should. Matthew can take the kids to my place with Vic, Bizz, and Stake. They'll be fuckin' safer there than anywhere."

He looked to Griz and then back to me. "I got shit I need to do, but I'll catch up with you sometime. Until then, Griz, Blue, and Pick will be with you, Hell Mouth, and Julian."

"I—"

"No, kitten. Do this. You need an outlet. As much as I'd like you to fuckin' use me, that ain't gonna work right now. All right?"

I nodded. "Okay, honey."

He smiled brightly and said, "Good."

CHAPTER FOURTEEN

TALON LEFT with the flowers and note—after, of course, a hot make-out session. And yes, it was in front of everyone. I was getting the impression he wasn't unfavourable toward public displays of affection. Something I was still learning to get over myself.

Maya and Cody were both fine with going to Talon's without me, and instead with Mattie and the bikers. I packed as Maya gabbed on about how unreal it was going to be staying at Talon's, that she was going to have a huge-arse—yes, she said arse, but only because Cody had—room to herself. I was going to have to have another word with Talon. Though, what had me forgiving Cody so quickly for cursing was when Maya told me that he'd said if she got scared through the night, she was allowed to go into his room, that he'd keep her safe.

Wasn't that just the cutest thing?

Before they left, I gave Cody a big hug for what he'd said.

It caused him to look at me strangely, because either he didn't know why, or he just wasn't used to a mother figure showing him affection.

Griz made himself at home on the couch, watching motorbike racing, while Deanna, Julian, and I sat at the kitchen table, organising the afternoon and night's events. We were arguing about whether cocktails or straight shots were going to be the main choice of beverage when the front door opened and in walked Blue and Pick. They sat down with Griz after a quick hello, and we went back to arguing while we made lunch for everyone.

In the end, we decided to do both. Once lunch was consumed— or wolfed away, where the men were concerned—Julian announced, "Massage time. Then we'll start a little drinky-poo."

"Whoa, hang on. I thought we were going somewhere for that massage," Deanna said.

Julian rolled his eyes. "Don't be silly, apple tart. I am actually a professional masseuse. I've got my table in my car and all. Girl, you won't know what hit you when I get my hands on you."

Julian, with the help of Griz, got his table from the car. Once we moved the lounge around a bit, we placed the table in the middle. None of the bedrooms were big enough to have it in.

The guys positioned themselves back on the couch and chair and continued to watch television. That was until Deanna came out in my robe. I had demanded—because it was my night—that she went first.

"Okay, lemon drop, lie on your stomach." Julian patted his table.

Deanna turned a glare on the guys, who quickly looked away, then lay down. She had Julian help her remove my robe so that all she was left wearing was her low-riding jeans. Her top half was naked. Not that you could see anything, thank goodness, or I wouldn't be getting up there. Julian squirted some oil onto his hands and rubbed them together. As soon as he placed them on Deanna's back and started to work out her knots, she moaned low in her throat.

"Jesus," Griz growled.

I grinned.

"I think I'm in the wrong job," Pick said.

I looked to Blue. He wasn't looking at Deanna at all. His eyes were on me, and once I'd turned to him, he said, "Looking forward to your turn, babe."

I blushed and had second thoughts about actually having a go.

"Blue," Griz barked.

Blue smirked and shrugged at Griz. "Can't help myself," he said.

Julian worked Deanna for half an hour, then wrapped the robe back around her; as she got up from the table, her eyes were hooded. That was when I noticed Griz adjust himself in his pants. He so wanted her.

"Come on, French fry, your turn," Julian said to me.

"Um, no. I think I'll be all right." I gave him a small smile.

"If I had to do it, so do fuckin' you," Deanna called from my room, where she was probably getting ready to shower to remove the oil from her skin.

"Unless you want me to do it, baby," Blue said.

"You are just askin' for it, dickhead," Griz snapped.

"It could be the only chance I'll get to have my hands on her sweet skin," Blue commented like it meant nothing, his eyes on me while my eyes were wide and worried.

Griz elbowed him in the ribs and ordered, "Get your stupid arse outside. Wildcat don't need that shit." He turned back to Blue. "And Talon will fuckin' kill you if you make this night crap for her."

Blue flinched. "Sorry, babe." He got up from the couch and left out the front door.

"Don't worry, Zara, he'll be all right. He'll still help out tonight," Pick said.

Was I right to feel bad for Blue? A part of me said no, and then another part said yes. What I didn't understand—even though they'd said some nice things about me—and couldn't comprehend, was that both Talon and Blue thought that I was an okay type of gal.

Maybe they were high most of the time?

That was all I had to explain their interest in me.

AN HOUR LATER, I had worked out that Julian was actually a god, and I wanted to chop off his hands and sell them on eBay. I could have made millions. But because I couldn't do that, I had a shower after my near-orgasmic massage, and was now dressed in a long black skirt, combat boots, and a black tee that read 'Rock On'. I put some make-up on and gunk in my hair to control the frizz. I piled it up, with the help of many bobby pins, on the top of my head—only Julian had to have his way and place a few ringlets hanging down. He was dressed in dark blue jeans and a teal-coloured shirt. Deanna looked amazing in tight black pants and a silky grey shirt. What we were dressed up for, I didn't have a clue, but once I started on my third cocktail, I didn't care. It was while I was on that third cocktail and fifth shot that I broke down crying when Julian mentioned my parents. Then I went from grieving to flat-out pissed off.

To say the least, I was so happy I had Deanna and Julian there to fuel my fire inside. We yelled and screamed. I quivered a bit and then whispered my worries to them both as we sat at the kitchen table.

Then I announced, "You know what? We missin' one of me gals 'ere. I'm gonna ring Vi."

"We 'on't need dat bitch," Deanna said. She was a little drunk.

Okay, we all were.

"Deanna," I sighed. "Honey lumpkin, you need to learn to play nice with others. I lov' ya, but life is all 'bout expanding. Look at me, I have a hot biker boyfriend, who I so want to have sex with—"

"Fuckin' hell," Griz growled from the lounge room.

"You said it, brother," Blue griped.

"They're kinda funny," Pick said.

"Don't listen in then, punks," Deanna yelled at them.

"Yeah!" Julian yelled as well and then, "Go on, cock ring, and ring her."

Julian's cute pet names, I noticed once he was drunk, turned dirty.

I reached for the phone on the kitchen bench and said, "All right, I'm gonna do it." *After a long drink of water.*

I rang her mobile number; on the third ring, she picked up.

"'Lo," she said

"Why 'ello there, Miss Marcus. You know I really should have taken notice of your last name more because it's just like Talon's."

"Zara?"

"Yeah?"

"Are you drunk?" I could hear the smile in her voice.

"Maybe a wee little bit, and I thought, I'm having a few drinks with Deanna and Julian, and I was missing someone, and that someone was you. Now get your behind here and drink with us," I ordered.

"I doubt Barbie wants me there—"

"Oh, don't mind her, she's all full of shit bein' a hater."

"No, I'm not," Deanna yelled beside me. I shoved her. She teetered in her chair, about to fall—and I would have laughed my arse off—but then she regained her balance.

"I can't, anyway," Violet said. "I'm still at work, and I've got some filing to finish."

"Hmm." I thought for a second and then slapped the table with my hand. "I've got it. We'll come to you."

"Yay, an outing. Ooh, I've got to get my shoes." Julian ran from the kitchen, yelling, "Has anyone seen my shoes? We're going out."

"Like fuck," Griz barked.

"I don't think you should do that, Zee. Someone doesn't sound happy about it on your end," Vi said.

"Oh, pish posh. Leave them to me. See you soon, hun, and we'll bring some grog." I hung up before she could complain about my idea.

Griz, Pick, and Blue stomped into the kitchen. They all looked good enough to eat, standing there in jeans, biker boots, tight tees and their Hawks vests, with their arms crossed over their chests.

"You know," I began, "you guys are pretty good looking."

"You ain't charming us into doin' this shit, Wildcat," Griz said. His dark blue gaze shifted from me to Deanna and narrowed.

"What? Don't look like that at me; it wasn't my idea. Still, it's a good one. We need to get out. No, scratch that, Zee needs to get out, have stress-fuckin'-free fun. It's what her bossman would want for her."

"Hey, yeah. Good point there." I nodded. "Call my sex-on-legs man. See what he says."

Griz stalked into the lounge; his voice was low enough we couldn't hear what was being said, but he sounded outraged. Looked to me like I was going to get my way. I grinned.

"Hell, baby, this is a bad idea, but you knew Talon'd let this fly for you," Blue commented.

I shrugged and tried not to look so pleased.

"Makes me kind of thankful it ain't me dealing with this shit. If you were my woman, I wouldn't allow this."

I bit my bottom lip.

"Nah, I'm still fucking jealous." He walked off as Griz came in.

"Let's roll then." He turned to Pick. "Go get your vehicle, you and Blue follow—"

Julian ran into the room saying, "Found them, thunder cunts. They were under the bed."

"Julian Jacob, do not say that word around me again," I snapped.

"Sorry, pussy flaps." He smiled sweetly. I rolled my eyes, and Deanna burst out laughing.

"You three are with me," Griz ordered.

Excitement ran through my body. I couldn't keep still in the car on the way to work, which wasn't far. Really, we could have walked, but I wasn't going to push that idea. Deanna sat in the front of the tough-looking black Chrysler, next to Griz; Julian was in the back with me. We kept looking at each other, smiling and giggling.

We pulled up to the office, and I got out juggling a bottle of tequila, a bottle of bourbon, and a cocktail shaker. Julian was carrying the glasses for us to use because I knew there were none at the office, well, besides coffee cups. But that just wasn't going to happen.

Griz came around the front of the car and barked, "Next time, you wait till I'm outta the car and the boys have pulled up and got out as well."

"Sorry, Griz," I said in a little girl's voice. Julian and Deanna laughed. Griz's eyes narrowed.

IT TURNED out to be a great idea of mine. Violet was a great person usually, but a hoot when she was tipsy. We were surrounding her desk, sitting in our own chairs, talking and laughing about our first time experiences in sex. The guys were sitting back a bit, pretending not to listen as they played cards.

"It wasn't until I met Travis that I was introduced to receiving it hard. God, I loved it when he used to pound into me and let me tell you, he was huge. Delicious." Vi licked her lips and grinned at the memory.

"Christ," Blue swore.

"I think I need a smoke after that," Julian said. We all laughed.

"What about you, Barbie?"

"The best time I've ever had sex was when—"

"Enough," Griz growled. "I don't wanna hear any more of this shit."

"Aw, but we haven't got to my turn yet," Julian moaned.

"No offense, man, but we had to hear about your first time; that was enough," Pick said.

"You know what?" I asked the room.

Vi, Deanna, and Julian all asked "What?" at the same time, causing us to laugh again.

"I need music."

"Yeah, that'd be a grand idea. I want to dance." Violet smiled, but then it quickly faded. "But I haven't got anything here to listen to it on."

"Not even a radio?" Julian asked.

"Nope. But hey, there's a bar just down the road—"

"Fuck no," Blue said.

"Yes. Yes, I like that idea." I clapped. "Come on, guys, it's just down the road, like five places away. We can walk. Nothing's gonna happen."

CHAPTER FIFTEEN

WE WALKED into the bustling bar. The atmosphere felt great, with dim lighting and someone singing at the karaoke machine. The pool tables were full; so were the booths and seating area at the bar.

Deanna dragged me over to the bar and squeezed her way in, shouting out to the bar girl in a tight white tee that she wanted four shots of Cock Sucking Cowboys.

Upon paying, she dished out the shots and on the count of three, down they went and up came my hamburger from dinner...nearly.

"Oh, I love this song. Let's dance," Julian shouted when Taylor's Swift's "Trouble" came through the karaoke machine, and some young girl started singing it with a not-too-bad voice.

We left Griz, Pick, and Blue at the bar, while Violet, Deanna, Julian and I went to shake our booties.

Two songs later, I glanced around for our guards, only they were no longer brooding at the bar. I looked around, but couldn't see them anywhere. Violet tugged on my arm, and while she jiggled what her mama gave her, she pointed through the crowd to a booth in the far corner where they were now seated—still brooding. Their arms were crossed over their chests and their eyes said 'don't speak to me or I'll bite your head off.'

It was only Griz's gaze that lasered into us. Though, I think that had something to do with the way Deanna was grinding against some innocent young man…um, okay, maybe he wasn't that innocent, considering the way he grabbed her boobs. I giggled to myself when she elbowed him in the ribs and pushed him away. She turned her gaze to me, grinned and shook her head.

Deanna, Julian, and I made our way to the table while Vi went to grab us some more drinks. I'd asked for water because I didn't think my stomach could handle another toxic mix. That was when Deanna called me a pussy and said to Vi that if she got me water, they'd be having words. Violet then proceeded to laugh in Deanna's face, and answered with 'Whatever.' I knew what I'd be getting —water.

I collapsed next to Pick. Griz and Blue stood so Julian and Deanna could sit, and then Vi when she got back. It was like they were protecting the President's daughter. Blue and Griz had their backs to us; both were standing straight and still, glaring out at the partygoers.

Wow, they must take their jobs seriously.

"You know, I kind of feel like Whitney Houston in *Bodyguard* right now," Julian said

I held up my fist to be pumped and yelled, "That's what I was just thinking." *Sort of.* Why I was yelling I had no clue; it wasn't so hard to hear in our corner.

"Yo, Vi. Oh, my God, I love you," I yelled—yes, again—when she deposited a bottle of water in front of me with a smirk directed at Deanna.

"Do you reckon Talon could be quiet during sex?" I asked.

Okay. Maybe I was a tad intoxicated still because yelling was all I could manage.

"Jesus," Blue hissed.

"Talon owes us," Griz barked.

Julian ended up spitting his drink all over the table. Violet groaned and banged her head against the back of the booth. Pick asked for me to move so he could escape, and Deanna sat with her finger tapping her chin, pondering my question.

"Given his hotliness and badarseness, I highly doubt it," Deanna said. "Why the wondering?"

I sighed loudly. "I wanna have sex. I miss the pounding, the closeness, and the connection," I whined. "Hey!" I shouted, pointing at Griz and Blue. "No comment from the spunky men," I yelled before they could even think of commenting.

"Uh, Wildcat. Please, please move," Pick begged.

While continuing my rant, I moved and sat back down after Pick had escaped. "Six years, people. Six long years. Holy haemorrhoid, do you think my well's dried up?"

"Fuck me," Griz snapped.

"You don't want me to," Deanna supplied. I thought it had been quiet, but Griz turned a surprised stare upon her, which quickly morphed into a glare. Then he went back to looking at the crowd.

"You can't tell me—" Vi began.

"What?" Julian asked.

"Nope, I can't say it. That's my brother, for gonad's sake." She shuddered.

"Oh, oh! I think I know where you're going," Julian said, clapping. "And, cock ring, you can't deny the male fuckableness your bro is. Anyway, what she was getting at…you can't tell us that you and Spidey haven't done squat in the bedroom department."

I think I just blushed. Or the room had turned up twenty degrees.

"What the fuck, bitch? You have done something with the bossman and you ain't told me? Where's the friendship? I told you *all* about my last one not that long ago."

Griz flinched. Deanna smirked, but then quickly sent me her deadly glare. Thankfully, I was immune.

"Shit," Blue said. "I am not stayin' here to hear this crap. We can watch 'em from the bar." Blue stalked off, with Pick and a grumbling Griz not far behind.

"Maybe I should join them," Vi added. "I *really* don't feel like hearing about what my brother gets up to in bed. It'd probably cause me to chuck."

"Block your ears then," Deanna said.

I had to laugh when Violet did, in fact, block her ears.

"Quickly spill, muff lover," Julian cried, leaning forward over the table.

"There isn't much to say. As you can tell, we didn't do the deed..."

"But? Come on, woman, don't leave me hanging," Deanna said.

I blushed again. "I'm still kind of sensitive about it. Icameinliketwoseconds."

"Say what now?" Julian asked. "Sorry, dick sucker, I don't speak drunk-virgin-hymen-grown-over girl talk."

Groaning, I hid my eyes with my hand. "He went... you know... down yonder, and I was... um, done quickly."

"Did he care?" Deanna asked.

"No. Well, I don't think so, especially not when I reciprocated."

"Whoop, fuckin', whoop, girl. I'm so proud of you." Deanna beamed.

Deanna cheering me on made me smile. I should be proud; I was lucky I lasted that long after *six years*, and Talon didn't seem to have minded at all.

I got in closer and whispered, "He is huge."

"I hate you." Julian glared.

"You—"

"Hey there, sweetheart," a guy in his late forties said, as he stood at our table with two others. They all wore jeans and tees, with leather biker vests over the top. It was hazy, but I read the words 'Vicious Club' on the top patch.

The older one sat down beside me. "How's your night been, beautiful?"

I studied him for a second, and it was his eyes that told me he was harmless; the crinkle around them showing me he loved to laugh, and his smiling mouth told me he was caring. The thick salt-and-pepper hair told me my fingers wouldn't mind running through it to see if it was as soft as it looked.

His friends, though, were another story; they looked mean and scary. Which was why I leaned into him and whispered, "You seem like a nice guy, and I honestly mean it when I say that one day we could be friends, but—I'm sorry to say that your friends don't seem all that nice."

I sat back and watched him throw his head back and laugh a deep belly laugh.

"Oh, you are precious." He smiled.

"Which is why she's Hawks property," Griz growled from beside us where he stood next to Mean One and Mean Two.

Property, smoperty. I wasn't sure I liked that word yet.

Mr Nice looked up at Griz and asked, "Whose?"

"Talon's."

But I like that word.

"Wildcat, go and dance," Blue ordered.

Now he just popped up out of nowhere. I rolled my eyes and scooted around the other side, where Julian, Deanna, and Vi were already waiting for me.

Leaning over the table, I uttered, "It was nice meeting you…"

"Rocko," he supplied.

I smiled. "Rocko, and remember what I said." I got closer still. "I think you may need new friends."

"Thanks, sweetheart." He chuckled and then winked. "I'll keep that in mind."

Griz sat down as soon as I was out of the way. I moved off to the dance floor with my peeps to jiggle my flabby bits once again.

I was determined to have a great night.

We danced, we drank, and we sang our night into happiness.

Rocko and his mates had left probably an hour earlier, but I still couldn't fight the feeling of unease.

Then I thought it could be because I had to pee. Violet had gone to grab a drink, and while Deanna and Julian were being enter-tained by the Tina Turner wannabe, I went off in search of the toilet.

CHAPTER SIXTEEN

I woke up in the back of a strange car. My eyes were a little blurry, but once they cleared, I saw a gun pointed at my face. The guy who aim it was the one I'd seen walk into the girls' bathroom behind me at the bar, and he was also the one who had tasered me in the back after saying his boss wanted a word with me. It was just before I had the chance to scream.

"I don't know your boss," I croaked and sat up slowly.

My mouth was dry, and the great buzz I'd had going on at the club had disappeared, leaving me with a very nasty headache.

Though, that could also be from being *freaking* tasered.

"Yeah, well, he knows you, and when he wants something, he gets it." The guy smiled, showing crooked teeth. If it weren't for those, he would have been an okay-looking man. He had a buzz cut, leaving dark-coloured fluff, and his eyes were brown. He had piercings in his lip, nose, and eyebrow, and seemed tall, slim and young. It was dark in and out of the car.

His companion who was driving was completely different. He had long dirty-blond hair; his build was larger, and he seemed shorter than Mr Talker.

I wondered if by now my friends knew I'd been kidnapped. I hoped they weren't panicking too much. My next thought was why wasn't I panicking? I felt a bit stressed, only relieved at the same time, because at least no one would get hurt when I was delivered to David. He'd already done many bad things to me; it couldn't get worse. Right?

I gulped.

At least Maya was safe.

The car suddenly stopped. It was then I realised I should have been taking in my surroundings to know where they were taking me in case of an escape. We'd pulled up outside of a huge house, one I didn't think was anything David would buy. It was old, yet beautiful. David loved new and exquisite things. My door opened. Mr Silent was there smirking in at me; he then jutted his chin out and up.

I stumbled out, and Mr Silent grabbed my arm, dragging me roughly forward and through the front door, down a hallway that took my breath away, and into a room that was a library. Books lined two walls from top to bottom. A large desk was in front of a huge bay window, where a man stood looking out. He turned with an intense gaze.

Oh. My. God. Where do they make these people? He was yet another good-looking older man, probably in his early forties, with dark hair and a few greys splattered at the sides. He had grey eyes and an athlete's form hidden behind a designer suit.

"Um, you're not David," I said, puzzled. What was I doing here and who was this guy?

"I hope my men weren't too forceful in getting you here."

"Do you call being tasered too forceful?" I asked with fake bravado, hands on my hips, glaring at him. On the inside I was chanting *I'm gonna die; I'm gonna die, and I never got to have sex with Talon.*

His fierce gaze turned to Mr Silent and Talker. "I told you to ask her politely. Did you even do that? Doesn't matter, get out of my sight," he snapped. "Please, Zara, have a seat, and I'm sorry for the way they treated you. It was not something I wanted."

Scepticism ran through my mind; still, I took a seat opposite him as he sat behind a large wooden mahogany desk that held papers scattered everywhere. "You have a nice home," I said. *Why am I being polite to the guy?* I cleared my throat. "Um, I mean, what am I doing here?"

"Thank you to the first." He smiled. "And to the second, I have some questions, to which I am sure you will have the answers."

"Sorry, but I doubt it. I don't know you." I looked down at my lap and adjusted my skirt.

"Pam, please come in," he called.

I turned in time to see the door open, and my jaw dropped. In walked the Pamela Anderson-wannabe from swimming that morning.

"You have got to be shitting me," I uttered. I watched her as she walked over to…heck, I didn't even know the guy's name, and stood beside him, smiling smugly.

"I can see that you recognise my girlfriend, Pam Knowles."

I snorted. I couldn't help it, and said, "Seriously, buddy, you need to find a new girlfriend."

He glared at me. "So what happened this morning was true? You verbally insulted and harmed Pam in front of my child."

I gasped.

"You see, Zara, I do not take kindly to this type of behaviour in front of my child, and I do not appreciate having my girlfriend mentally and physically hurt."

I slapped my hands on the desk and stood yelling, "Say what now? Look, buddy, I don't know who you are, and you seem like a nice sort of guy, but I can tell you now, I never did anything to your Pamela Anderson-wannabe."

"She's lying," Pam spat.

"Oh, my frigging God, are you really trying this on?" I glared and turned to her fella, offered an eye roll and added, "Buddy—"

"Travis Stewart," he supplied.

I sighed deeply. "Travis, I didn't even see a child with her. I only approached her because she was, and I'm sorry to tell you this, hitting on *my* man in front of *his* child. My man's son found me sitting down and he looked worried by it, so I got up to get rid of her. I may have called her a dog in heat, but other than that, I never did or said anything that was not appropriate." I raised my hands in the air and let them fall. "This is why I was tasered and brought here? Jesus, how bad is my luck right now? You know what? I really don't need this. I have enough going on." I flopped back in the chair.

"I'm sorry, Zara—"

"What are you apologising to her for?" Pam snapped.

Travis glared up at her. "Clearly, she is having a hard time in life right now." He stood to gaze down at her; she took a step back. "Tell me, Pam, is it true what you have told me, or is what Zara was saying true?"

"Travy, it wasn't like that. She's lying."

We all turned to the door when we heard a commotion outside of it. The door flew open, and in it stood Violet holding out her gun, pointing it inside the room.

"Travis?" She looked as though she knew him. She relaxed her form and stepped farther in.

I looked from Vi to Travis, and then back. Wait a cotton-pickin' minute. "That's *your* Travis?" I gasped. I turned back to Travis and appraised him in a new light.

"Violet. What are you doing here?" His tone held shock.

Vi shook her head and placed her gun away. *Hang on, should she be carrying a gun?* Because when I left, she was well on her way to being drunk. And where in the heck was Talon?

"I came for Zara." She walked over to stand beside me.

"Where are my men?"

Vi shrugged. "Unconscious. Travis, what's going on here? Why kidnap Zara?"

"Pam here told me Zara abused her in front of my child. I couldn't stand for that. I needed to have a word with her."

Vi scoffed. "Zara wouldn't hurt a fly." She jerked her head sideways to Pam. "She's lying."

"I am not," Pam screeched.

"Oh, just give up," I said to her, then to Travis, "Ask my man; he'll tell you."

"Travis," Vi said, catching his attention, "you *really* should have gone about this differenly."

"Why?"

"She's Hawks' property."

"Fuck," he hissed. "Whose?"

"Talon Marcus."

"Christ." He turned to Pam. Just from his look, I would have been scared as well. She was taking step after step away from him. "Get the fuck out of my house. You lied, and now I have this shit to fix. You're fuckin' lucky I don't kill you. You stupid bitch, in front of my baby, you whored yourself?" He ran a hand through his hair. "Leave. Now."

She ran from the room.

"Christ. Fuck!" Travis said as he paced the room, only to stop behind the desk again. "I am truly sorry for this, Zara." He looked at Violet. "When will I hear from Talon?"

"Not sure. He doesn't know yet."

Scoffing I asked, "How'd you pull that off?"

"I told the guys I'd be able to get you back before he found out. It was just lucky I saw those idiots leaving with you over one's shoulder. I followed and rang Griz on the way. He freaked. I told him I'd have you back soon, so we better get going."

"Wow, you're like a super-agent." I grinned.

"Yes." I watched Travis smile appreciatively, his gaze wandering up and down Vi's body. He turned back to me. "Please let me know if there is anything I can do for you. Again, I am sorry for the way my men treated you, and for this...terrible misunderstanding. I'm sure I'll be hearing from Talon soon."

"Don't worry too much; it wasn't so bad, and I'll let Talon know that. I'm just thankful you know what a...nasty person your girlfriend is now. No one needs that around their child."

"That's true. You sound like you speak from experience."

I smiled. "I have a six-year-old daughter. It was just lucky I got away from my nasty before it could touch her."

"Zara, we better go," Vi said.

"Maybe one day, when we have more time, you could explain further on that topic?" Travis asked.

I cocked my head to the side. "You know what, maybe one day I will. And I'm sure Violet would love to come along as well."

He smirked, knowing full well that I knew about their past. "That would be wonderful. Coffee with two beautiful women."

"Alrighty, I'll be in touch. It was nice to meet you, Travis, and I'm glad it was you who kidnapped me." I smiled brightly and walked to the door with Violet following as she laughed.

Travis cleared his throat and said, "I had heard Talon had claimed an old lady. Now I can see why he has done it so quickly. I look forward to seeing you *both* soon. Please remember that if there is anything you need, call upon me."

"You may regret that," I said.

He chuckled.

We got outside to a vehicle that wasn't familiar to me. I looked at Violet, who was staring back, smiling. "Whose is this?" It certainly was a beauty.

We both got in before she answered, "Not sure. I had to find something quick to follow. But at least I'll be dropping it back, and hopefully, whoever this baby belongs to, they will be none the wiser." We both giggled.

What a frigging night.

Arriving back at the pub, I could already see Griz, Pick, Deanna, Julian, and Blue standing outside waiting for us. As soon as we pulled up, my door was flung open, and I was pulled from the car by Blue, who examined my body for any signs of injury. Well, that was what I guessed he was doing when he ran his hands over me.

Deanna shoved him out of the way, saying, "You can cop a feel later. Bitch, what the fuck?" She grabbed me into a tight hug; a second later, Julian joined in.

"Guys, it's okay. It was *all* a misunderstanding. Travis didn't know his men were going to taser me—"

"You were fuckin' tasered?" Griz roared.

"Holy Mother Mary." Julian gasped, tears welling in his eyes.

"Arses. I'd like to have a chance at tasering them back," Deanna said with an evil look in her eyes as she rubbed her hands together.

"Shit, we need to tell Talon," Pick whispered. He looked worried.

"Don't worry, Pick. I'll explain it calmly and sweetly, and things will be fine," I reassured him.

Well, that was what I thought would happen. I didn't expect what did.

CHAPTER SEVENTEEN

Violet parked the car that she'd stolen back where it had been, and thankfully, no one was out looking for it. Vi ended up coming in Griz's car with us so we could drop her at home along the way. She sat between Julian and Deanna, as I was up the front with Griz that time. I think he was afraid to take his eyes off me in case something else happened and he'd then have to explain to Talon how he'd lost me a second time. Not that it would happen; my bad luck was done for the night... at least I hoped so.

On the way to Vi's, she explained a few things about good-old-rough-loving Travis. They'd met in university, both sharing a love of maths. They dated for a year, had mind-blowing sex—her words, not mine—but then he chose to move to Melbourne. He'd asked Violet to go with him; she said she wasn't ready for that. She loved the area and her family too much to leave it behind. He decided to go still; they visited and wrote for a while longer, but their lives eventually changed. They both became busy with their careers and drifted apart. I could tell it was something she had always regretted.

Travis was now a top-notch businessman. Well, he'd have to be to have security men working for him—who tasered people. I doubted I would ever get over that fact.

Travis also had that huge-arse house and expensive suit, which explained that he had money. So what had he been doing with a fluff-head like Pam instead of tracking down Violet? Someone had better talk with him. Of course, that someone had to be me. I smiled to myself and gave a mental pat on my back.

After dropping Vi off, we pulled up to the compound. I hadn't been watching where we were heading—again—so I wasn't expecting to be there. I just assumed Talon had left me to have a good night with the girls and had gone home to the kids.

Wow, that sounded fantastic in my head. *Gone home to the kids.*

So I was a little confused as to why Talon would still be here at one in the morning. And how had Griz known he was here?

Pick was ahead and he opened the door to the motorcycle club-house, a place I had never been inside before. What I had expected, which was a run-down, dirty and smelly hole, was so different from what I saw. As we entered, there was a small hallway with a room on each side. The doors were closed, so I didn't get to see what was behind them. The hallway led us into… I supposed you could call it the main common room. It was large. Two massive tables and chairs were off to the left, and just behind them was a bar where three bikers sat whom I hadn't met. To the right of the room was a row of couches where they'd sit back, chill, and shoot the shit. Right in front of us, across the empty wooden floor, were another two long hallways and along them were many other doors.

"Right on. I need another drink," Deanna announced and dragged Julian along to the bar. Pick followed and greeted his other biker brothers with a handshake and then what you could call a man hug with a slap on the back.

"Yo, where's Talon?" Griz called.

The first one, an older man with grey hair and a long beard, scanned me from top to bottom with an approving look. Another biker looked down at the floor, and the last guy, who stood beside Pick, with long dark hair and wild dark eyes, gestured with his head to the long hallway across from us.

I was a little disappointed Talon wasn't out here to see me, but then I had to remember he didn't know what had occurred as of yet.

No sooner had I felt that disappointment than it twisted into rage. A door at the end of one of the hallways caught my attention when I heard it click open. Out walked Talon with a woman clinging to the front of him as they hugged. Her back was facing me, and I watched as she looked up to my man, then Talon's head came down. It looked as if he was kissing her.

"Babe, not what you think," Blue whispered in my ear.

I call bullshit!

Enough! I'd had enough.

I found myself striding down the hall; some would have run the other way from a situation like that, but I was moving right into it. Talon must have heard my pounding feet approach, as he looked up with surprised eyes.

"Kitten, I—"

I wrapped my hand into the wench's hair and pulled her roughly back. She squawked in pain, and then I pushed hard, sending her crashing into the wall. A satisfied smile settled upon my lips.

"Kitten," Talon snapped.

"Don't you friggin' 'kitten' me, you arse. This,"—I pointed to the woman, who was leaning quietly against the wall while I yelled at arsehat—"this is what you've been doing while I was kidnapped and tasered?" I punched him in the stomach.

"That a girl," Deanna cheered.

"I should never have trusted you," I whispered. Tears filled my eyes. I went to punch him again for the hurt and betrayal I was feeling, but he caught my fist and pulled me closer to him, his eyes filled with fury.

He can suck his own dick. I am not sorry for punching him.

"You were kidnapped and tasered?" Talon's voice was a snarl.

Uh oh. I forgot calm and nice altogether.

"What the fuck, Zara?" His voice was a low outraged whisper.

"Everyone clear the room," Griz growled.

"Damn it, we're going to miss the fun again," Julian said.

"Call if you need me to kick his arse," Deanna yelled down the hall.

I didn't care. He didn't frighten me like David. He was pissed, but it wasn't at me. Well, not totally.

"Don't you 'what the frig' me, Talon Marcus, and get all alpha-angry. You don't get to be angry now! You didn't just walk in on me tonguing some guy."

"Hoo-wee. I like her," a deep voice said with a laugh.

"Colin, let's go," Blue said.

I heard some shuffling, and then doors being opened and closed.

Talon's grip gentled. "Babe, I just found out you were taken and tasered. Of course I'm gonna be pissed."

I got up close to him, nose-to-nose in fact, and snapped, "And I just found the guy I *was* with kissing some bimbo while all that went down. No, it's not the fact that you missed out on it all; it's the frigging fact that you had your tongue down someone else's throat!" I stepped closer again so our chests touched, and leaned my head back farther to keep eye contact. "There is no way you will ever get into my pants. I will deal with my stuff on my own. Now, I'm going to get Maya, and I don't want to see you again."

"Uh, sugar," the woman beside us said. I turned to glare at her. "It's not what you think, honey, we weren't kissing, and anyway, I'm—"

"Let's go into the office," Talon barked. He grabbed my wrist, spun and dragged me into the office with his tonguing friend, who closed the door behind us.

I pulled my arm free, went over to the far wall and sat on the dark blue couch with my arms crossed over my chest, glaring at them both. The room felt too small, having Talon and his hook-up in there with me, as well as two file cabinets that sat just behind the door. A desk had papers scattered all over it. *Someone needs to get organised.* Actually, the whole room needed a makeover; if felt gloomy. A few plants and a fresh coat of paint would do wonders.

Why am I thinking of decorating?

"Well?" I snapped. "I've got things to do. Hurry up and tell me your lies so I can be off."

"She's a feisty one, Tal. Perfect for you." Tonguer smiled as she perched her behind on the corner of the desk where Talon sat.

Good. Stay as far away as possible, arse.

"Zara, right?" she asked. I rolled my eyes. "I'm Livia. I manage Talon's strip club in Geelong."

"Oh, oh. How silly of me, so it was all a mistake. You were just here on a business date and they always end up with you two kissing each other." My voice dripped with sarcasm. I got up from the couch. "Now that we have all that settled, I'll see you guys around...like, say, never."

Livia grinned. "We weren't kissing. He's like a brother to me. We hug, talk close, but I promise you we weren't kissing."

"No." I shook my head. "I-I can't believe... it was too close, it looked... you were kissing." I was sure that was what I saw. "I-I knew you'd end up doing this to me." I closed my eyes, trying to control my emotions.

"Kitten." His tone was warm, soft.

"Zara," Livia said with a pleading tone. I opened my tired eyes. I just wanted to get Maya, go home and crash. "Honestly, for me, kissing Talon would have been gross."

Snorting, I shook my head and gave them a sad smile. Did she really think I could believe that? I stood and started for the door.

"I'm gay."

Tumbling around fast, I tripped over my own feet and fell to the floor. With wide eyes, I watched Talon grin, and Livia, with a smile, walked over to me and helped me from the floor and back over the couch, where she sat next to me.

She took my hand in both of hers and said, "I'm sorry that you thought you saw us in an embrace like that and it hurt you. I've known Talon for a long time, and I know he would never do anything on purpose to upset you in any way. He's like a brother to me, and *that* is all. Believe me when I say I'm 100% gay and I would rather have sex with you in a heartbeat than Talon any day."

I nodded numbly. She sounded like she was telling me the truth, but could I believe that?

"Livi, stop coming on to my woman," Talon said with an amused tone.

"Oh, shush. Tell you what, Zara, any time Talon and I have a business meeting, you can be there; and if you want, it can be you at the end who I hug."

"Christ. Livi, leave now before she thinks about letting you," Talon growled.

Livia giggled. "You're no fun, Tal." She kissed my hand, got up from the couch and went to the door. "Later, honey, and…" She winked. "I'll see you soon. Talon, now you have someone who'll make my visits worthwhile."

"Thanks." I winked back. "Oh, and sorry about being too rough with you before."

"That's all right. I enjoyed it."

"Jesus," Talon hissed.

Livia left laughing and shut the door behind her. The door I kept staring at because I didn't want to meet Talon's gaze. I could feel the heat of his stare, but I was embarrassed. Let's not forget tired from such a long, gruelling, and hard night.

"Kitten," Talon said softly.

"Yes?"

"Come here," he ordered.

"Nope, I'm all good here."

I heard his chair being pushed back. Excitement and worry coursed through my body as his footsteps approached. He sat next to me on the couch, and in the next second, I squealed, because I was pulled out of my spot and was straddling his waist. My skirt bunched up, and my exposed knees were around his hips. I looked at the roof with my arms crossed over my chest.

"Zara, look at me."

I shook my head. I could not look at him because I would cave. He looked and smelled too damn good.

"Kitten, please look at me."

"Why?"

"So I can tell you how fuckin' sorry I am. I wish you'd never seen that and I wish I could take the pained look I saw on your face, those tears that fell from your eyes, and wipe away any hurt you felt before you knew the truth." He reached behind my neck and pulled me closer so our foreheads touched and our eyes met. "It's you, kitten, ever since you rocked up to my door in a fuckin' nightie and combat boots. Now that I've finally gotten my arse into gear and claimed you, I'm never lettin' go. You are mine, kitten."

I breathed in a shuddering breath. "Does that mean you're mine?"

"In every way."

"No more... closeness with any other woman, even if they are gay."

He grinned. "No more, only and always just you."

CHAPTER EIGHTEEN

OUR LIPS MET in an urgent frenzy. I threaded my hands though his hair as he wrapped his arms tightly around my waist and pulled me closer. A moan escaped my lips. A deep growl left his, one I felt down to my toes.

I had never been kissed with such desire and passion.

Talon's hands fell from my waist and went to my thighs. Slowly and talentedly, he ran his hands up, sending a shiver throughout my body. I was already wearing an easy-access skirt, so I wasn't surprised when they dipped under and his thumbs gently rubbed my panty line.

Need surged through me, a need to rip our clothes away and have my wicked way with Talon once and for all.

He'd said he wanted to claim me by taking me; well I wanted the same. I wanted to claim everything about him so everyone knew he was mine and no one else's.

Especially if he kept up this teasing torture.

"Talon," I pleaded against his lips.

He smiled.

The arse.

His hands stilled, and then he whispered, "I won't have you here, kitten. Not in an office. You deserve a bed that I can lay you out on and fuck you until you scream my name over and over."

I rested my forehead against his shoulder and sighed. "No," I said, frustrated.

Talon chuckled. "What d'ya mean no, babe?"

Straightening, I crossed my arms over my chest and glared at him. "This is happening tonight and right frigging now."

"Kitten." His eyes warmed as he ran the back of his hand down my cheek.

"Talon. I mean it. We are going to have sex—" I leaned forward and hissed, "Now!"

"Jesus, babe, you're making this hard for me. I'm trying to be a fuckin' good guy here. You deserve care, time, and the right fuckin' place. I'm not takin' advantage of you."

"No, please advantage away on me, and you are a good guy, but if you don't do the dirty with me right now, you'll soon have a very pissed woman to deal with. We can take our sweet time another time and another place, with a bed and roses and songs. But right now, I want you to fuck me. Claim me."

His eyes flared, and from where I sat, something else flared in surprise. On a growl, he lifted me in his arms and off the couch. I wrapped my legs around his waist as he carried me to the desk where, with one hand, he swept all papers, the phone, and junk onto the floor to sit my butt on the edge.

"You want me to fuck you, I will. Really, I'm more than happy to, but next time we do it, we're gonna take our time so I can cherish every fuckin' part of your sweet body."

I gulped, nodded, and grinned like a fool. "I'm up for that, honey."

He closed his eyes and whispered, "Christ, I love hearing you call me that, kitten." Upon opening his eyes, he reached between my legs, which were still wrapped around his waist. He moved back, so they dropped, and he slowly pulled my underwear down and threw them away. "I'd love to taste you right now, babe, but my woman wants me to fuck her, so that's what I'm gonna do."

"Yippee," I cheered.

Talon laughed, shook his head, and his eyes turned serious. I watched him, and could have dribbled as he popped the button on his jeans and slowly slid the zipper down.

"Jesus, kitten, you turn me the fuck on just from the way you watch me." He licked his lips. "Are you ready for me, babe? Are you wet for me?" He ran a finger through my folds to see that, yes indeed, I was wet, ready and waiting. I shivered as I watched him raise that finger, place it in his mouth, and suck my juices off, causing a moan from Talon and a groan from me.

"Fuckin' beautiful," he hissed, and then surged his hips forward. In one quick swoop, he was bedded deep inside of me.

"Oh, God," I moaned. My head tipped back and my chest arched forward. I was in heaven. *Happy birthday to me; happy birthday, and Christmas, and all the other holidays, to me.*

"No, kitten, not God, just your man." Talon smiled. I swivelled my hips and that smile fell from his face. He pulled out slowly and plunged back in. "Goddamn, kitten, you're so fuckin' tight and wet."

After that comment, all hell broke loose. I grabbed Talon by the shoulders and pulled him forward so our lips met. As we kissed and bit, Talon pumped me hard and good, just the way I wanted it.

It was possible I would not be walking tomorrow, and at that point I did not care.

"Talon, oh, God, Talon." I groaned. It was building and it was a big one.

"Let it go, babe," Talon growled at my neck.

"Talon."

"Let it go."

"H-honey." I arched as my climax crashed over me, and I was sure I was going to black out. But I made myself focus and opened my eyes to see Talon still over and in me, pumping hard and watching me with hooded eyes. One, two, three pumps later, he groaned, swore, and collapsed on top of me.

"You're gonna fuckin' kill me, babe, but it'll be worth it." He pulled back to look at me, smiling. "So hot, so wet, so tight. Never had it like that before, babe. You're so fuckin' responsive; I'm never gonna wanna leave you or your pussy again."

I giggled. "That's okay, 'cause me or my...yeah, are never going to want you to leave."

I liked the way his eyes shone with more desire for me, until they turned teasing. "I fucked you hard, you screamed my name, and you still can't say pussy? Babe."

"Shud'up and kiss me."

He grinned and obliged.

"You need to get cleaned up, kitten. We got shit to talk about, once a-fuckin-gain, then we gotta get home to the kids."

I rolled my eyes, but did a happy dance on the inside, and then shoved him out of the way. "Yes, Talon." I moved off to the door, picking up my underwear along the way.

"Well, shit, babe. If all I gotta do is fuck you for you to be obedient, then be prepared to be on your back all the goddamn time."

"Whatever," I snapped. But smiled.

"Kitten—"

"Talon, honey. You want me to get cleaned so we can talk or what?"

"Bathroom's right across the hall." He smirked.

"I knew that." Although I hadn't, but he didn't need to know.

AFTER I CLEANED UP, went back in the office and had a make-out session with Talon, he informed me one of his men had dropped Julian back at his house. Then he told me that Deanna had gone to bed in Griz's room, as he dragged me down the hall past the main room I'd walked into when we arrived, which was now empty, and into what Talon called 'the meeting room'. It was just as big as the main room. Two large tables sat in the middle, wooden kitchen chairs piled around it, and they were mostly filled with bikers. A bar —of course, another one—was at the back of the room. Some old arcade games and a ping-pong table—yes, apparently bikers played table tennis, giggle—sat at the other end of the room.

As soon as we'd entered, and the bikers noticed us, they started clapping, cheering and swearing. One cheer caught my attention, "Christ, 'bout time you claimed all of her."

Holy shit.

Had they heard?

I knew my cheeks were flaming red, and I gripped Talon's hand tightly.

"H-how?" I whispered to Talon, but apparently I hadn't said it low enough because it was Blue who answered.

"Baby, Talon wouldn't walk in 'ere with a smile on his face after findin' out you'd been kidnapped. And you just confirmed what we guessed was happening."

I was more than embarrassed; I was annoyed and pissed. "Oh. My. God. Shut up. Seriously? Right, from now on, no one talks about me and Talon in front of me and Talon—unless, that is, Talon wants guy time and I've pissed him off in some way and he needs to vent. But that's it. We do not—" I turned to Talon, glaring. "—talk about our private time to anyone. Well, except for me, of course. I mean, come on, that's a given; I'm a woman and we talk about this stuff…I think *I'll* shut up now." I crossed my arms over my chest, stalked to the table and plopped down in the chair at the end while the room erupted in laughter.

"Shhhit, brother, where can I get me one of her?" someone asked.

Talon, grinning like a fool, walked over, pulled me out of my chair, sat down, and then tugged me down onto his lap. I tried to move, but he wouldn't have it.

"She's one of a kind, and what she says goes. No one is to embar-

rass her like that again. 'Less you want to hear her rant once more."
Talon chuckled as I jabbed him in his side with my elbow.

Seconds later, all joking left Talon's body. He stiffened, and eyeing Blue, Griz, and Pick he asked, "Right, who wants to start with why the fuck my woman was tasered, taken, and got free without me knowing about it?"

The whole room took on a tenser atmosphere, as if Talon was a lion and they were waiting for him to attack. Maybe that 'Talon and Zara happy fun time' hadn't sedated his pissed-off-ness.

"Honey, can't this wait till morning? I'm tired and I'm sure all the fellas are as well. It's been a long night. Can't we just go home?"

"No, kitten."

I rolled my eyes, sighed, and looked heavenward.

"Well, don't blame me if I pass out from exhaustion and hit my head on the table, get a concussion and then have to go to hospital."

"Babe." Talon smiled when I looked down at him. "I'd catch ya. Your head would never touch the table."

Oh, wasn't that sweet, but he was totally missing the point. I needed a bed and now.

"I'm spent. Being kidnapped, tasered, witnessing you tongue-bathing another woman, fighting, yelling, and mind-blowing sex can do that to a person."

Hands slapping the table, laughter, chuckling and shouting made me realise I had just said *that* aloud.

Holy crab cake.

With wide eyes, I looked down at Talon's satisfied face and uttered, "I said that out loud."

"Yep." He nodded, his eyes laughing.

"See?" I whined. "I'm tired. I need sleep, honey, and now. Plus, I want the kids to wake up with a parent home."

"All right, babe."

I grinned. "We're going home?" I asked as the bikers around the table talked and joked amongst themselves.

"You are. I need to find out what happened. I can't have anyone think they can do that shit to my woman without payback —"

"Talon, please. It was a mistake. Don't do anything to Travis—"

"I might just visit him, kitten. But if I don't like what he says, then we're gonna have problems."

"There won't be a problem. He's nice. He's got a daughter, and we're going to catch up for coffee one day—"

"What the fuck, babe?"

I sighed. "Don't worry, honey…hey, that rhymes—worry-honey." I giggled to myself. God, I was way overtired. "Anyway, you don't have to worry. He's got a thing for Violet, and a history. So she'll be coming with me when we catch up, a-a-and, if you want to work things out with your sister, it may be good not to *off* the guy she likes."

Talon shook his smiling face. "You make friends wherever you go, even after the guy fuckin' kidnaps you. Babe, get your arse home for that sleep before the kids wake up." He looked over my shoulder. "Pick, take Zara to my house."

"Sure, boss," Pick said, standing from the table, suddenly looking gloomy.

"Kitten, I need your mouth before you go. And don't worry, I won't off the guy."

"Thanks, honey." I grinned and kissed my man.

CHAPTER NINETEEN

PICK DROVE FOR A LONG, silent, fifteen minutes. He seemed to have something on his mind and any other time, I would have asked about it to see if I could be of some help, but I was beat. We pulled onto a dirt driveway that wound around to a massive ranch-style home. It was the prettiest white weatherboard house I had ever seen, with a large deck surrounding it.

"Wildcat, wait here a sec before we go in. I need to make a call." Without an answer, he climbed out of the car, shut the door, flipped his phone open, and placed it to his ear. I couldn't make out what was being said. He was speaking in a hushed tone, but whatever it was, Pick didn't seem happy about it at all. He waved his free arm wildly in the air, trying to get some message across that, obviously, someone wasn't getting.

I turned my attention back to the house. Most lights were off except the porch, and what I presumed would be the lounge. How had Talon afforded a place like this? It looked as though—from what I could see in the dark—along with the house, there was some mighty big acreage going on.

"Fuck," I heard yelled, bringing my gaze back to Pick just as he pounded the bonnet with his fist. He swung the door open and snapped, "Let's move."

Undoing my belt, I got out and met him at the front of the car. "Pick, are you okay?"

He grabbed my upper left arm and pulled me toward the house. "No, Wildcat, I'm not. I hate my fuckin' life right now. All I ever do is try to protect my ma, but she just keeps bringin' shit into her life, and then I have to fuckin' fix it. It sucks." We stopped just outside the front door as he turned me to face him. "Shit, Zee, sorry."

"Don't worry about it. You need to talk to get it off your chest, and maybe when I'm not so dog-tired, I could have some great advice for you, but right now, I doubt anything that came out of my mouth would be understandable."

He hunched and looked to his feet. "You're a great person, Wild-cat…and, I'm sorry—"

What?

The front door opened to a smiling Vic. "Come on in, sweet stuff." He reached out and grabbed my hand, dragging me forward, but I couldn't move my gaze from Pick. He seemed truly worried and remorseful. His eyes moved from the floor to me rapidly.

Finally, he met my stare and whispered, "I would never have done this if it weren't for me protecting my ma. Never. I'm sorry."

Shaking my head, I smiled. "Pick, what are you talking about?"

"Momma."

I spun so fast I would have fallen if Vic still didn't have hold of my hand. "Maya—" It was then I took in the scene in front of me, and I felt sick to my stomach. "W-what's going on?" I asked with wide eyes, staring at Julian and Mattie sitting on the floor near the far wall, cradling a scared Maya and Cody. I turned to Vic and noticed for the first time he held a gun.

"Have you worked it out yet?" He smirked.

"Not really," I hissed, ripping my hand from his grip. "But please, enlighten my tired brain."

He chuckled. "I can see why Talon likes you, showing balls in the face of danger. Please, have a seat while we wait." He shoved me to the couch near my family.

Straightening my clothes and myself, I looked over to the children. "It's going to be fine, okay?"

"Yes, Momma," my brave Maya said. Cody nodded.

Looking back at Vic and Pick—yes, any other time I would have laughed at the rhyming; instead I said, "I can sort of understand your reason, Pick. But, Vic, why?"

He shrugged. "I need the money."

"What's he paying you to deliver me?"

"Smart girl."

I shrugged. "Doesn't take a genius to work it out."

"I guess not. Between the four of us, we get fifty thousand each. Easy money really. All we have to do is keep you here till the delivery guys arrive. Easy as pie."

"Do you really think you'll get the money in the end?" I studied him. "Oh, my God, you do. Well, I guess you're as stupid as *you* look." I laughed, until he wiped that laugh from my face by slapping me. My head jerked to the side. Maya screamed. Mattie swore. "It's okay. I'm okay," I reassured them.

"He will pay or he knows I'll come after him," Vic screamed.

"Chill, man," Pick said.

"You fuckin' chill. I'm not the one chickenin' out. Now everyone shut the fuck up." He glared at me and took a step closer to say, "I may have to deliver you and the kids, but it doesn't have to be in one piece."

I gasped. "Kids? No, please no. Leave them here, please."

Vic chuckled a sardonic laugh. "I don't think so. At least then I'll know you'll behave for their safety. Not only for them, but if you try shit on the delivery, I'll kill your brother and his..." he looked at Julian in disgust, "...thing."

Jesus. What the hell am I going to do?

"W-why Cody too?"

"To shove it up Talon. Thinks he's hot shit. I'll show him."

"And you're okay with this, Pick?" I asked, tears threatening.

"No." He shook his head, again looking at his feet. "But if I don't get that money, my ma will be killed by loan sharks."

"Talon would have helped you. Why didn't you go to him?"

"I couldn't. I was…ashamed."

"And you thought this was the best way out of that black hole? To ruin other people's lives? Especially one who took you in, who looked out for you."

"Shut up, bitch," Vic snapped, hitting me in the back of the head.

"Vic, don't," Pick growled.

"Don't get a conscience now. Man up, fucker."

"God, please, please, just let the kids leave with Mattie and Julian. Please, I won't cause any trouble; I promise. I won't do anything; just let them go."

"Zara, it's no use," Mattie said. I turned my wet eyes upon them.

Regret.

All I could feel was regret, because they were here because of me. *I'm sorry*, I mouthed. I watched Julian's bottom lip tremble as he gripped Maya closer, and Mattie shook his head at me with a sad smile on his mouth.

"W-where are t-the others who came here? Didn't you get dropped off, Julian?"

Vic laughed. "Still holding out for someone to save you? Won't happen tonight. Your man will be very busy with the planned distraction."

"What?" I hissed, through clenched teeth.

"Yeah, I saw that bitch at the pool all over Talon. She didn't like to be dissed as nothing. So I approached her, asked her to help me out a bit. She went home crying to her fella. I rang her and told her where you'd be…after my man Pick had informed me. She mentioned it to her man, and he sent his guys to pick you up. Didn't think it'd be that easy, but you were stupid enough to go to the crapper on your own. So now, Talon will keep himself busy defending his woman, and while that's happening"—he laughed—"his life will be shattered right from under him."

The room fell silent.

All I could think about was scratching out his eyes. How dare he do this to Talon, to Cody and Maya?

Julian cleared his throat. "I was dropped off out the front, pumpkin. Walked in here blind to the trouble, just like you did."

"The other guys left when"—Mattie pointed at Pick—"he called them and told them it was fine to cut the guarding down to one. Vic offered to stay."

Shit. They had it all worked out.

I wanted to crawl up in a protective ball and cry, but then again, I wanted to rip their dicks off and slap them over their heads with them.

Oh, God. Talon.

He was going to go crazy, especially when he found out I'd dragged his son, his only boy, into this mess. He'd be on a warpath, and anything that crossed it was going to be destroyed.

I didn't even get to tell him I loved him.

Love him?

Yes.

Because I did.

Sure, to start with it was lust at first sight. But the care, the gentleness and protectiveness he had shown me…not only me, but Maya, and even Deanna, Mattie and Julian, had my heart beating in love for the first time in seven years.

All I could do now was suck up all my emotions and feelings, and stay sane and safe for the children. They were what mattered now.

What a fuckin' well-planned night.

I was just about ready to see my ex and punch him in the gonads for this.

I shook my hands out and rubbed my eyes. I was beyond tired, but I had to stay focused for the kids.

What about Mattie and Julian?

Yes, what was going to happen to them once we left? I looked over to my beautiful brother and brother-in-law. I wouldn't be able to handle it if something did happen, but I really didn't like our chances.

"It's okay, sis." Mattie smiled. Had he read the anguish in my eyes?

We all turned to the sound of a vehicle coming up Talon's dirt driveway.

"They're here," Vic said. He went to the window, looked out, and then walked out the front door to greet them, leaving Pick behind.

Duh. I had felt like saying, sarcasm was something I hid my fear behind, but now wasn't the time for it.

"Come on, poppet. Go to your mum," Julian said as he helped Maya stand on shaky legs. She hugged and kissed them both, whispering something in their ears, causing them both to pull their lips between their teeth. Maya then ran to me and climbed onto my lap, her tiny arms encircled my neck.

Mattie coughed to clear his throat. "Up you get, too, Cody," Mattie ordered. Cody mumbled something to them and they nodded.

Shit, shit, shit. I couldn't do this. I couldn't leave my brothers. I closed my eyes to fight the tears.

"Zee, honey." I opened them to Mattie. He ushered Cody forward, and Cody came to sit at my side. I placed my arm tightly around his shoulders while I held Maya just as tightly as I could with the other.

Looking back at Mattie and Julian, I forced a smile. "I love you, g-guys." I bit my bottom lip for control.

Mattie shuffled closer to a crying Julian and placed his arms around him. "We love you, too, sis. And we wouldn't change anything. We still would have come. We still would have stayed because it meant we got to spend more time with you. You, who I have missed for six years."

I closed my eyes and nodded, leaning my head against Maya's as she hid her face in my shoulder. I wasn't surprised that she hadn't cried. When she was under stress, like I had witnessed when she went to her first swimming lesson, she turned quiet. Her fear built inside her, and the only way she really showed it was through her body. She was shaking like a leaf in the wind. Just for that, and the fact that Cody showed his fear by being a silent statue, his form as stiff as a board, it made me want to buy myself a machine gun and shoot Vic while he tried to run for his life.

Though, I knew I wouldn't have it in me to harm Pick. I could tell that he honestly would not be involved in any of this if it wasn't to save his mother. Anyone could see that he knew this was the wrong choice. He was the one who was going to have to live with this regret...and that was only if Talon didn't get to him first.

Still, it also showed me that Pick was loyal. But in my opinion, he was being loyal to the wrong person. Yes, it was his mother, but a mother should never have dragged her own child into her mess. A mother was there to protect and provide for her child...not the other way around.

I felt for Pick, because in one way or another, he was going to be living his own personal hell.

Of course, I wouldn't allow myself to feel too deeply for him, because if he hadn't played a part in all this, I doubted I'd be in this situation.

Julian cleared his throat and clapped. "Enough of this crap. Honey, do not worry; we'll be fine, and you'll all be fine. Cody's superhero daddy will come to the rescue. Won't he, mate?"

"He will." Cody nodded with confidence.

I gave him a squeeze. He looked up at me and I winked. The front door opened and my mouth dropped open when Rocko's men, the ones I had seen at the bar, walked in.

I knew it.

I frigging knew it.

They were trouble, nothing but trouble.

More men added to the list I'd gun down in the bloodbath I was willing to orchestrate.

But how did they know about this? About me and David?

"Get up, bitch," Vic snapped. I placed Maya to stand on the floor beside me, and stood from the couch, pulling Cody up with me. I wrapped my arms around each child.

"We'll come, nothing will happen. We won't do anything…just, just don't hurt my brother and Julian."

"Yeah, we'll see." The glint in Vic's eyes sent dread to the pit of my stomach. "Keep me posted," Vic said to the two men. They gave him a chin lift in return.

I turned to Julian and Mattie. "I'll see you soon, yeah. Okay?"

"Of course you will, cupcake." Julian smiled.

"Be smart and safe, sis," Mattie uttered.

I nodded, because I knew if I spoke, I'd break down. Instead, I mouthed, *I love you both.* And even that caused tears to fill my eyes. I choked back a sob and pulled the kids in tighter.

With one man in front of us, and one behind, I followed them out to a black SUV. The man in front opened the door and we were pushed inside. The men got in and the scarier one with a scar running through his upper lip turned in his seat and threw something that landed in my lap.

"Put them on. All of you."

I moved my arm from around Cody and picked up the pieces of fabric. They were head sacks.

CHAPTER TWENTY

PICK

WHAT THE FUCK have I done? The front door closed behind Wildcat and I wanted to run out, shoot the motherfuckers, and save the day. But I couldn't, or my own ma would be dead by tomorrow. I needed this money. *This last time.*

No matter how much it had hurt to watch the dicks take them.

Fuck.

I'd never forget the look on Cody's face when I walked in and did nothing to help the situation. I let Vic hit Wildcat. I just stood by and did nothing...like the pussy I was.

I was scared, and that was all it came down to.

And it fuckin' hurt.

It hurt to see the pain in Wildcat's eyes. She felt betrayed by me, and it was justified.

Vic raised his gun and pointed it at the gay guys. "Right, change of plans. I have to get out of here now, so we gotta kill these fuckers."

I stepped forward, hands raised. "What? No way, man. That wasn't the plan. We need to stick to the plan."

"Can't. They can't live. You should'a figured that out from the start, brother. They know us and they'll run to Talon. Then, we're as good as dead."

"Please, no," Julian cried. Mattie stared at us with wide eyes. But his eyes also showed that he hadn't expected anything different to come from us. He closed his eyes as he pulled Julian closer, and rested Julian's forehead against his shoulder.

I felt disgusted in myself.

Fuck!

I couldn't let this happen. I would not have more blood on my hands. The only reason I let Wildcat go was because I knew her dickhead ex wouldn't kill her.

Yeah, you just keep tellin' yourself that.

I had to believe that. Or else I did all this for nothing. Really, I did it for nothing anyway. I already knew my ma wouldn't change, and it made me feel sick. Give her six months and she'd be back to owing, in more ways than one.

So why was I helping her now? After what she'd done? After the hell she'd put me through all my fuckin' fucked-up life. Who did that to their child?

Who sold their own child's body to be used by rich fat-arse bitches?

Jesus.

I couldn't let this happen.

"No, Vic."

He turned his hard stare on me, but I gave as good as I got and met his gaze with my own.

"What the fuck you mean, no?"

"This ain't happenin'." I pulled out my own gun from where it sat at the back of my pants at my waist, and pointed it at Vic. He didn't think I had it in me. That I'd shoot. I could tell, because he still held his gun at the gay guys.

"Don't do this, brother. Don't fuck this up for the both of us just 'cause you're a pussy and can't kill two fuckin' poofs."

"I should never have been involved. I should have manned up at the start and told Talon your plan, but I didn't, and I let Wildcat walk out. Christ, with her kids, and I'm gonna have to live with that. But I can't let you do this. I won't let you kill them."

One of them gasped, but I didn't dare look their way.

"You're pathetic. Why Talon ever let you join, I'll never fuckin' know. You could never handle the paybacks for the club. You're useless."

Scoffing to myself, I thought, *I guess he'll soon find out how useless I am.*

I watched his hand twitch and I knew.

I knew I was about to be shot.

But I had to get there first.

The sound of my gun being fired echoed through the quiet house.

Though, it wasn't only my gun.

I was knocked back when I was hit. My hand went to my chest as I stumbled backwards and then fell to my arse against the wall.

I smiled as I witnessed Vic fall to the floor, bleeding out from his throat.

We all watched silently as he took his last staggering breath and died.

"Holy shit," Mattie yelled.

"Mother Mary," Julian cried.

I snorted, and then winced from the pain. My hand was still holding my chest as the blood seeped through my fingers.

"G-get to Talon. Tell him," I said.

"We aren't leaving you," Julian uttered as he knelt down beside me. Mattie showed up with a towel in his hand, gave it to Julian, and then he disappeared again with a phone to his ear. I watched in slow motion as Julian moved my hand away and placed the towel and pressed against my chest, causing me to moan as the pain doubled.

"Right, there's an ambulance on the way."

"No," I whispered.

I was better off dead.

"Don't shit us. You're going to the hospital and that's final," Mattie ordered, and he knelt down on my other side, moved Julian's hand away and placed his in the spot. "You saved us. We save you."

I snorted again, but it turned into a cough. "N-no mouth-to-mouth."

They laughed a tired, stressed laugh. "You wish," Julian said.

"Handsome," Mattie said—I hoped to fuck to Julian. I glanced up and saw he was staring at his lover. "You need to go to Talon. Call Violet on the way; she'll need to be there. I'll stay here. We'll meet up later."

Julian shook his head. "I'm not leaving you. We can call him."

"No. We can't tell him this over the phone. Listen, here comes the ambulance. Go, Julian. Do this for Zee."

Yeah, finding out his brother betrayed him wasn't something to say over the phone.

Julian kissed Mattie quickly—not something a dying man wished to see. He got up and ran out the front door, yelling to the ambo guys on the way, "It's not my blood; in the house, get in the house."

CHAPTER TWENTY-ONE

TALON

I'D JUST PULLED up to the compound from visiting Travis when Pick's car came burling around the corner and skidded to a stop beside Griz and me. Only it wasn't Pick who got out, but Julian. Covered in blood.

My stomach dropped.

Pain filled my chest.

"What the fuck?" I roared.

"Inside now," Griz ordered to a pale-faced Julian. We ran. Julian ran straight for the bar; with shaking hands, he poured himself a shot and downed it.

I stalked over to him and yelled, "Tell me what the fuck is going on."

"Oh, God, Talon, shit, shit."

"Talk now, motherfucker, or so help me—where the fuck is my woman...fuck, the kids?"

"Brother, calm down," Griz said.

"Fuck!" I screamed.

"What the hell is going on?" Deanna asked, walking into the

room in shorts and a tee that she'd slept in. Her mouth dropped open at the sight of Julian. "No." she gasped.

Griz went to her, pulling her into his arms; she shoved him away and with her hands on her hips and cold eyes she asked, "What happened?"

"Vic," Julian said.

"What the fuck about Vic?" I asked as I started pacing. It was either that or I'd lose my fuckin' mind.

"H-he's got men delivering Zara and the kids to David right now."

I picked up a chair and threw it against the wall, shattering it.

"Where's Pick, Stake, and Bizz?" Griz asked.

"Shit, Talon. I'm sorry, man. Pick had called your house, even before I got there, and told them they didn't need to guard anymore. Bizz and Stake left it in the hands of Vic. Zee got back with Pick... shit. They had it all planned. Even tonight, the distraction of Travis —not that he knew, but his slutty girlfriend helped Vic set it up."

"Christ," I said to the roof. "My brothers betrayed me."

"Yeah," Julian whispered. "But then, Vic was going to kill Mattie and me once the others left with Zara—the others being Rocko's men, the ones we saw tonight."

"Motherfucker," I roared.

"How'd you get away?" Deanna asked as she stood there with her arms wrapped around her stomach. I knew she'd be feeling just as sick as I was.

Only hatred and fury filled me more, and I was willing to ride those fuckin' emotions to lead me to my woman, my son, and my Maya.

"Pick. H-he, God, he helped us. He didn't want to do this Talon. He hated every moment. But he's got some mother issues. He s-shot Vic, but got shot in return. Mattie's with him. They're going to the hospital."

"And Vic?" Griz hissed.

"He's dead."

"At least that's one less arsehole we'll have to kill," I said. "Right, Julian, go get cleaned up; I'll send someone down with clothes for you. Then get to the hospital with one of my guys to be with Mattie. No one takes their eyes off Pick. I'll need a word with him."

The door to the compound burst open, and in ran Violet, Warden, and Travis.

"What's going on?" Vi asked when she came to stop beside me.

"In short, I was betrayed by two of my brothers; Zara and the kids have been taken to David."

"Fuck," Warden whispered.

"Christ, no," Vi uttered.

"What can we do?" Travis asked. Any other time I would have told him to fuck off, but not when my family was involved.

Only nothing came to mind. All I could think about was hurting someone. I needed someone to pay for the gaping hole I was feeling in my heart.

Thank fuck I had Griz at my side. He barked out, "Violet, you stay here with Deanna and man the phones. Travis, see if you can find out where David is situated right now through your sources. Warden, you'll go with Blue. Once I call him in to the hospital, you'll need to talk to Pick. Talon…"

I smiled. "We're going to talk to Rocko."

Travis got on his phone. Griz got on his to call Blue. Julian took off to the showers; but it was Deanna and Violet both at the same time who yelled, "Fuck no."

Then Deanna added, "You can't expect me to sit on my arse while my best friend is out there having God-knows-what done to her by that fucker David. I'm not sitting here manning the fuckin' phones when you can get some of your boys to do it."

"I agree." Vi voiced. "You need me, Talon. We don't see eye-to-eye on a lot of things, but this, we work together on."

"Fuck, woman. I don't need this shit. I gotta go."

"Then we're coming with you," Violet said.

"Shit yeah," Deanna added.

"Jesus, whatever. Griz?"

"Jeremy's up. He'll call others to scout, and man the fuckin' phone. Let's roll."

A curt nod and we left.

Not fuckin' before I saw Travis—the biggest pimp in Melbourne —pull my sister aside, kiss her, and tell her something to have her eyes warm and nod.

Fuck, it was something to worry about when I got my family back.

Now it was time to fight for them.

CHAPTER TWENTY-TWO

ZARA

ALL I KNEW WAS that we drove for a very long time. Long enough that the kids fell asleep in my arms, leaning their heavy weight upon me, and it was long enough for me to doze off and on for quite some time.

I think my relaxed state showed the children not to worry, and in turn they weren't, so they could sleep knowing that I'd be there to protect them.

There were many reasons why I was relaxed. For one, alcohol still flowed through my body, and two, I knew Talon would go to great lengths to find us, and finally three, I was stronger in mind, body, and spirit to deal with an arsehat like David.

The only thing that had me worried, but I didn't let show, was how all this was going to be played out. What was David going to do? At least I was sure he would never harm a child. I—on the other hand—was a different story altogether. Though, I wasn't worried for myself, only and always for the children.

So to keep my relaxed state for the kids, I thought of Talon.

His eyes and how they grew soft for me.

His mouth when he smiled at me.

His hands and body, and how he always sought me out in a room.

Him.

The perfect, dominating, alpha bossy biker, who was a hard-scary-arse, beautifully hot, delicious man.

Sometimes, I had to focus, because my mind kept supplying me with other freaked-out thoughts of *Mattie, Julian, Mattie, Julian. God, I hope they're okay. I have to be good. I cannot rip into these guys like a momma T-Rex because...Mattie, Julian, Mattie, Julian.*

However many seconds, minutes, or hours later, the car came to a stop. The kids were roused from their sleep, and again, I reassured them that things were going to be okay.

"Keep the masks on," one of the men ordered. The doors opened and we were pulled out onto a gravel road. I took Cody and Maya's hands, and our feet crunched the gravel under us as we stumbled blindly along. A door was opened. Thankfully, there were no steps or I would have fallen flat on my face, bringing the children down with me.

"It's going to be okay," I said for the umpteenth time, and received a hand squeeze from both.

We were placed in a room in front of—I guessed—a couch, which I felt at the back of my calves.

"Sit," one kidnapper said. We sat, and I cradled the children close to me. The door opened again. Someone walked in and I heard a chair being slid back, the sound of *that* someone sitting in it. I knew who it was straight away. I could never misplace his strong, stinking cologne.

"Remove," David said, with a smile upon his mouth. I'd been around him enough to know when he was smiling.

Our head covers were whipped off. I blinked a couple of times to bring focus back. The kids rubbed at their eyes. I looked up and found David sitting behind a desk, his hands folded on top of it; his eyes gleamed with a 'gotcha' look, and his mouth was smirking at me. He looked the same as he had six years ago. The same ocean-blue eyes that had sucked me in, the same slim, tall form. The only difference was that his sandy hair had receded more on top.

"Hello, my dear Zara *Edgingway*." he gleamed.

"David."

"What, that's it? That's all you have to say to your husband? After all these years," he spat, disgusted. "Get the kids out of here. I want to talk to my wife."

"What? No, no, David. Please let them stay with me," I begged. I didn't trust the men standing behind the couch. Especially the one looking eagerly at my daughter.

David chuckled. "I doubt they'd want to hear what we have to talk about, darling."

"You leave her alone," Cody yelled as he stood from the couch.

"Cody," I said, pulling him back beside me. "It's okay, hun." I kissed the top of his head and looked at David again. "David, do you at least have someone who could be trusted with them? Please."

He did a full belly laugh. "Of course I do." He picked up the phone, pushed a button, and said into it, "Bring them in."

Moments later, the door opened and a guy in jeans and a long-sleeved black tee walked in. But I was more interested in the voice I heard in the hall.

"Are you bastards ever going to let us go? You know I've missed my tit appointment; not that I'd really want to get them squished into a vice, but it has to be done with a woman my age. Plus, my kids must be worried by now."

A sigh. "Nancy." And I knew that person would be shaking his head.

"Mum?" I called, shocked.

I stood as an older version of me walked into the room, wearing black pants and a red woollen jumper. Behind her was a brooding form of an older version of Mattie, only he was taller, with dark grey hair and warm, green eyes. Both of them looked a little worse for wear; there was a bruise on Mum's cheek and Dad had a black eye.

I felt sick.

David was going to pay.

"Dad?"

"Oh, my baby," Mum cried, and she ran at me.

"Mum, oh, God, Mum, Dad," I sobbed.

"Sweetheart," Dad said with tears in his eyes. They both wrapped me up in their arms.

"Oh, oh, is this my little angel, Maya?" Mum pulled away, picked Maya up, and hugged her to her chest.

"And who do we have here?" Dad asked. "Hey, buddy. I'm Richard, Zara's dad, and that loud lady is Nancy, Zara's crazy mum."

"I heard that, Richard, and I'm not crazy."

"It's so great to see you both," I cried. "A-and this is Cody. Talon's son."

"Really, and who's Talon?" Mum asked.

"He's my mum's man, Nanny," Maya informed.

"My dad's the one who's gonna come here and kick his arse," Cody whispered to my parents. I pulled him into a hug.

"Well, we look forward to meeting him."

David cleared his throat. "As do I. Now, isn't this reunion grand? But it ends now."

"No," I said. "Please, I just got them back. Oh, God, Mum, Dad. Mattie said you were dead, killed in a car accident."

"Yes, well. That's what the idiot over there told us, too. But it was his way of trying to get you to show. He thought you'd turn up at our funeral, and then he'd nab you there."

"Enough. Take them and the children out. I'll deal with them later."

Mum placed Maya's feet back on the floor and tugged Maya behind her body. Dad did the same with Cody.

"Mummy," Maya wailed. "I'm not leaving my mummy," Maya said, stomping her foot on the floor.

"Ha! I'm afraid so, daughter of mine."

"You're not my daddy. Talon is," she stated.

David's upper lip rose. "Get them out of here. Now!"

"I'll see you soon. It's going to be fine." How many times had I said that? I could only hope it was true. The great part was that I knew my parents would do anything to protect Maya and Cody, and they knew that I would understand that.

"Be smart and safe, sweetheart," Dad said.

Oh, God. Just like Mattie.

Snot a block—Mattie and Julian.

I nodded, tears threatening again. "Be good kids for your grandparents." I kissed Maya and Cody on their temple. "I love you both," I said, and it was then I saw for the first time tears in Cody's eyes.

"Love you, too, Mummy." Maya smiled. Cody gave me a chin lift...just like his father.

Mum hugged me close and whispered, "Don't give in."

"I never will." Not when I had Talon.

She picked up Maya. Dad placed his arm around Cody's shoulders, and they walked silently from the room with two guards, the one who came in with them, and one of Rocko's men. Thankfully, the one who'd eyed Maya stayed behind.

I slumped back onto the couch.

"No, no, Zara. Come and sit in this chair." David gestured to the chair Pervy Guy placed a foot in front of David's desk.

I rolled my eyes, hopped up, walked over, and sank into the wooden chair. Pervy Guy came to stand behind me. Hairs on the back of my neck rose. I looked over my shoulder at him and he grinned down at me.

"What's your name?" I couldn't keep calling him Pervy Guy, and I needed a name to seek my vengeance on.

"Call me Jeff."

I doubted that was his real name.

David stood, walked around the table, and stopped in front of me. My heart rate accelerated as *Jeff* grabbed both my arms and pulled then roughly behind the chair, holding them in place.

I winced. "Why all the fuss for me, David?"

He laughed. "I never like to let anything go, Zara, you knew this."

Whack. He slapped me across my already sore face.

"Obviously, I hired the wrong people to find you, for it to take this long. Wasn't it lucky these men contacted me and said they'd found my wife? You really should have turned up at the funeral, Zara. I might not have been as mad as I am now," he said, leaning over me with his hands on the armrests of the chair, our noses nearly touching. "But then again, you have really pissed me off." He leaned back.

Whack. A hit to the other side of my face forced my head around. Agony pounded in my face and heart.

At least he was being kind enough to not hit me in the same spot.

I licked my lip and tasted blood.

I don't know if I'm going to get out of this.

"Six years, Zara. You left me for six long years, and if you hadn't, I would have been fine. My plan would have been over by now, and I would be a rich man. But I'm not, all because of you."

Whack. I slumped in the chair and gasped, not just from David hitting me, but from being held in place, my shoulders and arms protesting against the angle Jeff had them in.

"Sit her up," David ordered. He sat back on the edge of his desk, eyeing me. It was starting to get a little hard to see; my face was already swelling. I felt the urge to vomit. The taste of blood and the pain churned in my stomach.

"So, we have a daughter."

I couldn't help but laugh. Now, he wanted to talk.

"Oof," I released with a gasp as David punched me in the stomach. I tried to calm my breathing, but ended up in a coughing fit. I spat blood onto the floor.

"Do not laugh at me." He opened a drawer in the desk and pulled out a wet wipe, wiping away my blood from his hands. He pulled out a knife, stalked back around, and in one move, he stabbed it into my leg.

I bit my lip, trying to stop my scream, but it still escaped.

He pulled it out slowly and ordered, "Rest her up a bit. I need to make some calls, and then we'll talk again."

I was roughly pulled from the chair just before I passed out.

CHAPTER TWENTY-THREE

TALON

"WHAT THE FUCK is going on here?" Rocko yelled, and stood from his desk. I stormed into his office in the nightclub he owned around midmorning. Griz, Deanna, Violet, and three other brothers were following close behind. Blue had called, informing me that he and Warden were at the hospital with Mattie and Julian. They weren't allowed in Pick's room, under doctor's orders. But he reassured me, as soon as no one was watching, he'd be in there.

With a lift of my hand, the three brothers slipped outta the room and closed the door, keeping an eye open for trouble that could come our way.

"What do you know, arsehole?" Deanna snapped. She stood next to Vi, both holding their hands on their hips.

"Sorry, sweetheart; I don't know what you're talking about."

I pulled a gun from under my Hawks vest and pointed it at his head.

He stood with his hands up in front of him. I followed his movements.

"Where are my boys?" he asked.

Violet scoffed. "You need new brothers, Rocko. They're all a bunch of pussies and incapacitated."

"Talon, what's the meaning of this? You want war? Is that it?"

"Two of your men have taken my woman and kids to hand her over to her ex, who beat and raped her. You tell me, do you want fuckin' war?"

"I know nothing about this. They have obviously gone out on their own. Who are they?"

"The guys that were with you last night," Deanna said.

Rocko smiled.

"What the fuck are you smiling at?" I roared.

Waving his hands he said, "Sorry, shit. I know it ain't a smiling matter. But your woman…" He smiled again.

"What?" Griz growled.

"She warned me last night that I needed to find new friends. Goddamn, she was right, and after just one glance, she picked it. Fuck. I should've never let them in. I was taking a risk on them. Other brothers had warned me, but I didn't listen. We needed new recruits. The Monty's motorcycle club from Melbourne wants our territory. Crap, I was only with them last night to see how they ran, and I didn't like what I saw. I was gonna cut them."

"How'd they learn about my woman and her ex?"

"I was the one who told Rocko. Fuck," Griz swore. "I'd asked him to keep his ear to the ground, see if he heard anything new. Shit, I didn't think."

"Jesus Christ!" I yelled. "Jesus Christ." I turned and put a hole in the wall the size of my fist.

"I'm sorry, brother," Griz said.

"Fuck, man, but it ain't your fault. You weren't to know," I answered, leaning one hand up against the wall.

I couldn't lose her. Cody and Maya…

It would kill me to lose any of them, most of all the three of them together.

I'd wasted so much time stuffin' around and waiting, trying not to scare her off. But I knew she'd been watchin' me the whole time as well. I saw the looks she gave me, the secret smiles that drove me fuckin' nuts. The way she'd blush at my words, the way her breathing would become faster when I was around.

I should have moved in sooner.

I should have claimed her months ago.

I'd thought the dicks in the brotherhood were crazy when they'd let their old ladies run their lives. Blinded by stupid love. I swore I'd never let myself fall again…never.

Until Zara. Until I fuckin' walked down that hallway to see a hot piece of arse standing there, glaring at me in a pink kitten nightie and combat fuckin' boots.

I was a goner.

From that day on, I knew I'd let Zara do anything.

She could talk, bitch, and complain about shit and it wouldn't faze me. She could harp about me swearin' around the kids, and still it wouldn't bother me.

Nothin' would, as long as she was at my side to do all that.

I had to find her. Them.

Jesus. The kids. I'd already missed out on enough of Cody's life. I wasn't missin' out on any more. And sweet Maya. There was so much more I wanted to learn about them both, so much I wanted to teach them.

I needed them all back.

They are my family.

And I fuckin' love them.

"Do you know where they have taken my family?" I asked Rocko.

"No. But I'll look into it. Maybe one of the brothers knows something." Rocko sat back down at the desk.

"You know I'll kill them."

"So be it. They are no longer Vicious."

My mobile rang and I answered, "What?"

"Nothing. I've got nothing," Blue said.

"Is Pick talkin'?"

"Yeah, he's talking, telling me lots of shit. None of it is any use to find them, brother. Cops have been. They want a statement on what went on in the house."

"Fuck. Has Mattie or anyone said anything?"

"Nothing, I told them to wait to hear from you. But you know the cops, brother. They won't wait long."

"Tell them to say it was self-defence. I had Mattie and Julian stayin' at my house. Pick called in and he found Vic holding them, ready to kill them. Vic was a hater of gays. Didn't like the way I was running things. No one says shit about my woman and the kids. We deal with this in-house. I'll be doing the clean-up."

"But the cops could help."

"No. They'll only hold me back."

"Right. On it. Then what?"

"Tell Matthew and Julian to head back to the compound—"

"Already have. They won't leave." Blue laughed. "They don't trust me and Warden around Pick. He saved them, brother. They're saving him back."

"Christ. All right, leave them there, and Warden, you get to the compound and see what they've found. Talk to Travis and see what's he's got. I'm heading to Vi's work."

"Right. Done," he said, then hung up.

I turned to Rocko. "Keep me in the know," I said with a chin lift. *In other words, if you don't, I'll fuck you over.* He nodded his understanding.

"I hope you find 'em, Talon. She's a rare beauty."

"I know. I fuckin' know. So are the kids. Let's move."

"Wait," Violet called, before I opened the door.

"What?" Rocko asked her; she was staring down at him.

"Do you know what they drive? Licence plate numbers, where they live? Maybe they're stupid enough to either use their own cars or take them to their place?"

"Great thinkin', sugar." He got up from his chair and went to a file cabinet to the right of his desk. "I had to shift my paperwork here while the office at our compound was getting detailed. Fuckin' lucky I did," he explained as he searched through the drawers.

Hell. How long did it take to find the information?

I just hoped these fuckers were just that dumb. And thank fuck my sister was here using her brain.

"Here." He thrust the files toward Deanna, the closest to him. "All the info I have on Jefferson and Zane. And while you're searching through it, I'll still keep looking here."

"'Preciate it."

Once outside, I sent my other brothers out searchin' the streets while Griz, Hell Mouth, Vi, and I got back into my Camaro to drive to Vi's station.

With the information we had, I felt a little lighter. The fist around my heart wasn't squeezing as tightly.

I just hoped it was going to lead us somewhere where my family was.

Payback was needing to happen, and I was looking forward to it.

There was no way I was gonna be some pansy-arse and pray... even if I wanted to.

Shit.

Fuck.

Why the hell not? Anything was worth it for them.

Yeah, um, God...

WE STORMED into Violet's work. Funnily enough, it was the first time I'd ever set foot in there. Things had to change. A lot of things. Violet booted up her computers while Deanna and Griz were talkin' quietly in a hushed tone, but I knew what it would be about. He was trying to reassure her, and I knew she wouldn't want that from him. Deanna was one hard chick to crack. Griz would have his work cut out for him when he got his act together. I should hurry him the fuck up—'cause you never knew what could happen.

"Anything?" I asked.

"Talon, I'm not that frigging fast, give me a minute." Violet groaned.

I paced in front of one of her desks while she worked on the computer; her fingers flew across the keyboard. I wondered where Zara sat while she worked. She hadn't been there long, but I knew she'd already brought some of herself into the business. The yellow sunflowers that sat on the windowsill. The scenic picture of the woods with a ray of sunshine shining through that hung on the wall. The colourful rug that sat in the middle of the floor. She'd always brightened up a place.

"I'll send Chuck to their houses, but I doubt they're there. They would have taken them to David straight away so they could be paid." She picked up the phone and rang her employee.

Griz walked over to me. "She's freaking. I'm worried she'll lose it soon."

I nodded. "She's not the only one." I sighed and ran a hand through my hair. "The thing I've noticed, though, is that Hell Mouth relies on Zara in more ways than one. Deanna not only helped Zara outta her past, but I'm sure it was the other way around as well. Not sure kitten knows that though unless she does and carries that burden, as well as Deanna." I looked over my shoulder to Deanna as she perched her arse on the end of Vi's desk. She looked in pain. "Anyone can fuckin' see that woman has been through some shit from that big iced wall she has built around her, and right now, it seems only Zara has a key."

I turned to Griz. "Good luck, brother; you're gonna need it." My phone rang and I grabbed it outta the pocket of my jeans, answering with, "Speak."

"Just got back to the compound. The brothers have nothing. No one's called in with shit, Talon. How's your end?"

"Violet, how we doing?" I was feeling antsy. I needed to be doing something instead of talking shit with Griz, or standing around doing crap. I felt useless, and it fuckin' hurt when it was my family out there in trouble.

"Zip. I've got Chuck on the line. There's no one at their houses. Their cars are in their frigging drives. I've got nothing else to go on. I'm sorry."

"Jesus Christ," I whispered.

"I'm guessing it's not good," Blue said on the other end of the phone.

"No. Fuck, brother. We have to find them—"

"Talon, wait," Blue snapped.

"Blue?" I heard talking in the background, but I didn't know what was being fuckin' said. "Brother?"

"Shit. Shit, boss, we've got them. Travis just came in. He's fucking found where they are."

"Text me the address. I'll meet you there," I said, and turned to the others. "Travis got a location. Let's go."

"Thank God." Deanna sighed.

"Christ, yes," Griz growled.

"Talon, wait," Violet called.

"What, woman? I gotta get my family."

"You and Griz need my guns. If the bullets are traced, I'm covered for being a PI. You're not."

I closed my eyes.

My sister was protecting me.

"I want one too," Deanna said.

"No way, darlin'. You get a taser," Griz barked and handed her a black taser from his back pocket.

"Seriously?" she said with an eye roll.

I ignored them as Violet approached holding three guns. She handed one to Griz and then one to me. I looked her in the eye and said, "There could be a lotta people goin' down today, Vi. You ready for this?"

"Fuck yeah." She smiled.

"Let's move then." I smiled back.

CHAPTER TWENTY-FOUR

ZARA

I WOKE LYING on a double four-poster bed in a dark room. I could see the sun shining through the gaps in the blinds. That told me it was still daytime, but I didn't have a clue what hour it was, or how long I'd been asleep.

I was sore all over. I needed water and something to eat, but I doubted I'd be able to keep it down.

Where was my family?

What was going to happen next?

I sat up slowly, wincing when pain stabbed through my head and leg. I looked down at the wound and found that someone had changed me into slip-on pyjama pants.

Why?

The door opened, and in walked a young girl around the age of sixteen with long red curly hair and a freckled face. She was short but slim, too skinny, actually. She carried a tray with a glass and a bowl upon it.

"Oh, you're awake." She smiled, but it didn't reach her eyes; it was all fake, a show. "Good. You'll be wanting some food and water, yes?"

I nodded. What was such a young girl doing in the house with David? She set the tray on the bed beside me. I took the glass with shaking hands and sipped it. The water helped my parched throat.

I looked to the door that she'd left open.

"You won't make it," she whispered as she stood beside the bed. A look of dread passed over her features.

What? Was she a mind reader?

"W-who are you?" I asked.

"I was homeless until David took me in." She glanced at the door, and then back to me. Bending over, so we were inches apart, she whispered, "You need to get out of here. He's going to kill you."

My eyes widened. Why was she warning me? I controlled my eye roll. *God, doesn't she think I already know that?*

"How can I get out?" I asked.

She shrugged. "That, I don't know."

"I wouldn't without my family anyway."

Her head cocked to the side. "Smart or stupid you are, but I can't work out which one. I know I'm stupid because I keep staying here. So maybe you're the same?" She smiled sadly.

Probably.

"Josie, what are you doing in here?" David came through the door.

Josie nearly jumped out of her skin, her cheeks turning a deep shade of red. "Nothing, Daddy. Um, I mean, I brought our guest some supper."

Oh, my flipping God. Was this for real? I mean I'd always wanted to role-play where Talon was a pirate and I was a damsel in distress…kind of like now.

But their roles were just fruited up.

Jesus, why hadn't I seen how crazy this fucktard was from the start?

He stalked across the room. Josie backed up until she hit the wall. "I told you not to call me daddy around people," he hissed through clenched teeth, and then slapped her across the face.

She whimpered and sunk to the floor. "I'm sorry, David."

"Don't be an arse," I said. He turned to face me.

Better me than an innocent girl.

His grabbed me by my hair and dragged me from the bed. I cried out when I landed on my knees in front of him.

"Don't," Josie screamed. She jumped onto his back, clawing at his face. He swore and flipped her off. She landed beside me with a *thunk*. He kicked her in her side and she groaned.

I punched him in the balls. It was his turn to groan, bending at the waist.

"Run," I yelled to Josie, but she didn't move, staying curled up in her protective ball.

"Jefferson," David called. In ran Jeff. "Take my *wife* to my office. I'll deal with her in a minute."

"You are nothing but a perverted cocksucker, David. Or should I call you daddy too? Isn't that what you like, you hairy sac sucker?" I yelled.

"Take her, now," David barked. Jeff dragged me up and threw me over his shoulder. I clenched my teeth at the pain.

We moved down a hallway, but I noticed David walk out of the room behind us and lock the door. I smiled to myself. I'd pissed him off that much? I guess he wanted to deal with me first. At least that left Josie alone... for now.

In the office, Jeff threw me onto the couch.

"Leave," David ordered.

Jeff smirked down at me, gave me a tap on the head, and left, closing the door behind him. David turned the lock into place.

He started pacing the room. "I used to think when I got you back we could have worked this out. But you've changed."

"Lucky for me, eh?" I sat up straighter and wondered why I

wasn't bleeding through the pants I had on. I felt my leg where David had stabbed me. It was covered by some sort of tape.

"Shut the hell up," he screamed. I felt like telling him he screamed like a girl, but I didn't think that would go down well. Though, my chances were getting slimmer by the second.

I love you, Talon. Tears threatened.

All I could do now was pray that he got here in time to save the children and my parents.

"I should have never been with you, David." I laughed. "I thought I knew what love was, but I didn't. Because now I know what love is. The love I feel for Talon is bigger than anything I've felt before—"

He ran at me, grabbing my shoulders, and roughly shook me. "Shut up. Shut up. Shut up. You are nothing." He spun away and walked to the desk.

Oh, shit.

He yanked open a drawer and pulled out a gun. "I would never have wasted my time in finding you, but your life insurance is going to make it worth it."

Say what, now?

"Um, hold on a second." I giggled. "Have you thought this through? Won't the insurance people know something's up if I'm riddled with bullets?"

Why am I helping him? Jeesh.

It was then I realised that I wasn't scared of David. I was no longer scared. What was in front of me was an old, mean man and nothing else.

"The police wouldn't question a break-in, where my dear wife was killed defending our home. Well, not home—seems you made me fucking travel a state away to kill you," he yelled and then shook his head. "Instead they broke into our new holiday warehouse here in Melbourne. Isn't it wonderful? I get a dead wife. I get money and a new place. Yes, I think I'll live here... with my two daughters."

"No!" I screamed.

He raised the gun and fired.

My body bounced back into the couch. I looked down as pain throbbed through my arm; blood started to soak my tee.

Damn it, I liked this one.

"Practice shot," he smirked. He raised the gun again.

CHAPTER TWENTY-FIVE

TALON

I'D ORGANISED to stop a block away, in an old, unused supermarket car park. I didn't want to rouse suspicion with Harley pipes, as well as all the large fuckin' cars pulling up to the warehouse.

I got out of my car just as twenty or so Harleys were roaring down the street and pulling in to stop. Blue was the first over to me, Griz, Deanna, and Violet.

"What's the plan?" he asked.

"We need to be fast, get in and get out. The warehouse is a block away at the end of a dead-end street. Not much goes on in these parts, so there shouldn't be any witnesses we'd need to buy off."

Fuck. I felt like I was wasting time standing there explaining. All I wanted to do was get in there, kill the fucker, and get my family back.

Violet stepped forward and rested her hand on my arm. "We go in on foot from here. We don't want them knowing we're coming." She looked over Blue's shoulder to a white sedan pulling into the car park. It stopped just behind the Harleys. "Good, just in time." She grinned as Warden got out of the car, went to the back of it, and opened the trunk. "Everyone needs to swap over their weapons for one of ours," Violet shouted to my brothers.

"Shit, Vi." I closed my eyes. "How the fuck are you going to explain firing off twenty or so guns to the cops?"

She shrugged. "We'll deal with that when the time comes." I shook my head as she added, "Do you think Zara would want her man in jail after just saving her? No. Do it for her, Talon."

"Do I get a fuckin' gun now?" Deanna asked.

"No," Griz growled. "You stick with me, princess."

She sighed loudly and rolled her eyes. "Fine. But I want a piece of him."

"We'll see," I said. I wanted him first. My hands itched to choke the fucker for layin' his hands on my family in the first place. "Right, let's load up and move out," I called.

VIOLET HAD me send Warden in first to remove—if there were any—cameras. Not that I believed a large motherfucker like Warden would get in there undetected, but he came back saying the coast was clear.

I spread my brothers out so we had the whole warehouse covered. I went straight to the front door with Griz, Deanna, and Violet. Then Blue came running around from the side to inform me, "We've taken out five men."

Then why the fuck wasn't the front covered?

I gave a chin lift in response and tried the front door. It was locked. I took a step back, ready to kick it in when Deanna stepped forward and knocked. I sent her a 'what the fuck' look.

Seconds later, the front door was opened, and one of Rocko's men, still in a betraying Vicious vest, stood there.

"Fuck," he hissed. He went to grab a two-way at his waist, but Deanna punched him in the face. He teetered back. Blue jumped him and held him to the ground.

"I'm sure Rocko wants to deal with this fucker himself." Blue grinned. "You guys go. I'll find something to tie him up with," he said while emptying the dick of weapons.

I bolted for the stairs, just as my other men came through the back door and went searchin' through the bottom area.

Taking three steps at a time, I climbed the stairs with the others following.

A gunshot sounded in the distance.

"Shit, shit," Deanna chanted.

We reached a hallway. I signalled for everyone to stay quiet and keep their eyes open. I opened the first door...nothing. Griz got to the second just as another of Rocko's men was walking out. He reached for his gun as Griz knocked him out with one punch.

"Leave him. One of the brothers will deal," I whispered.

Vi was at the next door to the right; she opened it, but nothing again. I wasn't there on a fuckin' scenic tour, so I took no notice of what was in the room and moved on.

The fourth door was locked. Violet pulled something out from her back jeans pocket and started working the lock; within seconds, it clicked open. She moved out of the way. I held the door handle and turned it. I threw it open while I stepped in with my gun raised.

A gasp, a sob, and a frightened squeal were what I heard first.

I looked around the darkened room and saw four bodies huddled in the right-hand corner.

"Dad?"

My eyes closed upon hearing Cody's voice. I lowered my gun, knowing Vi and Deanna had my back. I wasn't sure where Griz was.

"Told ya he'd come," Cody said with pride.

"Talon," Maya cried as she ran at me. I had enough time to brace as her little body hit me. I picked her up and hugged her close, gesturing to Cody to come to me.

"Richard? Nancy?" Deanna asked.

"Why, hey there, Deanna girl," a man said as he stepped forward into the hallway light.

"Oh, my God." Deanna gasped, tears in her eyes. I studied the man; he was an older image of Matthew.

"My, my, it's so good to see you, Deanna, and in the flesh, instead of on Skype." A woman stepped around Richard...fuck, she was an older image of my woman. "And you're just a hot piece of eye candy." She smiled, looking up at me.

Violet and Deanna chuckled. Griz came running into the room, and in his arms was a young teenage girl.

"Found her in a room. She's unconscious but alive." He laid her on the bed.

"Have you seen Zara?" I asked.

"Oh, my. No wonder my girl couldn't resist you with a voice like that."

Richard sighed. "Nance, focus. We saw her earlier, but that was a few hours ago. We don't know where she is."

Another gunshot sounded not far from where we were.

"Fuck," I hissed. I put Maya on her feet. "Stay here with your grandparents. Deanna, you gotta stay here with the girl in case she's gonna be trouble."

"Sure, boss," she said, taking out her taser. She looked itchin' to try that out.

"Keep 'em safe," I said to Richard as I handed him my back-up gun.

"Oh, sure, he gets a gun," Deanna complained.

Richard nodded when Nancy piped up about something regardin' me and grammar. I ignored it and knelt down to the kids. "It's gonna be good. I'll find your momma, baby girl, and then we can get outta here."

"I know you will." Maya smiled and patted me on the face.

"Good luck, Dad, and kill that fucker," Cody said.

"Boy, language," I growled, gave them both a peck on their heads, and ran from the room.

Another gunshot, but at least that time, I was able to pinpoint the location. It was the last fuckin' door at the end of the hall.

I tried the handle. Locked. I didn't waste time for Violet to pick it; instead, I kicked it open. With the gun held up, and with Vi and Griz at my back, I stepped in.

Fuckin' motherfucker.

I saw my woman on a couch, bleeding.

Shit, there was fuckin' blood everywhere.

"Who the hell are you?" David asked.

As I stared him down, he backed up, and Violet ran to Zara.

"Tell me she's breathing," I said.

"H-honey?" my woman said, but then started coughing.

"Christ, Talon. We have to get her outta here. She's got three gunshot wounds, and she's been beaten."

"You are not taking her," David yelled.

"Back the fuck up," I roared. I stalked toward him. "You bloodied my woman, you beat her, raped her, and fuckin' shot her. Fuck!"

Fury. All I could feel was fury. This fucker did not deserve it quick and painless.

He was going to pay.

He went to pick up the gun he'd dropped on the desk when we'd bound into the room, but I got there first and shot his hand away.

"Damn it!" he screamed, holding his hand to his chest.

"Talon! We have to go, and now," Violet screamed.

"Griz, take him. Clean this. I'm gettin' my woman outta here."

Griz smiled. "Sure, brother."

I stalked over to the couch. "Jesus, babe," I whispered.

"I-I k-knew you'd come. Kids? Parents?"

"They're safe. Now let's get you safe." There was no time for an ambo, so as gently as I could, I picked her up in my arms, but still, she cried out.

Pain laced through my heart.

"Vi, clear the way. Make sure the kids don't see."

"On it," she said, running from the room.

"H-honey…"

"Yeah, kitten?"

"I-I don't know…if this is gonna work. I-if I can—"

"Shit, kitten. Don't. You're gonna be all right, you're gonna be good. Fuck, babe. I know you're gonna be good 'cause I love you, and my fuckin' love for you is strong enough to keep you that way. So let's get you fixed, yeah?"

"Y-yeah, honey. You k-know, I love your alpha arse too." She smiled up at me and then passed out.

As soon as we reached the hospital, they took her away. They took her from my arms and told me to stay. The cops were called; still, my brothers got there first. The waiting room looked like a party at the compound. But instead of havin' a good ol' drunken time, everyone was sober and sombre.

I sat in a chair with my head in my hands as they worked over my woman. Zara's parents had the kids at her house, with more of my brothers watchin' them. They were waiting to hear from me. I just hoped to fuck I had good news to tell them.

No. It will be great, fan-fuckin'-tastic news that I'll tell them!

Griz was deflecting the cops, tellin' them what had gone down at the warehouse… well, our story of it. He told them that Zara had been kidnapped by her crazy ex and that when we turned up, David had taken off. We hadn't bothered chasin', 'cause we had to get her to the hospital. It was lucky enough that we had a witness, the young girl Josie, whom David had held hostage for the last three years. When Billy had brought her in, she'd said that she was willin' to tell the cops whatever we wanted, and she did. That, at least, brought me more time to sit and wait for my woman to get fixed. Though the cops said they'd still need my statement at a later date, as well as—how'd they put it? 'Miss Edgingway's, if she pulls through.'

If.

If she fuckin' pulled through.

That was when I punched a cop, swingin', and yellin' to get the fuck out. Blue had to pull me off him. The cop told Violet later that he wouldn't be pressing charges because he understood.

Not that I gave a fuck.

By the time the doctors came out, I had a child in each arm, and Zara's parents were sitting with me. They decided not to wait at Zara's house after all and came in after showering and changing. I couldn't blame them.

Deanna had turned up earlier, screamin' that she missed out on her shot, that she missed out on her retaliation on the fucker. That was when I'd whispered, "Not yet, you ain't."

She fuckin' grinned with pure glee and then sat her arse down to wait it out with us.

The doctor teetered backwards when she spotted the waiting room full of bikers.

"Uh…family of Zara Edgingway?"

"That's us," I said, standing. Zara's parents held the tired children close.

"Oh, okay. I just wanted to say she's through the surgery, and it looks like she's going to be okay."

I sank to my knees, and for the second time that day, I fuckin' prayed my thanks for savin' my life. 'Cause I knew I wouldn't have a life without my kitten in it.

EPILOGUE

FOUR MONTHS LATER

ZARA

I'D BEEN out of the hospital for two months when my mum turned up at Talon's house... though I should say our house because my man, being his bossy alpha self, had moved me in while I was still in the hospital.

My man loved to control.

But still, he had my heart in hand. He knew I'd be more than happy to have my family close, and I was.

Not only had my mum showed, but my father and Josie, who was my now adopted sister. She was still one mixed-up girl, but who could blame her after living with David for three years, and what he'd put her through?

I told her I'd help her along the way to recovery because we were sisters now. That was the first time I'd seen her smile. Not only had she attached herself to my parents and me, but she'd formed a bond with Maya, Cody, and Billy, the cookie-loving biker, one of Talon's brothers, who'd been her saviour by taking her to the hospital.

Mattie and Julian (who also joined the community of Ballarat and moved into my old place across the road from the compound) arrived with Deanna, Griz, and Blue.

Mum strode on through the door first with a small kiss to my cheek and hands full of dishes. Heck, it wasn't only her hands full but it was obvious she'd roped everyone else into brining something as well.

"What's this about?" I asked the last person through the door, my brother.

He rolled his eyes and said, "Just go with it, she's been cooking all day muttering about how her baby girl isn't eating enough. Apparently, you need more protein and vitamins to help you heal so you can give her grandbabies."

With wide eyes, I asked, "Please don't tell me she said that to everyone who walked in the front door just now?"

"Okay, I won't." He laughed, kissed my cheek and followed the rest to the kitchen.

It was then Talon walked from down the hall into the living room, where I was still standing with the front door open.

"Kitten, you're lettin' out all the warmth. What you doin', woman?"

"They just turned up. I didn't know they were coming and my mum's told everyone I need to heal to give her grandbabies... why are you smiling? You do know she'll be on your case soon because you're the one who has to impregnate me. Oh my God, she'll want to know things like when I'm ovulating, or I've got my period so she can work it out... she used to be a nurse; she's going to make our lives hell if she's already thinking about grandbabies." I'd been ecstatic when my parents told me they were moving to Ballarat... now I wasn't so sure.

"Babe." My man rolled his eyes at me. I snorted and shook my head at him. He didn't know; he hadn't been around her long enough to know my mum was...viciously crazy. Talon walked over to me, he took the front door out of my hand and closed it. Then he leaned in and kissed me soundly. So soundly I forgot what I was freaking out over.

"Wow," I uttered.

"Damn right. Now get in the kitchen and help get the food ready so we can eat, they can leave, we can put the kids to bed and then we can fuck like rabbits."

Biting my bottom lip, I admitted, "That sounds like a good plan."

He chuckled, touched his lips to mine and shooed me into the kitchen. I looked over my shoulder and asked, "How come you can't get in here and help as well?"

"Kitten." He chuckled and then said, "I have a dick, and all men with dicks sit back, drink, and watch their women do the work."

"Cheers to that," my dad yelled.

"Richard, don't you even think about doing nothing. Get your butt over here and carve this meat up. Talon can have a break, that good-looking man has been helping our baby girl nonstop."

"Jesus, Nance. I should get a break for just putting up with you."

Stopping in the doorway of the kitchen, I turned back to Talon and bulged my eyes out. As if he didn't care my family was crazy, he just smiled back with a shrug.

Maybe he was crazier for putting up with it all.

Or he loved me as much as I loved him.

Smiling to myself, I stalked in to help Mum before things got out of hand.

AN HOUR later we all surrounded the twelve-seater kitchen table. Griz, Deanna, Blue, Mattie, and Julian all sat on one side, my parents, the quiet Josie and the children on the other. Talon and I were at opposite ends. The food had been consumed and I loved it all. Mum always made a fantastic roast. Even the guys were raving about how good it was.

Watching everyone interact was amazing. Having my parents there and alive even better; seeing the way they had already bonded with their grandchildren, Maya and Cody, was something special. It brought tears to my eyes. The day would forever be in my memories.

Talon suddenly stood from the table. He cleared his throat. "The real reason I asked everyone here—"

"Wait, you organised this?" I interrupted, confused.

He smiled widely. "Of course, kitten." He started walking toward me, behind my parents and children.

Had I done something wrong?

Was he getting rid of me in front of everyone?

Was my heart about to explode in my chest?

If it did, it was all his fault.

Talon stopped at my side. He leaned over, took my shaking hand in his, and then... Oh my God, he got to one knee. My free hand went over my mouth, tears filled my eyes, and my body started to tremble with nerves.

"Kitten, no more stuffing around. The day I thought I'd lost you was... fuckin' painful. I know from then, hell not even that, from the day you moved onto the street, I knew I'd want to claim you in every way. You, Kitten, are my life, you're my soul, and I'd be nothing without you. Would you do me the honour of becomin' my wife?"

Speechless. I couldn't say anything, I couldn't move. I was in shock. This fine specimen of a badarse man wanted me in his future. He wanted me to be his wife.

Holy crap.

Talon Marcus wanted us to be his future.

Just like I had, but I'd never, not ever thought he would ask me to marry him.

"Kitten, you're killin' me here."

"Iloveyousomuch," I mumbled behind my hand.

"For the love of God, talk normal and give the poor man an answer," my dad yelled.

"YES!" I screamed and then jumped him.

He landed with a thud on the floor with me on top of him. My mouth attacked his, and he took it all with a chuckle.

Everyone started clapping and cheering.

I pulled back so I could see Talon's warm, soft, happy eyes.

Maya was the first on the Talon and Zara huddle; she climbed onto my back, leaned over my shoulder, and said, "Now you really will be my daddy."

TWO MONTHS LATER

"Talon," I moaned.

"Jesus, kitten." He groaned as I rolled my hips. We were in his room, at his...*our* house. The kids were at my parents', and it was time for us to have a private party for two. He was sitting up against the headboard, naked as the day he was born. I was just as naked, besides some rocking heels my man had bought me for my birthday last week.

I was working my inner-cowgirl magic, riding him like I was meant to.

Leaning forward, I kissed him.

I was never going to get enough of him.

Never.

"Babe," he groaned.

"Not yet, honey."

"Fuck, kitten."

"Not yet," I uttered through clenched teeth. "Oh, God, honey. Now." I gripped the headboard behind him as he pounded his cum into me, and I climaxed around him.

Exhausted, I rested my head against his shoulder, breathing hard.

"Christ, woman. We are never doin' that position again. I come too fuckin' quick."

I giggled. "Hell to the no. I love taking control."

"Only in the bedroom you can, and only when I let you," he growled.

"Whatever," I said, pulling back so he could see my eyes roll. He grinned. I got out of bed and went into the en suite to clean up. When I came back out, Talon was lying down with a sheet covering his bottom half. I ran and leapt right onto the bed. He chuckled at my antics. I turned off the lamp on the bedside table and snuggled in. Then I wiggled as close as I could to him, knowing he'd curl me into his arms just like he always did.

"You happy, kitten?"

"More than happy...but worried."

He laughed. "No need to be, 'ca I'll be here right alongside you. Always."

"I know, honey. That's why I love you."

"And I you, babe. Now sleep."

"Yes, boss." And I squealed when he slapped my behind.

I was worried because that morning at my doctor's appointment, we found out we were having twins. Talon had grinned down at my shocked face and said, "Fuck yeah. Kitten, when I do something, I do it good, and you got it good."

That was still debatable.

I had been just getting over the fact that we weren't sure I'd be able to have children after David had shot me twice in the stomach. You could say that Talon was over the frigging moon we'd be having a child together. He'd said that I'd been through enough shit in my life to last me till I was old and grey, and now that we were finally over the speed hump, we could live our lives to the fullest, each and every day.

Well, our lives would certainly be filled.

Of course, after the news, I ran and cried on Deanna's shoulder, telling her that Talon had supersonic sperm and that he'd sonic-ed his way into my... fandola, and shot me up with twins.

Her response was, "Well, fuck me."

I thought another hot-crisis issue would have gotten her out of her funk. But it hadn't.

She was worrying me because these days I hardly saw her, and when I did, she always seemed to have something on her mind... only she wasn't sharing.

It was if she'd been altered when I'd been taken, and it wasn't something she was getting over. Though, I still doubted it was that alone. Something else was in her head, and I was going to get to the bottom of it.

We'd been keeping a close eye on Maya and Cody since the incident, but they seemed to be handling it okay. We'd had Cody every second weekend until that stopped and we got full custody.

And that was because Cody had rung in the middle of the night recently, and we'd found just what his mum and stepfather had been up to.

Talon woke and picked up his phone. I'd woken when I heard a gruff, "Talk." And then he paused and said in a growled voice, "They're what?" I sat up quickly beside Talon and placed my hand on his back. "I'll be there soon."

He climbed out of bed and donned a tee and jeans before he turned to me and hissed, "Bianca and fuckhead are havin' a party. That was Cody. Let me just say it's not a party a kid his age should be witness to. We're gonna go get 'im." I was out of bed in seconds and threw on jeans and a hooded, long-sleeved top.

Maya was already having a sleepover at my parents' house, so there was nothing to delay us getting into Talon's car and driving the ten minutes to Bianca's house.

As we drove down the long driveway, we could already hear the music pounding from the house. I knew nothing of Bianca's new husband other than the fact he was someone who had money, and Talon called him a dick.

Talon skidded to stop. He handed me a small devise and said, "It's a Go-Pro. I need you to film what we see in there and we'll be takin' that fucker to court. I want full custody of my son."

"Okay, honey." I nodded. He kissed me hard and quickly and got out of the car. I was out and at his side as we stalked up to the front door.

Talon turned to me, his face dark and scary. "You'll be safe, they'd know not to touch you, or I'd fuck with them. Stay close though. We get in, get Cody and get out."

"I'm with you." I smiled.

"Fuck, how'd I get so lucky?" His lips pressed to my forehead before he spun, grabbed the front door handle and slammed it open.

Hmm, I guess it isn't locked.

"What. The. Fuck," Talon roared when he stepped in. I came around him with the Go-Pro held high and I soon found myself wishing I couldn't see.

In the large open-plan living room in front of us were...bodies. So many bodies and they were all naked, rolling around each other and doing things that shouldn't be happening when a child was in the house.

Suddenly the music was cut off, and Bianca was in front of us. Thank God she had a robe on.

"What are you doing here with *her*?" she demanded.

Talon took a step forward, leaned in and snarled in his ex's face, "Get rid of your 'tude, Bianca and tell me, do you think this situation is good for our son to be near?"

She rolled her eyes. "He's up in his room, I told him to stay there. He won't see anything."

"What's going on, darling?" A man of about fifty walked up.

Oh God. He was as naked as the day he was born and it was not a pretty sight. His bulging belly and chest hair were enough to put me off my food for a year, but when his hand ran along his small prick while eyeing me I just about dry heaved.

Talon was in front of me to hide the sight. Thank Jesus. I arched my hand around him with the Go-Pro so I could still capture everything.

"You look at my woman with your hand on your tiny dick again, I will fuckin' end you." My man was tense, he wanted to fight and take lives, but I knew he would hold himself back because his son was in the house. A house he should never have been in.

"Honey, I like the way you think, but that's not good for the camera."

He looked over his shoulder and smirked. "We'll edit it out."

"Camera?" Bianca gasped.

Talon turned back to her and said, "Yeah, bitch. My woman just took all this shit in and now I'm takin' my son outta here without any fuckin' trouble." He crossed his arms over his chest. "You won't fight me this time, Bianca. I'm getting' full custody of Cody. You no longer exist for him. If you balk at anything, the cops will see just what goes down in here."

"He's my son, Talon."

"Not anymore," Talon growled. "No mother would do this shit with a child in the house. You just lost him, Bianca."

The stupid woman shrugged. "Go and get him. See if I care."

I stepped up. "How could you—"

"Kitten, she ain't worth it." He was right, she wasn't. Talon took my hand and we starting walking through the house.

Thankfully, we got Cody out of there without him seeing anything. When we were in the car, on our way back home, a quiet Cody asked, "Am I going back there?"

"No, Cody. Never. You're with us from now on."

His smile was bright. So bright it caused me to get teary.

"Good," he said.

Turning in my seat, I told Cody, "You'll be happy with us."

His nod was immediate. "I know, Zee."

Things were now going to be full in our house, and I was looking forward to it. Of course, it wasn't always going to be roses and chocolates; we were two totally different people, arguments were bound to happen. Our first one wasn't long after I was released from the hospital, and it was regarding Pick. Mattie and Julian had told me what Pick had done for them. Talon wanted Pick gone from the brotherhood. Mattie, Julian, and I told him to give him another chance. Eventually, we'd worn him down, and he said he'd consider it. Meaning Pick was still in the brotherhood, and in the end, it was Talon and Mattie who helped Pick cut the ties his mother had on him.

I used to wake every night while I was in the hospital, but that stopped as soon as I had Talon sleeping next to me.

I'd always have scars, but they were something that made me stronger. To prove that I was over what had happened and that I was stronger for it, I did something that scared me. I got my first tattoo to cover the smallest scar—which hurt like a mother-fruiter. And that was when Talon and I had our second argument. He didn't want my body inked. That was when I yelled, "What's good for the goose is good for the gander." His reply was, "What the fuck does that mean?" I flashed him my tattoo on my lower stomach, a picture of a hawk, and underneath it was written 'You flew into my life, but I've got my claws into yours.'

The next day, he'd come back with his own tattoo, a picture of a kitten digging its claws into his skin.

"Jesus, kitten. I can hear your brain churning again. Get to sleep. Everythin' will be good."

I smiled into the dark room and knew that everything would be good because I had my badarse biker beside me.

CLIMBING OUT

OUT BALLARAT CHARTER LILA ROSE

Climbing Out Copyright © 2014 by Lila Rose

Hawks MC: Ballarat Charter: Book 2

Editing: Hot Tree Editing
Interior Design: Rogena Mitchell-Jones

All rights reserved. No part of this eBook or book may be used or reproduced in any written, electronic, recording, or photocopying without the permission from the author as allowed under the terms and conditions under which it was purchased or as strictly permitted by applicable copyright law. Any unauthorized distribution, circulation or use of this text may be a direct infringement of the author's rights, and those responsible may be liable in law accordingly. Thank you for respecting the work of this author.

Climbing Out is a work of fiction. All names, characters, events and places found in this book are either from the author's imagination or used fictitiously. Any similarity to actual events, locations, organizations, or persons live or dead is entirely coincidental and not intended by the author.

Second Edition 2019
ISBN: 978-0648481676

To my family, who has encouraged me to continue doing what I love.

PROLOGUE

DEANNA

As I watched Zara and her new husband twirl on the dance floor at their wedding reception, I wanted to throw up. Then again, I was also so fucking happy for her; maybe that was why I felt sick to my stomach.

She looked absolutely beautiful in her designer gown, even if her tiny two-month baby bump showed. It was as though she pulled her dress from a page in a princess storybook and slapped it on herself. Bitch.

Only she deserved this happy day, and so many more after the hell she'd been through. Even though eight months had passed, it still felt like yesterday when I'd come out of Griz's room at the compound to find Zara had been taken. The thought that I'd possibly lose my best friend shattered many things inside of me.

Yes, she pulled out of it, but I knew what something like that could cost you mentally. Sure, she seemed fine on the outside, but the inside would be a different matter. At least she had her boss-man to take care of her, and I knew he would.

Sighing, I sat back in my chair, and even though my insides were playing turmoil, I felt myself smile. Zara would soon be whipped away for her honeymoon in Fiji, the vacation they never got to have because everything turned into crazy-arse wedding planning mode. She was so excited about it, and when she got excited, other people also joined in on her thrill ride.

From the look in boss man's eyes, I knew she'd be on her back in a matter of time. I chuckled to myself. There was no way I'd ever want to be in that situation. Okay, so yeah, I could do with the part of being on my back, just without the being married and knocked up bit.

My eyes searched out Griz. He stood on the other side of the dance floor, casually leaning against the bar; his eyes were on me. I squeezed my legs together. Goddamn did I want that man, but he kept fighting it, and right then I was glad he did.

My life for the next seven months or so was going to be busy. I didn't need the distraction, and I knew as soon as I had my hands on Griz, I wouldn't ever want to let go.

I looked to my bag and saw the letter sticking out. I pushed it back in and zipped it up. That was the second letter; I got the first one when Zara's shit had started. Both were like a knife to my stomach. I thought I'd gotten rid of him from my life—obviously, that wasn't the case.

I had eight months before he came looking for me.

I could only hope my plan would work.

If not... I'd be dead.

CHAPTER ONE

FOUR MONTHS LATER

DEANNA

CLICK, click, click. The sound of my fingers flying over the computer's keyboard was starting to annoy the fuck out of me. I turned up *Roachford* on my iPod sitting in its dock on my desk. My attention quickly went back to the monitor. *Buy, buy, and buy.* It was all I could think of.

Some thumps on my front door sounded over the music. I rolled my eyes because I already knew who it was. Groaning to myself, I put a halt on my online retail therapy and slid my chair back so I could bang my head against the desk. She was never going to get the fucking hint I wanted to be left alone for a while. I didn't want to taint her happiness with my... bitchiness.

"Open the flipping door, Deanna. I'm a woman on edge. I had a large slushy on the way over, *and* I'm six months pregnant. Do you want me to pee on your doorstep for all your neighbours to see?" Zara yelled.

Fuck it.

I shouldn't have turned up the music because now she knew I was definitely home, and *I* knew she wouldn't be ignored this time.

"Come on, cupcake; she's going to blow," Julian joined in on the yelling.

Scoffing, I got up and started for the front door of my two-story house. On the way, I took in the sight surrounding me. There was no way I could hide anything in the next two seconds, so I opened the door and prepared myself for hell.

"You." Zara glared as she cupped her hoo-ha with one hand while the other was pointing a finger at me. "We have some talking to do, wench, but move, 'cause I've gotta go." She pushed past me and ran for the bathroom that was down the hall off the lounge room, only her steps faltered before she reached the hall's doorway. "What the truck?" She gaped at everything around her.

"Incubator, we'll talk about how crazy our girl is after you pee," Julian said as he stepped through the front door and kissed me on my cheek.

I shut the front door and was geared up to knock myself out when Julian squealed behind me. I spun around and saw him clutching the *Ouran High School Host Club* DVD box set to his chest.

"Oh, my gawd! I-I've wanted this for years, but Mattie said if I got it he'd turn me out. Holy capoly, girlfriend, be prepared to have me living at your house so that I can watch this day-in and day-out." He sighed.

"Keep it," I said.

Julian eyed me suspiciously. He leisurely took me in from head to toe and then back again. "You look like shit."

I rolled my eyes and went back over to my desk, sat down and hit buy. A notice popped up on the screen announcing I was now the proud owner of a house in the Grampians.

Even though my eyes were still on the screen, I knew exactly when Zara had come back out. She stood behind me and slapped me on the back of the head.

"What the fuck?" I spun my computer chair around and glared up at her.

"What the duck, indeed," she hissed. "What is going on here, Deanna? I haven't seen you in two, nearly three months, and this is what I find when I finally catch you at home?" She gestured to the room around her. "Are you starting your own Target store? What is with all this crap?"

All this crap was the only thing I hoped would keep... him from coming after his—well, what he thought was his—inheritance. If I spent nearly every penny, he'd have no reason to hunt me down.

However, I couldn't tell Zara any of that. She was in a happy place after having been through her own hell. I wouldn't bring her down again.

I shrugged. "Just doin' a little shopping."

She turned to Julian, who was still fawning over his DVDs. "Do you believe her lies?"

"Hen pecker, I believe her lies are so big I could roll them in a joint and be high off them for a year."

"See? We don't believe you." She pulled me out of my chair and studied my face. "Hun, please, please tell me what this is all about. And I mean everything—why you've been avoiding us, and why your house looks like a... a hoarder's place."

"Do you guys want a coffee?" I asked instead of answering. Though, making a quick escape to the kitchen didn't work; they followed me.

"Don't make me bring in the big guns to get you talking, Deanna Drake."

I laughed. "What, your mum?" I walked around the bench and readied the coffeemaker, and then turned to them as they sat at the kitchen counter.

"No—" she began.

I interrupted her. "Is that where Maya and Cody are?" I asked. Zara and Talon had won full custody for Cody two months ago, and they were ecstatic about it. So was Cody; he loved Zara, even more than his own mother. Though, no one could blame the kid; his mom was a slut.

"They're at school. Do you even know what day it is?"

"Sure, I was just fuckin' testing you, making sure you knew where your kids were. 'Cause you know, once your tribe pops out of you, you're gonna have to be on your toes."

"Bullshit." Julian coughed into his hand, then waved it in the air. "Basic manoeuvre to change the subject."

"That's the truth." Zara glared. "That's it. If you don't start talking, I'm calling." She grabbed her phone from her jeans pocket and opened it, fingers ready to dial.

"It's nothing you need to worry about, bitch."

"Five seconds, Deanna."

"Seriously?"

"Four seconds," she chimed.

"Who the fuck are you gonna call?" I snapped.

"The boss-man." She smiled.

"No," I gasped and shook my head.

"Yep. My hubby is already on speed dial. Four seconds, hun."

"Jesus, lamb chop, you're up to three seconds. Preggo brain strikes again," Julian said and sighed.

"If you call him, I will seriously be pissed at you," I informed her, and then leaned against the kitchen bench with my arms crossed over my chest.

"I'm willing to take your pissed-off mood if it gets me to the bottom of what's going on with you."

I closed my eyes and sighed. "Zara, *please* just leave it be."

"Oh, shit," Julian gasped. "She sounds serious, baby doll. S-she said please, and without cussing."

Zara nodded and said to me, "I know, but I can't let you deal with whatever you are on your own, Deanna. Friends don't do that. Also, if I recall correctly, it wasn't that long ago you were at my side through all my hell, and you wouldn't listen to me when I wanted it left well enough alone."

"Sing it, sister. Testify!" Julian yelled.

With a roll of my eyes, I said, "But look at how well all that turned out. And that was nearly a year ago."

"Tell me, Deanna," she pleaded.

I shook my head. "It's fine—nothing."

"Deanna!"

"Zara! Just let this blow over, and then everything will be back to normal." *I hope.*

"Let what blow over, buttercup?" Julian asked.

Shit!

"Nothin'. Look, I got crap to do, so both of you can just fuck off outta here."

Zara frowned, shook her head and then uttered, "One." She pressed her phone to her ear.

Fuck no!

I ran around the bench intending to tackle her for the phone, but she must have known that would have been my first move. She ran from the room.

"Hey, honey," I heard her say into the phone as I chased after her.

"Zara!" I yelled. "Don't you fuckin' dare." I glared as she stood on the other side of the couch.

"That's just Deanna in a bad mood."

"I will kill you," I hissed through clenched teeth.

"Why, you ask, is Deanna in a bad mood? Well, honey, I'm not sure, but there is something wrong here, Talon. I'm worried."

Motherfucker.

I knew I had no chance now. If Zara was worried, Talon would try his best to squish that worry for her—in any way he could.

I was done for.

Shit. No, I wasn't. I was Deanna Drake, and I didn't let anyone tell me what to do.

"Yeah," she said into the phone. "Thanks, honey. I'll see you soon." She flipped the phone closed, and put it in her pocket while biting her bottom lip.

Yeah, she should be worried. I was going to do what any tough, don't-fuck-with-me woman would do.

I ran from the room, up the stairs and locked myself in my bedroom.

My door shook as it got pounded on. "Open the fuckin' door, Hell Mouth," Talon barked.

There was no way in hell I was opening my door. I was sure I could wait out the lot of them.

"Just leave." I groaned from where I lay on my bed with my arm over my eyes.

"You know I won't. You're worrying my woman, Hell Mouth. I can't let that happen. Not only fuckin' that, but who her people are, now are Hawks' people, and you're one of 'em. We help each other, and that means either come out here and tell me what in Christ's name is goin' on, or I come in there."

I snorted... and wiped away the stinking tears that broke free while I thanked fuck no one could see how his words had turned me into some stupid emotional woman.

But they had.

Because of Zara, I now had a family, one that was alive and willing to help. Jesus, I knew I had become a raging bitch when Zara wouldn't let anyone help with her problem, and now I was doing the same.

Ironic. Insert eye roll.

But this was different.

Now I understood why Zee was so damned determined to keep others safe from her crazy ex because right then, I was willing to do the same. The only difference was that the wanker who would soon be after me wasn't an ex.

Fucking hell.

Was I stupid with this act? Probably.

But I didn't want anyone to see the scared fucker I was becoming underneath this facade. I thought I could take on everything.

I was wrong.

I was weak.

And I hated it. I hated myself.

David, Zee's weirdo ex, helped prove how much of a wuss I was.

It was a week after Zee's episode with him that Talon called me in the middle of the night asking me if I wanted my payback, and if I did, I had to get my ass to Pyke's Creek.

What I thought I was prepared to do ended up being different than what I did do.

CHAPTER TWO

GRIZ

I WAS SITTING opposite Talon in his office at the compound when his phone rang.

He looked at the screen and smiled. I knew straight away who it was before he answered it with, "Kitten, what's up?"

His smile dropped. "Who the fuck is yellin' in the background?" He waited for his answer, and then said, "Why is she spazzin' out?" He sighed. "You need me?" he asked, and then added, "I'm comin'."

He threw his phone to the desk and then must'a thought better of it; instead, he pocketed it as he stood.

"What's going on, brother?"

"Zara's at Hell Mouth's. Somethin's going on, so I'm headin' over there."

I also stood and asked, "Mind if I join you?"

He gave me a knowing smirk and chuckled. "Sure, Griz."

I ignored his reaction, followed him out of the compound and stalked across the gravelled path to our Harleys.

"When are you gonna snap the fuck outta your shit and take what you want?" Talon asked as he placed his helmet on.

"Don't know what you're talking 'bout. There ain't nothin' I want." I sat astride my bike and belted up my helmet.

"Motherfuckin' bullshit. Wake the fuck up, brother. Hell Mouth won't be available forever."

"You of all people know I don't need another bitch to deal with." My bike roared to life.

"She'd be different," Talon yelled over the rumble of our bikes. "I think you know this, and that scares the fuck outta you more." With that, he kicked the stand up and took off.

Following him, my mind couldn't help but wander off, thinking 'bout princess. Talon was right—she would be different, and that did scare the fuck outta me because I've never felt the attraction I did for her for anyone else.

As if to prove the point, my dick hardened.

Christ, now wasn't the time to get a hard-on like some fuckin' little boy.

I got enough shit to deal with in my life than worrying 'bout her, but it had been too long since I'd seen her. For some reason, she'd been absent from everyone's lives for the last couple of months. I often heard Wildcat complaining about it.

There had to be an explanation. Anyone could see the love Deanna had for Wildcat, so for her to keep her distance like she had been, there had to be a huge fuckin' reason.

Maybe if I could find out what crap she was dealing with and fix it, then I could stop thinking about her and worrying every minute of the damn day.

And my shit won't stink either.

We pulled up to her two-story brick home in fuckin' suburbia. I bet her neighbours had their blinds twitching, searching and wondering why Deanna had two criminal-looking bikers walking up her drive.

Talon didn't bother knocking; he walked right in, and I followed to find Wildcat and Julian sitting on a couch with a ton of shit surrounding them.

Talon let out a low whistle as I took in all the crap, from toasters to books to—was that a fuckin' vibrator sitting on top of the desk? I was afraid to look.

"What the fuck is all this shit?" I asked.

"That's what we want to know," Wildcat said. I glanced at her and could see the concern showing in her eyes.

"Where is she?" Talon asked as he made his way to his woman. He helped her from the couch and twisted her, so she was in his arms.

"Once she knew you were coming, hunk, she took off to her room and locked herself in there," Julian explained.

I seriously wished he'd quit with the damn pet names.

Talon looked back at me and I nodded. We made our way down the hall—which was also full of shit—and up the stairs to her room. I didn't ask how Talon knew which room hers was, 'cause I sure as hell didn't know, and it kinda already pissed me off.

It had to be because Wildcat told him.

It had damned well better be!

Talon banged on her door and barked, "Open the fuckin' door, Hell Mouth."

"Just leave." We heard with a groan of annoyance.

Talon started to say something else, but I was too occupied with my own thoughts to listen. What was going on with her? Why couldn't bitches just say whatever the hell was wrong with them, and then fix the fuckin' problem instead of doing this childlike shit?

After Talon's speech, silence met him from the other side. I was sure I heard a sob but then thought, *that couldn't be right.*

But what if it was? I—we had to get in there to find out what was going down with her before she stressed the fuck outta us even more.

Talon turned back around and looked at Wildcat, who had followed us down the hall.

"See what I mean? Usually, she'd be out here ranting and cussing like a sailor at us instead of this act," she said with a sad tone.

"She even said please before," Julian added, and Zara nodded in agreement.

Fuck. We all knew that word would never pass Deanna's lips unless it was serious.

"Do you reckon she'll let us have it if we break her door down?" Talon asked with a smile playing on his lips.

A shit-eating grin spread across my own.

"I don't think it'll be a good idea to poke Satan and test her," Julian said.

I chuckled. "I think it's fuckin' brilliant. Step back."

CHAPTER THREE

EIGHT MONTHS EARLIER

DEANNA

I'D MADE my way out to Pyke's Creek, to the destination where Talon had told me they'd be. I pulled my Mustang up, turned off the engine and then made my way behind an old, run-down boating house. The night was cold and misty; I wore jeans and a hooded jumper. I wasn't sure if this was killing clothes... what would one wear to kill someone in? I didn't know. I knew why they had chosen this area though. It was secluded. Nothing surrounded it except for bushland. The only road in was the one I just travelled. They could easily tell if someone was approaching.

Four large vans were parked there, and about ten bikers where standing around talking. Talon must have spotted me because he appeared out of nowhere right in front of me.

"You ready?" he asked.

I thought I had been, so I nodded. Talon gestured to someone, and the back door to one of the vans opened. One of his men dragged the beaten form of David out and threw him to the dirt ground.

"You can't fucking do this to me!" David shouted.

"Bullshit." Blue laughed. "You fuck with Hawks; we fuck back harder."

Talon took my arm and pulled me over to the bikers now circling David.

"What's she doin' here?" Griz growled from the other side of David.

"She wanted her chance. I'm givin' it to her," Talon said.

Griz shook his head and hissed, "Jesus, Talon."

Talon just ignored him and called, "Pick."

My eyes widened as the bikers parted, and Pick shuffled forward. He looked tired and seemed as though he was still in pain from getting shot. He was also showing signs of new bruising. I guess Talon hadn't been too happy with him after all. Though, no one could blame him.

"For the shit you caused, this is your payment. Do you accept?" Talon asked. "But realise this—if there are any blow-backs from killing this fucker, it'll all be on you."

Pick met Talon's hard gaze, and then stood taller and said, "I accept."

"He should fuckin' die like this piece-of-shit too," someone shouted.

Blue chuckled. "No one can touch him, or Wildcat will have Talon's balls for it."

Everyone laughed.

Pick winced. I bet he hated it was Zara and a couple of gay guys who saved his arse.

"All right. Let's do this so I can get home to m'woman," Talon ordered, and then turned to me. "Hell Mouth, you get first shot." He pulled a knife from the back of his jeans and held it out to me. "He stabbed Zara in the leg first, so I think it would be appropriate if we return what was done to her, to him."

I took the light-weight, agile fighting blade and smiled down at it. I felt pumped and excited for the fact Talon had let me be involved with this, even though Griz was obviously disgusted by it —I could tell from the scowl upon his handsome face.

Gazing from the knife down to David, my stomach churned.

"Hell Mouth?" Talon questioned, but my eyes stayed focused on David. He looked scared; his body trembled, and sweat-beads showed on his forehead, but there was a cocky glare in his eyes. He smirked up at me.

Had he already known I was second-guessing myself?

"Just stick it in, sweetheart," someone said.

I wanted to.

I itched to.

But I was scared.

Me... scared.

Not something most would believe.

Though, they didn't know my past. They didn't know that every time I saw the colour red, I had to fight a panic attack.

And that was something I wasn't willing to do in front of Talon and his hot biker brothers.

I didn't know how long I stood there, staring at the knife and then at David. It wasn't until I felt warm arms circle my waist and heard in my ear a soft whisper of, "Darlin'." That it had been long enough for Griz to move around the circle to me.

To give me strength? I wasn't sure.

He took the knife from my hand, passed it back to Talon and then took my hand and dragged me from the group of leather-covered giants to my car.

That was when I heard Talon say Pick's name, followed by blood-curdling screams coming from David.

"Princess, look at me," Griz ordered, and when I didn't comply, he took my chin in his hand and forced my head up. "Get outta here and go home."

I shook my head, disappointed in myself. "I-I should have

done it."

"No, you shouldn't have," he barked.

My eyes snapped to him, and I sent a glare his way. "Yes, I should have. I'm a strong bitch, and I should have been able to gut the fucker, but...." I tried to pull away—to think—only Griz wouldn't have it.

He met my glare with an amused look on his heart-stopping, sexy face, which had been tanned by the sun and wind from riding that Harley of his. "It just means, darlin', that you have a heart."

I gasped. "I do fuckin' not, you-you arse!" I took a step back from him and watched his large, calloused hand fall from my face.

Regret filled me. I liked his hand on me. I sure as hell wanted more of Griz on me.

"I'm going. I have to go." I opened my car door and said over my shoulder, "You're a dick. You know that, right?"

"Sure, princess." He smiled a smile that made me want to drop to my knees and beg him to shove his dick in my mouth.

I shook my head and added, "No one fuckin' says a word, or... I don't fuckin' know. Maybe I'll send Julian upon you all for a year."

"Shit, no. No biker would ever want that to happen."

A surprised laugh escaped me as I watched him shudder. "Damn right," I said.

Gunshots echoed in the background, making me jump. I looked over toward the area where David was about to take his last breath, and I felt nothing but annoyance at myself for not doing what I so wanted to do.

"Get home, Hell Mouth," Griz uttered, which brought my attention back to his concerned eyes.

I grinned wide to show I wasn't bothered by what happening just beyond the wooden shed.

"Don't tell me what to do, you prick."

He burst out laughing, shook his head and walked off.

PRESENT TIME

Bang. I jumped from my bed to the other side of the room while holding a hand to my heart.

What the fucking hell? My door was kicked off its hinges, and the culprit stepped into my room.

"Griz, what the fuck?!" I yelled.

"Well, maybe next time you'll open your damned door," he growled.

What is he doing here anyway?

Talon, with a scary-ass-biker scowl across his face, walked around him, as did Julian and Zara.

"You made me do this. I had no other choice," Zara sighed dramatically.

"That's fuckin' it! I'm taking back the Harleys I bought for your little aliens," I said.

"Hang on a minute," Julian started, hands on his hip. "You bought her and Mr McSlap-my-arse's spawn Harleys, and they aren't even born yet, and all I get are some DVDs? Let's talk about that." He stomped his foot.

"No," Talon barked. "Let's talk about why in the fuck you're spendin' all your money."

Zara gasped and caught everyone's attention. She then proceeded to slap her forehead and say, "I'm such a flipping idiot."

"I won't fuckin' argue," I offered. Talon sent dagger-eyes my way.

She looked at me with sadness in her eyes. "I get it now. I'm such a bad friend. Shoot, Deanna. I'm so sorry. Of course this is why."

"Zara," I warned.

No. No. No. I never thought she'd remember. She was as drunk as a skunk when I had told her. How in the hell could she remember?

"Kitten, you want to tell the rest of us?" Talon asked.

"Don't!" I hissed just as Griz's phone chimed.

"Fuck me, what now?" Julian sighed.

CHAPTER FOUR

GRIZ

I LOOKED at the screen and my stomach turned. I wanted to put my fist through a wall. It was her again. This was becoming more frequent, but who was I to deny it?

"Gotta go?" Talon asked. He must have read my face.

"Yeah." I sighed. "Fuck!" I clipped and looked up from my phone to meet Deanna's curious gaze. My brows furrowed and I turned to Talon. "You'll catch me up later?"

"Course, brother," he said with a chin lift.

"There will be nothing to catch up on," Deanna snapped.

I scoffed. "Sure, princess." I walked to the doorway— where the door was now hanging from its hinges—and said over my shoulder, "See ya later."

And I meant it in every way because I knew whatever was going down with Hell Mouth would be yet another situation where shit would happen.

She would need someone at her side.

Whether she liked it or not, that someone was me.

Shit.

And that was going to be more trouble I didn't need.

Guarding Hell Mouth's person was going to be a test all on its own.

I KNOCKED on the front door, but there was no answer. That had never happened before, so one could say I was already on high alert. Kathy always had the door opened within seconds when I pulled up. She'd listen for my bike and be ready and waiting, eager to get the fuck outta here.

So where in the hell was she when it was only ten minutes ago that she'd rang?

I pounded on the door this time, and yelled, "Kathy?"

Nothing.

Not one fucking sound.

That was when I heard it.

A faint cry.

I kicked my boot through the second door of the day and ran into the house.

The crying got louder as I got closer to the back of the messy house and into the bedroom.

"Fuck," I growled.

Stepping over Kathy's prone body on the floor, I picked up Swan, my two-year-old daughter, from her crib.

"It's okay, baby. Shh, everything's gonna be fine," I cooed and murmured to her as I walked her out of the room, down the hall and into the dirty kitchen.

Fuck!

Was she dead?

She had to have been.

Jesus. Was the mother of my child laying on that floor dead?

In front of our baby?

Stupid fuckin' bitch. What in Christ's name had she done now?

Why the fuck did the house look like a bomb had hit it, and smelled like it as well?

I glanced around the kitchen, from the dirty floor to the bench tops, and some crap sticking outta the oven. The fridge door was open and empty.

Flipping open my phone, I looked down at Swan. She'd calmed down enough to stare back up at me.

"It's gonna be okay, baby," I whispered.

Her little hands reached up and wrapped around the back of my neck. She buried her tiny head into my shoulder and sighed.

She knew.

She knew her daddy was here and was gonna make it all good for her.

Putting my phone to my ear, I rang Blue, because Talon had enough on his plate right then.

"Brother?" he answered.

"I found Kathy lying flat on her face in our kid's room."

"Be there with Stoke and Killer. We keepin' it low?"

"Nah, I gotta call the cops, man. People saw me walkin' in. But try and get here first."

"On it. I'm five or ten minutes out."

"See you soon."

I'd give him five minutes before I called the cops, and in that time, I left Swan in the lounge playing happily while I went to check what I already knew.

Kathy was dead. She must have passed after her call to me. I found her phone under Swan's stuffed animal-filled crib.

Quickly grabbing Swan some clean clothes and a new nappy, because her other one was soaked through, I went back out to take care of my girl and called the police.

How long had Kathy been on the floor like that?

Shit, fuck! I could only hope that Swan never remembered what she saw when she was older. What type of blow-back could she have for seeing her mother lying dead on the floor? She was already not talkin', unlike most kids at that age who would have already tried to bleed your ears out with their constant babbling.

But my Swan stayed quiet.

I had asked Kathy to take her to the doctor's. She was forever telling me it was all okay, and that for some kids it took longer.

I'd bought that story for so long.

Now? Not so much. Something else was going down, and I was gonna get to the end of it.

After Swan was clean, I wrapped her in my arms and held her tightly. She liked that, always had, ever since she was born.

Christ. My heart was bleeding for her.

I should never have left her with that bitch, but all women seemed good at the start, until they'd try and control you. I wasn't having that, so I left, and then she'd told me she was pregnant. I was actually happy. Even though we weren't together, I thought it could still work. I thought even though Kathy was not meant for me, maybe she was meant to have a baby, to be a good mother in her own controlling ways.

I was wrong.

She never wanted Swan.

She still liked to party, and the few times I caught her trying to have a party in the same place my daughter was—let's just say things got ugly, and Talon ended up having to drag me away before I killed the bitch.

At least she wasn't dumb enough to cross Talon. Once he made an order, she followed through. The people were kicked out, and Swan was brought to my house for the night.

What I didn't understand was why she kept coming back for her. I'd told Kathy a million times over I'd keep Swan full-time. Only she wouldn't have it. Told me a man should never raise a girl on his own and that she needed her baby girl. She'd be lost without her.

Then, over the last ten months, things had gotten strange. Kathy would call and tell me to get my arse over to the house or she'd leave Swan on her own.

'Course I'd bolt over, and as soon as she'd heard the pipes of my Harley, the front door was opened and Kathy was disappearing into a cab. I'd take Swan to my house and tear Kathy a new asshole when she'd come to pick her up the next day, looking like shit.

But it was the same story every time—just that she needed a night out, needed to feel free, and we'd argue about letting me take Swan permanently. But of course, like the sucker I was, I gave in every time, because I'd never want my baby girl to grow up without a mother.

All that was about to change though.

And honestly, I couldn't be happier.

Fuck. I sounded like a dog for saying that shit, but I was. I was happy, because I knew Swan would now be in a tightly secure family. It was a family who took care of one another no matter what.

It was obvious something had gone down in the house last night, and the fuckin' knowledge my baby girl was here for it made me sick. Nothing like this would have ever happened at the compound, or even in the brotherhood. We party, but we don't it with the kids around. They were always safe at home with someone trustworthy to take care of them.

The front door opened, and in walked Blue, Stoke and Killer. They came over to the couch where I sat with Swan, who was now asleep in my arms. "Check the house, brothers. See what needs to be hidden, and what gives us clues on what went down. We've got about five minutes before the cops show."

"Done," came from Blue.

"On it," Stoke growled.

And Killer gave me a chin lift. He was the silent type. Didn't utter a word unless he felt it necessary, and he knew now was no time for talking.

They spread out and went on the hunt for me, while I sat back with my resting baby girl, thinking of the next step.

CHAPTER FIVE

DEANNA

Worry seeped into me. What was Griz involved in that had him running every time he got a phone call? It had to be something shitty, and if it was, no matter how much I wanted to tap his fine arse, I wouldn't.

Maybe just once? Get it outta my system?

No. I couldn't.

I looked up from the floor and into three sets of eyes that were all focused on me.

Fuck.

"Kitten, start talkin'," Talon bit out, and then shook his head. "Damn, but that shit sounds familiar. You two can't keep doin' this—keepin' things from me and my brothers so we can't help you."

"Hey," Zara snapped. "Don't go all angry-man at me. I only *just* remembered what all this is about."

"You can go angry-man on me anytime," Julian offered. I couldn't help but smirk; that fucker was always bringing a smile out of me when he'd say shit that would usually never be said, especially to an alpha male like Talon.

Zara turned to Julian and glared. He took a step back, hands held up in front of him and said, "I'm just saying. Whoa, momma bear, you are scary when preggo." He coughed into his hand. "Overprotective much?"

"Stop hitting on my man then," she grumbled. "Then I wouldn't feel the need to pee on him. It happens all the damn time. Whenever we go down the street, how do you think I feel when he's walking next to a waddling duck, while all the skanks' eyes are checking him out and thinking he could do soooo much better."

Fucking hell. She was on the verge of tears.

"Zara," I said, "get your hormones under control."

She stood straighter and said, "Right, yes. We're here about you."

Damn, I shouldn't have said anything.

"Kitten," Talon barked. We all looked at him to see he was tense, but his eyes were warmly focused on his wife. He took two steps and had her in his arms. "You don't have anything to worry about. I don't give a fuck if there are ten thousand women checkin' me out, and you shouldn't either, 'cause I fuckin' love the way you move, the way you look and the way you tell me off. No one will ever gain my attention for the rest of my life the way you have."

"Oh. My. Gawd," Julian whispered.

Something dropped onto my cheek. I looked to the ceiling to find what it had been, but nothing was there. It was then I realised my eyes had tears filling them, and one had escaped.

Fuck.

What was wrong with me? Why in hell was I leaking over shit like that?

I could only come to one conclusion—I must've been PMSing.

"Honey." I watched Zara melt into Talon. She whispered something into his ear that had him chuckling, and if I knew my girl like I knew I did, she was promising him something steamy in bed.

She turned in his arms back to me. "Now how about we all go to our house, hun? We'll have dinner, some drinks and we'll get all this sorted out."

"No, thanks. I'm all right here. You guys go ahead though." I walked around my bed and out of my bedroom, down the stairs and into the kitchen. I knew they were following me.

I stopped at the coffee pot and offered, "Anyone want one before you hit the road?"

"Hell Mouth," Talon hissed through clenched teeth. I turned to find him on the other side of the kitchen bench with Julian and Zara.

"Yes, boss-man?"

"If you don't get your arse in Zara's car, I will carry you outta your own house kicking and screamin'. What's it gonna be?"

"You know he'll do it. You've seen him do it to me," Zara added.

Sighing, I looked down at the floor pretending to think about it, but really, I just wanted to annoy him for butting into my shit.

Though, I couldn't really blame him. No, it was his wife I was gonna smother in her sleep.

Glancing up, I rolled my eyes. "Oh, all right."

DINNER AT ZARA and Talon's house was always something I enjoyed, no matter what kinda funk I was in. Honestly, who wouldn't? What I presumed would just be Talon, Zara, Julian, Mattie and the kids, actually turned out to be all of them, plus Zara's parents with their foster daughter

Josie, and Talon's sister Vi, and her boyfriend Travis. Thankfully, Talon's house was huge enough to have us all there.

It was loud, messy and fun.

Until the front door opened, and in walked Blue and Killer. From just one look at their tense faces, Talon was outta his chair and in their little huddle at the front door.

"Oh, my. I'll never get over seeing so many delicious men in a room," Nancy, Zara's mum, said, causing Josie to giggle, and Richard, Zara's dad, to sigh loudly.

"Mum," Zara snapped and made wide eyes, gesturing toward Cody and Maya.

"Oh, what? It's not like I said they were—"

"Nancy," Richard interrupted. "Let's get these munchkins ready for bed." He stood from the table. "Josie, want to help, honey?"

Josie was still quiet around a large group, but if she was on her own, one-on-one, you could never shut her up—unless that someone was a male. She was still very timid around any man, even Mattie. Though Julian was girly enough, she never flinched any longer when he'd get near her. Still, there was one exception, and that was the youngest Hawks member, Eli Walker, or as we called him 'Billy The Kid.' Anyone could see the major crush Josie had on him. We could only hope he'd never be stupid enough to break her heart. But most of us were sure it was bound to happen, because he was such a womanizer.

Nancy, Richard, and Josie disappeared with the kids from the kitchen and down the hall. They must have sensed something was going to go down because in the next second, a piercing cry sounded at the door, bringing everyone's attention back to the group of delicious bikers.

Talon, Blue, and Killer moved aside, and in walked— Holy hell. It was Griz carrying a beautiful, little blonde girl in his arms who kept screaming like a banshee.

What in the hell was going on?

I didn't know, but damn he looked good in jeans, biker boots, a white tee and his club's vest over the top. His eyes were a little more grey and hard, and his salt-and-pepper hair was a mess, but seeing it made me want to run my hands through it—just like every other time he walked into a room.

And honest to fucking God, he looked sexy as hell carrying that gorgeous little girl in his arms... even if she wasn't shutting up.

"Oh, my," Zara whispered.

"Zara," Talon called. She got up from the table and went straight into his waiting arms. He said something quietly to her and I watched—though I was sure it wasn't only me watching—as her eyes grew wide, her hand flew to her mouth and she nodded.

"New drama is a-blazing," Julian sang.

He was sure as fuck right.

CHAPTER SIX

GRIZ

WATCHING Zara being informed I not only had a kid, but that kid's mother had just died hurt me more than I thought it would—especially when she turned her eyes toward me, which were now filled with sympathy and pain.

But I didn't deserve it.

I hated the bitch who died, and right then, even though Swan was balling her eyes out, I was one fuckin' happy man. I had my girl —my baby—to myself, to raise in the way I wanted her to be, surrounded with people who cared about her more than anything, even more than their own life. That was what the brotherhood was about, and that brotherhood extended to their old ladies and rug-rats.

"Hey there, pretty girl," Wildcat cooed, capturing Swan's attention, who immediately settled a little. "Are you hungry?"

"She doesn't talk, Wildcat, but I'm sure she's hungry. Thanks, sweetheart."

Zara nodded, clapped her hands out to Swan and I was goddamn surprised when Swan reached out with her own small arms to be taken.

As Wildcat walked off with Swan, I watched them the whole way and was damn glad I did. Swan looked over Zara's shoulder and smiled. She smiled. My dead heart started to fill from that one little expression, only to skip a beat when my gaze landed on Deanna.

Fuck. She looked sexy. She sat at the table with Mattie, Julian, Vi, and Travis, and while they all talked, her attention was only on me, and the look she was giving me—like she wanted to rip my clothes off—caused my dick to harden.

Shit.

"Griz, brother, wanna fill me in on what went down?" Talon asked.

"Like I already said, I found Kathy dead in her house. Swan was crying, so I broke in. I got the brothers to come first, and then the cops came and questioned us. It was obvious she'd OD'ed on something."

"Did they accuse you of anything?"

"They would have liked to, but a neighbour stated she'd had a crazy party last night, and that she saw me pull up not long before the cops did."

"Fuck, man." Talon sighed. He turned to Blue and Stack. "Did you find anything?"

Blue looked at me. I nodded, giving him the go ahead to talk. "Yeah, Talon, we found a member's vest... an old one."

"What the fuck do you mean?" Talon hissed.

"It was Maxwell's," I said.

Max was the one who left our club when Talon had taken over and cleaned the brotherhood up. Max still wanted to deal in hookers; he couldn't get enough of it. He loved the money they brought him, the attention and the pussy.

"We gonna have a chat with him?" Talon asked.

I ran a hand over my face. "Not tonight, man. I'm tired, and I want Swan to have my attention all night. I don't wanna leave her."

Talon nodded. "Fair enough. But tomorrow, we go talk with our old pal."

I smiled, because I sure as fuck had questions for Maxwell, like why the fuck he would allow Kathy to have a party with my little girl in the house in the first place.

Jesus. The thought made me sick to my stomach. What in the hell had my baby seen last night?

"Calm down, brother," Talon ordered. "We'll find the answers."

Giving a chin lift, I turned my attention back to the table. Talon would have known how I was feeling, because he'd feel the exact same way if it had happened to his kids.

"What's the situation with Hell Mouth?" I asked.

"Don't fuckin' know yet. Everyone turned up for dinner and we didn't want to talk about shit in front of the kids, but whatever it is, she'll need protection."

I'd guessed as much.

"I need her keys," I said, while watching her at the table admiring Swan, who was sitting in Wildcat's lap eating some meat and vegetables.

Talon chuckled. "Kitten?" he called. Zara eyed her husband, handed Swan off to Vi and made her way over.

"Yes, honey?" she asked as she wrapped her arms around Talon's waist.

"Babe, I need you to get Hell Mouth's keys on the down low."

Her brows arched; she looked from her man to me, so I supplied her with the reason why. "We're guessin' that whatever Deanna has to come clean about is serious enough to need protection. That right?" When Zara slowly nodded, I added, "So I'll have to move some things in, and if she knows before I get my shit to her place, she'll put up a huge fight. But if my stuff's already there...."

Zara smiled. "I'll get them."

Talon laughed. "That'a girl." He smacked her on the arse as she walked off.

"What about Swan?" Blue asked, his eyes shining with humour.

"I'll be taking her with me. Once Zara gets the keys, I'll need you two to go to my place and pack what you think I'll need from my room and Swan's—her bed and all. Then you'll need to go to Deanna's, fix her bedroom door if ya can and load all my shit in. If you can find fuckin' room."

"What you mean by that?" Killer asked.

"You'll see once you get there. You two okay with doin' that?"

"Pleasure." Killer grinned.

"Yeah, I just wish I could see Hell Mouth's face once she realises." Blue chuckled.

I couldn't wait to see it either.

CHAPTER SEVEN

DEANNA

MY STOMACH WAS IN KNOTS. Zara's parent had left with Josie, and I knew the time was coming for me to talk. Everyone was expecting it, and I knew if I didn't supply them with the reason why I was going bat-shit crazy, Zara would.

But something else was going down as well. I could sense it. Zara was being cagey—one second she was with us at the table helping Swan eat, the next she was with Talon, and then next she'd disappear into the kitchen, only to return and walk back over to the guys still huddled at the door. Then Blue and Killer left, but not before staring at me with... amusement in their eyes.

Yes, something else was happening, and I think that something was at my expense.

Now, we were all sitting back at the kitchen table, with Griz joining us after he took Swan from Vi and sat her on his lap. The kids were in bed watching something on their TVs, and Zara had just come in from the kitchen once again—this time with Julian—and handed out coffees for everyone.

"All right, Hell Mouth," Talon began, and then took a sip of his coffee. "Enough time has passed. Let's have this out."

"Looks like we came on the right night for dinner," Vi said, rubbing her hands together. I glared at her.

"Vi," Travis warned. He knew of our hate-hate relationship. Actually, I was sure everyone knew of it. It wasn't like I totally hated her—she had helped Zara in a huge way—but I hated the thought of anyone new stepping between what Zara and I had.

Was I jealous?

Fuck yeah.

Because I couldn't lose Zara. She was my rock.

"Yeah, well, feel free to fuckin' leave," I said.

"Deanna!" Zara snapped and looked to Swan.

I rolled my eyes and muttered, "Sorry."

"Let's just get this sorted so I can get my girl home," Griz clipped.

Shit. My heart skipped over and stalled. That was something I'd wish Griz would say about me. 'Get my girl home.' Yes, fucking please.

Instead, I glared at Griz, and asked, "Any chance you wanna fill us in on why the... *heck* none of us knew you had a kid?"

"No," he stated like there was never going to be an explanation, but I wasn't going for that.

"I knew," Vi said.

"Jesus." Travis sighed. "You can't help yourself," he said with a smile. "Precious, I think it's time we left."

"No way! I want to find out what's going on." She glared at him and crossed her arms over her chest.

"I'm sure you'll be filled in sooner or later, but it'll be less tense without us here, and anyway, we should get home to Izzy. The sitter can only stay for so long."

Violet actually growled under her breath. "You spoil all my fun."

"Thanks, man." Talon grinned.

"Yeah, thanks." I smirked.

"Hell Mouth," Griz said with a warning tone.

"So here it is, and I'm not going to repeat it, so listen—beep—carefully," I said, once Travis had left with an annoyed Vi. Zara giggled at my attempt of adding in a swear word, but I had to add in something. It was killing me not to, but when I looked at the sleeping form of Swan—Griz's flipping daughter—something in me wanted to behave like a grown-up.

I fuckin' hate doing this. I goddamn hate that I didn't know Griz had a kid when I want to be the one to have his babies... Holy shit, where in the hell did that come from? I want his kids? Fuck no! I'd be no good as a bloody mother.

"Sinner of all sins, how about you spit it out before hunter-man has a breakdown?" Julian suggested. I looked next to me at Griz, who had his jaw clenched and was glaring at me.

"Fine." I sighed. "I grew up in foster care, going through family after family until I came to the Drakes' house. They actually put up with my bad mouth and attitude enough, even going so far as to show me... love. Until, that was, their son came home from traveling. He didn't like me. I didn't like him. Jesus, do I really have to?" I whined the last part.

"Yes," Griz growled.

"Okay, okay. He came into my room one night and said if I didn't put out for him, he'd kill his own parents."

"Fuck," Griz bit out, and then yelled, "Fuck, fuck, fuck!"

Swan stirred in his arms. Mattie jumped up from the table, and with tears in his eyes, he swept Swan out of Griz's hold and out of the room.

"I thought no swearin'?" I teased, trying to lighten the mood.

"Sweetheart, don't," Julian uttered.

Zara had tears in her eyes. Talon was as stiff as a board, and

Griz... emitted a different kind of heat. His hands were clenched on his thighs like he was just waiting to hit something.

My heart sank and sputtered to life.

Fuck me.

They cared... and I couldn't handle that.

"Keep going, hun," Zara supported.

I nodded and stared down at the table. "I didn't know what to do, but I knew—I knew he was fucked up enough to do just that. And I would never want anything to happen to the Drakes, so I... I gave myself to him."

Shifting in my seat, I felt all their eyes on me and I didn't like it. I hated attention. "I let it go on for a year. Then I thought of a plan. One night when he came into my room, I'd hidden a video camera. I told him no—like I had every other night—so he forced me. The next day, I thought I was the smart one and went to him, telling him to leave and stay to the fuck away or else I'd go to the cops and show them what he was doing. I-I should've fuckin' known. He went into a fit of rage, but then he left, so I thought I'd won."

I took a deep breath to steady myself. There was no way I was going to cry. I had cried enough.

"Mrs Drake overheard our conversation. She was devastated her son could do something like that. She wanted me to go to the police, but I didn't. I didn't want anyone to judge the Drakes for what their son, Jason, had done. Two months later, he broke into the house, and after he killed his father and tried to kill his mother, he came into my room—with blood all over him—to kill me too. Only Mrs Drake was still alive, and she called the cops. They came and he went to jail. Mrs Drake lived for another week on life support, and then passed away. It wasn't until I was at the reading of the wills that I found out—the day before their son had come home—they'd changed their wills and left everything to me."

I rubbed at my chest and then my eyes.

That had hurt.

It wasn't like I wanted to forget them, but if I let the memories get to me, I'd be crazy. I was nearing crazy when I met Zara three years later; she'd helped me and dragged me out of my darkness.

Julian's breath hitched, and I watched Zara wipe away her own tears while I waited for someone to say something.

It was Griz's hard voice that supplied a question to the silence. "How old were you when it started?"

"Sixteen."

"The fucker gets out soon, doesn't he?" Talon hissed through clenched teeth.

"Yes, and this is why I've gone a little crazy with shopping. I was hoping that he wouldn't come and look for me if he knew I've spent all his money—or the money he thinks is still owed to him."

"Are you sure he'll come looking for you?" Julian asked.

"Yeah. He sent me a letter about nine months ago."

"When all my stuff was happening?" Zara gasped. "Oh, God, Deanna. Why didn't you say anything? I'm such a bad friend." Talon pulled her out of her chair and into his lap.

"What did the letter say?" Griz asked.

"'Looking forward to catching up and my payment,'" I quoted. I witnessed Griz and Talon share a look. "What was that?" I asked. "What was that look about?" Because for some reason, I didn't think that look would mean good news.

"Nothing. Let's talk about this shit another time. Right now, I gotta get my girl home." He stood from the table and looked down at me. "I'll give you a lift."

I was sure I heard Zara giggle, but when I turned to her, she was straight-faced.

"That's okay. I'm sure Julian won't mind," I said, standing myself to stretch.

"Not at all, she-devil." Julian smiled, only it looked forced.

"No!" Zara yelled. We all turned to her. "I mean, I need Julian here. I'm really tired."

Julian's brow furrowed; I was sure he was thinking the same thing I was—how strange that sounded.

"Okay, weirdo." I shrugged. "I'll just grab my bag while you get Swan," I said to Griz, and with a chin lift, he left the room.

I bent over the table and whispered to Zara, "I don't know what you're playing at, but it ain't gonna work."

She smiled brightly and giggled. "We'll see."

CHAPTER EIGHT

DEANNA

SWAN SLEPT all the way to my house in her car-seat in the back of Griz's Jeep Cherokee. As we pulled onto my street, I noticed two Harleys and one van parked out the front of my place.

"What's going on?" I asked, more to myself, but Griz answered with a shrug.

Stopping the car, I grabbed my bag and hopped out, and then leaned back in and said, "Thanks for the lift." Only Griz wasn't still in the driver's seat. He'd also gotten out and was now opening Swan's door to—I guess, get her out as well?

What the fuck?

"What are you doin'?" I asked as I slung my bag over my shoulder, but before he got to answer, I heard the sound of feet stomping down my drive. I turned to find Blue.

"What are *you* doin'?" I asked with my hands on my hips and a glare in my eyes.

Blue chuckled. "Not much, Hell Mouth." He walked right up to me and handed me my keys.

Hell. What is going on?

"W-what? How? Why do you have my keys?" I screeched.

Blue looked over the car to Griz. I looked over the car to Griz too, who was now holding a tired-eyed child in his arms. The men communicated something through head nods and chin lifts, and that just pissed me off even more.

I turned to Blue, pulled back my leg and kicked him in the shin. "Why do you have my keys?"

"Fuck, Hell Mouth. Christ, why'd you do that?" he hissed as he bent over and rubbed his shin.

"No one is answering me or the main question I keep askin'!"

"They moved my stuff in, princess," Griz said.

My body froze. Had I heard him right?

Looking over my shoulder, I hissed through clenched teeth, "No way."

He grinned. The arse grinned, shifted Swan in his arms, walked around the car, got close enough that our noses just touched and whispered, "Yes way."

Stepping back, I turned to shove a laughing Blue out of the way and stomped up my drive.

"Good luck, brother," I heard Blue say to Griz. "You're gonna need it."

Not wanting to hear his reply, I opened my front door just as Killer and Stoke were coming out. Upon one look at my face, they both smiled widely and moved out of my way.

"Have a nice night, Hell Mouth." Stoke laughed as I picked up a cushion and threw it at him. They walked out the front door and closed it behind Griz.

Oh my God. Was Griz really staying here?

My heart took off out of control regarding a certain thought of seeing Griz every night and morning, walking around my house in nothing but his boxers.

My hoo-ha sang for joy.

I had to have proof.

Dropping my bag to the couch, I made my way down the hall

and up the stairs. I opened the door to the first spare room. What was full of shit this morning, now held a kid's bed with some side cushion-thingy on it. I guess that was to stop Swan from falling out.

Wait a goddamn minute!

Swan was staying here as well?

Oh, shit.

Fuck.

I couldn't have a kid around. It'd learn bad shit from me. What was he thinkin'?

"I see you found Swan's room," Griz said from behind me, causing me to jump.

"Jesus, a warning is nice before you sneak up on someone." I looked to Swan in Griz's arms; she seemed so tired, with her blue eyes blinking up at me and her head resting against Griz's chest.

I wondered if he'd let my head rest on his chest too?

Shaking my head, I looked up to a smiling Griz. What the fuck was he smiling about?

"Look, you can't do this. You can't just move you and *your daughter* in here. This isn't going to work." I shook my head.

"Its fine and it's staying this way until your shit is over," he said in his don't-give-me-any-bullshit voice.

"You wanna risk your daughter?" I asked.

"She won't be at risk. During the days while I'm busy, she'll be with Wildcat until I can get a sitter or organise some childcare. Then at night—well, I'll be here, so no risk will come to her... or you."

Why was my heart beating like the *Jaws* soundtrack?

Because this was going to either kill me or—yeah, let's not go there because that thought was even scarier.

I was sure Griz was shocked that I didn't argue with him. I muttered a final "whatever" and left the room. There was no point anyway, not when he held an exhausted Swan in his arms. Plus, there was always tomorrow. For now, I'd let him have his way and crash in my spare room.

Though, as I changed into my cami and boy shorts for bed, my mind wouldn't stop wandering from the thought of Griz sleeping in my house—sleeping not far from me.

What is he dressed in?

How far is the sheet pulled up over him?

Does he have a sheet on at all?

Should I check if he even has a sheet on?

Fuck! This was really playing with my mind.

There was only one thing for it. I rolled over on my side, opened the bedside table and pulled out Vinny.

Vinny the Vibrator had many times entertained me enough to forget whatever else was going on around me. I could only hope he would fulfil his job tonight, or else Griz may just call the cops and accuse *me* of rape.

Pulling the sheet back over me, I quickly wiggled out of my shorts and was just about to go to town... when I heard my bedroom door open.

"What are you doing?" I yelled at Griz.

"Goin' to sleep, darlin'. I'm buggered."

He took off his vest and pulled his tee over his head, showing me he was ripped and tattooed galore over his pecs and upper arms.

Frozen in my state of admiration, and thanking myself for leaving the curtains open enough, I could clearly see him unbutton his jeans and tug them off, leaving him in black boxers. He pulled the sheet down a bit and hopped onto the bed next to me, lying on his back.

"Um—"

"Don't start, sweetheart; let's just sleep."

"But—"

"Darlin', I don't want to fight."

"Why aren't you in the room with your daughter?" I asked, and yes, still with Vinny waiting patiently at my entrance.

"I don't know if you noticed, but there was only her bed in there."

"I have other spare rooms."

"Yeah, with that much shit in there, no one could fuckin' breathe."

"Griz, I really don't think this is a good idea," I stated, even though I was ready to throw Vinny away, jump onto Griz's rhythm stick and go for a ride.

"Too bad, darlin', 'cause I ain't movin'."

He rolled onto his side, so his back was toward me. What in the hell was I supposed to do now? I had a hot male—who was tired and seemed in a mood—sleeping next to me, while I lay with my legs apart and my vibrator ready for the green go-sign.

Decisions, decisions.

Can I continue with what I so want and need? Or should I do the proper thing and put Vinny away for another night.

To hell with it.

My hoo-ha yelled in victory.

Flipping the switch, Vinny buzzed to life, and with one thrust forward I moaned as he slipped into my willing, wet pussy.

"What the fuck?!" Griz yelled. It was in seconds, I was sure, that he'd flipped over to face me, went up on his giant, muscular, tattooed arm and threw the covers back with his other hand. "W-what?" He looked down at Vinny, and then up at me with a look of lust, anger, and desire all in one.

"Well, you fuckin' came in at the wrong time, and there is no way I'm willing to stop," I supplied.

In my little rant, my hand moved Vinny and a groan left my lips. I arched off the bed and settled down, only to open my eyes to meet the hooded grey stare of Griz.

"Fuck," he hissed.

In yet another second, he was off the bed and over in the corner of the room.

"Y-you can't do that shit while I'm in here." He glared and then looked away to the floor.

"Bullshit. It's my room; you came in here, so suffer the consequence." I giggled, but it quickly turned into a moan as Vinny hit just the right spot.

"Jesus!" Griz groaned.

I found that I was turned on even more than usual having Griz in the room and watching me with hungry, but pained eyes. I pulled Vinny out, only to push him back in swiftly, and hissed when he reached that wonderful spot inside of me again.

I opened my eyes as I pulled Vinny out and laid him against my clit. My breath hitched; I knew I was close.

It was the fastest I would ever have been able to make myself come in my whole life.

But I wasn't ready quite yet.

I needed to play with Griz a little more.

Moving Vinny away, I looked over at Griz, who was still standing in the corner with a tent in his boxers watching me. "You could come and join me?" I whispered to the quiet room.

He shook his head. "W-we can't do this, princess."

I pouted. "And why the fuck not? It's obvious you want me, and I've been forward enough to let you know I'd do you. So what's stopping you?"

"My child in the other room," he growled.

Pulling the sheet over me, I shook my head and said, "No, I don't think that's it. 'Rents have sex all the time with their children in the house. It's something else, but what?"

"You're too young," he said.

I scoffed, "Get over it." Throwing the sheet back off me, I grabbed Vinny tightly and plunged him into my still-wet pussy. A moan filled my mouth as I grabbed my breast and arched. "Oh, God, Griz. You better hurry before I come."

"Shit," he uttered and then cleared his throat. "Darlin', you better fuckin' stop."

"Hell, Griz. I can't. It feels so good, babe." Vinny and I were having the time of our lives as he slid back and forth into my wet tunnel.

"Fuck, darlin'. Fuck." Griz groaned. "Two can play at this," he growled quietly.

Looking back over at him, my eyes widened as I watched him pull the front of his boxers down and palm his large, hard erection, and then proceeded to masturbate.

Holy shit!

CHAPTER NINE

GRIZ

I COULD NOT FUCKING BELIEVE what I was doing—standing over in the corner of the room with my dick in my hand—and as I tugged it, I watched with pure voyeuristic desire as Deanna's pussy engulfed her vibrator laying in her bed where I was just beside her.

Actually, that was what she *had* been doing... until I took my cock in my hand.

Now, her greedy eyes were trained on me and my body, and her vibrator was set aside.

She rubbed her legs together, got up on her elbows and licked her lips.

A groan fell from mine. I wanted more that any-fucking-thing to take a leap and have my dick buried inside of her willing snatch.

But I didn't.

Why?

Many reasons, but the main one was that once I was in her, I wouldn't want to leave.

Ever.

That was a fuckin' scary thought.

Shit. I was so close to coming just from watching her watch me. I needed to stop, or at least slow the fuck down so I didn't embarrass myself and come too quickly.

"Griz," she moaned. "Please."

Jesus Christ!

"Call me by my name, darlin'."

Her eyebrows rose. She didn't understand what I was asking. Instead, she said, "Griz."

I shook my head and slowed my hand down even more. "No, princess. My real name."

I bet she didn't even know it, and the thought of that fucking hurt. Why in the hell would she want to screw someone whose name she didn't even know?

I watched her face light up, and she licked her lips. She ran her hand over her breasts, down her stomach and finally spread her legs, dipping her fingers into her juices. "Please come and fuck me... Grady."

Motherfucker.

With a growl, my boxers hit the floor and I was on the bed in seconds, hovering over her on all fours.

A smile spread across my face as I watched her lay back and laugh.

"You should have told me that's all I needed to do, and I would have uttered your name a long time ago." She grinned.

I brought my face closer to hers and hissed, "Say it again."

She licked her lips and whispered, "Grady." Only to end with a moan as my fingers slipped into her wet core.

"Fuck, darlin', you're so wet for me," I growled.

She panted, "Only for you." It was then she reached up, wrapped her arms around my neck and pulled me down to her. Our lips collided in an urgent frenzy, and then our tongues entwined together while my fingers fucked her.

Pulling away was one of the hardest things I've ever had to do, but I wanted something else even more. Plus, I needed oxygen, because right then, it seemed my body wasn't getting enough.

"Jesus, Dee," I growled as my chest rose and fell at a rapid speed. At least mine wasn't the only one. I watched as Deanna's perky breasts rose and fell just as quickly. "I need to taste you." That statement was a rumble from my chest. "Fuck, I need it more than air right now. Will you let me?"

"What're you askin' for, babe?"

"Some women don't like it." *Where I loved to give it.*

She ran her hand over my cheek and grinned. "Grady." *Hell, I loved hearin' my name on her lips.* "I want you to taste me. My pussy needs the attention of your mouth. Can you do that for me?"

With wide eyes, I clipped, "Christ." Giving her a quick, hard kiss, I moved down her body and spread her legs to accommodate my large frame as I laid my body down. I pulled her ass up with my hands and dove my face into her snatch. Even if my dick was begging to be where my mouth was licking, biting and sucking, there was no way I was gonna miss out on the chance to taste her sweet juices. Because I knew once my cock got his way, we'd probably be over in a matter of seconds.

Dee's hands slid into my hair and held me tightly to her, but she needn't have worried—there was no way I was goin' anywhere until I felt her come on my tongue.

She moaned, hissed and swore as my lips, tongue, and teeth drove her crazy.

To watch her beautiful body arch as she yelled my name was something else. And it was something I would never get enough of. She was sexy—a real, hot piece of work.

Fuck.

I was in trouble.

"Grady, damn, Grady, I'm gonna come," she moaned.

Jesus, I was pretty sure I was gonna come myself. What didn't help was that I was thrusting my cock into the bed, and the friction of it, as well as watchin' and tasting her, wasn't doing me any good. I was seconds away.

"Do you wanna come on my tongue or my fingers?"

"Hell... oh, God. Um, fingers. I want your fingers. Is that okay?"

"As long as I get to clean it all up with my mouth, it's fuckin' fine with me, darlin'." I pulled my face back and inserted my fingers back into her tight pussy. She groaned loud and sweet as my fingers drove back and forth and my thumb rubbed at her clit.

"Grady, fuck. Faster, babe. Oh, hell."

Shit, she was so damn hot.

Her eyes met mine and that was my undoing. As she came all over my fingers, I pumped my hips into the bed and blew my load all over the sheets, causing both of us to cry out. After she'd come down, I removed my fingers, and she watched me and whimpered as I licked them clean and then bent my head to clean away all her come with my mouth and tongue.

I got up on all fours and made my way back up so I was over her where we'd started.

"Now it's your turn." She grinned.

I felt my cheeks heat and I knew she'd seen them because her eyes widened a fraction. "Too late, darlin'. Watching you and your hot body move under my face and fingers had me shoot my load onto the bed like some fuckin' eager teenager."

Her mouth opened in shock. She threw her hand over her mouth to cover the giggle that escape, but it was too late; I'd heard it.

"You laughin' at me, woman?" I mock-growled. She nodded and rolled to her side, though she shouldn't have, because now I had the chance to smack her arse good and hard.

She stopped laughin' straight away and ended up moaning. "Fuck me. My darlin' likes rough play," I groaned.

She looked up at me with pleading eyes. "Wanna try again, Mr Teenager?"

I rolled to the side and pulled her close. She rested her head on my chest. "Jesus. You're gonna kill my old body."

"Don't say that."

She sounded so serious I brought her head up with my hand under her chin to see the look on her face. She had said it with a somber expression.

"Darlin'?"

"Please... fuck. Just don't say shit like that. I-I can't have you dying on me too."

Stupid fuckin' dick—that's what I was.

"Sorry, sweetheart."

"Great." She hit my chest. "Now I've put a downer on what was the best head-job in my whole life."

I grabbed her hand and said, "No, you haven't. And seriously, best?"

"Well, let's not get ahead of ourselves. There still could be better out there."

I rolled her on top of me so she lay flat along my body. My dick went straight to attention, but I wasn't gonna start anything again tonight. We needed to take this slow.

Instead, I smacked her arse again and growled at her lips, "You have been good and fucked by my mouth and fingers, darlin'. No one, and I fuckin' mean no one, is gonna have a chance to do the same while I'm in the picture." I squeezed her arse in my hands. Her eyes widened. "You get that, darlin'? No one. Because I plan to stick around for a long fuckin' time. Now that I've tasted you, I want nothing else."

"Even if this scares you?" she uttered.

It was my turn for my eyes to widen.

How in the fuck had she known?

She sighed and laid her head on my chest. "It scares me too, Grady," she whispered.

Well damn.

CHAPTER TEN

DEANNA

STRETCHING in the morning after a good and proper tongue-lashing felt great. I reached over to the side Griz…Grady occupied last night, with a smile on my lips, only to find it empty.

It was then I heard voices and the TV coming from downstairs because my bedroom door was open. I realised then that Blue, Stoke, and Killer must have fixed my bedroom door, as well as moving Grady and Swan in last night. That was nice of them.

Oh, hell, when did I ever fuckin' think nice things? It was happenin' already. I was—and felt—less bitchy. I wondered what would happen to me if I truly got fucked by Grady.

A laugh escaped me. I couldn't wait to find out.

After stretching again, I then ripped the sheet from my naked body and got out of bed. I headed straight for my en suite and started the shower.

Though, maybe I shouldn't have had a shower first. Maybe I should have gone downstairs to see Grady instead, because now, as I washed my blonde hair, I had more time to second guess…everything.

What would happen if things had changed for him? What if he didn't really mean what he said last night? *No, it wasn't a dream. He had said he wanted something to start between us.*

But then, what happens if this—us—did start... seeing each other? There was Swan to consider in this. It wouldn't be just a relationship with Grady, but his daughter as well.

I wasn't good enough to be around her.

Was I even good enough for *him*?

Fuck. Now I felt like shit, and mean. Maybe I shouldn't have started anything last night.

Crap. I just didn't know.

There was only one way to decide—go down and face the music. I'd learn how he would be with me and see if he wanted me around his daughter.

I turned off the water and got out of the shower. After quickly drying myself, I dressed in black slacks and a white shirt; I had to get to work at the library in two hours. With wet hair hanging loose and bare feet, I made my way downstairs.

Walking into the lounge, I found Swan sitting on the carpeted floor playing with two dolls and some blocks, while some cartoon played on the TV.

What was I supposed to do, keep walkin' or talk to her?

I need to grow some balls. So I walked over to her and sat down beside her.

"Morning, Swan."

She looked up at me and smiled shyly, and then went back to her toys.

"Do you wanna build something with me?"

She shook her head and pointed to something on the other side of her—books. I reached over and picked one up. "Do you want me to read this to you?"

She nodded. I could do that. I read *Spot Bakes a Cake,* and then we moved on to another Spot adventure. But when I started *Whose*

Nose, that was when Swan moved to sit on my lap, and my heart constricted when she rested her head against my chest.

After her last three books—all *Hairy Maclary* ones, which I loved—she looked up at me, smiled and uttered in such a soft sweet voice, "Ta."

I helped her hop off my lap and back onto the floor and then said, "I love reading, Swan. So maybe later, when I get back home from work, we can read some more?" She beamed up at me; I guess that was my answer.

Standing up, I turned to go and find Grady, only to see him standing in the kitchen-lounge doorway, leaning against it with his arms crossed over his black-teed chest.

Damn, he was hot.

With a chin lift, he turned and walked back into the kitchen. I followed.

He was on the other side of the island bench, and once I walked in and over to stand on the opposite side, he said, "I was gonna come wake you. I'm glad I didn't have to...because what I saw in there—you with my daughter, reading to her—means more to me than you'll ever know."

"Um."

"Get your arse around here," he ordered on a growl.

I got around there, and when I did, he pulled me against him and attacked my mouth like a starved man. I wrapped my arms around his neck and went on my tippy-toes to show him what he just said meant more to me than *he* would ever know.

He pulled away and looked down at me. "Fuck. You look hot, darlin', looking all professional."

I grinned up at him and said, "You look hot yourself, biker-man. So hot, I'm wet already."

He closed his eyes and groaned. "Shit, Dee. I want my fingers in you so much right now, so that I can taste you again."

"It'll have to be later, babe. Now that Swan's awake, we have to be careful."

He tilted his head back and let out a roar of laughter. I hit his chest. I didn't know what in the fuck he was laughing at, but I knew it was at my expense.

I tried to move out of his embrace, but he held strong, and after he'd calmed enough, he looked down at me with amused eyes. Though, they also held a sweet heat that had my hoo-ha convulsing.

"Darlin', you saying that, wanting to protect my daughter makes me fuckin' happy." He grinned. "Makes me realise I was being a stupid dick being worried about our age difference. But most of all, what you just said turned me the hell on, and now I've got to have a taste before I take Swan over to Wildcat's." With that, I found his hand down my pants and in my underwear. I gasped at the abruptness and then whimpered when his eyes took on a wicked gleam as his fingers ran along my folds and then inserted into my already wet pussy.

"Hell, darlin', I wish I had time to wet my dick with this," he pumped his fingers in and out, causing me to moan, "with your sweet pussy, but I don't, so this will have to hold me off." He removed his fingers, and my eyes grew as I watched him raise his hand to his mouth to lick and suck my juices off. A growl escaped his chest. He closed his eyes in what looked like ecstasy.

"Jesus, Grady," I hissed and whimpered. I was so turned on I needed a release, or I'd be one cranky bitch all day. "Please tell me you have time to fuck me. Tell me you'll go drop Swan off now, come back here and fuck me hard and good."

He smiled down at me and shook his head. "Sorry, princess, I've got shit I have to do, but at least I know you'll be ready for me tonight." He stepped back, slapped my arse and walked out of the room chuckling.

"You leave me like this and you won't see anything tonight," I yelled to him.

"Yeah, right, we'll see," he yelled back.

Yes, we would see.

CHAPTER ELEVEN

GRIZ

FUCK, it was so hard to walk out the door with Swan and not go back to screw my woman like she wanted. Hell—like *I* wanted. But as I said, I had shit to do, so after dropping off Swan at Wildcat's, I headed to the compound. Upon walking through the front door, down the hall and into Talon's office, I knew he knew I'd be coming, because not only was Talon there, but Blue, Killer, Stoke, and Pick were there also.

"I guess you already know what I want," I said.

"I do, brother, 'cause I'd want the same goddamn thing." Talon nodded. "The brothers here all agree; we're going with you in case it gets ugly."

I looked to the group of men around me, fuckin' proud and happy I had these men, these brothers, in my life. "All right, let's do this. Let's go see our old member for some answers."

We all loaded onto our Harleys and left the compound to head across Ballarat to Lal Lal, where we knew Maxwell resided. He lived on a dead-end street, but a street that was busy with houses and families. Though no matter where he lived and who saw us approaching, I still had to find the truth, and he'd better fucking give it to me, or he'd soon be a dead motherfucker.

No sooner than we stopped out the front of his run-down brick home, the door was opened and Maxwell ran out to meet us on his front lawn.

"I heard, I heard. It wasn't me. I had nothin' to do with your woman's death." He held his hands up and out in front of him, shaking them from side to side.

"Funny, Max, how in the fuck do you know what we were coming here for?" I asked.

"People talk, brother. I heard. She had a party and we fucked, but that was it. I left and she was fine."

Talon stepped forward. "This is not something we need to fuckin' talk about out in public. In the house, now," he ordered, and when that happened, people knew to follow. Maxwell turned and led us up the concrete path to his house. Stoke, Pick and Killer stayed out front, while Blue, Talon and I entered. The stench of pot, mildew, and pussy filled our noses.

"Damn, Maxwell, clean up the fuckin' place; it stinks in here," Blue said with his upper lip raised in a grimace.

Max laughed. "Yeah. Just been a busy time for me, brothers. Busy time. Got new whores I been testin' out; they're in some of the rooms. I'd be happy if you guys wanted to have a go at them."

I looked at *my* brothers, his no longer since he left the club, and saw they both held the look of disgust I knew I had.

Blue whispered something to Talon, who nodded in return, and then I watched Blue walk to the front door. In the next second, Pick was in the house and heading down the corridor to the left. He was paying the whores a visit with, no doubt, a little warning.

Talon walked over to the kitchen table, and in one sweep of his arms, everything on it fell to the floor in a loud clatter. He leaned his arse against it and said with a chin lift, "Max, come and have a seat. Griz has some questions, but I have something to say first." Talon waited until Maxwell was seated in the seat closest to him. He waited until Maxwell looked up at him, and then he took a breath, glared and said, "You no longer have the right to call us brothers. You left the club to deal with your whores and, I guess, run your fuckin' life down the shit hole, but that was your choice. So you live by it."

"All right, sure. Okay, bro—sir... um, Talon."

We all laughed at how pathetic he was.

Pick cleared his throat behind all of us. We turned, he gave a chin lift and then he left the house. It was the all-clear for us to do what we had to, meaning—the whores were too high to know what was going on.

I walked over to the table and stood just in front of Maxwell.

"Tell me, Max; why in the fuck would you have a party at my ex's *while* my daughter was in the same damned house?" I bellowed in his face.

"Look, man, I-I... shit! She... she needed some extra money. So, you know, I paid her for the night to fuck some customers, and then before we left... I had a go with her."

"You pimped her out while my child was there?" I roared. Someone grabbed me from behind because they knew I was ready to jump this fucker and rip his worthless head off.

"Why'd she need money, Max? Griz was giving her enough to help with the cost of their kid," Talon asked.

"Um, shit. Ah... your woman—"

"She ain't my woman, but she was still the fuckin' mother of my child, so talk, dickface," I growled. Blue let go of me and stepped back. He took out his phone, flipped it open and hit record. It was the same process we took every time we questioned anyone for anything.

"All right, okay. You see, she—ah, she got to like... a bit of crack."

I grabbed him by his dirty white tee and pulled him up so our faces were only inches apart and his feet dangled off the ground.

"You meanin' to tell me you sold crack to my ex?"

"Fuck no, man. I don't deal with that shit—I promise, but... my new partner does."

I threw him back into his chair and turned my back on him. "Tell me who."

"I can't, Griz. I can't; he'll kill me. He's one mean motherfucker."

Blue snorted. "And we won't kill you if you don't tell us?"

"Hell, please don't do this."

"Enough," Talon clipped. "Max, they're selling crack in our territory. They will be dealt with, so just give us his name."

"Whatever you do, he'll want payback."

"We'll see," Blue said.

"Shit. All right, but it didn't come from me. Can you promise me that?"

"Sure, Max. Sure." Talon smirked.

Fucking dipshit. Did he not see Blue recording this?

"His name's Ryan Little, and he lives over in Delecombe."

"Thanks, mate. We'll figure out the rest." Talon stood tall and pulled his gun—with a silencer—from his back holster and pointed it at Maxwell's head.

Max raised his hands and cried, "Wait, wait! Please, please don't kill me. I told you who it was. I told you!"

Talon lowered his gun and sighed. "I guess that's true." He nodded to himself. In the next second, he fired his gun and hit Max in the left knee. As Maxwell screamed, Talon picked up a cloth from the floor and stuffed it into his mouth. "That's for lettin' this shit happen in the first place. No one brings crack into my territory. Pass the word on." He stood tall, turned and walked toward the front door, but I hadn't moved. "Griz, brother," Talon called. "Do what you want." He glanced over his shoulder and walked out of the house with Blue following.

In his haste to get away, Maxwell fell to the floor shaking and holding his knee, still moaning in pain from the gunshot wound. I raised my foot and planted it in the side of his head. He fell to his side, whimpering like some lost little kid.

"You really should have never crossed my family and me even if she was my ex. But what broke the respect I still had for you, was the fact you were stupid enough to do shit around my child. That—I can never forgive."

It was my turn to remove my gun, which was also prepared with a silencer on the end, from my side holster. I aimed at Maxwell and fired a round into his other knee, and then another into his left arm. As I watched him roll around in pain, I smiled. At least the fucker, who played with not only the brotherhood but my family, now knew not to.

I leaned over and hissed, "Keep the fuck outta trouble, Maxwell, or we will be back, and you know what will happen then. If I see your face again, there'll be a bullet between your eyes."

Before parting, I fired another shot into his stomach. Hopefully, he'd die before his whores found him.

CHAPTER TWELVE

DEANNA

AFTER BEING at work for an hour, I was, for once, enjoying the silence. I loved working here. I loved the smell of the books and watching what people chose to read. But on some days, the silence did get to me... only not today.

In the last twenty-four hours, I'd had my fill of noise, tension and company—well, except maybe Grady and Swan's.

Oh, well, would you fuckin' look at that? I counted Swan in the mix of things.

Strange.

The library doors opened, and a regular came in. I was sure she was here every day—at least, every day I worked she was. Someone always accompanied her in, holding her arm and then seating her at a table with some audiobooks to listen to. It had taken me my second day of seeing her a month ago to realise she was blind, and the person who helped her in here had to be her sister. They looked alike in many ways. Both were slim, tall and red-haired, only the blind one's hair was shorter, styled in a pixy cut, where her sister had long hair, which was usually plaited down her back.

The only thing that annoyed the hell out of me was the way the one who wasn't blind would speak to her sister. It was like she was the dirt under her fingernail she wanted to get rid of. It took all my strength not to say anything.

What also annoyed me was the fact it was obvious the bitch sister had advised the other on what to wear. Where the bitch looked immaculate—perfect hair, light green eyes, flawless make-up and designer clothes—the blind one always wore tracksuit pants, baggy tees or hooded jumpers. Her hair was always scruffy-looking like she'd just gotten out of bed.

The bitch left with a glare, and like every day I saw it, I wanted to go over and find out what in the hell was going on, but I had enough of my own shit to deal with, rather than adding someone else's to the mix.

One day I would, or I'd never forgive myself.

It was after lunch, and I was working the floor, replacing the returned books to their shelves when the automatic front doors swished open, and in walked Julian. He always looked good; today he wore a red polo shirt with dark blue jeans and black leather boots. I watched him scan the front desk and then the floor. When he spotted me, a smile lit his face and he bounced on over.

"Hello, bitch-face," he said stopping in front of me.

I sent an eye roll his way and turned back to the shelf. "After-noon, cum-sucker. What brings you here?"

He giggled, but then it abruptly stopped. I looked at him to see he was studying me.

Oh, crap, what's going to come out of his mouth now?

He gasped. "No way."

"What?"

"O-M-G, no way." He pulled his phone from his back pocket and dialled a number. "Hey, sugarplum, you know how I was going to the library to see how our Deanna was after last night and being blindsided by what she was going home to?" He waited for an answer. "Yes, well, I'm here and guess what I see... our woman's glowing like she got some nom-nom last night!" he squealed.

"Julian," I snapped.

"I know," he screeched. "Hang on, I'll put you on speaker." He clicked a button and held out his phone. "Deanna Drake," Zara's excited voice called out. "Tell me now what went on last night, and tell me why you haven't called me already to tell me what happened last night. Hun, I should have been the first one to be told. Holy cow, babe! Finally—you and Griz! This is so awesome. Oh, wow. I can't believe this. I'm so excited for you. Was it good? Did he treat you right?"

"Up-the-duff, if you'd let her actually speak, you'll hear what she has to say," Julian said.

I sighed. "You losers will have to wait for the juicy details. I'm at work, and this is not the place to be talking about these things."

"Deanna," Zara whined, but Julian pressed a button again and held it back up to his ear.

"Baby Maker, I see the seriousness in her eyes. She's not gonna budge. What? Oh, oh, good idea. Okay, I'll see you soon." He ended the call and turned to me. "She'll be here when you finish up; we're going for a coffee down the road. This is exciting; I can't wait to hear it all," he gushed, and then he turned, grabbed a book and walked over to the table where the blind woman sat.

I looked at the clock that sat above the attending desk and saw I had two hours left of work before the cheer crew wanted all the details. It wasn't that I didn't want to share, but I also didn't want to jinx what had happened with Grady. Maybe if I said it out loud, it could change things. Though, I also knew they wouldn't give up without hearing everything.

Damn.

As soon as the clock hit four, Julian was up at the front desk smiling like he'd just given a head-job to his favourite actor. After clocking off, I walked around the desk and toward the front door.

"Zara said she would meet us at the coffee place. She just has to drop the monsters off with Mattie and Swan, and then she'll be here. Oh, and do you know that gorgeous woman I was sitting with is blind?"

"Yes."

"I think she was really scared to talk to me at first, but then—you know how everyone loves me—she ended up opening up and talking back."

"What's her deal?" I asked as we walked down the road.

"She has to come to the library every day while her sister works because it isn't safe at home for her. I asked her what she meant by that, and she said her sister doesn't trust she's capable at home on her own. I called bullshit and told her that. Sure, she may be blind, but a lot of blind people live in their own houses and can easily take care of themselves."

Entering the coffee house, we found a seat to wait for Zara; although it wasn't hard since the place was quiet with only a few business people scattered around.

"I've seen her sister, and she seems like a real bitch." Julian raised an eyebrow at me. "A bigger bitch than me even. Always bossing her around, never smiles.... I don't know. I wouldn't trust her sister. She needs to get out of that situation."

"That's what I said, but she won't. She said she has no money and her sister takes care of all that by working."

"Maybe we can see what we...." I snapped my mouth closed and thinned my lips when I spotted a person in the far corner. "How long has Billy been following us?"

Billy was the youngest member in the Hawks Motorcycle Club... or as Zara would call him, the cookie-loving biker.

"Oh, he was out the front when I arrived."

"Dammit, Grady's already got people following me, and Jason isn't even out of jail yet."

"Who's Grady? O-M-G, that's Griz, isn't it? I never knew his real name, but that is so hot for him. Why doesn't he go by that all the time?"

"Not sure," I said and sent a glare to Billy, who ignored it.

"Give the kid a break. He's only doing what he's been told."

"Exactly."

"Honey, don't be too hard on Grady. Isn't it obvious he just wants to keep you safe? I think it's sweet, actually."

"I guess," I grumbled. In retrospect, I knew I shouldn't be upset by it, but it had kinda put a downer on my good mood. *Grady had better make it up to me tonight.*

The front door opened, and Zara, in a long skirt and black tee walked—okay, waddled was more like it—in. She spotted us, clapped and ran-slash-swayed over. It was a funny sight to see.

"Hoo-wee, I can't wait. Spill! Spill now, woman."

"Can't I get a coffee first?" I smiled.

"Sure." Zara grinned, and then called over her shoulder, "Billy, can you get us two lattes and a hot chocolate, please?"

I rolled my eyes.

"Sure, Wildcat," Billy said with a deeper voice than I expected.

"Now you can talk."

"I don't want to go gettin' your hopes up or anything; this thing with Grady—"

"Oh, wow, you're on first name basis? It's serious!" Zara gushed, interrupting me.

Another eye roll from me. "But...you know things could change. I know I'm not the easiest person to get along with." Both of them snorted. "So it could all go to shit, and I worry if I act like a woman and rave about how last night was the best night in a long time for me...yeah, I just worry."

"Hun," Zara started and placed her hand on mine. "Live in the moment. We can both see the shine in your eyes—a shine that has been lost for a long time—coming back, and it only happened after what occurred with you and Griz last night."

"And if anyone can put up with Satan herself, it would be hotman Griz," Julian added.

"He's right, Deanna. Griz has had his eye on you for-freakin' ever, and I don't know how, but he finally got over the age difference and took what he's wanted since you walked into his life."

"I think he held that pause button of his because it also had a lot to do with his psycho ex. May she rest in peace," Julian said and crossed his chest in silent prayer.

"But," Zara said, "he knows you are nothing like her. Nothing."

I looked over Zara's shoulder to Billy. He silently placed the drinks on the table. With a thank you from all of us, he gave a chin lift and left to go back to his seat across the room.

"Now, that's all sorted; spill the beans, woman." Julian grinned.

Lifting the warm cup to my lips, I took a sip to hide my smile. They were right; I had to live in the moment, and if Griz hadn't run already from the way I was, then I guess I was lucky and I'd run with what we had—whatever that was.

Placing the cup back down on the table, I cleared my throat. "Okay, last night I went to bed after finding out Grady had not only moved himself in, but Swan as well." I turned a glare on Zara. "And by the way, thanks for the heads up—*not*."

"Oh, pfft. I think I know what the outcome was, so I'm glad I did it."

"Anyway, I went to bed in a state of shock as Grady was putting Swan down to sleep. I expected him to sleep with her in her room or the other spare one, and then my thoughts started running wild—"

"Like how such a hot piece of male was only metres away and you wanted to jump his bones? Well, one for certain." Julian cackled and then sobered. "Wait, should we be talking about this in front of...." He gestured with his head to Zara.

"What do you mean? Of course, I can hear this," Zara snapped.

"Not you, the babies. Should we get some ear-muffs and place them on your belly to block all this out?"

Zara and I looked at each other and cracked up laughing.

"Whatever, mofos. Fine, corrupt the young, see if I care."

"I love that you do care, Julian, but I promise they won't remember anything being said here." Zara smiled warmly at him.

I took a breath and continued, "As I was saying, I was making myself horny, so I pulled out Vinny, but just when I was about to get into it, my door opened, and in walked Grady."

Zara covered her mouth, though I'd already seen the huge smile she was trying to hide behind her hand. While Julian gestured with his hands for me to keep going, his eyes shone with glee.

"I asked him why he was there and he said he was tired. I said there were other places to sleep, and he told me to be quiet because he was exhausted. He got into bed, and I thought *fuck it*, and continued with what I was doing."

"You didn't." Julian laughed.

"Wow," Zara said, her eyes as big as saucers.

I grinned widely and said, "I did. He freaked, jumped out of bed and was over on the other side of the room in seconds."

They both laughed with me.

"Then what?" Zara asked, leaning forward as much as she could with her round belly.

"I kept going and asked him to join me. He said no, but I could tell he wanted to by the large tent he had going on in his boxers." I smiled at the thought. "After a while, he ended up shovin' his boxers down and said 'two can play at that game', *and then* he started to tug his chain."

"Holy crap, that is so hot," Julian moaned, and Zara nodded in agreement.

"In the end, he couldn't resist any longer and came over to give me the best head-job I've ever had. I swear, I would have seen angels singing above my head if my eyes were open."

"Yes!" Zara clapped.

"And?" Julian drew out.

I giggled, like an actual girly woman, as I teased, "I wanted to finish him... but...."

"But what?" Julian screamed. Zara shushed him.

"He'd already finished. Apparently, just going down on me had him so worked up, he'd pounded his spunk onto my bed."

"Shit. Oh... damn. I need a fan or I need to come." Julian sighed and leaned back in his chair.

"That is so cool." Zara beamed, and I beamed right back at her.

It *was* totally cool, and I couldn't wait to do it again, even if he had teased me that morning and left me wanting him more than anything all day long. I mean, of course he would pay for it; he *had* to pay for it. I'd been so soaking wet all day, that I shoulda brought an extra pair of underwear.

Great, now it was even worse just thinkin' about what the night might entail.

CHAPTER THIRTEEN

GRIZ

MY BODY HUMMED WITH ANTICIPATION; I needed to get home to my woman, take her in my arms and then plant my cock inside her.

Especially after the day I had. Going from Maxwell's house, Talon called reinforcements in after we found where Ryan Little lived, and travelled our way to his place in Delecombe. It was only seconds after we pulled up to his two-storey home when another ten brothers pulled their own Harleys up and surrounded the jack-ass's house.

The little, bald, fat prick was smug enough to let us in. He had about eight men who sat, stood or leaned around the living room as we talked about what we wanted. The choice we gave him was either he stopped dealing in our territory, or he'd end up a dead man. He laughed and said he'd consider it. Then the dick turned to me and informed me that since my woman was dead, the money she'd clocked up using *his* drugs now fell on me.

That was when all hell broke loose. The fight was bound to happen; it was just sooner than we thought. Talon stood by my side as I beat the shit outta Ryan and told him he'd never see his money. The other brothers each fought their own battle against Ryan's men.

Once things calmed down, we left the house with a promise it'd be worse if we found out he was still around and dealing.

We all went back to the compound to clean up and have a sit-down. It was decided to keep a close eye on the fucker; we needed to know what his next move would be if he was game enough even to make one. But I was sure he'd be shitting himself right now and packing himself up to leave town. If he didn't, the fucker was just asking for a bullet.

After the meeting ended, I rode my Harley to Wildcat's place, where I'd left my vehicle and daughter that morning. Talon had ridden next to me, keen to get home to his wife and kids, but once we arrived, she was nowhere in sight. Instead, Mattie had the tribe of kids in the living room playing and watching TV. I could see Swan had taken a liking to Maya, as they were playing with some weird looking dolls.

"Where is she?" Talon asked Mattie.

"Zara and Julian are with Deanna having a pow-wow."

Talon laughed. "Shit, brother, you're fucked," he said to me.

I rolled my eyes and shrugged. I didn't care what Deanna told the other two, as long as she was happy when I saw her next.

The front door swung open, and Zara stood there with a frown upon her face. My heart picked up, and worry took over my body.

I took a step toward her and barked, "What's wrong?"

She looked at me quickly, and then back at Talon. "Did I just hear you swear in front of the kids?" she scolded.

Worry slipped from my body and I chuckled.

Fuck. I had been so wound up, my chest hurt. I rubbed at it.

"Dad's gonna get it," Cody chimed in behind us from the couch.

"Shut it, Cody," Talon said.

"Talon Marcus, don't you tell Cody to shut it. Tell me instead—did you just swear in front of the kids?"

He rolled his eyes and sighed, looking like he was praying for patience. "Kitten," he growled with a tone of warning.

"Don't *Kitten* me, and don't do it again, Talon, or you will get a tongue lashing in front of the kids, *again*." She moved forward and Julian stepped in behind her; he closed the door and turned, and then looked at me blushing.

What. The. Fuck?

"It won't be me gettin' the tongue lashing tonight," Talon said with a lift of his eyebrow.

"Jesus, Dad! I'm here ya know, and I know what you mean. Gross!"

Talon hit Cody in the back of the head and stalked to Zara. He pulled her into his arms, whispered something in her ear and she melted into him.

"Just don't swear again," she said. "Also, you can't talk like that in front of them." She bit her bottom lip worriedly.

"How can I help it when my woman is so fu—freakin' hot?"

"Don't think you can charm your way out of this." She turned in his arms and her eyes fell on Cody. "Cody Marcus."

"Uh-oh," Cody uttered.

"If I hear you use that J-word once again, I will wash your mouth out with soap. You hear me, boy?"

"You sound like Grandma when you say that."

Shit.

Zara hated being referenced with her mum. Though she loved her mother, even Zara thought she was bat-shit crazy at times.

Zara gasped. "Cody Anthony Marcus! You take that back."

"Now *you're* gonna get it," Talon sang, and then laughed when Zara elbowed him in the stomach.

Cody stood up with wide eyes. Damn, he was a tall kid for a thirteen-year-old. "Sorry! I didn't mean it. Sorry, Mum."

Zara's hand went to her mouth, her eyes welled with tears and she sobbed.

Hell, that kid knew how to work it. It was the first time he'd called her mum, and he'd just saved his arse from getting into deeper shit by doing it. I was sure Zara knew it, and I could see Talon knew it from the proud smile on his face, but both of 'em didn't care at all.

Mattie and Julian had somehow disappeared, and I didn't even want to think about what they were doing. It was my turn to head out as well to let Talon and his family have this moment, while I went home to my woman and had my own moment.

I picked up Swan from the floor, kissed a usually-loud Maya on the forehead as she silently watched her new brother and parents with warm eyes, and then walked to the door.

"I'm out," I said to the room.

They all turned to me; I thought I'd escape without an incident, but Zara ran over to me, pulled Swan and me into her arms, and cried, "Oh, Griz, thank you, thank you for bringing my best friend back to me." Shit, with the number of tears leaking outta her, my shoulder was getting wet.

"Uh, sure." I looked over her head to Talon. He shrugged and said, "Pregnancy makes her crazy."

Zara spun around. "Oh, shush it." She looked over at Cody and must have remembered what he'd just said before I'd announced I was leaving. She sniffled and ran over to the poor kid, bringing him in close and hugging the shit outta him.

"Dad," Cody whined, though anyone could tell he was happy.

"Good luck with that," I said with a chuckle, not only to Cody, but to Talon as well, and then left.

I lifted Swan into my car and onto her seat, and after strapping her in, I smiled down at her. "Did you have a good day, baby?"

She looked up at me and smiled. I could see her brain ticking something over in her mind and then in the next second, she blew me away. "H-home."

"Yes, sweetheart, we're going home to Deanna." I kissed her head, closed the door and took a breath to get myself under control. I needed to get home to my woman.

CHAPTER FOURTEEN

DEANNA

I NOTICED the house was dark and quiet when I pulled into the drive. I'd thought Grady would've been back by now, especially when he had Swan to think of. Then I wondered if they'd eaten... and if I should make something for dinner.

Well, have a fuckin' look at me. I'm all Betty homemaker, thinkin' of the family. I chuckled to myself.

I was just about to put the key in the lock when Billy called out from behind me, telling me to wait. I bit my tongue so I wouldn't argue. Yes, it had hurt me to do so, but I didn't want him to get chewed out by Grady.

So instead of me entering the house first, Billy made his way in and told me to wait outside. Five minutes later, he came back out and told me it was all clear.

With an eye roll, I said, "Thanks. Um... do you want to come in?"

His eyes widened. "Ah, no thanks. Griz would kick my arse if I did." That didn't explain why he looked so shocked when I had asked him.

Shrugging, I replied, "Okay." I then turned and shut the door behind me.

After changing into jeans and a red tee, I went downstairs and looked through the cupboards and fridge for something to eat... for everyone.

It didn't take long to see I had to make a shopping trip for groceries the next day, but I was lucky enough to find all the ingredients for chow-mein.

The pot was boiling by the time I heard the front door unlock and two steady, heavy booted feet made their way into the kitchen. I looked behind me and my heart sped up at the sight of Grady holding Swan in his arms, both of them smiling at me.

"Hey." I grinned.

"How you doing, darlin'?"

Damn, that sounded nice. A thrill was sent straight to my core. "Good." I nodded. "Dinner is nearly ready." I looked at the clock above the fridge; it was just about six-thirty. "You guys must be hungry, eh?"

Grady sat Swan in her seat that was attached to a kitchen chair at the table. He rounded the counter and pulled me into his arms.

"Dinner would be great. Next time, I'll be home earlier so Swan's not eating so late. Yeah?"

Home.

Fuck. He'd said home.

I thumped my forehead against his chest so he wouldn't see what that one word had done to me. I hated anyone seeing I was becoming mushy, but I was.

Fuck it, I *really* was. Stupid cock-sucking emotions.

"Dee?"

"Home early would be great," I muttered into his chest.

He squeezed me and pushed me back, his eyes searching mine and his grin widening. "Good, now kiss me."

"Grady," I hissed and looked at Swan, who was watching us with her adorable, little head tilted to the side.

"She won't care, but I will if I don't have your mouth on mine in a second."

After a sigh, I was ready to argue the point, until his lips met mine in a demanding kiss. Forgetting everything, I wrapped my arms around his neck and pulled him close.

"H-home," I heard a soft whisper say.

I moved back a step and gazed at Swan in wonder. Had she really just said that?

Grady moved in behind me, wrapping his arms around my waist, and his chin rested on my shoulder as he whispered, "She shocked the shit outta me when we were leaving Wildcat's place and she said the same thing. She likes it here, darlin'."

I nodded, fighting my damn emotions once again. "W-well." I cleared my throat. "I had better get dinner finished. Why... um, why don't you get Swan ready for bed, and by then everything will be done?"

He must have known I needed the distraction from the situation at hand because he moved from me with a pat on the arse and a look that read there was more of that to come later, as he went to Swan and took her to get changed.

I was in seriously deep shit.

HAVING people at the table in my own house for dinner was... overwhelming. Fuckin' tears, sobbing and screaming all wanted to leak from my body. Since I'd lost the Drakes, I'd never *felt* so much in one night, and never felt a connection to a family. Watching Grady and Swan together warmed me in so many ways.

I knew then I was one lucky bitch.

Sure, Zara had welcomed me into her family—her whole tribe had, and I was more than grateful for it—but even that was different to what was in front of me now.

Only, there was no way in hell I was turning into some *Meet the Cleavers* family.

"Dee?" Grady's voice grumbled beside me.

"Huh?"

"I'm gonna get Swan into bed and read to her for a few. Why don't you get ready for bed too?"

My body tingled with anticipation. From the heat and wetness I felt from my hoo-ha, I was more than ready for bed.

With a small nod and a bite on my bottom lip, I watched Grady's eyes darken. He stood, got Swan from her chair and placed her on her feet. She padded her small feet around the table to me, and before I knew what she was going to do, she wrapped her arms around my waist and hugged me tightly.

My heart shattered, only to be put back together wholly with a new, sweeter beat to it made by a certain little girl.

This time, there was no stopping the tears that pooled in my eyes. I bit my lip tighter and looked up at Griz; he was watching the whole thing with warm eyes and a beautiful smile brightening his face.

My hand on its own accord reached up to run down the back of her head. With that, she pulled away and started into the living room. I knew Griz was waiting for my eyes to reach his, but I couldn't give them. "There's only so much emotional crap this woman can take for the night. You'd better work it outta my body later."

A manly chuckle filled the room. "I'd be glad too."

Fuck. I looked up at him and asked, "I said that out loud?"

"Sure did."

"Great, now I'm turning into Zee."

With another laugh, he left the room to go see to his daughter.

Two hours later, I had cleaned the kitchen, filled the dishwasher, took a shower, got into my boy shorts and a cami and then changed the bed sheets.

Turning around from the bed, I was about to head back downstairs to grab a drink but found Griz leaning against the doorframe.

"How's Swan?" I asked.

"Asleep. We played for a bit, I read her some books, and she went out like a light."

"Good." I nodded. "That's good. She looked tired."

He stood straight and took a step forward. "I've decided we're all going out tomorrow." Another step forward, but the fiery look in his eyes had me backing up a step.

"Um, where?"

"Wildlife Park. Always wanted to take Swan there, have never gotten around to it. Now I will." Another step forward and he slipped his tee over his head.

I bit my lip to stop myself from groaning as I eye-raped his beautiful, muscular, tattooed chest.

I licked my lips, and he watched my tongue. "Well, I'm sure Swan will enjoy that."

Another step and he was in front of me. "You're coming," he quirked an eyebrow and added, "in more ways than one, but tomorrow you are coming with us."

"But—"

"No buts, woman."

"Whatever." Now was not the time to argue; I needed, and so very fuckin' much wanted, his body to fill me *in more ways than one.* "Enough talk, let's fuck." I grinned up at him. His eyes were hooded, and he sighed.

"No, darlin'. The way I'll make you feel, the way my body will possess yours, it's more than just fuckin'."

Holy hell.

"Okay, stud. Prove it."

He grinned wickedly at me. "Gladly."

CHAPTER FIFTEEN

GRIZ

I CLENCHED my fists at my side once again. No matter how much my dick wanted inside her, I wouldn't allow it. I meant every word I'd just said. I wanted her to be fully aware of who she was about to have in her body, mind, and soul.

"Take your clothes off. Now," I growled.

Her eyes widened. I was waiting for her to argue back, to tell me to get fucked, because I knew she hated being told what to do. Though, I also knew I was possibly the only one who could get away with it.

She removed her girly top and shorts quickly and quietly.

Yes, I was in there. She may not totally know it yet, but I was embedded deep in there.

Hiding my grin, I told her, "Get on the bed on all fours and face me."

"You're fuckin' lucky I'm in a good mood, Grady."

Hell. I loved it when she said my name. "I know," I admitted.

She climbed on top of the bed and turned, so she was on her hands and knees facing me.

I took a step back, flipped the button on my jeans and then slowly slid down the zipper. She watched every move I made with an eager look upon her face. My jeans dropped to the floor with my boxers, and I kicked them off and stood before her.

My hand wound around my cock and started to stroke it. "I saw last night that you liked how I handle my dick. Am I right?"

"Grady," she groaned on an exhale.

I had been right, so I kept tugging myself, just out of reach in front of her. The sneaky woman ran her hands over her beautiful boobs, down her stomach to her pussy, which I knew would be wet for me.

"You keep touchin' your sweet spot, you won't get my cock."

She glared, but then pulled her hand away and rested it back down on the bed. "You had better give it to me *now* then, or I'll finish all this on my own."

I smirked. "Bullshit. Tell me you want my cock in your mouth."

"Grady," she said with a warning tone.

"Tell me," I growled.

She licked her lips. We both knew she wanted this, and if she didn't hurry the fuck up, I'd blow yet-a-fuckin'-gain too early from just thinking about how wet her pussy was.

"Babe, I want to suck, lick and devour your cock inside my mouth right now."

"Christ," I bit out and moved forward. With my hand in her hair, I slowly slid my rock-hard erection into her sweet mouth and groaned. "Shit that feels good." Pulling back out, I pushed in again quickly. She moaned, and the hum of it sent a pulse through my dick.

With a tighter grip on her hair, I pumped my cock into her mouth over and over again.

Hell. I had to stop, or I was gonna come.

Loosening my grip on her hair, I ordered, "Move." She did by sitting back on her knees. I got on the bed and laid flat. "I want you to fuck my face, darlin'."

Her breathing picked up, and I knew she liked the thought of that. She climbed over to me and positioned her snatch above my face, her knees on each side of my head. I grabbed her thighs and lowered her delicious-tasting pussy to my mouth. It didn't take her long to take control. She moved her hot body over my mouth, running her pussy back and forth over my tongue.

"Jesus, Grady, Jesus," she moaned. "Fuck, babe. I'm gonna come."

I pushed her up and barked, "No. Not fuckin' yet. Not until my cock is inside of you."

"Yes," she hissed and moved off my face to lay her head on her pillow.

"Wrong again, darlin'. Get up on all fours."

She smirked but did as I asked... or I should say *told*. She flipped over and got up on her hands and knees once again. I crept up behind her, so fuckin' eager to have my cock deep within her tight core.

"Shit, tell me you're protected."

She nodded.

"I need to hear it, darlin'."

"I'm on the pill and clean. I've been tested, recently," she said over her should. Her lust-filled eyes upon mine.

"Thank fuck. So am I."

She laughed. "What, you're on the pill too?"

Little minx. I slapped her arse and she moaned loudly. "You know what I mean," I growled. "I'm clean." And with that, I forced my cock balls-deep straight into her, knowing her pussy would be wet and ready enough for me to take, and it was. Both of us hissed and groaned.

"Hell. I knew you'd feel good, but this is way fuckin' better than I fantasised." I pulled out and pushed back in over and over again.

"Damn, Grady. Christ, you feel so good in there. You belong inside me."

Shit.

"And don't ever forget it," I said through clenched teeth. I was close; there was no way I could hold off for much longer. The way her tight walls milked my cock—it was fuckin' bliss.

I reached over her, grabbed her shoulders and pulled her up, so her back was to my chest, all while still pumping into her twat. As I held onto her with one arm across her chest, I reached with the other and found her clit with my fingers. She whimpered and put her arms above her head, reaching to the back of my neck to hold on.

"Fuck, darlin'. Tell me you're close." The more I played with her button, the wetter she became; I was sliding in and out of silk.

"I-I'm really close. Oh, God. Grady."

I picked up speed and pounded harder into her. On a scream, she came undone and cried out my name. Two hard thrusts later, I came right along with her as her walls still clenched around my cock.

CHAPTER SIXTEEN

DEANNA

WHAT THE FUCK?

Griz woke me up the next morning, ordering me to get me sweet arse outta bed so we could get to the Wildlife Park. My body was so relaxed I didn't even bite his head off, and I was excited to go somewhere with both of them. I had such great sleep I hadn't even heard Swan wake at—what Grady told me—seven that morning.

By 10 a.m., everything had gone to shit... literary.

Grady had paid for us at the door. We got bags of food to feed the animals given to us as we walked in through a little gift shop, and now I gaped up at Grady, who was pushing Swan in her stroller. It was a damn hot sight—a biker man with tats, wearing a short-sleeved black tee, his club vest over it and tight-ass black jeans. I was ready to lie on the ground, spread my legs and beg to have his cock in me once again.

Damn, I had totally missed the point and gone Grady-crazy instead. But that could be understood, I was sure.

Back to how everything went to shit...it was when we walked

outta the gift shop and entered the Wildlife Park, where kangaroos and God-knows-what-else ran wild. There was shit—their *shit* —everywhere.

Now, I was no prim-proper lady, but *there was shit! SHIT*, people —everywhere. I was scared.

"Suck it up, princess. It ain't that bad." Grady chuckled at my shocked, scared face.

"Grady, babe, I don't know where to step. Stuff it; you'll have to carry me. No, I've got it—I'll get in the stroller with Swan; she can sit on my knees."

That was when Grady burst out with a deep, manly laugh, which turned me the fuck on. How could a guy's laugh turn me on when shit surrounded me?

All right, okay, I may have exaggerated. There was shit every-where, but once I saw how excited Swan was, I calmed my own freak-out down and watched as Grady let her out of the pram and walked with her over to the nearest kangaroo. He crouched down with Swan between his legs, and then proceeded to open the bag and show her how to place her hand out flat to feed the roo who had come right up to them.

The sight before me was amazing, and I wouldn't have changed it for anything else in the entire world.

"Dee," Grady called, "get over here."

I tentatively strolled over, worried I'd scare the roo away, but it took no notice of me. Grady grabbed my hand and pulled me gently down to crouch beside him. I looked down at Swan, and her smile of pure joy made my heart cry. She was beautiful.

Grady turned his head toward me and grinned. I knew my own smile matched his. It was fuckin' wonderful. He leaned over and placed his lips upon mine for a quick kiss.

Besides the crap everywhere, it had been the best day I'd had in such a long time. We saw crocodiles, emus, turtles and so much more. There were also koalas; one I actually held—after Grady pestered me to—for a photo.

We ate lunch at the cafe there, and then after that, we entered the snake enclosure—which freaked me the hell out, all while Grady and Swan got close, pointed, smiled, laughed and learned about the ugly-looking fuckers.

By the time we made it home in the late afternoon, I was sure, not only Swan, but Grady was just as tired as I was from walking around the thirty-seven some-odd acres of the wildlife park.

After I threw the shitty shoes out the back, I went to get changed before starting something for dinner. I was in my walk-in closet when Grady found me standing in my underwear, searching through my clothes for something comfortable to put on.

"How's Swan?" I asked. "I'm just gonna get changed and get some dinner on for us. I'm sure she'd need an early night after the amount of walking she's done today." I was bent over, going through my bottom drawers when I felt heat at my back. I turned my head to the side to see Grady's hungry eyes roaming my body. From the bulge in his jeans, I knew he liked what he saw.

In the next second, a gasp was pulled from my mouth as Grady's hand slid straight into my panties and into me.

"Fuck, darlin', how are you already wet?" he growled.

"Because I've been around you all day," I answered truthfully. I went to stand, but his other hand went to my shoulder to hold me down.

"Stay," he ordered.

Damn, his voice sent me wild. As his fingers slid in and out of me, he used his other hand to slowly pull my panties all the way down, and then before I could protest, he slapped my arse hard, ripping a moan from my throat. He then kissed where he had spanked; he was driving me insane, and he knew it.

"W-where's Swan?"

"Downstairs, watchin' some girly cartoon show. So we have to be quick." He turned, never removing or stopping his fingers from fucking me senseless, switched on the light and closed the door.

"Damn, you're beautiful," he said as he pulled his fingers outta me, and they went straight into his mouth. Groaning and growling while he sucked my juices off his fingers, he used his other hand to undo his jeans and free his cock.

He stepped up behind me and slapped my arse again with both hands on both cheeks, causing another moan from my lips to erupt. As he rubbed his palm over the sting, he rubbed his cock through my wetness.

"Fuck, darlin', I can't wait any longer."

A whimper escaped me. I needed his dick inside of me now, too.

He must have known this because one hand disappeared from my hip as he grabbed his dick and lined it up with my centre. A scream tore outta me as he plunged his thick rod balls-deep inside of me.

"Fuck, shh, princess. Shh."

"Grady, Jesus. God. That felt so good."

"Hell. Hold on to your ankles, darlin'. I won't let you fall, okay? But I gotta fuck you hard. So fuckin' hard. You trust me, right?"

Was he crazy? Of course I trusted him.

"Yes. Shit, yes."

"Thank Christ," he hissed. He pulled out of me and thrust back in hard and fast, but he didn't stop—he never stopped. He held onto my hips tightly as he entered me— in and out, over and over, again and again.

"God. Oh, fuck, Grady. Keep going. Don't stop."

His breath escalated, and I knew it wouldn't be long before he filled me with his seed. But that was okay, because the all-too-familiar tingle started in the base of my belly, going lower and lower until....

"Oh, oh. Hell. Yes. Yes, Grady."

"Damn. Fuck. Your sweet pussy is milking me, baby. Ah, fuck," he growled as he slammed into me one last time, filling me with his hot come.

With him still inside of me, he reached over and pulled my

exhausted body up, so my back was to his chest. "That was fucking perfect. Tonight, we go slower. I can't wait to eat you out, darlin'. Do not shower before it; I wanna taste us inside you."

Holy hot, shit, and damn—that was the hottest thing anyone had ever said to me.

CHAPTER SEVENTEEN

ONE WEEK LATER

GRIZ

SUNDAY MORNING, I heard Swan making noises from down the hall. I turned my head to look at the clock on the bedside table. It was only six. Too fucking early, but I knew once she was fully awake, there was no stopping her. I looked down at Dee, who was curled up around my body. Her head was resting on my chest, an arm slung over my stomach, and her legs were tangled around one of mine. I would've loved to wake her by fuckin' her hard and fast before Swan started crying, but there wouldn't have been time. Instead, I untangled myself; she sighed and shifted to roll on her other side.

She is so goddamn beautiful.

How in the fuck did I get so lucky?

And why in the hell did I spend so much time running from this, rather than takin' that leap and jumpin' straight into it with her?

Though, now that I thought about it, if we had fucked when I wanted—when she wanted—it wouldn't have worked out like it had. We were too fucked up back then. At least, I knew I was. I still had Kathy to deal with; there was no time for pussy besides one-night stands. I guessed that was also another reason I held off. I didn't want Deanna to be just a random one-night pussy. Maybe I knew she'd be more.

Fucking glad I waited. Even if it near killed me the time we went head-to-head in Wildcat's kitchen when I'd ordered her to stay in my room at the compound.

A smile formed on my lips just thinkin' of it. She'd told me, 'You'll be tugging your chain every time you think of my arse.' And damn it if she wasn't right. I couldn't count the times I'd jacked off thinking of her—her mouth, her body, her attitude.

Ever since the time I was walking away and she'd called me handsome.

I thought she was just teasing. Why in the hell would a young, hot bird like Deanna find me—an old, cranky guy—attractive. But the looks she'd given me and the small smiles told me that she was not shittin' me.

She did, in fact, want me, which shocked the shit outta me.

And now, here I was in a bloody relationship with her, and I couldn't be more fucking happy.

I moved my naked self from standing next to the bed, watchin' my woman like some trained puppy, to throw on a tee and some cut-off track pants. After pissing and washing my hands and face, I made my way down the hall to Swan's room.

When I opened the door, my eyes went straight to her crib. She was already standing up and smiling with a soft fabric doll in her hand.

"Mornin', sweetheart. You ready for some breakfast?"

She jumped up and down with her arms in the air, ready and waiting for me to grab her. I did, and in one swoop, I had my baby girl in my arms, and we made our way downstairs. Once in the kitchen, I sat Swan on the bench next to me as I made her some porridge. It was her favourite—I would swear most kids thought it was gross; my girl couldn't get enough of it. Fuck, I even hated the taste of it—reminded me of paste.

I grabbed the milk out of the fridge and noticed we needed some more. A grin came over me, caused by the thought of Deanna, Swan and myself walking through a supermarket together as a family. That was something we had to do today.

After I'd finished getting Swan's breakfast and tested that it wasn't too hot for her, I sat the bowl with a spoon in front of her and kissed her on the forehead. She smiled up at me. I could honestly say these past few days were the happiest I'd ever seen my daughter. Even with Kathy, it'd been like she was too scared to do anything, never feeling secure enough to open up and be what I thought normal kids were like. Here though, she was more out there, full of smiles, touches, and happiness. I reckoned it had a lot to do with the atmosphere because Deanna was so…bright—not that I'd ever say that to her face—though it wasn't just that. She'd welcomed us into her house—after we forced our way in, of course —and now it felt like this was our home.

Thinking of Deanna, I got the coffee pot ready, because I knew how much of a bitch my princess could be if she didn't have coffee as soon as her feet hit the kitchen. Thank fuck we weren't outta that, but we'd still have to stock up.

"Dadda," Swan called. I turned from staring out the kitchen window to see that Swan had finished her meal and was waiting for me to get her out of her chair.

"You had enough, baby girl?" When she nodded, I shoved the bowl away, pulled her chair back and lifted her into my arms. "We'd better get you dressed," I said with a kiss on her cheek.

As we were walking out of the kitchen, through the living area and to the hall that lead to the stairs, there was a knock on the front door.

I turned back and called, "Who is it?" but it probably came out more like an annoyed snap.

"The man of your dreams."

Fuck. Julian was here; it was too early for this shit. I liked the guy, but... yeah... he could be a bit much. I mean, there was no way in hell I'd ever say anything. The women loved him, and we'd— meaning me and Talon—get the shit kicked outta us if we ever tried to change him in any way. It wasn't that we were worried they'd literally kick the shit out of us... it was more that we were concerned they'd cut us off from their pussies. That could never fucking happen.

"Hello, sweetmeat!" he called through the door. I hurried to open it in case the neighbours thought I was havin' it off with him. Very fuckin' unlikely though—they knew I was here for my woman... but still.

Flicking the lock and opening the door, I was greeted by a grinning Julian and a quiet Mattie.

"Yo," I said.

"Oooooh, look at you, beautiful." My eyes went to Julian as he squealed this, just to make sure he was talking to my daughter and not me. Thank Christ, his excited face was directed at Swan. He clapped his hands out to her, and she was more than willing to be taken by him.

What was it with women and kids? They fucking adored this guy.

He pushed his way in, and I had to back up or he would've rubbed himself against me. Mattie followed behind him and gave me an apologetic gaze, but anyone could see he also adored the guy —in more ways than one.

Something I would not even think about.

"Sorry to come by so early; is Deanna still in bed?" Mattie asked.

"Not anymore, with all the bloody noise." She walked out of the hall and into the living room in hot fuckin' short-shorts and a light blue tee. My dick strained to get to her.

"Oops. Sorry, blossom. I didn't know you were in the room," she said as she walked up to Swan in Julian's arms and gave her a sweet peck on the cheek. Swan beamed up at her.

"Princess," I growled. I wanted—no, *needed*—her mouth on me as soon as my eyes caught sight of her each morning.

With an eye roll, she walked over to me. I wrapped her up in my arms and kissed the fuck out of her. She was finally getting used to doin' it in front of an audience.

She turned in my arms with a slight blush on her cheeks and met the guys' gazes.

"You do know that we're gay, right? So you don't need to mark your territory in front of us," Julian teased.

Deanna laughed. "He isn't doing it for you; it's what he wants, and if he doesn't get a kiss every morning, he gets cranky."

Mattie chuckled, and Julian smiled and said, "That is so awesome."

"What are you guys doin' here?" I left out *so fuckin' early.*

"We wanted to take Swan to see Zara and the kids. Is that okay?" Mattie asked.

Deanna looked up at me and raised her eyebrow. I shrugged. "If it's okay with Swan," I told the men.

"Do you wanna go, sweetheart?" Deanna asked her. Swan nodded. "Then you can go. Do you have a seat in the car for her? If not, you can borrow ours. She can't go in a car without a seat; it's unsafe… what?" she snapped at the end after she noticed all of us smiling widely at her.

"Just happy to see you caring for Swan," I said and then looked at Mattie. "And you can take my car." I looked back down to Deanna, "We're taking yours to the supermarket; we need shit for the house."

"Oh, okay," she mumbled.

"Great!" Julian grinned. "Let's go get this monster organized for a day with her uncles, and then we'll get out of your hair. I'm sure you'll like that." He chuckled when Deanna gave him the finger after Swan turned her head away.

"I'll help," she said and followed Julian to the hall door, no doubt heading up to Swan's bedroom to get her dressed.

While they did that, Mattie and I went into the kitchen to shoot the shit about random stuff. Now *he* was more than normal, and very easy to get along with. Look, I didn't give a fuck if a person was gay or anything, but sometimes Julian just shoved the fact in your face and flirted shamelessly; Mattie didn't. He was quiet, and just sat back and watched what was goin' on around him. I supposed Julian was damned lively enough for the both of them.

"Mattie," Julian called from the front. I walked with him out into the living room to see Swan was now freshly dressed and lookin' happy. I walked over, kissed her on the cheek, and said, "Be a good girl."

"Oh, I will, but only if you kiss me." Julian smiled.

Jesus.

"Never gonna happen, and you know if my daughter is harmed in any way in your care, I'll come for blood."

"Grady, stop it. She'll be fine; won't you, sweet girl?" Dee cooed and kissed her on the cheek of her own. Swan nodded, waved and left along with a final farewell from both Mattie and Julian.

"You know, the more you cringe and react, he'll keep being over the top," Deanna explained as we watched them place Swan in my car.

"I highly doubt that. No one could knock that shit outta him; it's just who he is."

She laughed. "Yeah, that's true. Now, are we going back to bed to fuck?" She turned in my arms and raised her chin to look up at me with hooded eyes.

My hands went to her arse, and I gave it a pinch. She hit me in the ribs. "I'd love to be buried inside of you right now, but we gotta go do some shopping. After we get home though, there will be nothing to stop me from having my cock in you."

She rolled her eyes. "You say such sweet things."

I chuckled. "And you love it." Her eyes turned serious as soon as 'love' left my lips. I wanted more than anything to tell her I loved her with everything I had, but we just weren't ready yet.

She closed her eyes, smiled, and then whispered, "Maybe." With that, she moved from my arms and stalked into the kitchen, her hips swaying in a way that had my cock hardening once again.

We weren't ready yet, but it was coming soon. Very fucking soon.

CHAPTER EIGHTEEN

DEANNA

I COULD NOT BELIEVE I was in a supermarket, with my man, shopping like some average Joe. It shocked the shit out of me that he wanted to go food shopping with me in the first place. Though I knew as soon as I saw him walkin' down the aisles pushing a trolley, the sight would make me wet, and I'd want to jump his bones. And it did. My hard, grey-eyed man with salt-and-pepper hair, tattooed arms, wearing biker boots, jeans, and a black tee looked more than fuckin' hot in a supermarket pushing a trolley and collecting food to feed his family.

I went up behind him while he studied a package of pasta, wrapped my arms around his waist and stood on my tippy-toes to whisper in his ear, "I am so wet and ready for you; it's ridiculous."

A soft growl erupted from his chest. "Do not fuck with me right now or I'll take you on the floor right here and right now. I don't give a fuck who watches." His lips crashed down onto mine. I hated public displays of affection, but when it came to Grady, I didn't give a fuck.

"Deanna?" I heard over my shoulder. I was pissed someone had interrupted our make-out session, but when I turned around my stomach dropped, and I knew some shit was about to go down. There stood one of my exes, Nate Derick. He and I went out for six months just before Zara and her stuff went down. I broke it off with him because he wanted to get serious and I didn't. There was also the fact he wasn't that great in bed, but I wasn't a big enough bitch to say anything. He still looked good with his sandy-coloured hair, dark blue eyes, and his tall, slim body. He wore black trousers and a white shirt, dressed to impress as usual, and I supposed he had to for his job as the owner of a car dealership.

"Nate, um… hi," I said.

"It's great to see you, Deanna. I've been thinking about you heaps." *Oh, shit.* I felt Grady tense behind me. "Who's this? Your dad?" *Oh, fuck.* "Hi, I'm Nate, Deanna's ex… for now." He grinned and then held out his hand to Grady, who stood as still as a statue behind me.

"Are you fuckin' shittin' me?" Grady growled low and deep.

Nate straightened, put his hand down at his side—*thank God, or he would have lost it*—and with a puzzled look, he asked, "About what?"

Instead of answering, Grady glanced down at me and asked, "Is this dickhead for real?"

I licked my lips.

"Excuse me, but what is your problem?" Nate snapped.

Holy crap.

Grady took a step forward, bringing me with him because I stood in front of him. "My problem, assface, is that you have the balls to ask if I'm her daddy when I was not even a second ago sucking her face, and she was enjoying every minute of it. Now, did that look to you like I'm her fuckin' father?"

"Well, I just presumed you could have been an affectionate family because it didn't make sense to me that Deanna would be interested in someone so old, when she could have someone like me."

Jesus Christ. Blood was about to be spilled.

Grady's eyes widened, turned to me and he barked, "And you let this fuckhead inside of you?" He seemed sick by the idea.

"Do *not* look at me like that, Grady Daniels. God knows where your cock has been, so don't fuckin' start judging me," I snapped with my hands on my hips, glaring up at him. How dare he?

"Deanna, I'm sure you can do better than this; this guy isn't worth it," Nate said from behind me. I felt him take a step closer and place a hand on my arm. "I'll get you out of here if you like."

I closed my eyes as soon as a vicious hiss started coming from the direction of my furious biker boyfriend. "You take your goddamn hand off my woman or I will kill you."

"Who in the hell do you think you are?" Nate spat.

"You'll soon fuckin' find out *if* you do not remove your hand."

I'd had enough. We were starting to attract attention—okay, I was being naïve; we drew attention as soon as Grady bellowed out that first time.

I shrugged out of Nate's hold, turned and leaned my back against Grady. Even if he had pissed me right the fuck off, there was no way I was letting some guy from my past look down on him or speak to him like shit, because Grady was my future.

"Nate, you need to get lost. You knew Grady wasn't my father, but you had to come over and act all tough and big to see if you could win me over. What you don't know is that Grady may be an arse and piss me the hell off, but I care for him. He is more of a man than you could ever be." He went to argue, but seriously, enough was enough. I held up my hand in front of me. "Don't. I really don't want to hear anything else from you. You need to leave."

He glared. "Deanna, you don't know what you're talking about. You'll regret going with him and not walking out with me. One day you'll come crawling back, and I don't know if I'll want you then."

This guy was deluded. I hadn't seen him in for-fucking-ever, and now he wants to cause this shit? What in the hell had come over him? I knew he never liked to lose, but this was plain stupid.

I sighed and decided to play dirty to get this jerk away from me. "Nate, I never did introduce you to my man... who gives me orgasm after orgasm. Nate, meet Griz, the Vice President of the Hawks Motorcycle Club."

His eyes widened, his face visibly paling in front of us. I heard Grady chuckle behind me. Nate took a step back, and then another.

"I-I...."

"Yeah, fuck off, dickhead, and if you ever sniff around my woman again, you'll pay the price," Griz snarled.

Nate spun around and stalked off. I was surprised I didn't see a wet patch on his pants; I was sure he'd shit himself.

Grady pulled my back closer to his front with an arm around my waist, and with his head on my shoulder, he uttered, "Bloody idiot."

I stepped away, turned around, and glared. "Grab what we need for now. I want to leave."

He looked shocked by my hard tone. "Princess?"

"I do not want to have this conversation at the fuckin' super-market in front of everyone. I want to go home."

"Fine."

I knew by his sharp tone that he thought he'd done nothing wrong, but he had; I was pissed enough to know he had. Sure, Nate was a dick, but I didn't need it thrown in my face that he had been inside of me in front of not only Nate, but other people as well. We both had people in our past I was sure we regretted, but the way Grady said it was as though I was scum. He was disgusted by it, and that fuckin' hurt.

So as soon as we got home, after a silent ride in the car the whole way, I let him have it, and his reply was, "I didn't like the fucker calling me your daddy. What did you expect from me, to let it slide?"

"No, of course not, but that's not the point, Grady," I said as I slammed food away in the cupboards and fridge with force. "Yes, he pissed you off, and yes, he said you looked older than me. I wouldn't care if you punched him in the face for it. What I do care about is that you got jealous over the little—yes, younger than you—prick enough to take it out on me in front of said little prick and other people. I don't throw your past in your face, so I'd appreciate it if you didn't do it to me. Ever. If you're jealous, use it in another way. Show them that you have me. Show them I'm *yours* now. Mark your territory. Show them why I'm with you."

I sighed and faced him where he stood, leaning against the kitchen bench with his arms crossed over his chest and a scowl on his face. "You know that no matter what anyone says about our age, I just don't give a fuck, right?'

He grunted.

"Jesus, Grady. Don't let this get to you. You're the one I want." I gulped and laid it out there. "The only one I'll *ever* need."

His eyes flashed something, but I couldn't see what it was, because in the next second, I was in his arms and his mouth was assaulting mine.

And I loved it.

He pulled back, and said, "Next time some punk gives us shit, I will take you right in front of 'em to show that you are mine."

I rolled my eyes and giggled like a schoolgirl. "Sure, handsome. Now let's have sex before we go and get Swan."

He threw me over his shoulder and made a dash for the stairs.

CHAPTER NINETEEN

THREE WEEKS LATER

DEANNA

IT WAS BOUND TO HAPPEN. We'd been going great after our last fight
—one that could have been prevented if Grady hadn't been a jealous
fuck.

Only this time, I knew it was my fault for the fight that was
going to brew as soon as he walked in the door. I'd done something
I shouldn't have, and I knew it, but it was something I had to do
because I had been worried. Swan wasn't up-to-speed of what a
two-year-old should have been, so I took her to see a paediatric
specialist. I came away with great news, but—and that's a huge
fucking but—I shouldn't have done it without telling Grady about it
first. I knew it, but still, I went ahead and did it.

And now, I was going to suffer from what would come from it.

I could only hope I wouldn't lose them in the process.

I was sitting at the kitchen table with a cup of coffee when I
heard the front door open. Swan was out with Nancy, Zara's mum. I

felt she and Zara were the only ones I could confide in. Both of them told me I needed to tell Grady, get it out in the open, and they were right. I'd been sitting on it for a week, and it was eating at me like a living thing.

The front door opened, and his heavy footsteps paused. I knew what he was thinking—the house was too quiet. Usually, he'd walk in and find Swan sitting in front of the television while I was getting dinner ready. Instead, the only light on was the one in the kitchen, where I was waiting for my doom.

Fuck. My heart rate sped as he called out my name, a dot of worry in his tone.

"In the kitchen," I answered.

His keys hit the stand just beside the front door, and he made his way in. He stopped just inside the archway. "What's wrong? Where's Swan?"

"She's fine." I tried for a smile, but it slipped from my face as quickly as it appeared. "Ah, she's out with Nancy for a bit. I need to talk to you."

His body was tense; I could see it in his furrowed brows, clenched jaw and tight muscles under his white tee, club vest, jeans and his usual biker boots. He pulled out the chair next to me and sat down.

"I'm fuckin' stressing here, princess. What's going on?"

"I've done something I shouldn't have." I nodded to myself, looking down at my nervously wringing fingers in my lap.

"You slept around on me?" he growled.

Glaring, I snapped, "No, dickhead. Oh my fucking God, why in the hell would you think that? I'd never, *ever* do that."

"Shit, sorry, okay. Look, I've seen you stressed, but this—what I'm seeing in front of me—is a state worse than I've ever seen you in. So please, just tell me what the hell is going on."

It was true. I knew I was showing how scared I was. I even felt sick to the stomach. I didn't want—no, *couldn't* lose them.

Ever.

"Sorry." I took a deep breath and went on. "I took Swan to see a specialist because I was worried she wasn't developing the way normal two-year-olds do. I know I should have told you, but I was worried you'd say no. But the good news is that she's going to be fine. Yes, she's a little behind and still very quiet, but she isn't missing anything. She's a bright young girl, and with our help, she'll be up to the standard soon." I looked up from the table. The first thing I saw was that his fists were clenched on the table in front of him, and as he leaned forward on his elbows, he brought his angry face in front of mine.

"Who in the fuck do you think you are? She is *my* girl, *my* daughter, and what she does has nothing to do with you. I would have done it. I was getting there, but then you just had to go and prove to everyone I'm a shit father to my own baby girl."

Tears filled my eyes. "No one knows," I uttered.

He shoved the chair back with a foot and stepped away from the table.

"Bullshit. You wouldn't have kept your big trap shut. Fuck. You need to stay outta my business, and that means my daughter. Not yours. Do you damn well get that?"

I knew it would be bad... just not *this* bad.

Standing, I clenched my fists to control myself because I so wanted to punch him and also wail like a baby at the same time.

"All right, Griz." His head moved back, his eyes widening at the way my voice was...sad, and because I'd called him Griz. "I'm so fuckin' sorry I involved myself in *your* business." *You fuckin' arse.* Couldn't he see he was doing the same goddamn thing by moving in here in the first place? *The two-faced fucker.* "It won't happen again," I said and left the room.

"Where are you goin'?" Grady yelled. He stomped after me.

I picked up my bag and keys near the front door and looked over my shoulder. "I think you need time away from me. I'm going out for a while." I opened the front door.

"I don't fuckin' think so. You're staying; we need to talk."

"Don't you mean you need to yell at me more? I'm not staying for that." I took a breath and faced him. "In my heart, Grady…." I tapped my chest "….in my heart—the one you and *your* little girl made whole—I was trying to do what's best. I can see I was wrong and I'm sorry for it… no, fuck that. I'm *not* sorry. Now I know what I have to do to help Swan." I laughed sadly. "Oh, wait, now I know what *you* have to do to help Swan. I'll be sure to let you know. You're a great father, Grady. I've never said any different to anyone. I just wanted to help… isn't that what families are supposed to do?"

Spinning back around, I quickly made my exit, shutting the front door behind me before he could say anything else. I was in my car and pulled onto the road before the dam broke.

Sniffing and wiping my nose, I pulled over and grabbed my phone. She answered after two rings.

"Hey, hun. What's happening?" Zara asked.

I bit my lip and took in a deep shaky breath.

"Deanna?" She sounded panicked now.

"I-I… can we talk? Can I come get you?"

"Sure, yes. Drive safe."

"See you soon," I whispered. I hung up, only to dial a different number.

"Satan girl, how are you doing, my lovely?" Julian answered.

"A-are you up for a girls' night?"

There was a pause on the other end. "You okay, sweetie?"

"No," I answered honestly.

"I didn't think so, and you know I'm always up for a girls' night. Do you want me to meet you somewhere?"

Blinking hard to fight the tears, I said, "I'll come get you. I just have to pick up Zara first."

"Okay, I'll be ready. What are you wearing?"

Looking down at myself, I realised I was only in jeans and a tee. That wouldn't matter though; I wanted to go somewhere quiet.

"Jeans and a tee, why?"

"So I know what to dress in. I don't think boxers would go over really well, and doll, I have to look better than you—can't have all the guys spying on your lush form."

I snorted a laugh. "Th-thanks, Julian. I needed that."

"I know, biscuit. I'll see you soon."

CHAPTER TWENTY

GRIZ

Fuck, shit. What had I done? Yeah, I was pissed, but I was more pissed at myself for behaving the way I did. I raised my goddamn voice at her and told her to mind her own business.

Dammit.

This *was* her business. Swan and I were hers.

She was right; this *was* what families did for each other, and I knew—once I had calmed down—all she was trying to do was help.

Still, at that moment, I'd seen red, which I fucking regretted it hugely.

She wasn't like Kathy; she wasn't like the other gold-digging, controlling bitches I'd had in the past. No, Deanna was different, and yet here I was, treating her like she was the same as those other hoes.

Motherfucker. I was the biggest idiot in the whole world.

As I sat on the couch with my head in my hands, thinking about how I was gonna save this, the front door opened. I was off that couch in seconds, but when the door came further open and in walked Nancy with a sleeping Swan in her arms, I growled and then sighed. My shoulders slumped as I walked up to them to grab Swan from Nancy without saying a word.

"What did you do?" Nancy glared and spun Swan away from me. "No, wait, don't tell me just yet. I want to tell you off good and proper without a child in my arms. I'll go put her to bed. You go and make me a cup of tea." Without an answer from me—not that I could have fuckin' given her one, since I was gob-smacked she'd spoken to me that way; I was fuckin' forty for God's sake—Nancy moved from the room to the hall, and then I heard her footsteps on the stairs as I made my way into the kitchen.

I was leaning against the bench with a cup in my hand and staring at the floor when I heard Nancy approach the kitchen.

"How'd you know I'd done something?" I asked as I looked up to see her walking to the other side of the bench.

"Pfft, please. I know a wounded, this-is-all-my-fault look from a mile away. Richard has them all the time."

Setting the cup of tea in front of her when she sat in a chair at the bench, I asked, "I guess you know what she did?"

"Yes, and…?"

"She should have come to me first. I should have taken Swan, not her."

"Don't give me that shit, young man," she snapped and sat her drink back down in front of her once again. Fuck, from her glare I could tell I was in for a lecture—one that I was too old for, but probably deserved.

"Tell me, Grady. Who was it that moved into Deanna's house? Who was it that had forced himself *and* his child onto Deanna without taking in any of her feelings?"

"It's not like she argued about it," I replied pettily.

She scoffed. "Of course she didn't. She knows who she has to deal with when it comes to you alpha males in the biker club. She knew she didn't have a chance. But it wasn't that. She knew not to fight, because this—you and Swan—is what she wanted. She's had you living here for some time now, and she has adapted to become a part of that little girl's life up there." She pointed to the ceiling, indicating Swan's room above us. "Still, anyone could tell it worried her that she was going to be a bad influence on Swan. But it was *you* who showed her she was more than just a loud-mouthed young lady. You let her in also, Grady Daniels. So, of course she's going to open her heart and soul to not only you, but that precious baby, and do things for you both—sometimes without thinking, but she does it because she cares so much for you both. But now you've thrown some of it back in her face… haven't you?"

I looked away. Fuck. I had, and I'd done a lot more. I'd shoved her out of what we had—our family.

"I know I was wrong, and I can only fuckin' hope she'll forgive me for it."

Nancy cleared her throat, and when I looked over at her, she smiled. "Of course she will." She laughed. "It may take some time… and begging, but she'll forgive you. You may just need to use that nice body of yours. Seduce her." I choked and spat what coffee I had in my mouth out onto the floor.

"Ah, okay. Thanks, Nancy."

"My pleasure, dear. Oh, and speaking of pleasure, I must get home to my Richard. Thanks for the cup of tea, and be a good boy."

I was forty-years-old, and I was going red from embarrassment. How in the hell had Wildcat survived growing up with her and not turned out strange? Although, Wildcat did have her moments.

DEANNA

I picked up Zara, who waddled out to the car with Talon following her. Blue and Stoke were standing out on the front porch looking on as the boss-man threatened me if I didn't bring his woman home safely. Though, his threat was a mild one to what I'd seen in the past because once he saw my tear-stained face, he knew something big had gone down and I needed my girl.

We drove on silently and picked up Julian. I'd asked Mattie to come, but he was already in bed asleep; he hadn't been feeling well. Julian got in the car, looked at me and then Zara, and then back to me and asked, "Who do I have to hurt? I've never seen our girl like this—well, besides... nope, not even then."

I snorted.

"I know. It's even worse than when we found her with a department store in her house. Tonight, she let Talon rip her a new one—though he did it gently—and usually she'd bite back big... but nothing. She hasn't spoken, like, at all. I think she's dead."

Biting my lips, I mumbled, "No, but I do feel like it. And stop talking like I'm not in the fuckin' car."

"There she is." Zara smiled as she grabbed my hand. "What's the plan?"

"To talk about my feelings and shit," I said with a snarl. I hated this crap, but I needed advice. Even if he didn't like me talking—no, *opening my big trap and telling people*— he could go and get fucked by a donkey.

"Don't worry, pumpkin. We'll get you so drunk you won't even know your name."

"Sounds like a plan." I started the car and drove to the nearest pub, which was two blocks away.

Zara and Julian chatted while I consumed five shots and two rum and cokes. I was on my third when it went down the wrong way and I started coughing.

"Maybe you need to burp her; get you some practice till the peanuts are out of you."

Turning my head, I saw Zara shrug and move her arm to my back. "If you try it, I'll post that picture you took when you were drunk and running around naked out in the backyard."

She glared, uttered 'Bitch' and placed her hand back on the table. I had to laugh; her belly was just touching the table in the booth we'd sat in. Looking around the small, somewhat-clean pub, I found I liked it. It was loud and bustling with people. The jukebox was playing softly, there were two other guys at the bar, and Blue was sitting in a booth three down from us. Apparently, Talon didn't trust me all that much with his wife… or had it been Grady? If it was, did that mean he still cared?

I looked back at Zara, who sat next to me, and then to Julian, who sat across from us. They were the *bestest* friends anyone could have.

Okay, I may have been a bit drunk. It sure would have explained why I burst out with, "I fuckin' love you two. I do. I know I can be the biggest bitch, but you guys put up with me, and I really appreciate it." I sighed and leaned my head against the table.

"Um, hun, you could catch something from doing that," Zara said.

"Why do I have the song, 'Ding dong the witch is dead. Which old witch? The wicked witch,' playing around in my head when I see her like this?" Julian asked.

"Screw you." I laughed and sat back up. "My life ended tonight. I told Grady about takin' Swan to see a specialist behind his back, he went ballistic. I've never seen him that mad, guys, and it was all because of me and my stupid, interfering, big trap. He hates me. He does. He's gonna move out now," I whispered, and tears slipped outta my eyes and down my cheeks. "He's gonna move out and take that gorgeous little girl with him. Then I will have nothing." I took a breath and sighed. "Jason may as well come and kill me."

"Don't you dare say that, bitch," Zara hissed. "He was just in the moment. I'm sure he's gotten over it and feels sorry for the way he's spoken to you, hun. I'm sure of it. Men talk and rant before even thinking about the situation."

"That they do. I know; I'm one of them… well, sort of. But Mattie does it all the time. One second he's yelling at me for something, and then later, he sees I was right all along because I am. Then he apologizes, and we have make-up sex. You just watch—you'll get home later, and he'll be all sorry, and the sex will be crazy mad." He leaned over the table. "And I wanna hear about it all tomorrow. Don't even think about leaving anything out."

"He's right," Zara said.

"See? Always right." Julian smiled and winked. I snorted.

Zara rolled her eyes. "Well, this time he is. He'll be begging for your forgiveness, and then you will do the deed in the hottest way yet, and then, yes, I also want to hear all about it. I'm not getting enough; Talon's scared he'll do damage to the babies with his 'ginormous'—his words, not mine—'perfect pecker'. I'll never live that saying down." She sighed but grinned.

"You really think so?" I asked.

"Yes," they both replied.

"Come on, cupcake from hell. I'll drive you both home, and you'll see that tomorrow will be a brighter day." Julian clapped.

I hoped to fuck so.

CHAPTER TWENTY-ONE

GRIZ

I DON'T KNOW how long I'd been sitting at the kitchen table after Nancy had left, but I'd keep sitting and waiting for my woman until she was home so I could crawl up her arse and tell her how sorry I was. The phone rang, and my heart jumped into my throat as panic settled in. Had something happened? A car accident?

I reached for the phone on the table. "Deanna?" I answered.

"What in the fuck did you do to her?" Talon growled down the line.

Shit.

Ignoring his question, I asked, "Where is she?"

"Probably out drinkin' her sorrows away with Zara. Again, brother, what did you do? I've never seen her look so... fuckin' defeated. Like her world had ended. Not even when she'd told us the story about her past. Fuck, man, I'm seriously thinkin' I need to come over there and beat the livin' shit outta you for putting that look on her face."

Sighing, I rubbed at my temple with my free hand. "Maybe you should. Jesus, Talon, I really fucked things up." I sighed. "Still, I did get a stern talking-to from Nancy when she dropped Swan off. Then she proceeded to tell me she was going home to pleasure her husband."

Talon's loud laughter filled the phone. "Goddamn, brother. I seriously don't know about that woman's sanity sometimes."

"I know what you mean."

Talon's voice was back to the gruff, harder tone when he said, "So, what in the hell are you gonna do to fix this?"

"Christ, anything at all. Anything."

"Good luck with that. And if my woman comes home pissed because of you, I'll fuckin' kill you."

"Sure, but I guess I'll be dead soon anyway when Deanna gets her fight back in her." I heard a click at the front door. "I've gotta go. Talk soon." I didn't wait for a reply; I hung up the phone and listened closely to hear Deanna come inside.

What was taking her so long? Instead of waiting, I went to the front door and opened it. Deanna was standing there with a tear-stained face and worried eyes.

"Sorry if I woke you," she said and brushed past me, heading for the stairs.

"Darlin', we need to talk."

"I smell like smoke and booze, Grady. I need a shower," she said over her shoulder and continued upstairs.

Fuck.

I hated seeing her like this. Where was her fight? Why wasn't she yelling in my face, calling me every name under the sun?

Making sure the house was locked up, I made my way upstairs. I could hear the shower running from the en suite in our room. I quickly checked on Swan; she was sound asleep. I pulled her blanket up over her more, and gently rubbed her beautiful blonde hair out of her face.

"I'll make this better, baby girl," I said quietly.

Leaving her room, I made my way down the hall and walked into our room, shutting the door behind me. I pulled my tee over my head, and took off my jeans and boxers. The bathroom was misty when I entered, some of it slipping out the open door. I opened the door to the shower and stepped inside. Before she could say anything, I wrapped my arms around her waist and brought her naked, smooth, wet back against my chest and out of the hot spray of the water.

"I'm sorry, darlin', so fuckin' sorry. I shouldn't have reacted like that."

"S'okay," she uttered. "I shouldn't have done it."

"Don't. You had every right. Fuck, princess, I was pissed, because I should have been the one to do it. I should have made it a priority, but I didn't, and I was—I don't know—jealous in a way. I never should have spoken to you like that, and you should have told me so. Turn around and hit me, swear at me, anything, and everything —just so I know we're okay. I need us to be okay, darlin'." I kissed her neck. "I love that you did this for us, for Swan, for *our* family, and I'll never do or say anything otherwise ever again. Swan is as much yours as she is mine. I knew this when I went off, but I couldn't stop myself. I'm an arse, princess."

She sniffed. *Damn, is she crying?*

"You *are* an arse." She shifted in my arms and turned to face me. "It's why I walked away. I knew you needed time to get your anger under control, and I was proven to be right." She smiled. "But, Grady, if you ever fucking speak to me like that again, I will castrate you." One of her hands wound around my cock and balls, squeezing hard, drawing a gasp from my mouth.

"Fuck, darlin'." I closed my eyes, only to open them seconds later. "Does this mean you forgive me?"

"For now." She smiled, got up on her toes and kissed me. Her tongue slipping over my bottom lip, I opened and our kiss deepened. My hands ran over her amazing body. I moved my mouth from hers and kissed down her neck, surprised to find her breath already heavy. I made my way with my mouth down to her left nipple, sucked it in between my lips and gently bit. She gripped my hair and the base of my neck. It was painful, but goddamn enjoyable.

After paying attention to her left breast, I moved to the right, causing a moan to fall from her lips.

Damn, my woman was hot. I gripped my dick in one hand and started to stroke, while the other hand slid between her thighs, fondling her trimmed, course hair there. She spread her legs wider and I slipped two fingers in; she was wet and ready.

"Grady," she hissed as my finger fucked her in and out. "Grady, I want you. Please."

I took a step back, my hand still around my dick, and I continued rubbing it up and down its length. She licked her lips as she watched me. A growl left my throat from the look in her eyes. She fuckin' loved to watch me, and I loved to please her.

"Darlin', I'm so damn hard for you."

"Yeah?" She smirked.

"Yes."

"I want you to fuck me, Grady. Now." She glared.

"Anything...God, fuckin' anything for you." Letting go of my dick, I gripped her wrist and pulled her against me, claiming her mouth with mine. She held me tightly, her hand fisting my hair as both my hands went to the backs of her thighs and I lifted. She wrapped her legs around me and continued our kiss.

Turning, I put her back to the wall. She gasped around my mouth from the cold, but as soon as I reached between us and placed my cock at her entrance, she moaned and then cried out when I slammed into her willing pussy.

She tore her mouth from mine, her head falling back against the tiles.

"Grady, God, yes! That feels so good."

"Damn, darlin'," I growled as my cock drove in and out of her hard and fast. This was what we needed—to dominate one another, to let our bodies say this was how it was supposed to be.

I was so fuckin' happy she'd forgiven me, and all I could do was show her my appreciation with my words and body. She drove me crazy, but I fuckin' loved it.

Her head fell to my shoulder, her arms encircling my neck more tightly and she hissed out, "Fuck, you make me feel so good, you arse."

I chuckled. "That I am, but one who will always fight for your forgiveness."

"Oh, Grady... just don't piss me off; though this was worth it... oh, God," she groaned as I shifted and tilted myself up more to touch that sweet spot inside of her.

"Yes, babe, right there."

"Darlin', hell, I'm gonna come soon."

"Me too. Keep going, please... d-don't stop. Yes!"

Two pumps later, she was gone, crying out and raking her nails down my back. A loud groan fell from my mouth as I released my seed inside of her.

"Wow," she mumbled against my neck.

"You got that right." I smiled and kissed her temple. "Maybe I should yell at you more often."

"Don't even fuckin' think about it." She pinched my back.

"I hope when I say never I can mean it," I said as I slip out of her, making sure she was steady on her feet. "But I know I can be bad-tempered. Just remember, I'll always be sorry, and eventually, I'll tell you that, once I've cooled down."

"I know, babe. It's why I'll keep you around a bit longer."

I grinned down at her and wondered if it was too soon to talk about babies.

Shit, where in the hell did that thought come from? I was a bloke, for God's sake—a guy doesn't think about kids before the chick does.

Christ! I was a fuckin' goner for this woman.

CHAPTER TWENTY-TWO

TWO MONTHS LATER

GRIZ

I WAS SITTING in Talon's office with him, Blue and Stoke just shooting the shit, but I could not stop fuckin' smiling, because I kept thinking about the way Dee had woke me up that morning.

Before I even had my eyes open, my dick was in her mouth, her hand was between her legs and she masturbated as she blew me, and what a fuckin' perfect sight to wake up to.

The thought of staying in bed all day with her crossed my mind many times, just like it had in the last two months we'd spent together. We now moved in a certain, day-by-day routine. The days she worked, Swan was at Wildcat's; the days she didn't, she offered to have Swan with her. Not only did Swan love it, but so did Deanna. I felt like such a cock over how I reacted to Deanna taking her to see someone. I'll regret my reaction and the pain I saw in her eyes every fuckin' day. I was still grateful she forgave me and we'd moved passed it. I'd do my best to make sure I'd never do that to her again.

It was beautiful seeing her with Swan, with *our* baby girl.

One night, I was nearly brought to my knees when Swan came up to me as I was sitting on the couch watching a football game on TV. She hopped up on my knee, looked up to my face and started singing the alphabet song. As she continued, my eyes and mouth grew wider and wider.

Once she'd finished, I heard clapping from the kitchen doorway and found Deanna with a proud smile upon her face. She bounded over to Swan, picked her up in her arms and spun her around, telling her how perfect she was.

My chest ached, and for the first fuckin' time in my life, I had tears welling in my eyes.

Fuck, I was a man for God's sake. I was not supposed to feel shit, and if I did, I wasn't supposed to show it.

From that day on, Swan bloomed into a beautiful, chatty young girl, and I had no other person to thank but Deanna. My woman.

And believe me, I thanked her every night. I could not get enough of her sweet, tight pussy, and she knew it and loved it.

"Griz?" Talon's bark brought me back to the room.

"What?" I answered with a slight jump.

They all laughed.

"Your mind seems to be elsewhere; should we take this meetin' up another day?" Talon asked.

"Nah, it's cool."

"You sure about that, brother?" Blue queried and looked down at my crotch.

What. The. Fuck?

I glanced down to see I had a boner. A fuckin' boner in a fuckin' meeting.

Shit.

"Ha! The fucker's blushin'," Stoke teased.

"Screw you," I growled.

"Well, if that's what you were thinkin' about to get hard—"

"Do not finish whatever you're about to say, dickhead," I warned. They all chuckled.

"All right, settle. Let's get back on track," Talon said, just as the office door opened and Pick stuck his head in.

"You needed to see me, boss?" he asked Talon.

"Get your arse in here," Talon ordered.

I noticed Pick paled. I couldn't blame the guy. Ever since he got outta the hospital after being shot, he'd been weary of not only Talon, but all the other brothers.

He had every right to be. No one looked at, treated or spoke to him the same, all because he was stupid enough to betray the brotherhood.

Damn well lucky Talon was married to Wildcat, and Pick was the one to save her brother and his lover's lives that night, or else he would've been a dead man also. Just like Wildcat's ex.

But no, instead, he was still in the brotherhood and still fuckin' living... only on a tighter rope.

"Pick, any news on that wanker Ryan?"

He stepped into the room but came no further. He swallowed and said, "No. Killer and I watched him pack up two months ago and drive outta town, down toward Geelong Way. I've kept an eye on him myself, but he hasn't done shit. Just sitting low in a fuckin' huge-ass house on the beach."

"Anyone come and see him?" I asked.

Pick turned to me and nodded. "Yeah, one time. Maxwell. It was about a month ago. He was all bandaged up still from our visit. He went in, stayed an hour and then left again. Other than that, nothing."

"Maybe we should have closer eyes on him," Blue suggested.

"Whadya mean?" Stoke asked.

"Have Warden, Vi's worker, get in and set some cameras up."

"Not a bad idea. Get on that," Talon said to Blue, who nodded in return.

"Still can't believe that monster of a man can sneak into any place undetected."

"I didn't either until I saw it myself," Talon said. His brows furrowed, obviously remembering that day—the day he nearly lost his woman.

"What about Maxwell?" I asked.

"Would he really be stupid enough to do anything?" Pick asked.

I looked from Talon, to Blue, and to Stoke. "Yes," we all said in unison.

"All right, inside eyes on him as well. I know we got others on him day and night, but I'd feel a lot fuckin' better if we had eyes on him at all times. What would be even better is if either of them would make a goddamn move already. I hate this waiting shit," Talon said, and everyone nodded.

"We still got his phone tapped?" I asked.

"Yeah," Stoke replied, "but that's also givin' us shit all."

"Okay, let's get to doin' the crap we need to," Talon barked.Everyone but the two of us disappeared from the room. Blue was the last to leave, closing the door behind him.

"How's business?" I asked.

"Pickin' up every fuckin' day, so it's good, but you didn't stay around to ask that. What's up, brother?" he asked, leaning back in his chair and crossing his arms over his chest.

"You're right, but it ain't nothing. I gotta go fix that Harley that was brought in yesterday. Catch'ya later."

I went to stand until Talon growled, "Sit the fuck down."

With a grumble, I complied. "What?" I asked.

"If you don't tell me what's on your goddamn mind, I'll spread the word about your boner to everyone."

"Fuck you. Besides, not like Blue hasn't already told everyone already."

Talon chuckled. "True that."

I shifted my weight in the hard seat, contemplating if I was really gonna tell Talon.

"Brother, just spill it."

"Fuck, I feel like a little girl talkin' about this shit."

Talon's eyes widened. "You askin' Hell Mouth to marry you?"

"How? What? Fuck. Yes."

Talon's wild, wide smile was catching.

"Shit, Griz. I knew it right from the start. The way she watched you, and the way your eyes followed her every fuckin' move, I *knew* this day would come. And I couldn't be more damned happy for you."

"Fuck." I grinned and looked down at my boots. "Thanks, brother."

"When's he gettin' out?" he asked, obviously changing the subject so I could stop feeling like a pussy.

I growled, "In a month."

"We'll up the security then. We'll get the bitch before he even breathes her air."

I looked up at him and knew my eyes were hard. "Yeah, we will."

Talon chuckled, and I looked at him with a questionable gaze. This wasn't a laughing matter.

"Damn smart move, though," he said.

"What?"

"Moving in with her before her shit actually started. It gave you both time to get to know one another."

I laughed. "It was more than smart; it was fuckin' brilliant."

CHAPTER TWENTY-THREE

DEANNA

It was Sunday morning; Grady had gone to the compound for a meeting, and I'd organized to meet up with Zara and the monsters at a play centre with Swan.

Walking in, I spotted Zara... I mean, who wouldn't? She looked like she was about to burst out the little devils any second; she was that large. Not that I'd tell her—she'd either start crying like a fool, or she'd kick my arse.

I looked to the person next to her and smiled; I should have known she'd bring her posse—Julian, Mattie, Nancy, and Josie.

"Well, have a look at this proud mamma bear," Julian grinned. I made sure none of the kids were watching and gave him the middle finger.

"Ooooh, and she's temperamental like a bear too. Must run in the family—seems her man is the big tough Grizzly."

"Cut it out, Julian," Nancy scolded. I smiled as he rolled his eyes. As I placed Swan on her feet, Nancy bent to her level and said, "Hello, sweet Swan. Maya and Cody are out there playing somewhere. You wanna come find them with me?"

Swan looked up at me. I smiled and nodded. "Hang on, squirt. You have to take your shoes off." I sat her on the chair and undid her runners. As soon as they left her feet, she jumped up and ran on with Nancy following.

"Hey, Mattie and Josie." I waved as I sat next to Zara at the long table. "And how's the whale today?" I asked her.

"I swear, if there were no kids around, I would," she picked up her bottle of water, "stick this up your arse and sit you back down."

We all burst out laughing.

"Isn't it funny how they've changed roles? Deanna's now the non-swearing, calm, nice one, and Zara's turned into hell on wheels," Mattie stated.

"It's amazing what children can do for you," Nancy said as she sat back down next to me. "Josie, you should block your ears around Zara now. She's been so vile lately."

I watched Josie giggle into her hand. "I think it's funny," she said.

"Deanna," Nancy started; I looked around Zara, "I just wanted to say, sweetheart, that I'm very proud of you." *Oh, shit. Shit, no. I cannot take this.* "I've known you for some time now, even before Zara went through that terrible business. When I met you over Skype, I knew you'd be a true, trustworthy friend for my baby girl, but I also knew from your foul-mouthed attitude you had your own stuff to deal with. I know you still are, but the way you've grown these last months is amazing. I am very proud, and I'm positive you have a great thing going with that hunk of a man of yours and beautiful girl over there." I turned my wet eyes to see Swan sitting in a ball pit with Maya and Cody, laughing and smiling.

"Thank you," I uttered. Zara placed her hand over mine on my thigh and squeezed it.

"Mum, enough of the sweet words. My emotions can't take it," Zara said.

"Oh, shush."

"Now, if I weren't taken, I'd be all over that," Julian piped in, lifting his eyebrow in the direction of the entrance. We looked toward the door to see Pick walking in. I turned back to the other side of the table in time to see Josie blush and look down at her lap.

Hmm, what was going on there? I had thought she was still infatuated with Billy.

Zara stood up and asked, "Is everything all right, Pick?"

"Yeah, Wildcat, sorry if I scared you. Talon just wanted me to hang for a bit. I... ah, didn't want to do it outside, in case someone got the wrong impression seeing a biker sit out the front of a play centre full of kids."

She smiled at him. "That's fine. Take a seat."

"On my lap," Julian said. Mattie hit him in the shoulder as Pick rolled his eyes and chuckled. He chose to sit at the end of the table next to Josie, on a chair, of course, but backwards. "What?" Julian asked Mattie. "I was just offering." He grinned, and then said under his breath, "Like you weren't thinking it."

I think ever since the day Pick had saved them, they both had a soft spot for him, and it was that soft spot that kept him alive.

Holy shit.

As Nancy started complaining about the prices of food, I noticed the small, but intense look that Pick was giving... *Mattie?* What was that about?

Oh, no. Fuck. Please do not tell me Mattie was cheating on Julian. Please. I loved them both; they had to stay together.

I felt sick all of a sudden.

Mattie looked over at me, and I glared. His eyes widened and shook his head, and he moved to pull out the chair next to me.

"Deanna," Zara snapped, and I turned to face her "I need food. Feed me, please."

I forced a smile and said, "You're effing lucky you're preggo."

She grinned. "Oh, I know."

I stood. "Would anyone else like anything?" After they gave me their orders, I stepped away from the table.

"I'll help you," Mattie said.

Of course you would, you cheating, lying, little fucker, who I was gonna kick the living shit out of.

We stepped up to the long line and waited.

"Will you stop glaring at me?" Mattie sighed.

I hadn't realised I was, but now that he said it, I felt my brows were furrowed, and my eyes were squinty.

"Give me a fuckin' good reason why."

"Well, at least I know if you're pissed enough, you go back to swearing." He laughed.

"This is no laughing matter, cocksucker. What in the hell, Mattie? You make me want to feel like crying, and you know I hate to cry and feel shit."

We stepped forward before he said anything. "I know. Damn, I know. Look, can you just believe it isn't anything and leave it alone?"

"No."

He sighed and looked to the floor. "Deanna, you should know I would never jeopardise my relationship with Julian. I love that man with my whole heart and soul."

"Mattie, I know, which is why I don't get what that look was about, but I know it was intense enough for me to doubt that love you have for your man," I explained.

He shook his head. "What I'm about to say cannot be passed on to anyone. And I mean *anyone*, Deanna, not even Griz."

Shit. That was hard, but I had to know if I still had to beat the hell out of him.

"Okay." I nodded.

Mattie pulled me out of the line and pointed over to the toy machines. He was putting on a show for anyone who was looking our way.

"We better make this quick before Preggo-zilla comes ballin' us over, hunting for food," I said.

He smiled. "That's true." We stood in front of the machine, and I placed my gold coins in to see if I could win a stuffed toy.

"Mattie, talk," I snapped.

"He's confused," he said.

"Who? Pick?"

"Yes."

"About what?"

Mattie looked at me; I looked back. "Oh," I said.

"I think it has something to do with the fact that Julian and I helped him through… everything. He knows he'd be a dead man if I wasn't the brother of his boss's woman."

"Oh," I said again.

"He thinks he likes me, but he also thinks he likes Josie. You know how Ma is; she knows we were helping him, and in return, she thinks she's helping him by inviting him over for dinner. Sometimes I'm there, sometimes not, and he gets to spend time with Josie."

"Mattie," I whined.

"I know. I've told him that nothing can happen. I've also told him he only thinks he likes me because of everything that happened, but he's not sure. Ever since he's cut ties with his mum, he's leaned on not only me but my parents as well."

"What are you going to do?" I asked.

"Nothing. There is no way I would leave the other half of me. Julian is my life. Pick knows this and accepts it; he just has trouble hiding his feelings at the moment."

"Well, this has blown me outta the water." I shook my head and sighed. "Pick thinks he's gay."

"No," Mattie said.

"What?" I gaped. More? There was fuckin' more to this?

"Apparently, he knows he's bisexual."

"How?"

"Um…."

"Mattie," I growled again.

"No, no, nothing like that. I didn't do anything."

"Then what?"

"He, um... he told me he knows, because he still loves to...." he coughed and whispered, "fuck women and... he, um... he went to a certain club and... yeah. You can guess what happened there."

"With a man?"

"Yes."

"Oh, wow. Okay, I mean, not that anything like that bothers me. It's just... it's Pick. He's a biker. I didn't know there were bi bikers."

Mattie burst out laughing. "Honey, there's bi, gay or curious in all walks of life. Oh, look you won." He pointed at the machine, and yes, I had indeed won a freaky-looking bear. Still, I knew Swan would love it.

"Deanna," Zara bellowed across the room. I shifted around to look over at her. She pointed to her belly and then her mouth. I chuckled, took the bear in one hand and Mattie's hand in my other and moved back to the line before Zara went on a killing spree.

"You won't say anything?"

I rolled my eyes at him. "Of course I won't. To anyone. I promise. I'm just happy I don't have to hurt you now."

Mattie laughed. "Yeah, me too."

CHAPTER TWENTY-FOUR

GRIZ

Fuck, I hated Mondays. I hated leaving Swan with Wildcat while Deanna went to work. I hated leaving Dee in bed alone before she had to get up for work. At least I had the chance to wake her up early enough—before Swan was even awake—for some morning entertainment.

Shit, I really had to get my body under control.

Just thinkin' about how wet she was for me had me hard, and now wasn't the time. I bent over the hood of the Chevy to try and work out what the fuck was wrong with it.

But yet again, my mind drifted to Dee and that morning, because it had been different. Instead of fuckin', screwin' or just getting my jollies off, we'd made love. It was slow, sweet and damn unbelievable. I knew she'd felt it too; I saw it in her eyes.

She'd woken up on a moan, with my hand in her panties flicking her clit. "Griz," she'd moaned.

"Darlin', you don't call me that here in this bed while I'm playing with you."

She'd nodded before my finger took her over the edge. I'd got to my knees, my hard-on pointing in the direction it wanted to go. So I pulled her panties down and off as she lay on her back and watched, with lust-filled eyes and a cute smirk on her mouth. In a quick rush, my boxers were gone, and I was between her outstretched legs.

"Grady," she'd snapped because I was holding back. I had my dick just at her entrance, my arms and hands braced on the bed beside her waist. I hovered over her. She wanted me to plunge in, but I didn't. Instead, as I kept her gaze, I slowly pushed my cock inside her tight, wet pussy. She saw it then, what it was I had intended. I needed this—the slow, passionate warm-up for making love to my woman. Her eyes filled with tears, and as I withdrew from her warmth and sank back in, I bent and kissed her tears away.

"Fuck, darlin'," I growled as I got back up on my arms to watch her. "You feel so, so good."

"Grady," she moaned.

"Slow and easy, princess. Shit, this is us, darlin'. This is what we've got," I said and witnessed the warmth seep into her eyes.

She knew. She got it.

"Babe," she'd uttered and wrapped her arms around my neck, tuggin' me down on top of her. "I-I love this—us," she whispered, and then pulled me into a fierce, smouldering kiss.

My dick, still moving slowly in and out of her, knew it was only seconds away from shootin' its load. Only, there was no way I was lettin' my woman—my old lady—fall behind. I went to reach between us but stopped when Deanna grabbed my wrist and brought it up to link our hands and fingers together.

"I'm nearly there, babe. Hell, so close, just from you—from your dick."

"Fuck," I groaned.

"Oh, damn. Grady." Her tight walls clenched around my dick, and grunted moans fell from my lips as I planted my seed inside of her.

GODDAMN IT. I threw the spanner down to the concrete floor and stood up straight. My mind was definitely not at work. I needed to be embedded in my woman's pussy. My dick was aching for release, but there was no way of getting it. Deanna was at work; otherwise, I would've ridden straight home and had my way with her, and she'd be more than fuckin' happy to oblige.

I looked down at my hard cock, thanking my damn lucky stars that the garage wasn't full of other brothers. Only a few were scattered here and there, but no one who'd take notice I was palming my dick through my jeans.

Christ. I was palming my dick at work.

What the fuck had my woman done to me?

There was only one way to fix it so I could get some work done. I walked outta the garage and over to the compound.

Another blessing—no one was around while I walked through the building and into my room. I closed and locked the door, and then leaned against it.

Shit. I can't believe I was gonna do this, like some stupid, horny kid.

With my fingers on my zipper, I pulled it down, undid the button, reached in and grabbed my hard cock. A moan slipped past my lips. I pulled my dick outta my boxers and started stroking it as I walked over to the bed and sat down.

Up and down, my hand slipped with ease. A picture of Deanna popped into my mind, spreading her legs wide for me like our first time. I imagined her playing with Vinny, as she called her vibrator, rubbing it over and over across her clit and then down, pushing it in and out of her dripping hole.

"Shit," I groaned. With my other hand, I pulled my black tee up and over my head, leaned back on the bed on one elbow and watched as my hand moved faster and faster stroking my dick.

A picture of Deanna riding my cock was what ripped a moan from my lips and had me coming all over my own stomach.

Fuck. I was feeling the need to stay in bed and sleep for a while after coming so hard, but I had shit that needed to be done. So I grabbed an old tee I must of left there a while ago from the other side of the bed and cleaned myself up.

A smile etched across my face. I really needed to play out that first time with Deanna again, and even have Vinny join us. After cleaning up in the adjoining bathroom, I made my way back out.

As I was just getting through the door to the garage, Town, a younger club member with shaggy blond hair and beady eyes, stepped up to me.

"Hey, brother," he said.

"What's up, man?"

"Not much. I gotta work on a bike some bird is bringing in later. Though, I'd rather work on her, if ya know what I mean." He chuckled.

I rolled my eyes. "Yes, Town."

"Hey, do you know where Talon is?"

"I saw him this mornin'; he said he was doin' shit at home today. Why you need him?"

"Oh, no reason. Just wanted to shoot the shit."

Like Talon would fuckin' want to. He couldn't stand this little shit, but he was good at what he did—fixing bikes.

"So what's been happenin' with you, brother?" he asked.

"Just the usual stuff."

"Any, you know, *secret stuff* I can help out with?"

"What the fuck are you talkin' about?" I was starting to lose my good vibe after comin'.

"Oh, you know... drugs."

I got in his face and hissed, "Listen here, you little shit. You've been here five months; you should know by now we don't deal with that shit, and if you ever fuckin' try to bring it in or on our territory, which you are a goddamn part of, I'll rip shreds through you—after Talon is done with you, that is."

"Yeah, all right, brother. Cool it. I didn't mean anything by it; I just thought all motorcycle clubs dealt with that sorta stuff. I didn't hear anything about it, so I just assumed I wasn't high enough in ranks to hear about it. But now I fuckin' know. Damn, you don't need to put my balls in a vice about it."

"Town, grow the fuck up."

Walking off, I looked to my side to see he was following. I stopped at the Chevy, picked up the spanner again and started to work on it.

"Soooo...."

"Town, go find somethin' to do," I growled.

"Come on. I just wanna get to know you."

Sighing, I said, "There ain't nothing to know."

"Sure there is. I heard you got yourself a sweet piece of arse, but that she can be a ball-busting bitch. At least you've got a replacement mamma for your offspring. I bet that's all you're with her for, right?"

I needed this fucker to get outta my space, or I was gonna punch the arsehole out.

Which was why I said, "Yeah, brother, that's why I put up with her; she's a nice replacement-mum for Swan."

"Oh, shit," Town laughed.

"What?" Why in the hell I was encouraging him to talk, I didn't know.

"Is your woman blonde, with a smokin' body and blue eyes?"

Standing, I moved closer. "I'm startin' to get sick of you talkin' about my woman. As I said, grow the fuck up and you may find something special like I did. No, she ain't a replacement. She never was. I was just lucky enough she was interested in me. Now you say one more word about her, I swear you'll be breathin' by a machine."

His eye widened. "Fuck."

"What?"

"Man, don't kill me, okay? She, your woman, was just here, and she just heard your earlier replacement comment."

"*What?*" I yelled.

"Sorry, brother. She was just here, but ran when she heard that."

I pulled my fist back and clocked him in the jaw. He cried out in pain and fell to the ground.

"Never call me a brother again, and you'd better goddamn pray nothin' comes of this little fuck up."

Running to the door to hopefully catch her, I was stopped short when Zara waddled in looking angry as all shit.

"You." She pointed. She walked up to me and stabbed me in the chest with her finger over and over again. "You wanna tell me why my best friend just left here crying?"

I grabbed her finger, and said, "It was all a mistake, so don't stress before you squirt the little people out. I'll fix it. That dick," I gestured with my chin to Town, still lying on the ground with several brothers standing around him laughing. "Was annoying the... I don't have time to explain. I have to go find her. Wait, why are you here?"

"Ma came and got Swan this morning; she wanted to take her to the shops. Talon wanted me to get out of the house, so he sent me to grab some stuff from his office. He said I was driving him crazy, Griz, but all I wanted was sex. I heard it brought on labour, but he wouldn't have it. Oh, no... I mean, he had me once, but he wasn't doing me the second time." She chuckled. "Okay, we did it the second time, but—" My hand went over her mouth.

"Wildcat, I love you like a sister," I began, and tears shone in her eyes, "but I do not want to hear about my *brother* givin' it to you."

She nodded, so I let my hand fall from her mouth.

"You love me like a sister?" she cried and wrapped her arms around my waist. Well, she tried to, but her huge belly wouldn't let her. "That means so much to me, Griz."

"Wildcat," I said and patted her on the back. "As much fun this is, I have to go find my woman and explain."

She pulled back and stepped away. "Of course. You'll need to grovel. She hates crying, so be prepared to shift mountains for her forgiveness."

"Will do… and, Wildcat? Do me a favour, besides never talking about your sex life, go and give that arsehole a piece of your mind for causing Deanna to cry."

She grinned, and said, "My pleasure."

CHAPTER TWENTY-FIVE

DEANNA

Stupid cocksucking wanker. To think I was there because I couldn't get him out of my mind and wanted to screw his brains out. Stupid him, and his stupid way he loved me that morning. Just thinkin' about it had me near coming on the spot.

But now all I wanted to do was rip his beautiful cock off.

I was crying once again, for God's sake. Crying! I hated it.

If it wasn't one way—where he was yelling at me to butt out—it was another—saying I was just a replacement for Swan. Maybe that was why he apologised so quickly?

It couldn't be; I was probably overreacting, and he probably didn't mean it that way. That idiot with him probably goaded him about the whole situation.

But damn, it had hurt.

He wouldn't be far behind me.

Though, from the look on Zara's face, he could be delayed for some time after she gave him a good scolding, which she was good at. I often felt like a five-year-old when she'd do it to me.

Serves him right.

He was sure as shit gonna pay for it when he got home for making me cry again!

Even if I was ready to cut the shithead loose after the pain that stabbed me in my chest when I heard those words fall from his mouth, I couldn't do it. I knew there had to be a reason, so I just had to sit back and wait for him to come grovelling.

Naked.

Damn, that sounded good.

I wondered what else I could make him do before I let him off the hook.

I pulled my Mustang up out the front of my house, got out, locked it and then saw that Violet fuckin' Marcus was standing on my front porch when I rounded the hood.

"What in the hell do you want?"

"Well, hello to you too, Barbie."

"Seriously, Vi, what are you doing here?" I asked as I stepped around her and slid the key in the lock.

"Why are you upset? You've been crying."

"No I haven't, and if I had, it would be none of your fucking business," I explained and turned back to her with my arms crossed over my chest. I sighed, and asked again, "What are you doing here, Vi?"

"I wanted to have a chat with you."

My eyebrows shot up. She'd shocked the shit outta me enough it was a wonder my eyebrows even stayed on my face.

"What about?"

"I think its best we go inside and have a coffee for this conversation."

Shit. This sounded bad. If she was willing to come to me, be in my presence and be willing to enter my house, it had to be some bad shit.

"Fine." Turning back, I unlocked the door, opened it and entered.

Only once I was through the threshold, I was grabbed around

the neck, flung sideways and held against the wall next to the front door.

With my hands holding the one hand that was around my neck applying pressure, I watched Vi pull her gun out and around, but in the next second it was knocked out of her hand by another guy, and then he hit her. Once she was on the ground, he was on top of her, holding her hands behind her back.

The hand around my throat tightened enough to make me cough.

"Kenny, ease up a little. We can't have her dead," the tall, thin guy with dirty blond hair said from the floor as he continued to subdue a kicking Violet.

The hand around my throat eased enough for me to get a big breath in.

"Who the hell are you? Deanna, do you know them?" Violet asked with a hard tone.

I looked from the guy with long black hair and dark brown eyes in front of me, and then back to the one on the ground.

"No," I choked out.

Fuck!

Who in the hell were these guys and what were they doing at my house?

"Doesn't matter if you know us or not. Someone wants to get to know you, so you're coming with us," the guy in front of me hissed in my face. Kenny, wasn't it?

"Boss said to only grab the blonde," the one on Vi said.

"We'll have to take both. Can't have that bitch running off to tell someone."

"No," I uttered. Obviously this was my shit if they only wanted me, so I wasn't bringing anyone along for this fucked up ride. "She won't say anything. She hates me anyway. It'll be no loss to her if you take me. Alone."

"Bullshit," Kenny spat.

"Take her out the back to the van. I'll bring this one."

"Sure, Nathan."

Shit, shit, shit.

I couldn't let this happen.

Kenny's hand slid from my throat, down over my breast and gripped my wrist tightly as he pulled me forward, heading to the back of the house.

"Violet?" I asked. She'd know what to do; she had to, right? This was what she did for a living. Well, not exactly this, but....

"It'll be all right, Dee," she called.

Fuck. That really didn't ease the tension running through my body. It didn't ease the fright running through my veins.

Goddamn it.

I started digging my heels into the ground, forcing my weight backwards.

There was no way I was going without a fight.

"Bitch, fucking move your arse."

"No." We were passing the kitchen bench where a plate was laying. I picked it up and clobbered him over the head with it.

He let out a curse, spun and backhanded me across my cheek.

Damn it all to hell; that had hurt.

I kicked out his knees, and when he went down I turned to run, only he grabbed me by an ankle and the next second, I was on the ground with his full weight over me.

"What is going on?" Nathan yelled as he walked into the kitchen with Violet in front of him. He still had her arms pinned behind her.

She smirked down at me and gave off an eye roll.

Man, I so wanted to kick the shit outta her. Punch her in the boob. Why in the fuck was she so calm?

Then it hit me.

She had a plan.

She must have one, right?

"Get her up, dipshit, and contain her."

The weight behind me left, and I was pulled off the ground and held like Nathan was holding Violet with my arms behind my back.

"Violet?" I asked again.

Kenny spat, "Shut up, slut." He leaned over my shoulder and whispered in my ear, "You'll get payback for what you just did. I'll make sure the boss will give you to me, and after I fuck you, I'll kill you."

Shit.

Whatever Violet's plan was, it had better be good, because I was sure as shit about to pee myself.

CHAPTER TWENTY-SIX

GRIZ

I was just out the garage doors when my phone rang. I grabbed it from my jeans pocket, flipped it open and answered with a barked, "What?"

"Get the fuck back in the garage," Talon bit out.

"Brother, I have to go find my woman and make sure she ain't setting traps to kill me in my sleep."

"I need you, man. Turn your arse around and get to *my* woman. I trust no one there but you with her."

By the scared tone in his voice, I spun and ran back into the garage.

"What in the fuck is goin' on, Talon?"

"Kitten's water just broke. I've called an ambo and I'm on my fuckin' way, but I want someone with her, brother."

"I'm on it," I said and hung up. He needed to concentrate on getting here without any other stress to freak him out.

I rounded a corner, as a blood-curdling scream tore through the garage. I ran into the room to see a puddle under Wildcat as she bent over a counter, legs apart. One of her hands braced her bodyby one hand holding her up, while the other one had Town by the balls, and from the look on his face, he was in a large amount of pain.

Stoke, Killer, and Memphis all stood around her, trying to hide their smirks.

She took a deep breath in and out, and then said, "If you cock-sucking men get a woman pregnant, I swear I will hunt you down and cut off your dicks."

"Wildcat?" I asked, easing up behind her.

"Griz, what the hell are you doing here? Go find Deanna and do her. Or I'll... oh, shit." She ended with a scream and leaned her head on the bench.

"Jesus, man. Please, please make her stop," Town cried as he gripped her wrist, trying to break her hold.

Fuck. What in the hell was I supposed to do?

"Wildcat, you wanna let go of the guy's nads?" I asked gently and then moved to rub her lower back with my palm.

"Ah, Griz. Yes. Oh, damn, that feels so good," she moaned.

"Why do I feel a hard-on coming on?" Stoke laughed. "You keep moanin' like that, lady, and you'll give us all boners."

She turned her head to glare at him.

"Shut the fuck up, dickhead," Killer barked.

"Griz," Wildcat whimpered. Christ, they were close, the fucking contractions were coming fast.

"Wildcat, let go of his balls and I'll keep rubbin'," I said and put more pressure into the motion of my hand on her back.

Her hand dropped away, putting it on the bench with her other and Town left in two seconds flat.

"Shit a brick. Oh... Hell!" she cried.

"Breathe, woman, breathe that shit out. Do the he-he-ha breathing they teach you," Stoke said. We all looked at him, even Wildcat. "What?" he asked. "I've seen it in movies."

"Idiot," Killer uttered.

"Tool," Memphis chuckled.

"It's all right, Wildcat. Talon's on his way; he called an ambulance. They'll be here soon."

"Good," she snarled. "They need to be here when I kill Talon for doing this to me."

"You need anything, woman?" Killer asked.

"No!" she snapped. My hand stilled on her back as I listened to hear the sirens and the pipes of a Harley coming up the road.

"Griz, if you don't start up your hand again, I'll have to hurt you, and then Deanna will be pissed at me." I quickly started rubbing again, and she groaned.

Heavy footsteps pounded down the hallway; I looked over my shoulder to see Talon with a worried expression come running in, and two EMT men entered seconds after him.

"Kitten," he called.

"You!" she yelled, stood and turned to face him while holding onto her belly.

"Shit, he's a dead man," Stoke muttered.

The EMT men reached her sides, and one said, "Come on, sweetheart, let's get you to the hospital."

"You fuckin' touch her again and call her sweetheart, I'll kill you." Talon moved himself in, gave me a chin lift and I moved in on her other side, and with our help, she waddled her way out.

"Don't go all Neanderthal on me right now, Talon Marcus. Let these nice men do their jobs; you're in enough trouble."

"They can do their damn job at the hospital. Until then, I've got you," he barked.

"I don't appreciate that tone right now, Talon." She looked over her shoulder to the smirking ambo guys. "Do you have another bed for my husband? Because I'm about to beat the shit out of him." And with that, she slogged her fist into Talon's stomach.

"Hell, woman. Whad'ya do that for?"

"You and your stupid sperm! That's why. Now get me to the damn hospital." She stopped and hunched over while Talon and I held her weight, and she screamed through another contraction.

"Kitten?" Talon's tone was gentle. Once we started moving again, she looked over at him. "We'll get through this together. I hate that you're dealing with this pain on your own; I wish I could take it away, but I can't. Just think though, kitten. Once this is done, we'll have our beautiful kids with us."

Tears shone in her eyes. "We will." She smiled. "But until then, be prepared for the ultimate bitch to be here."

"I'm ready for her, baby."

"Good."

We helped her up into the back of the ambulance, and just as I was shutting the door, Talon grinned with fuckin' joy. "Thanks, brother."

I gave him a chin lift and said, "Anytime."

"Griz?"

"Yes, Wildcat?"

"I asked Deanna to come to the birthing suite. I need my girl there. Bring her, please."

"I'll go get her."

As I watched the vehicle leave the car park, my phone rang. "Yo?"

"Griz?" A deep male voice asked.

"Yeah."

"This is Warden."

My brow furrowed. "What's up, man?" Why was this guy calling me?

"There's been a situation. Violet has set off her safety button in her pocket."

"You need help? I can't talk to Talon. He's just left with Wildcat; they're about to be parents." I smiled.

"No. I... fuck, man. She was at Deanna's when she set it off."

My body stilled, my heart stopped, and by fuck, I wanted to scream at the sky.

"I'll be at the office in five," I snarled.

"See you then."

CHAPTER TWENTY-SEVEN

DEANNA

VIOLET AND I WERE THROWN—LITERALLY—INTO the back of a black van. We could hear the door being locked behind us. I quickly tried the side door. No luck there, it was also locked tight.

I turned to see Violet sitting calmly.

"What the fuck, Vi?" I hissed.

She pulled something outta her pocket and smiled. "It's a silent alarm that sends its signal back to the office. It's also a tracking device. By now, Warden will be rounding up the troops to come find us."

"Fuck," I whispered.

My fists went to my eyes, and I flopped to my back on the steel floor. Even though it hurt, a sense of solace swept over me, because I knew that Warden would call Griz.

My man would be hunting for me.

Damn, that felt good—no *great*... fan-fuckin'-tastic to think of.

"But just because we know the cavalry is coming doesn't mean you can cause shit. You need to keep your mouth shut and do as they say. That way, neither of us should get hurt."

I felt my cheek; I knew it was already bruising from how tender it was. "Okay," I said and sat up to face her, where she sat at the back of the van.

Violet smirked. "What? You're not going to fight me on this?"

"I don't have the energy. I've got enough shit to worry about."

"Like your foster brother?"

My eyes widened. "Who told you?"

Violet rolled her eyes. "Come on, Barbie. I knew something was up that night we were all around for dinner at my brother's house. Even though I didn't get to stay for the information, it doesn't mean I wouldn't check."

I shrugged. "So, you know. I really couldn't care."

Violet studied me. "What else was wrong when you got to your house before?"

"Nothin' you need to know about."

"Did someone ring you about Jason Drake?"

"No, why?"

"He's out, Deanna. He got out a month early; he was released yesterday."

Panic surged through me.

Shit, just what I needed.

I scoffed. "Well, aren't you just a bringer of good fuckin' news? Glad you told me now? What, did you want to see the worry, the panic in my eyes, so you can go back and tell Travis and have a good laugh about me? About how it freaks me the hell out to know the man who murdered the only parents I knew did it all because of me? Great, thank you. Fuck!" I punched the side of the van.

Oh, God. I just wanted to curl into a ball and forget everything. But I fuckin' couldn't.

"That wasn't why I came to tell you, Deanna. I wanted to warn you."

I snorted. "Yeah, okay."

She sighed. "Look, I don't give a shit if you believe me or not; at least *I* know what my intentions were. Now tell me, do you think these idiots who took us have anything to do with Jason?"

"Hell, it hadn't even crossed my mind. But honestly, no. He'd want to do his own work. He's never trusted anyone else. This has to do with something else, Vi, and I wouldn't have a fuckin' clue what."

"Doesn't matter. We'll figure it out. If not us, the guys will."

"Where do you think they're taking us?" I asked.

"Not sure, but it's obvious it's not someplace in Ballarat."

I crossed my legs and sat straighter as I watched Vi move to lean against the side of the van. "Look, I can't help but be a bitch, and I'm not sorry for it, but I am sorry for having you dragged into this. Whatever this is."

"Aw, Barbie, you do love me." Vi laughed.

"Fuck you."

"No, thanks. I get enough at home."

I cleared my throat. *Damn, was I going to do this? Have a bloody normal conversation with my nemesis?*

"How are things with you and Travis?" *Yeah, I guess I was.*

It had to do with the fact that my emotions were fucked. They were going haywire inside of me. I was scared, angry, worried, pissed, annoyed and did I mention scared? Not only about this stuffed-up situation, but the fact that the man who would have killed me many years ago is out walking the streets.

A free fuckin' man.

It wasn't right. No man should have been released after the crime he committed, but it showed just how crazy the system was.

In my eyes, he hadn't paid enough for what he'd done. Which was why, in some ways, I did hope he came for me so that I could enforce a better punishment.

I may have failed Zara for not following through with what I wanted to do to David—at least he was dead now—but I would with Jason. He was a sick prick who needed to be eliminated.

"Are we really going to have this conversation?" Vi asked, bringing me out of my thoughts.

Shrugging, I said, "What else is there to do. I'm not gonna sit here and play truth or dare, or braid your fuckin' hair."

Violet actually laughed. I fought the smile from my lips.

"All right, things with Travis are good."

I waited for more. "What, that's it? That's all you're going to say?"

It was her turn to shrug. "What do you want me to say?"

"I don't know, but something more at least. How are you, the PI, handling that your man is the top dog in Melbourne for selling women?"

She rolled her eyes and then glared. "Nothing is sacred in our little family, is it?"

I shook my head. "No, not really."

"How about you tell me what was up your arse when you got home, and then I'll talk to you about... that."

"Deal." I smiled. I didn't care; my information wasn't juicy gossip like hers was.

CHAPTER TWENTY-EIGHT

GRIZ

Before I left the compound on my Harley, I called Killer and told him to get Stoke and Blue to meet me at Violet's office. Then I called Nancy, Wildcat's mum, who had Swan.

"Hello," she answered.

"Nancy, it's Griz. I need you to watch Swan for a while longer."

"Sure, honey, as long as you don't mind me taking her to the hospital. You know my baby girl is gonna have her babies? I'm so excited."

"Yeah, I know. Look I gotta go—"

"Griz, what's wrong?" she interrupted to ask. How in the fuck she knew I didn't have a clue.

"Nothin' that can't be fixed."

"Do you need help?"

Damn, she'd actually brought a smile to my face when it felt like my heart had dropped into my arse and I was about to shit it out.

"No, woman, I'll deal with it," I said and slipped my leg over my Harley.

"Deal with what, young man? What's going down; is someone hurt? Griz, do not leave me worrying."

"Nance—"

"Griz, Richard here. What's going on? Why does my wife look pale all of a sudden?"

Fuck, I had no time for this.

"Richard, shit, sorry to upset your woman. I don't know how in the hell she knew something was going down, but it is, and I gotta cut this short so I can get things done. Long story short—my woman and Talon's sister have been taken. We know where they are, so I'm going to go get them back."

"Right, son. I'll keep things here under control. You go do what you gotta, unless you need an extra pair of hands. I've still got that gun Talon gave me."

"No, I've got my brothers help, but I really have to head off."

"See you at the hospital to meet my grandkiddies after you get the women back."

"Richard, what's happening? You tell me right now or I'll...." I heard in the background.

"Woman, shut it and get everyone in the car. Zara's probably holding her legs together keeping those kids in, waiting for us to get there." He took a breath and then said into the phone, "Be careful, son."

"Right," I said and hung up. With a kick, my Harley roared to life. I was finally on my fucking way to kill whoever put his hands on my woman.

STRIDING INTO VIOLET'S OFFICE, I found Warden and Travis, Violet's man, standing at a desk; they both looked up from the computer and gave me a chin lift.

"What's the deal?" I asked.

"The tracker hasn't stopped, so we don't know their final destination. As soon as we do, we'll be on the road," Warden said. I looked at Travis; he seemed just as strung out as I was—any fuckin' wonder. Who knew what was going on with our women? Fuck, now I knew how Talon felt when he had to sit around waiting for information about where Wildcat had been held.

It not only fucking hurt, but it made you even crazier as the seconds ticked by.

"What area are they at now?" I asked.

"Heading their way to Geelong."

"Christ," I bit out.

"What?" they both snapped.

"I know where they're goin'. Let's head out, and I'll explain on the way."

We all jogged out, and while Travis and Warden jumped into Travis's Hummer, I went to the back of it where Blue, Stoke, Killer, and Pick pulled up on their Harleys.

"What's happenin'?" Blue asked.

I ignored him and looked at Pick. "Why haven't you spoken to Warden about an inside watch at that jackass's place in Geelong?"

"I had, Griz. I swear I had. Fuck, is he saying something else? I went straight to him that day I left the meetin' and told him what we're after. He said he'd get on it. I thought he had. Hell, I haven't done anything. I swear."

"All right, calm the fuck down." I shook my head. I could understand the panic in his eyes. He knew if he betrayed us in any way, he'd be a dead man. "Looks like Ryan wanted payback after all. That's where the women are being taken."

"Pick, you know the way?" Stoke asked.

"Yeah, yeah, I know it."

"Okay, you lead the way. Park a street away; we'll go on foot from there. You boys know the drill."

"Yeah, course, brother," Blue said. "Should we say anything to Talon?"

"No. He's gonna be busy and worried enough with Wildcat givin' birth."

"She is?" Blue grinned. "Right on."

I turned to walk off and get in the car with a no doubt impatient Warden and Travis.

"Griz," Pick called.

"What?" I prompted over my shoulder.

"Find out why Warden hasn't done the job. Please. It wasn't me stuffin' up, brother. I swear."

I shifted to look at him and gave him a chin lift.

"Rest easy, brother," Killer said to Pick.

Yeah, we all knew Pick wasn't dumb enough to try anything behind our backs. He was back in the fold of the tight arms of the brotherhood.

CHAPTER TWENTY-NINE

DEANNA

"I'D OVERHEARD Griz saying he was with me only because he needed a replacement-mum for Swan."

She snorted. "And you believed that?"

"At the time, yeah. It had hurt, but then the more I thought about it, the more I realised he was probably just talkin' shit in front of his biker buddy."

"That would be more like it."

"I know, but fuck, that still stung. I mean, why in the fuck would he want me—the dirty-talkin' sailor—around his daughter."

"Um, duh. Jesus, Barbie, everyone knows your bark is bigger than your bite. Underneath all that, you're just a big softy."

"Do you want me to fuck you up?"

Vi rolled her eyes. "Whatever. It's the reason I put up with your hating attitude toward me. I know deep down you really care for me."

I coughed out, "Bullshit."

"Again, whatever." She smirked. I covered my mouth to hide my own smile.

"I guess you're not too bad," I said.

"See, all we needed was a bonding moment by getting kidnapped together for us to speak civilly to each other." She grinned.

"I still hate you though."

She laughed. "Oh, the feeling is mutual."

"Okay, enough of this gooey shit. What's the chop with you and Travis?" I asked, moving into a position of crossing my legs and leaning back on my palms.

She stretched her neck and back, and then started with, "At first, I thought I could be with him, but after one night, when we were out in Melbourne, two of his whores spotted him, and when they came over for a friendly chat I decided I couldn't deal with his business."

"Why?" I asked.

"He'd been sleeping with them, not when he was with me, but before. Still, the hookers made sure I knew about it. He saw how uncomfortable I was, but did nothing about it. Instead, he continued laughing and flirting with them."

"Damn. What an arse," I said with disgust.

She nodded and looked to her hands in her lap. "That night, when we got back to his house in Melbourne, I left while he was in the shower."

"So how'd it get to where it's at now?"

She smiled to herself. "He became a pain in my arse. He rang, sent flowers, emailed and popped into places I was at—even when I was out on a date with Jim Binton. Do you know him?"

"No." I shook my head.

"He's a cop, and a good one, but just not a great guy to date. Anyway, we were at a restaurant talking and eating, and then in walked Travis. With a glare, he stalked right up to our table, pulled up a chair and sat down."

A laugh escaped me. "What happened next?"

She grinned and then snickered. "Jim asked him if he was all right. Travis ignored him, grabbed my hand, which I tried to pull away, and then proceeded to tell me everything he loved about me. How he couldn't see his life without me in it and now that I was back in it after so many years apart, he was not willing to lose me again. He said he would do anything to keep me in his life, and then continued to inform me, in front of a cop, he no longer dealt with hookers. He'd passed his women on to another he trusted."

"Holy shit. What'd the cop say?"

"At first, he was shocked, but then he actually laughed. He stood from the table and wished me good luck with my future and said he could not compete with him. He threatened Travis that he would be keeping an eye on him and his dealings. Also...." she laughed. "He asked Travis if he'd be willing to tell him who was now in charge of his women in Melbourne. Of course, Travis didn't."

"He's lucky he didn't get his arse taken to the station for questioning."

"I think he didn't because of me. Jim had a soft spot for me, and apparently, from what he told me when he rang the next day, he could see the way I felt for Travis from the look upon my face, and there was no way he could crash my hope in the form of any legal proceedings."

"Damn." I smiled. "And I guess from then on out you two have been attached at the waist."

"You could say that, but I'm not stupid; I've kept a close eye on him, and he's kept his word. He's now just the owner of his construction company, and the women are a thing of his past."

The van came to an abrupt stop, only to start off again. I quickly gripped the side rail, as did Vi on the opposite side. They turned sharply, the van's tires squealing on the concrete road.

"What the fuck?" one of the guys yelled the front of the van.

"Who in the fuck are they?"

Violet and I looked at each other and smiled.

The guys had come.

That was when we heard the sound of Harleys in the distance, but coming up fast.

"Shit, Christ. We got bikers coming up," Nathan yelled.

"I'll fuckin' worry about them after I lose that damn car first," Kenny barked. "What should I do? What in the hell should I do? Boss will kill us if we bring this to his doorstep." His tone grew louder with worry.

"Fuck!" Nathan screamed.

"Either way, we're gonna end up dead," Kenny yelled the obvious.

"Slam on the brakes," Nathan spat out.

"What?"

"Hit the brakes. NOW!"

I gripped harder just as Kenny pushed his foot down on the brakes. My body twisted around with the force and I wasn't able to hold on; if I had, I would have broken my wrist. I let go and went flying to the front of the van. My head collided with the back shelf.

"Deanna? Barbie, are you okay?"

I sat up slowly, my head spinning as the car came to a stop. "Was that concern in your voice, bitch?" I asked.

Violet sighed and then laughed. "Well, damn. I guess it was."

"I'm okay. It'll just be a bruise."

"Get the fuck out," we heard a gruff and hard voice order. I pulled my aching head up to meet Vi's eyes.

"Griz," I uttered. She smiled and nodded.

Harleys came to a stop wherever we were. My heart beat with excitement from having a chance to see my man in hero-mode.

"Move it slowly, and hand the keys over," Griz growled. "Blue, hit the doors, brother."

The back doors were unlocked and then pulled open; both Vi and I blinked until our eyes got used to the shining sun.

"Is she okay?" Griz asked.

Blue looked in and smiled widely. "Hello, sweetnesses." He then yelled around the van, "Looking good as always, brother."

"Fuckin' lucky," Griz clipped.

"Violet?" Travis yelled.

"I'm fine," she called back.

And we were. We were fine now that our men were there, even though we could have kicked some arse ourselves.

"You ladies had better get your sweet booties out of there for your men to see for themselves before a bloodbath hits the streets," Blue suggested.

Vi and I shared a secret smile between the two of us before making our way to our guys.

CHAPTER THIRTY

GRIZ

WARDEN HAD JUST EXPLAINED from the back seat that he had been meaning to set cameras up in both Ryan and Maxwell's place, only the business had been so busy he'd been caught up in other situations. After cursing for five minutes, he said whenever we needed something again, it would be a top priority. He didn't want the same mistake to happen again.

I agreed and turned around to face the front. Pick was up ahead, and my other brothers were a few car spots behind us. I was surprised the cops weren't after our arses; Travis was driving like a maniac—it was fuckin' great.

"Take the next left," Warden yelled after lookin' down at his tracking system.

"What? Why? Pick's going that way," he growled back.

"They've turned off. Turn, motherfucker, turn."

"Shit, hold the fuck on," Travis yelled. I gripped the seat and dashboard and saw before we spun around the corner that Pick had hit his breaks.

"With your driving, we've nearly caught them," Warden said. He looked down and then up again; his hand pointed out the front windscreen. "There, that damn van. It's got the women."

A couple of cars up the road and across a lane was a black Holden van with no number plates. For some reason, it must have spotted us; it's speed picked up.

"We ready to catch them?" Travis asked.

I pulled my .44 auto-mag pistol from its holster under my club vest. "Let's do this. They're turning. They're turning!" I yelled.

"I can fucking see that," Travis bit out. He took the next lane, cutting off a car who laid on its horn, and then we were around the corner in seconds. "Bloody idiots." He smiled. I looked up from my gun and out the front to see the van parked at a dead end street.

We all jumped outta the car when Warden said, "Nothing around but empty industrial warehouses." He grinned.

I stalked around the front of the van with my gun pointed directly through their window and at their heads. "Get the fuck out."

The rest of our little army came around the corner on their bikes; they stopped and were surrounding the men in a matter of seconds, all with their own guns out.

"Move it slowly, and hand the keys over," I growled. The one who had driven held the keys high. "Blue, hit the doors, brother," I ordered. Blue grabbed the keys and ran to the back of the van.

"Is she okay?" I asked.

Blue yelled around the van. "Looking good as always, brother."

"Fuckin' lucky," I hissed at the fuckheads.

"Violet?" Travis yelled.

"I'm fine," she called back.

As Travis, Stoke, Pick and I each held a gun on the two fuckers as they knelt on the ground, Killer patted them down and threw their phones, knives, and handguns aside. I waited patiently—even if I wanted to get trigger-happy—until I could get my eyes on my woman.

My head rose as I heard movement behind the van, and then Deanna and Violet walked around the corner of it. "Fuck!" I snapped. My woman had a bruise shining on her cheek and a red bump on her forehead. What did they fuckin' do?

Stepping forward, I kicked the one who had driven in the stomach; he bent over coughing. "Who laid their hands on my woman?" I snarled down at them.

"Griz," Deanna called. I looked up, and she was in my arms. I stepped back with my arms around her waist, and she wound hers around my neck. "Fuck, woman. Fuck," I whispered.

"I'm okay. I'm fine," she uttered. She said she was okay, but I could feel her body shaking.

I pulled back, placed my hands on each side of her face and searched her eyes. "Who touched you, darlin'?" I asked.

"Wait," the guy who was still kneeling—in other words, the one who I hadn't kicked—pleaded. He went to get up, but Killer was behind him, and with a hard hand, he thrust him back to the road. "Wait," he said again. "We were just doing a job. I hardly know the guy."

I shifted Deanna behind me and said, "Then which of you was it who laid a finger on my woman? Was that in the goddamn job description?"

"It wasn't me."

"Well, fuck," the guy who was still trying to breathe got back up to his knees, "Yeah, it was me. What you gonna do about it?"

Fool.

My brothers laughed behind him. Out the corner of my eye, I saw Violet step away from Travis, and Warden then walked up beside me.

"When Deanna tried to fight back—"

"Violet, no," Dee gasped behind us.

Vi turned to her. "They'd find out anyway. In this world, Deanna, in our world with *our* men, we have to do what we have to, and that's standing by them and telling them everything they need to know."

I watched my woman close her eyes and nod. Violet looked up at me and said, "He was going to ask his boss for her. He wanted to rape her and kill her."

"Shit," Blue clipped.

"Fuckin' A," Stoke said.

"Dead man breathing." Killer grinned, and right there was the reason he was called Killer. He loved to be the one to do it, but this one was on me.

I looked down at Violet. She took a step back from the hatred in my eyes. "What about the other one?" I asked.

"I think he was just hired help. He was... nicer, gentler."

With a chin lift, I stomped back to Deanna. "Darlin'...."

"What are you going to do?" she asked.

"What I have to. No one touches what's mine; no one lays a harmful hand on my woman and still lives." I told it to her straight; now it was up to her to choose to still be with a man like me... or not. If she chose she couldn't, I'd understand; it would fuckin' kill me, but I'd understand, because I had blood on my hands from my past, and I was sure in my near future.

She studied my face and saw the truth of my words. I expected her to flinch and turn away in disgust. What I hadn't expected was her to nod and say, "You do what you have to, whatever you deem necessary."

Fuck.

I stepped close to her, and I carefully placed my hand under her chin to bring her face up as I leaned down. "You are my woman."

She grinned. "I know, and you're my man... but I can't be here for this."

"I know, and I would never expect it." My gaze explored hers and I saw it. Fuck, did I see it. "You know I love you right? And I'd only do good by you."

Tears shone in her eyes. I knew now wasn't the time to confess my feelings—with an audience and with what I was about to do—but I couldn't hold it back. I couldn't *not* tell her.

She nodded and gave me a sweet, soft kiss. I pulled back and turned. "Pick, you need to leave your bike and take the women to the hospital."

"I don't need to go," Deanna said as she came up to my side and placed her arms around my waist. I moved to fit her as close as I could get her next to me with my arm around her shoulders.

"Just get it checked, and besides… Wildcat's waiting for you. She's popping out her kids."

"What? Shit, fuck. I need to go. She'll need me there. Pick, get your arse in that car. You too, Violet," my woman ordered. She nearly tore my head off as she pulled my head down, kissed me hard and said, "See you there?"

"Yeah, darlin'." I laughed. "We won't be long."

"Travis?" Violet called from the car.

"I'll meet you there," he said. She looked concerned, but nodded, and got in the car.

I was ready to complete the next stage of my plan.

CHAPTER THIRTY-ONE

DEANNA

Pick got us to the hospital in under an hour. It could have had something to do with the amount of abuse spilled from my mouth if he didn't get us there on time.

I just hoped like fuck Zara held those little monsters in until I arrived.

He dropped Vi and me off at the door and went off to park the car. We raced in and straight up to the elevators. It seemed to take forever for one to arrive on the ground floor. People who stood with us waiting, backed up a bit as I swore and cursed the slow-moving machine.

On the fifth floor, we spotted the birthing suite and saw Zara's parents waiting out the front with Josie, Mattie, Julian and the kids.

Swan popped up from the seat; as soon as our eyes met, she ran at me. I got down on one knee and braced for her lunge. Her arms wound around my neck, and she hugged me as tightly as I was her.

Tears filled my eyes. I had been so worried I'd never get to see her again.

She pulled back and touched my cheek. "Sore, Mummy."

Oh, fuck.

Oh, shit.

Goosebumps broke out all over my skin. I had heard her right, hadn't I? She'd called *me* mummy.

"It's okay, sweetheart. I'm okay," I said through a choked-up voice and tears.

She smiled and kissed my cheek gently. Nancy came up behind Swan, and I looked up at her. She had her own tears shining in her eyes. "You'd better get in there, honey. She's been waiting for you."

Nodding, I looked back at Swan, and said, "I'll be back out soon, okay? You stay with Nancy."

"Okay, Mummy."

Hell. That precious girl had just made my shit day so much better and brighter. Now all I needed was to have my man at my side.

God, I hoped he was okay.

As I stood, Mattie and Julian came up. "Are you good, sugarplum?" Julian asked.

"I am now." I smiled, bent over and kissed Swan on her forehead.

I walked through the doors to the front desk and asked for Zara's room. A male nurse smiled and said, "Follow me." We started off down a hallway. "You must be Deanna. She's been screaming at her husband to get you here."

I laughed. "Yeah, that's me."

He pointed. "Right in there, and good luck." He grinned as a scream came from the room I was about to enter.

"Huh, thanks." I stepped forward, took a deep breath and pushed the door open.

"I swear, Talon, I swear you're having your balls removed. I am not doing this again."

"We'll see, Kitten."

Zara was bent over the double bed, the side of her face planted into the mattress, as Talon stood to the edge of her and rubbed her lower back. Another nurse, this one female and young, stood on the other side of Zara, holding a tube that was hooked up to a machine.

Talon saw me first and smiled, only it faded as he took in the bruise on my cheek and the bump on my forehead. "What the fuck happened to you?" he growled.

I shook my head and mouthed, *I'll tell you later*. I was here for Zara, not anything else.

"What the hell do you mean? You knocked me up, dickhead!" Zara yelled.

I laughed; her head popped up and met my gaze. "That's right, bitch. It's all your boss man's fault."

"Deanna," she breathed. Tears overflowed from her eyes and she sniffed. "I thought you wouldn't make it," she whispered, wiped her eyes to clear the tears and glared at me. "Where have you been, wench? W-what happened to your face?"

I moved forward to lie on the bed and get close to her face. "I'll tell you all about it after you've laid your damn eggs."

"De—oh shit! Give me that machine!" she screamed, and snatched the tube from the nurse, placed it in her mouth and breathed through it over and over through her contraction.

After it passed, she threw it to the side. "Oh, man, I love that stuff." She laughed and looked at me. "You know when we got stoned that time, that," she pointed at the machine, "gives me a wicked buzz. Is my voice funny? It sounds funny."

I rolled my eyes. "No, dipshit, your voice isn't funny. Maybe Talon and I should try some of that stuff?"

"Don't you dare," she growled. "I'm still mad at the both of you—him for impregnating me, and you for being late. So you can suffer through this."

The nurse moved, put gloves on and her hand disappeared under Zara's pink nightie.

"What are you doing?" I yelled. "Don't put your hand up there

LILA ROSE

when the monsters are trying to come out. Jesus." Thank fuck I
missed all this shit and waited in the waiting room when she had
Maya. No wonder my brain told me I'd be scared to watch this
shit stuff.

"Calm down, Hell Mouth. She's just checking how far dilated she
is," Talon said.

"Whatever that means. Hey, Zara?"

"What, hun?" She sounded so tired. I glanced up at Talon to see
he had worry in his eyes.

"At least you can say you've had a lesbian experience now."

She chuckled and said, "Fuck you. Oh, oh. Tube me, tube me!"
she yelled. I quickly passed her the sucky thingy. She latched onto it
like it was Talon's dick and sucked hard.

"Not long now," the nurse said after Zara's pain had passed.
"When the next contraction hits, try pushing, okay, Zara?"

"No. You try," she hissed.

Talon leaned over her and whispered, "Come on, Kitten. You can
do this."

"Yeah, bitch, show me how tough you are," I added.

"I'm not. I'm tired, Deanna. So tired."

Talon and I looked at each other. Both of us, I knew, were
wishing we could help her more through this, but we couldn't.

"You wanna lay on the bed?" I asked.

She nodded. I moved outta the way as Talon scooped her up into
his arms and laid her down.

I lay next to her on the bed, and Talon knelt beside it on her
other side. We both took a hand of hers each.

"You know I love you, wench, but there is no way I'm getting
down the other end and lookin' at your hoo-ha."

She smiled and closed her eyes, only to open them seconds later
when the contraction hit.

"Push, Kitten. Push, baby, please."

Her hand gripped ours tighter, and she screamed, "I am pushing, you motherfucker." And she was; she bore down and pushed so hard, I was surprised her eyes didn't pop outta her head.

Just as I was thinkin' there was no way in fuckin' hell I was ever going to go through this, a cry hit the room.

"We have a boy." The nurse smiled and passed him off to another nurse I hadn't seen enter the room.

"A boy! A fuckin' boy, Kitten." Talon grinned and followed the nurse who held his son. "Be careful with him. Fuck, woman, are you supposed to do that? You fuck him up, I'll hurt you."

"Talon." Zara smiled tiredly. "Let them work."

"Just take a breather, and then we'll do it all again on the next contraction," the nurse next to us said.

"Is he okay?" Zara asked.

"He's a fuckin' champ. Big and loud, baby," Talon said as he knelt back down next to his wife. He certainly was loud—the kid hadn't shut up—but then again, I'd be upset coming into a cold world after living in a warm squishy waterbed too.

"Talon," Zara cried as another pain hit.

"Kitten, baby, push again and we'll get to meet our other youngin'."

She nodded and bore down once again, ending in a scream that a smaller, quieter one replied to.

"It's a girl," the nurse said before she turned to take her over to a table.

"Kitten, fuck, I am so proud of you. So fuckin' proud," Talon whispered into Zara's hair. He pulled back, and that was when I saw the tears in my boo's man's eyes.

"I love you, Talon Marcus," Zara muttered.

"I love you more than my life," he said and kissed her softly on the lips.

"Good. Now check they aren't swapping our kids over. And quit all the cursing…they can hear you now," she ordered.

Talon laughed and replied, "I'm on it." He moved from the bed and went to check his twins.

Zara turned her head to me. "I love you too, wench."

I bit my lip and nodded as tears filled my eyes. "You saved me, Zara. I would have been lost without you. But you saved me, and I'm so happy you let me be here for this miracle. I love you too, bitch."

CHAPTER THIRTY-TWO

GRIZ

AFTER THE WOMEN HAD LEFT, we collected the sweating men—who were now shittin' themselves—back into the front seat of the van. As Killer held a gun on them, Blue and Stoke moved the bikes to the side of the road. Travis, Warden and I climbed in the back of the van, and once we were in position with the divider open and a gun on the two up the front, Killer came around and got in with Blue and Stoke.

"I'm sure by now you can guess what the plan is," I said, "but in case you're dumb fucks and haven't—which you must be to take the women in the first place—you're taking us to Ryan's. Now start driving." The one named Kenny started the van, did a U-turn and started off.

"How far are we from the destination?" Travis asked.

The one in the passenger seat, Nathan I think, replied, "About ten minutes."

"How many men has Ryan got at the house?" Warden asked.

"Not many, about five," Nathan said.

"You need to shut the fuck up," Kenny growled.

I hit him in the back of the head. "No, dickhead, you need to."

"You know what?" Blue started. I looked over my shoulder to see him leaning against the back of the van, but I knew once the time came, he'd be more alert and ready for the fight that was about to come. I gave him a chin lift to continue, and he did. "I reckon Trav and Warden would make great brothers. We should swear them in."

I looked at Travis beside me, and then to Warden, who was holding onto the safety bar just behind Travis.

"I'm happy where I am," Warden said. "I got enough shit goin' on workin' with Vi. No offense, but being in a biker group ain't my thing."

"None taken, but I'm sure the offer is still there, even when we tell Talon," I said. "What about you?" I asked Travis. He'd be a good asset; he's got sources in Melbourne. It was obvious he'd do anything to protect what was his, and he didn't crack under pressure.

"I'd have to talk to Violet about it," he said with an amused smile.

I chuckled, as did my brothers. We got that; Violet was another hard, ball-busting woman.

"We're nearly there," Nathan said.

"Fuckin' nark," Kenny hissed.

I hit him in the head again, making him swear.

Blue got up on his knees with his hand on the backdoors, ready to pop them open. Killer and Stoke were beside him, which left Warden, Travis and me to get out the side door.

The calm atmosphere in the van intensified into a harsher anxious one. Everyone was ready.

Duckin' my head down a bit, we pulled into a drive. Kenny went to stop there, but I ordered him to take it into the garage that was already open. Ryan's huge motherfuckin' house was in the suburbs; we couldn't risk an audience. We needed to take the fight inside.

With a hard shove on the back of Kenny's head from my gun, he finally did as I told him, and slowly drove the van into the garage. As soon as we were through, the automatic door behind us closed.

I smiled. Ryan obviously didn't want an audience either, seeing how he still thought he was kidnappin' my woman. It was pure fuckin' luck we caught them before they arrived here because it had worked out beautifully for us.

A door in front of the van opened, and Ryan outlined the lit opening.

"What the hell are you waiting for?" he yelled.

Just as I turned to give the go-ahead to the boys up the back, dickhead Kenny screamed, "Watch out!"

It all went into chaos. My brothers jumped out the back as I knocked Kenny out with the end of my gun. Warden opened the side door, got out with his weapon raised and pointed it at Ryan. He moved aside to let Travis and myself out, and I stepped up to Ryan and smiled. His eyes widened comically.

"It was the wrong move trying to take my woman, arsehole."

A shot at the front of the garage fired off. "We've got incoming," Blue called.

"They're coming in the side door, Griz," Travis said.

More shots got fired. Travis ran to the back to help out while Warden and I eyed Ryan. For some reason, he wasn't running.

He moved aside, and a few more men ran in shooting at whatever moved. I shifted back into the van, as did Warden.

"What do you want to do?" Warden asked.

"I want my hands on that motherfucker," I growled. The noise in the garage grew louder from guns, fists, and voices.

"Go get him then." Warden grinned. He silently moved out of the side door of the van once again and crept to the front, where the men with guns were now standing. Warden shot and one fell; the next turned and fired on Warden, but I dove from the side of the van, fired off a shot and clipped him. Warden ran and tackled the guy to the ground as Blue came up from the other side of the garage and took down one more.

I ran for the door and went straight through. A loud clutter came from the left, so I went that way, following the wall down the hall closely, so if anything came around the corner, they wouldn't see me first before I killed them.

As I crept closer to the entryway to what looked like a living room, another loud clatter sounded, accompanied by swearing.

"Fuck, where in the hell are my keys?" Ryan cried.

I turned the corner with my gun held high and asked, "Missing something?" He was over near a black leather couch, a cushion still in his hand.

"Griz, come on. Let's forget this. You don't owe me money any longer, and I promise I won't go after your woman."

I laughed. "Too late for that—your guy already touched her in a way I didn't like. She'll have a bruise from it for a couple of days, which means she'll remember what happened for a couple of days, and I don't like that."

"What do you want? You want money? People? I can find anyone who has done you wrong and have them gone."

"Jesus, you are stupid. I want nothing from you; I take care of my own business. No one who has crossed me or mine has lived to see another day."

"What about Maxwell?"

"Don't worry about him; he's on my list." I glared. "Get on your knees," I snarled. He was pathetic, trying to bargain his way out of the inevitable.

He took a step back, his hand raised in front of him, and he looked down as a wet patch filled the front of his slacks. "Griz," he squeaked. "I-I'm sure we can work something out."

I shook my head at the sight in front of me. It was all the same. As soon as the shoe was on the other foot, their tough exterior faded and left a weak, useless one behind.

I scoffed, "Nothin' to work out."

"I'm sure we can figure something out." A gun got shoved into my back. I looked over my shoulder to see Kenny standing there.

Well, shit. I should have just shot the dick.

"Not today," another voice said; this time, it was behind Kenny, who in turn let out a grunted groan and fell to his knees, his gun dropping to the ground beside him.

Nathan stepped up with a knife in his hand. "He's getting away." He gestured with his chin to Ryan, who was looking frantic as he neared the front door.

I sighed, aimed and shot. Ryan fell onto his back to the wooden flooring, just out of reach of the front door.

"Because you had my back, you go. Now, before my brothers catch you," I said to Nathan as I started my way over to a moaning Ryan.

"Thanks," he said and moved off to where, I guessed, the kitchen and back door was.

"Don't thank me; you haven't made it yet."

I stopped and looked down at Ryan. The fucker was crying as he held his stomach.

His eyes widened as I raised my gun once again and shot him in-between his eyes.

"Griz, brother, we gotta go," Blue called from the other side of the living room.

I looked up to see him with a bleeding nose and a busted-up lip. Running forward, I asked, "Everyone all right?"

With grim eyes, he shook his head.

Fuck.

Shit.

"Who?"

"Stoke. We gotta get him to a hospital. He was shot in the gut and he's bleeding out pretty bad. I think it hit something vital."

"Goddamn it," I uttered. We hit the garage just as Killer and a limping Warden were loading Stoke into the back of the van.

After Travis climbed in the driver's seat, Blue hopped in the passenger one and I ran around to the back to get in.

Warden closed the door behind me. I made my way to Stoke's side; Killer was on the other, holding a folded up towel over Stoke's wound.

The garage doors opened and we took off. Both Killer and I supported Stoke, trying to keep him as still as we could as Warden watched from the backdoors of the van.

"Brother," I said, taking his hand in mine. "Dammit, Stoke, dammit."

"S-s'all good, Grady. You know I'd do it over again if I had the chance. Always at your back, brother. Alwa—"

"Stoke. Shit, brother?"

Killer crouched over him. "He's only passed out, but his heart is slowin'."

"Fuck! Travis, drive like you did before; get us to a hospital."

CHAPTER THIRTY-THREE

DEANNA

I LEFT the happy couple to head back out the front where everyone else was waiting. Talon wanted me to announce the monsters' arrival while he helped Zara get cleaned up; they wanted to bond with the twins over breastfeeding.

Opening the doors, eight pairs of eyes were instantly latched onto me.

"We have a boy and a girl." I smiled. Clapping filled the space along with wild cheers. I searched further to see if my man was there, but he wasn't. My shoulders slumped in sadness. I would've loved to have shared this moment with him. Worry took over my body. *Was he okay? Was he hurt? Where in the fuck was he?*

I pushed it all back and slapped on my happy face. A nurse stepped out behind me and said, "Only a few visitors for now, but they're asking for their children, Zara's parents and his sister to come in."

A tired Violet, Richard, Nancy and Cody, who took Maya's hand, walked past me as Josie and Swan came to stand in front of me. I smiled and asked, "Are you guys excited to meet..." *Crap, I didn't even know the names of the brats yet.* "...the bundles of joy?"

"Yes, very." Josie grinned behind her hand; she was often doing things like that. If she laughed, she covered her mouth, but if she forgot to at the time, she'd duck her head at the end and blush. I could only hope one day her self-esteem issues would evaporate.

"W-when?" Swan asked.

I looked over my shoulder to the doors. "I'm sure you can soon, baby. Besides, they have to announce their names." I glanced over to Julian and Mattie, who were sitting in the waiting chairs hugging. "Do you guys know what they're gonna name them?" I asked.

They looked at each other and then shook their heads.

"No," Mattie said. "It's all been very tight-lipped."

A half-hour had passed when the doors finally opened again; Violet and Zara's parents walked out with the kids, happy tears shining in their eyes.

"She wants all of you in there." Nancy smiled. "They're absolutely beautiful; I could just eat them up."

Violet walked up to me and whispered, "I'm going to catch a taxi, head home to shower and come back with Travis. I'm leaving his car here in case you need it to get Swan home."

"You're being nice again," I stated.

"I know, and believe me—I'll throw up for it later." She smiled. I smirked at her and shook my head.

I understood her need for a shower; I really wanted one too, but I'd wait. So with a thanks and a nod from me, she took off after a goodbye to everyone else.

"We're taking the kids to the cafeteria to get something to eat. Do any of you want anything?" Richard asked.

With a no from everybody, they made their way to the elevators, and Mattie, Julian, Swan, Josie and I went back into Zara's room.

She was sitting up in her bed, and even though she looked beat, she was obviously happy. I could see it in her shining eyes and the smile that played on her mouth.

I stood back with Swan, holding her hand as Julian, Mattie and Josie all gushed over the twins being held by their mum and a very happy dad.

After they stepped back, I moved forward and sat Swan on the bed beside Zara.

"Hey there, sweetie," Zara said to Swan. "Do you like the babies?"

Swan nodded, and then her head turned on its side as she asked, "Names?"

Talon cleared his throat and was about to say something when the door to the room opened and in walked Grady. My hand went to my neck as I took him in. He was in one piece, but he had a grim look upon his face, though it quickly changed once he saw Swan and me.

Swan jumped down from the bed and ran for her father, yelling, "Daddy!"

He scooped her up in his arms and held her tightly, and then one arm came out as he eyed me. I went straight for it. I wrapped my arms around both of them, burying my head into Grady's neck.

"You okay?" I uttered.

"S'all good, darlin'. We'll talk soon."

I nodded and moved back so I could reach up and peck him on the lips.

"Will you two stop groping in front of your child? Let's hear the announcement of the names, and then we can take Swan down to the cafeteria too," Julian said.

Grady had a silent conversation with Talon through nods and chin lifts. I would never begin to understand how that worked.

"All right," Talon started, "we've been going over some names for a while, but we've finally decided, and even if you hate them, we won't give a fuck. For our son," he lifted his arms cradling the sleeping boy, "it's Drake." His eyes held mine as stupid, ugly tears filled my own eyes. Holy shit, why would they do that?

"Hun, we wanted to pass on the Drake name in some form. I knew how much they meant to you and how much you mean to me.

From what you've told us, they were amazing people who deserved to have their name preserved, so that's why we chose it."

I could only nod. If I opened my mouth, I was likely to cry.

"And for our beautiful girl, her name is Ruby," Talon said and smiled. "Maya and Cody helped with that one. We were sure damned surprised that they actually kept it to themselves." He chuckled.

"They're really nice," Josie commented.

"They're great," Mattie said.

"I love them!" Julian clapped. "Right, now come on, sweet pea," he said to Swan and took her from Grady's arms. "Let's go get some food."

Mattie gently grabbed Josie's hand, who I saw flinch, but he ignored it and started for the door. "We'll be back soon," he said, and then left with the rest.

As soon as the door closed, Talon growled, "Now, you wanna tell us what in the fuck is going on?"

"It's been handled, so you don't need to worry about it right now."

"I don't give a shit if it's handled. Explain, brother."

I stepped out of Grady's arms and went over to sit on the edge of the bed. Grady came up behind me and rested his hands on my shoulders, and I leaned back into him to absorb his warmth.

"Violet was at my house—"

Zara gasped. "Is she still alive?"

With an eye roll, I said, "Very funny, wench, and yes, you just saw she was. She came to tell me Jason got released early."

"You didn't tell me this," Grady snapped.

"Well, I didn't actually have time now, did I?"

"Griz," Talon said. I lifted my head to see yet another fucking silent conversation was going on. I was sure this one said in their caveman ways, *She'll need more protection,* with a response of, *I'm on it. Ugg, ugg, grunt, fart, and groan.*

"Anyway," I said, "we went into the house, and two men were there waiting and took us." Zara gasped once again. "It's all good, as you can see. Violet had a tracking device; the guys found us and we came here."

"Then who put that fuckin' bruise and bump on your head?" Talon asked.

Grady grunted, "One of the guys."

"Where is he now? And who in the hell would take Hawks' property?"

"He's dead. It was Ryan's smart idea to try and get money out of me."

"Tell me he failed," Zara asked. Holy shit. Did she mean what I thought she meant?

Grady nodded. "He's also dead."

"Good," she said, and then glanced at me. "Oh, don't look so shocked. Being around him," she gestured to Talon, "for so long, I learn what's good for our family and what's not. I don't like most of it, but if it's to protect what's ours, then it has to be done."

"I agree," I said, and I did.

"There was one problem though; Stoke's being operated on as we speak."

"Fuck. What happened?" Talon asked.

"Bullet to the stomach. It must have hit something vital."

"The bastard better pull through," Talon uttered.

"I'm sure he will," Zara said and placed her hand on Talon's, which was holding Drake's. He met her worried gaze and nodded.

"We better head off, brother," Grady said. "I'm sure you're both tired."

"Pfft. He's not the one who gave birth to two watermelons. Both kids had huge heads... must have their father's ego." She always liked to lighten the mood, and it worked.

Talon grinned at his wife and then turned to Grady and me. "Thanks for coming, Griz. And you too, Hell Mouth."

"Always a pleasure when I'm around." I grinned and then sobered. "We'll keep you updated with Stoke." I looked to Grady for confirmation, and he nodded.

We said our final goodbyes and then made our way to the cafeteria.

CHAPTER THIRTY-FOUR

GRIZ

NANCY SAW how exhausted both Deanna and I were—mentally and physically—so she offered to mind Swan for the night, and Swan was more than happy to go with her.

I had Pick drive us home in Travis's car; everyone else wanted to stay a little longer, so Pick was gonna head back after dropping Dee and me home.

Even though it felt fuckin' weird, I got in the back with Deanna and brought her close to me, leaving Pick up front alone like some damned driver of the rich and famous.

"Have you heard any more about Stoke?" Pick asked.

"Nah, not yet. I'm sure Killer will ring as soon as he knows."

"Do you want to head back there? After Pick drops us off, we can take my car," Deanna offered.

"Darlin', it's so fuckin' sweet of you to ask, but not tonight. Ask me again in the mornin'." What I wanted and needed the most was to lay down between the sheets and in-between my woman's legs. I needed to feel she was there, safe and in our house.

It made me feel like an arse about Stoke, but I was sure he

would've done the same. There was nothing I could do for him at the hospital. If and when we heard the outcome, we would deal then. We would take care of him one way or another. If I knew how to fuckin' operate on a body, there would be no way I'd be in the back of this car, but I didn't, so as I said, there was nothing I could do for Stoke right then.

The car pulled to a slow stop out the front of our house. I gave a chin lift and thanked Pick as we got out, and with dragging feet, we made our way up the walk.

"Griz?" Pick called.

"Be back in a sec, princess," I sighed to Deanna. She smiled, gave me a quick kiss and moved off to the front door.

I turned around and was walking back to the car, when I saw something shining in the living room window—something that shouldn't have been there, something I had never seen before.

Ignoring Pick, I started to make my way back to Deanna just as she was unlocking the door. She opened it and took a step inside. I watched as her body startled. She looked back outside to me with tears in her eyes, shook her head and closed the door in my face.

Fuck, fuck, fuck.

He was in there. Jason Drake was in the house with my woman. Alone.

No matter how much I wanted to bust down the door, I didn't. I couldn't, because there was no telling what kind of situation Deanna was in.

I stepped back, and the curtain twitched. He was watching, waiting for me to make a move. Did he know I was aware he was in there? I wasn't sure.

"Fine, bitch, be that way," I yelled.

Christ, I hoped to hell he bought this shit acting.

"I'll be back in the morning for my stuff," I called. It damn near burned me inside to turn back around and walk back down the path to the still-waiting car I climbed into.

"Trouble?" Pick asked.

"He's in there," I hissed. "Drive around the corner and park. We're going in through the backyard on foot."

"Who's in there, Griz?" he asked.

"Her foster brother, the man who killed his own parents and is about to harm my woman. Fuck!" I yelled.

"We need back-up?" he asked as he put the car in park and I jumped out.

Pick was around the car in seconds, and I replied, "No. Too late. We're doin' this...unless you don't want to?"

"I'm there, brother." He nodded.

"Right. Let's kick it."

Adrenaline pumped through me. Even though I was dead on my feet, the need to save my woman overran my body and pushed any other feelings or thoughts out. Pick and I jumped over four backyard fences and finally reached the small, familiar yard that belonged to Dee. The back deck was dark, as was the house, except for one light in the living room. I was used to the house, so I knew what I was looking at coming from the kitchen window—the lamp that sat next to the couch in the front room was on.

I signalled for Pick to keep his eyes and ears open; he gave a swift nod and went around the side of the house. I crept to the back door with my keys in my hand. My grip was on the handle when I heard a scream.

TEN MINUTES EARLIER

DEANNA

Unlocking the front door, I was more than ready for bed; I was ready for my man to take me slow and deep to release some of the stress that had built up as I waited for him to arrive at the hospital.

I stepped through and turned halfway, so I was facing the living room. My eyes hit him straight away. Jason was standing near the window smirking at me.

My heart hit my feet.

Shattered. That was how I felt. Tears filled my eyes because I knew this was the moment I was probably going to die or try my fuckin' hardest not to.

I had people to live for; I just hoped that'd make me strong enough to get through… without bringing anyone else down in the process.

I glanced back outside to see Grady making his way back up the footpath, a stern, worried look held within his eyes. I shook my head and closed the front door in his face, quickly locking it.

"Fine, bitch, be that way," Griz's booming voice rang through the room. "I'll be back in the morning for my stuff."

Jason raised an eyebrow at me. "Smart move, Deanna," he said.

He looked the same as he had eight years ago, with the same dark red hair and light green crazy eyes. He was still tall and thin, but I could tell he must have been working out while in jail. His muscles were more defined now.

Fuck.

Did that mean he was stronger?

"I don't have the money, Jason."

"Don't bullshit me. I know you've tried to spend it, but the amount they would have left you could not be spent in one lifetime. Though, that's not all I want Deanna. You should know this."

I nodded. He wanted my life.

"I just can't understand why you would be so stupid to move to a holiday house *my* parents owned. You made this so easy for me."

"I know."

He studied me where I stood behind the couch.

"Why don't you seem… scared?"

I pretended to think about it. "Honestly, I'm not sure. Maybe it has something to do with the thought it won't be *my* life ending tonight."

Shit, fuck, shit. Please buy the crap I spew.

He laughed and took a step forward. "I highly doubt that. You see, I learned many things while I was in prison."

"I'm sure you did. A time well fuckin' spent for the crime you committed, eh?"

"Oh, you still haven't broken out of that habit. It's ugly, Deanna; you need to control your language." He casually reached over to the chair next to him and ran a finger along it as he smiled. "But then again, I won't have to put up with it much longer."

"Hmm, probably not, because you'll be dead."

He chuckled. "Are you really going to try, Deanna? Or is it that you're stalling? Do you think the man you arrived with will come back and save you? Is that it?"

My eyes widened. He had better damn well not be. I'd have to hurt Grady if he tried anything. This was my fight.

"No," I said. "You heard him."

He crossed his arms over his chest. "Even if he were, it wouldn't bother me. It would just be another person to kill, and I've missed that, Deanna. I've missed slicing my knife through flesh and bone, and the way my victims would cry or hiss their pain. I would love to see what that man would do."

"You won't get the chance, Jason," I growled.

"Maybe, we will see."

"You're a sick bastard you know that? Sick," I yelled, only to jump to the side to miss the knife that whizzed past my head and embed itself into the wall near the hallway to the stairs. With a thump, I landed on the ground with my head just past the couch. I glanced from the knife back up to see Jason grinning.

"Tut-tut, Deanna—language."

"Fuck you," I yelled, and then screamed when another knife was thrown my way. I ducked down and reached under the couch to where the gun I had strapped to the bottom of it waited. I pulled it free and stood.

"You need to stop, J-Jason," I said, and then damned my voice when it shook.

"Deanna, oh dear, sweet Deanna, you see, I don't think I do. You won't pull the trigger."

"I will. I fuckin' will," I yelled and brought my other hand up to help the one holding the gun because it was shaking like shit.

Stupid, cocksucking nerves.

I can do this. I need to do this. It will bring me peace. It has to.

"Deanna?" I looked out the corner of my eye to see Grady with a gun held high, and just like mine, it was pointed directly at Jason.

"What are you doing here?" I hissed through clenched teeth. "Th-this isn't your fight; it's mine."

"No, darlin', it ain't just yours. It's ours. If you want justice for what he's done, *we* will bring it."

Oh, fuck. Shit.

Tears filled my eyes.

"Grady," I sighed.

"Isn't this sweet?" Jason cooed. His eyes landed on Griz. "Move another step toward her and she dies." He pulled a knife from the back of his pants, and with it in his hand, he aimed it at me. "I'm great at hitting my target." He smiled.

"You fuckin' hurt her, I will—"

"What...kill me? I've been dead ever since she came into my life. If I die here tonight, at least I know I'll be taking her with me," he sneered.

"No, you won't," Grady growled. His gaze came to me; I could feel the heat of it on me. "Dee, walk slowly over to me."

"No," I uttered, "I-I have to do this." The damned gun in my hands was shaking so badly, I didn't know if I'd actually hit anything.

"Deanna," Grady said, his tone holding that familiar warning.

"This is great and all, but I'm bored," Jason sighed. He flung the knife just as a boom echoed in the house and a loud crash of glass breaking filled the room, all of it happening in seconds.

I went crashing to the floor when a large form tackled me.

Dazed and confused, I looked up at Grady where he stood above me. If he was there, then who in the fuck was on me?

Blinking, I turned my head to see Pick staring back.

"You all right, Hell Mouth?" he asked. I nodded.

"No time for sleepin', you two. We gotta do a quick clean-up. I'm sure one of your neighbours has called the cops by now, darlin'," Grady said and reached a hand down, and as Pick got off me, I placed my hand in it and he pulled me up to stand.

I looked over to Jason, wondering why he wasn't saying anything, only to find my answer.

"Dammit, Grady, you killed him," I snapped and stomped my foot.

He chuckled, grabbed me and wrapped his arms around me. "There was no way that fucker was going to wreck what we've got."

I gave him an eye roll. "Well, I know that, but you could have let me do it."

"Next time, darlin'. You were just lucky that knife didn't plant in your head." He gestured with his chin. I looked over my shoulder to see a knife in the wall behind where I had been standing.

Fuck me. I could have died if they hadn't been there.

"Thank you," I muttered and glanced to Pick, who was now wrapping a dead Jason up in some plastic. Where he got it from, I didn't know, and I didn't care. "Both of you, thanks."

"It's what families do for each other," Pick said.

"Ain't that right." Grady smiled. I grinned back up at him.

"I love you," I said.

His eyes transformed in front of me; they became hooded and heated. His smile widened into a shit-eatin' grin.

"We choose some funny moments to tell each other."

I laughed. "I know, but I love it—this, you and every moment we have, no matter the situation—as long as we're together."

"Fuck yeah." He squeezed my body. "As long as we're together."

"Now get your sweet arse to helping Pick. I hear some sirens on the way," I told him with a wink.

"Bossy, bitch."

Grinning, I said, "And you love it."

EPILOGUE

ONE MONTH LATER

DEANNA

EXCITEMENT AND NERVES swirled through my body. I felt all girly and shit, wanting to squeal, clap or jump up and down. My man was on his way home, and I had a surprise for him. Two, actually. One, I wasn't sure how he'd react to... okay, I wasn't sure how he'd respond to either of the surprises, which was why I was so fuckin' nervous as well.

Everything had settled down after that night after the cops left believing our story. We told them Grady had been drunk—which he acted out fuckin' superbly—and had fallen through the window, and once they saw he was no threat to me, they left. Pick ended up bringing around Travis's car. They loaded up Jason, and as far as I knew, they found a special place to get rid of the body—a place I was told no one would find. I didn't want to know where exactly, because I didn't care.

I was free.

It was as if a weight had lifted from me. No, it would never help the grief I still felt for the loss of the Drakes, but it did ease it enough I knew my life would now be lighter.

Also that night, Grady had gotten a call waking us in the middle of the night; it had been Killer. Stoke had pulled through his operation and was on his way to mending. Things couldn't be better— well, unless Grady liked his surprises, then things could get even better.

I heard the front door open from where I stood in the kitchen.

"What in the goddamn hell is that?" Grady yelled.

I grinned. He'd found my first surprise.

Heavy footstep pounded and I looked to the doorway. He came in wearing his usual jeans, tee and biker vest over the top. He started straight for me.

"Deanna Drake, what is that fuckin' *thing* in the living room in a playpen?"

I backed up. He stopped at one end of the kitchen bench, and I was at the other end smiling like a fool.

"That, babe, would be your surprise."

A tiny yip came from the living room.

"What is it?" he growled. "No, don't fuckin' tell me. It ain't staying. It's damn ugly, woman, and I don't want Swan gettin' attached to something that isn't staying around."

With my hands on my hips, I glared. "It fuckin' is staying, arsehole. Swan is going to love it, just like I do, and I know you will... eventually."

"No, I won't," he yelled, and then calmed enough to ask, "Where is Swan?"

"She's at Zara's. Drake and Ruby love her. We'll get her soon. Plus, I told them I wanted to surprise you with Oscar."

"What's Oscar? That *thing*?"

"He is not a thing. He's a Pomeranian and cute as a button."

"Fuck. Do you hear yourself? *Cute as a button?* My woman doesn't say that shit. He's changing you already."

"Well, it's time I did, and besides, I got him for a good reason."

"What? To use as a fuckin' mop? It's that damned fluffy enough."

I giggled. "No, smartarse, I thought..."

"What, darlin'?" he prompted when I paused.

"I... he, um. I thought... that, well... he'd be good practice. I mean, he's a puppy, and he'll have needs and shit, so I thought we could have a bit of practice for when the time came when we'd... um, maybe have a baby."

Holy shit. That was harder than I thought it would be.

I glanced up to see Grady's eyes were wide.

Maybe it wasn't a good surprise after all. Goddammit, I shouldn't have gone off the pill. I only missed that morning's, so I could do a catch-up. We'd have to not have sex for twenty-four hours... or some shit like that.

I jumped when I felt a hand caress my face. With his fingers under my chin, Grady turned my head to look up at him.

He seemed calm now. "You mean, you want to have a kid with me?"

"Um... yes?"

He grinned so wide his molars were showing. "First things first," he said, and I raised my eyebrow at him.

He got down on one knee.

My heart wanted out. I was sure it would have crawled outta my mouth if I wasn't clenching my teeth together so hard. Tears filled my eyes. Was this really happening?

"Deanna Drake, the moment you came into my life, it changed. I love how you fight back. I love that you don't take a shit and that you know when to be sweet, sexy, mean and bitchy. But most of all, I love *you*, every fuckin' way you are—and yeah, even when you're moody. I want to know if you'd be willing to put up with me and the way I am. Will you marry me?"

"Damn you for making me cry, but it's a yes. Hell yes, I'm more than willing to put up with you and your demanding ways." I smiled. His eyes softened as he pulled out a gold ring with a beautiful princess-cut diamond out of his club-vest and slid it on my finger.

As he stood, my tee came up and off and thrown to the side. He kissed me hard, sweet and long.

Coming up for breath, I asked, "W-what are we doing? We have to go get Swan and introduce her to Oscar."

"Later, I'll let those two meet, but right now, we gotta get down to business," he said and kissed my shoulder. His hands reached around to unclasp my bra. He pulled it from my shoulders, threw it to where my tee was on the floor and then palmed my breasts.

"What business?"

"Making a baby. I want this to happen as soon as fuckin' possible. I cannot wait to fill you with my seed and for it to stay there to make a miracle."

Well, hell. When he said it like that, how could I resist?

I ripped his tee over his head and dropped it to the floor. My hands went to his jeans. Popping the button, I slid down the fly and gripped his hard cock tucked inside, making him hiss.

My jean shorts were undone and pushed down my legs with my underwear.

"Spread 'em," Grady growled. I did; I moved my feet apart enough he could run a finger over my folds. With ease—because I was so fuckin' turned on and wet—his finger slipped inside, and then pulled out to rub against my clit.

"Shit," I uttered. My head fell forward to his chest as I gripped his dick harder and ran my hand up and down his length.

"Step outta your pants, darlin'," he ordered.

After I did just that, he wrapped a hand around each of my thighs and picked me up to sit on the kitchen bench, my hand falling free of his boxers—not that it bothered me, because I knew what was coming next. I watched as he rid himself of the rest of his clothes.

He stood back, his cock at full attention and his eyes on me. He licked his lips and then grinned. "Put your feet up on the edge of the bench, knees wide for me."

"Grady," I warned. I didn't want to play games; I wanted him now.

"Deanna, do it." He glared.

With an eye roll, I brought my legs up and opened them so far apart the most intimate area of me was on display.

"Beautiful," he hissed. "Fuck, please play with yourself," he asked and wrapped his large palm around his dick and started to stroke it.

I ran my hand over my breast, down my belly and outlined my folds with a finger. His heated, hungry eyes ate it all up.

Dipping one finger into my hole, my head fell back and I moaned, only it turned into a gasp when my hand was pushed to the side, and Grady's mouth was on my pussy, licking and tonguing me all over.

"Jesus. Fuck, that feels good, Grady," I hissed when he gripped my hips tightly and drove his tongue straight into me over and over.

"Oh, hell. I'm gonna—"

"Not yet," he growled. He stood with his cock in his hand and stepped forward. He lined his dick up and slowly entered me, and his thumb slid over my clit. There was no way I could have held off. My walls gripped him tighter as I came around his entering dick.

"Darlin', Christ," he snarled. He reached for me, and with a hand on each arm, he pulled me up. I wrapped my arms around his neck as his folded around my waist. Our lips met and as we kissed; the taste of myself on his mouth was something erotic. Grady slid back and forth in an agonizingly slow motion, and I loved every fuckin' second of it.

His lips left mine, and I met his warm gaze. "Are you ready?"

"Yes."

"Fuck, woman, I'm gonna come any second. We're about to make something special."

I gripped his arse and smiled. "May not happen the first time."

"Fuck that," he growled. "It will work with my swimmers." He grinned. "Christ," he hissed as he moved his hand from my hip to in-between our bodies, and with one flick on my clit, a moan left my lips as I came once again. With a grunt and then a groan, Grady pumped his seed into me.

He pulled back and looked at me. I knew I was smiling like a fool; I liked the thought of having him inside of me. Even though we'd done it many times, this time was exceptional.

It was something else.

It was us.

"We're in this together," Grady said.

"Together." I nodded and reached my hand up to touch his cheek. "I can't wait."

"Me neither. Even if you do drive me nuts, it'll all be worth it." He smiled. I gave him a light slap on his cheek.

His eyes widened. "You wanna play rough? Give me a minute, and we'll play it my way."

I laughed. "We can't. We have to get Swan."

"Bullshit. She won't mind waiting," he said as he slowly slid his cock out of me.

"We have to check on the dog."

"He can wait," he said with a hard thrust back inside. "We're busy."

"Grady," I snapped and then rolled my eyes. I knew there was no way he would listen. I felt his dick harden even more within me.

I guess Swan and the dog could wait just a little bit longer.

FINDING
OUT

BALLARAT CHARTER LILA ROSE

Finding Out Copyright © 2014 by Lila Rose

Hawks MC: Ballarat Charter: Book 2.5

Cover Photo: Rachel Morgan
Editing: Hot Tree Editing
Interior Design: Rogena Mitchell-Jones

All rights reserved. No part of this eBook may be used or reproduced in any written, electronic, recorded, or photocopied format
without the permission from the author as allowed under the terms
and conditions with which it was purchased or as strictly permitted
by applicable copyright law. Any unauthorized distribution, circulation or use of this text may be a direct infringement of the author's
rights, and those responsible may be liable in law accordingly.
Thank you for respecting the work of this author.

Finding Out is a work of fiction. All names, characters, events and
places found in this book are either from the author's imagination
or used fictitiously. Any similarity to persons live or dead, actual
events, locations, or organizations is entirely coincidental and not
intended by the author.

Second Edition 2019
ISBN: 978-0648481683

To Jessica and Chris, the best cover couple, thank you for your help and putting up with me through it all!

CHAPTER ONE

ONLINE DATING. Some were for it and some against. Me? I was somewhere in the middle. You see, I joined the *'Find Your Soul-Mate'* dating site six months ago. Although, I'd never been on since filling out the form, until today. The reason being, I had no other choice now. I was desperate. My cousin's wedding was creeping up slowly, and I had a just over a week to find a date to take.

The truth, I had lied, and now it was coming back to bite me on my huge arse. I'd told my bitchy cousin Leanne I was bringing my long-time hot, successful boyfriend Max. The only problem was he didn't exist. This left me scrolling through the list of potential victims who could accompany me on this date and pretend we'd been an item for two years.

The door to my office—out the back of the café I owned—opened and in strolled Helen, my best friend since we wore diapers. She looked great in her pantsuit. The sight of her had me thinking that I wished I'd have said I was a lesbian. At least then, I could have taken Helen, and we would have had a fun night. Instead, it was just going to be awkward. Especially since my parents were flying in from Sydney to go to the wedding, and they couldn't wait to meet my *serious* boyfriend.

Yes, I had lied to them as well. In my defense, my mum kept hounding me about marriage and babies. They thought having a twenty-eight-year-old single daughter was wrong. That was only because my younger brother and sister were both happily married off.

Arguably, the happy part was still debatable.

Dragging the chair in front of my desk around next to me, Helen sat down. She slapped my hand away from my mouth because she hated my habit of chewing my nails, seemingly oblivious to my worrying over my whole life falling apart.

She pulled her long blonde hair up and tied it into a ponytail on the top of her head. She was beautiful, with her sexy hair, bedroom deep-blue eyes, and Jessica Rabbit figure. Turning gay was still an option; I could just say that Helen won my heart away from my serious, fake boyfriend.

She cleared her throat before she spoke. "No, I will not take one for the team and become gay for you, even for one night."

"Poop," I sighed.

"Come on, Ivy. You'll find someone perfect who will make your she-bitch-from-hell who-is-actually-a-guy and sucks-cock-like-the-dirty-tramp she is cousin choke on her own tongue."

Did you feel the hate? Not that I could blame her, Leanne did steal Helen's fella, who she was now marrying. I even hated my cousin for it, and I refused to go to her wedding until my mum rang and threatened that since I was the only cousin living in Ballarat, I was to attend no matter the situation or else she was going to post on Facebook that she wished me well on my sex change. Yeah, my mum could be a bitch.

"I can only hope," I muttered and slumped back in my seat as Helen pulled my laptop closer to her.

"Oh, look at this one. He's got a nice profile picture. It says, 'Hi, my name is Nick, and I love pussy.' Okay, maybe not that one," she giggled. I rolled my eyes. Some men were true idiots. "Look at this.

You haven't even opened your message box. Mr Right could be sitting in there waiting for you. Let's see."

I didn't bother looking. Helen lived an orderly life and I hoped she'd help...all right, take control of this and just point me in the right direction. Though, I was actually surprised people had messaged me. My profile picture was not that good. I'd uploaded the one where Helen had just said something funny, and I was laughing hard while we were out at a park with my German Sheppard Trixie. My brown eyes were squinty, and my long, wavy, mousy-coloured hair was blowing in the breeze, which meant it was everywhere, including over my face and a bit in my mouth. Still, six months ago Helen had insisted on that photo. She'd said it would let a man know that I was fun and full of life. I honestly thought she was full of shit. Now I thought she was only half-full of shit. I had messages in my box. I wish I had something else in my box...it had been too long since it was last filled.

"Right, you have two potentials out of ten. The other eight are just scary and will not be worth mentioning."

I sat up and adjusted my jeans and tee. Just because I owned a café, it didn't mean I had to dress like the boss. I would hate to wear something like Helen wore every day at her journalism job. My café was all about being comfy. If I was happy and comfy, then I hoped it meant my workers would be, as well as my patrons.

"Hit me with the good ones then," I said. She moved the laptop so we could both see the screen. When my eyes landed on the profile picture in front of me, I uttered, "Holy shit, I wish I was a virgin again so I could lose it to this guy."

"I know," Helen sighed. She shook her head and continued with, "Here's what he's written about himself. My name is Fox Kilpatrick. I'm thirty-eight years old, and I work in construction. I'm looking for someone who is fun and lively. I like to go to the movies, cook and clean."

I snorted. "No way would a guy say he likes to clean. Either his sister filled this out, or there is something seriously wrong with the man."

Helen shrugged. "Maybe to both, but even if there was something wrong with him, just imagine turning up to *her* wedding with that on your arm."

This was true. Fox was definitely a fox. His eyes shone blue, and he had shaved head that showed his dark blond colour. To top it off, like frosting on a cake, he had a small smirk upon his full lips that said he had a sense of mischief inside of him.

Me wanty.

"Before you fall for this one, take a look at option two. His name is Jim. He's a doctor, works long hours but is looking for someone special enough to understand that what he does is important. In his free time, he likes to ride, eat out and also relax in with a good movie, while cuddling."

"Oh," I sighed. "He sounds nice and a doctor is very important, so I already understand he'd be a busy man."

Helen turned to me and asked, "What did you tell your family your mystery guy did for a living?"

Biting my bottom lip, I mumbled, "A cop."

"Ivvvvy," Helen whined. "You shouldn't have told them anything. Next time, and yes I know there will be a next time, be vague. Say he does a bit of this and that."

"I was under pressure. You know I don't work well when under pressure. It was the first thing that popped into my head when mum asked. Plus I was watching *CSI* at the time she called."

"Well, thank God, you didn't say pathologists."

Raising my eyebrows, I queried, "Huh?"

Rolling her eyes at me, she smiled and answered, "A person who works on dead people."

"Oooooh, well, I wouldn't have said that. That's just gross."

She shook her head and laughed. "You're an idiot. Now, I suggest having a date with both of them. That way after meeting them, you can pick out which one would be better at lying to your family."

"Good thinking ninety-nine. But for now, I better get back out front before Justine and Manny kill each other." My employees were school dropouts, and no one had given them a chance to prove themselves in a job. Therefore, I did. If it weren't for the sexual hate/love tension between the two, things would be perfect.

"All right, but you will message them back tonight? You need time to work on them both before doom-day."

"Totally, I will not fly solo to this gig and have all my happiness in life sucked from my body."

"Glad we have an understanding." Helen smiled. We did our usual secret handshake and butt slap, and she left me to go save my shop.

After I shut down the computer, I walked out of my office and into the front of my café just in time to hear Justine hiss at Manny, "I'm going to kill you slowly and painfully if you stuff up another coffee." I didn't mind the death threats. I was used to them, and so were my regular customers. They even got a chuckle out of it, and I was sure sometimes they only came to get the free entertainment for the day.

I stood beside them as they glared at each other before I placed a hand on a shoulder each. "Justine, you can't kill Manny."

She rolled her eyes and snapped, "Why?"

"I'd hate to train anyone new, and I'm sure you would too."

She puffed out her cheeks and sighed, "Fine."

"Miss M, you also forget that Justine would be lost and lonely without me because she loves me so much, which is why she's always a raging bitch." Manny smirked at Justine.

Before she could find something to stab him with, I quickly said, "Manny, go and get the cupcakes from the back kitchen that I made earlier and load the sandwiches into the fridge before the lunchtime rush. Justine, please go and serve the customers and I'll make coffees for a while. Sound good?"

"Sure, Miss M." Manny grinned. He patted me on the shoulder

and slapped Justine on the butt quickly before he ran out the back to safety.

"One day I will murder him," Justine announced.

The waiting customer turned to her friend and whispered, "And one day she will screw him."

"You!" Justine yelled at the blonde businesswoman. "That will never happen, and if you say something like that again, you'll be on my shit list. Now, what in the hell do you want?"

They laughed because they knew, like Manny and I knew that Justine's bark was much worse than her bite.

I loved my workers, regulars and even those customers who popped in just for a quick coffee on the run. Most of all, I loved my café. I'd bought it five years ago when I was fresh out of university after receiving a business degree. Back then, it had been a corner milk bar, but it just wasn't busy since a supermarket moved in down the road. I think it also had to do with the fact that the owners were now in jail for selling drugs as a side business from the store.

Now instead of the gloomy look it had, it was all bright and full of life. I had pretty much gutted the inside, thanks to all the money I had saved selling my homemade jewellery online. People were sad when I stopped doing it, but to make my café successful, I had to put all my time and money into it. I was so glad I did. I wouldn't say 'Ivy's Brunch' was booming, but I am now living comfortably and have two great employees when they weren't trying to flirt in their own weird way.

The day turned out like it had every other day: we worked our butts off, me especially when Justine caught Manny staring down her top. Let's just say that Manny may come into work tomorrow with a limp. After cleaning and closing the shop, I walked the block home and relaxed in the bath with Trixie—who was happy because I fed her as soon as I got home—sitting beside me. She waited like the loyal, sweet dog she was.

Later that night, as I sat in bed, I fired up my laptop and sent a quick message to Fox and Jim. They weren't online, and before they could get back on, I quickly shut it down and then left myself pondering if they had yet replied. I eventually fell asleep in the early hours.

Bleary-eyed, the first thing I did when I woke was check the computer. Okay, that was a lie. The first thing I did was pee, and then I made myself a coffee. While I waited for that, I turned on the laptop at my kitchen table.

My heart beat like a maniac. I had two messages. I opened Jim's first. For some reason, I was more nervous about Fox's response. Jim had typed back—to my asking him for coffee at my work, not that I said it was my business place, but I just felt safer meeting strangers there. He said that he'd love to meet for a coffee and that he was available this Saturday. I replied with 'Great, I'll meet you there at ten am.' That would give me time to chat before I helped out with the lunch.

Now my hands shook as I clicked on the next message. Fox replied to my message with a short answer of, 'Yes, see you at 2pm Saturday.' I giggled with glee. Why did I have that reaction with one man and not the other? All I knew was I couldn't wait until two pm Saturday. What I had to do now was keep myself occupied for two days, figure out what to wear and pray that Justine and Manny would behave themselves enough while I had my blind dates.

I was on my way to work when I texted Helen telling her that I was all organised for Saturday with Foxy and Jimbo. She asked if she could pretend to be a customer in the background while she checked them out. I told her that was fine because it would also help my nerves. She was also a good judge of character and could help me determine which would be more suitable to put up with my effed up family.

CHAPTER TWO

SATURDAY CAME TOO SOON, and I found myself sitting at a table with sweaty palms, dressed in a dark blue sundress and sandals. God, I hoped to Christ Jim didn't want to shake my hand. If he did, we might be stuck together from the amount of sweat my hands were producing. I looked over at Helen. She sat three tables away dressed in jeans and a tee. She caught my eye and mouthed, 'Relax.' I nodded, picked up a napkin and wiped my hands for the fourth time. Jim was late. It was now 10:15. I hated people who couldn't be on time, but then I had to take into count that he was a doctor and could have been called away on an emergency.

So as I waited, I looked around my café to the long front counter that was off to the right of the entrance. It held the coffee machine and the cabinet of cupcakes, cookies, sandwiches, and croissants. I loved to bake. Justine and Manny were serving customers; there was a line-up of four people. Still, my eyes took no notice of them and moved on to the seating area. I had managed to fit in four booths along the opposite wall to the counter and had tables and chairs scattered here, there and everywhere in the flooring space that was left. In the long shop window, to the left of the entrance, I had a bench with chairs, where I sat papers and magazines off at both ends.

I looked back at the clock that sat just behind the register. It was now ten-thirty. It was time to give up; Jim wasn't coming. Just as I stood, Helen was beside me and said, "I just logged onto the site. He's sent you a message. It says that he can't make it, but he'd love to reschedule for Monday at the same time."

Nodding, I said, "I kind of guessed that. Can you send a quick message back saying okay?" She gave me a chin lift and typed something into her phone while I added, "Doesn't matter. I just hope Fox turns up."

She looked up at me and smiled. "I can tell by your voice that you already have a mild crush on him."

"Oh no, Helen, it's lust. Just from his picture my woman bits are crying to be near him."

She laughed. "I completely understand that. Listen, I've got to go and run some errands, but I'll be back here before your next date."

"Thanks, babe," I said. We did our handshake, and after she left, I spent my time doing what I loved: working.

"GOOD LUCK WITH THIS ONE," Justine started as she placed a latte on my table. "The offer still stands. If you wink twice, I'll come over here and pretend to be your jealous girlfriend to get you out of the date."

Maybe I should just take Justine to the wedding. Then the night could end up with her in jail when she discovers what douches my family members were.

"Thank you. I'll let you know." I smiled up at her.

"Great." She grinned, turned and went back to work behind the counter—after punching Manny in the arm.

It was five minutes to two and Helen had sent me a text saying she was running late; she'd be there as soon as she could. So when the bell over the door jingled, I looked up from my latte expecting it to be Helen. Instead, in walked a man who made my cooter want to jump from my body to run over and rub up against his leg. It was in heat. He also caused my breasts to tingle, which has never happened before. I shook my fogged head and realised that the man who walked in, dressed in dark jeans, a black tee—that showed off his wonderful tattooed arms—and motorcycle boots, was the man of my porno dreams and Mr Fox Kilpatrick himself. All of a sudden, my mouth went dry. I assumed it was because all the liquid from my body had travelled south to pool in my panties from the mere sight of the man before me. I watched his eyes scan the shop and then land on me.

I gulped, and with wide eyes, I watched him stalk his way over. He stopped just beside me, and in a deep voice, with a hint of a growl, he said, "Ivy, right?"

And I said, "Huh?"

His serious face stayed serious, still I caught the little lift in the corner of his mouth. I only saw it because I happened to be staring at his mouth-watering lips. He pulled out the chair opposite me and turned it backwards to straddle it. His hands rested on the top of the chair, and he stared a piercing stare straight to my heart.

"So?" he said.

That was when I vomited, not actual spew, but in a sense, only with words. That's right… I vomited words right in his face.

"Hi, yes… I'm… ah, Ivy and I guess you're Fox, right? I mean, I hope I don't have that wrong, you are Fox, right?" He sent me a chin lift, and I continued puking works, "Thank you for agreeing to meet me, you…um…I mean. I didn't think you would. You are extremely good looking and, well, you saw my photo. I don't really know why I joined the site. I mean I do. It's been a long time since I've had sex. Oh, my God, I did not just say that. I did. God, I did." My hands went to my glowing cheeks.

"Let me explain. I didn't join the site to just have sex with random guys." I grabbed my latte for something to do or else they would be running through his thick hair. "I joined...dammit; I may as well just come out and say it. I need a date...not for sex, though that would be good." I reached my hand up and shook it in front of me. "Not that you have to have sex with me. What I'm trying to say is I joined ages ago but was too scared to get on, and now I have no choice." I took a breath and placed my hands in my lap. "I'm really nervous if you couldn't tell...did I mention you're good looking and that it's making me nervous and the way you're staring at me without saying anything...I ramble in situations like this, and I can't seem to help myself." Another breath. "I was meaning to tell you...that I need a date, for my bitchy cousin's wedding that's coming up. *That's* why I got the courage to get back on that site."

I snapped my lips shut. Oh God, was I getting an eye twitch? Hell. Yes, I was. There it went again and again. Shit.

Next thing I heard was something being slammed down, and then Justine was stomping our way. Oh, sweet Jesus and Joseph. She thought I was winking at her. I waved my hands up in front of me, and with wide eyes, I said, "Justine, no it's fine. At least I think it is." The poor guy hadn't even said a word. I just knew he was going to run for the hills.

Justine stopped beside us and asked, "So I don't need to pretend to be your gay partner?"

Fuck me.

Sighing, my head flopped forward, so my chin rested against my chest. "No, Justine, but thank you," I uttered.

"Well good," she said and leaned closer to me. "He is sex on legs, Ivy. I'd stoop him." With that, she turned and walked off.

Holy shit.

"I hav'ta get goin'," Fox said and stood up, moving to the side of the table.

I didn't look up at him, only nodded and whispered, "I understand." He was way out of my league.

"Tonight, I'll pick you up here at five. We're going out to dinner."

My head snapped up. "Are you crazy?" I asked. After everything he just witnessed, I was sure I'd lost any chance of anything.

Crossing his muscled arms over his chest, he grunted. "No. I like what I see in you. We go out and talk. 'Bout your cousin's weddin', 'bout why I joined the site and...'bout us havin' sex."

I swore as soon as the word sex left his sweet mouth I was jabbed in the snatch by an invisible dick because I nearly came on the spot.

He smirked. "Five?"

I nodded and then whispered, "Five."

His parting word was, "Good." Then he left.

Two seconds later, Helen walked in, she took one look at me and uttered, "Shit, you're a goner." She came over and sat in the seat Fox vacated. "He wasn't here long. Was he an arse? It doesn't look like he was. You're all... moony."

"No—" I began, only to stop when Manny walked up and placed a piece of paper on the table.

"Miss M, this was left for you on another table."

I smiled up at him. "Thank you." I unfolded the paper that held my name on the front. It read, *The way you acted with that man was disgusting.* Scoffing I scrunched the paper up and placed it in my coffee cup.

"What was that?" Helen asked.

"Nothing really, I think it was from one of my family members popping in to annoy me." I rolled my eyes.

She snorted. "Annoying." Helen sang, and then smiled. "Come on, I need you to tell me the sweet stuff. Tell me *everything.*" She leaned forward, her head in her hands with her elbows on the table.

"Well...." I started only to stop when there was a loud commotion at the front counter.

"I don't give a fuck about the policy and that you can't divulge information like that. I know the fuckin' owner is Ivy Morrison. Just point me in the right goddamn way to see her," A beautiful blonde yelled at Justine over the counter.

"Fuck you," Justine hissed with a glare in her green eyes.

The blonde laughed and said, 'I like you. You got fire. But, sweetheart, you won't win against me.'

"Jeesh, Satan with a pussy, the girl is doing her job. Leave her be," a tall, obviously gay man said from beside the blonde.

"Dee, calm down and listen to Julian," a dark-haired woman sighed. "Miss, thank you for your help—"

"She wasn't any bloody help," the girl named Dee snapped.

Before she could scare any customers away or before Justine jumped the counter and attacked the foul-mouthed woman, I stood from the table and called, "Excuse me." The three of them turned to face me. "Is there anything *I* can help you with? I am the owner, Ivy Morrison."

"Well fuck me sideways," Dee smiled.

"Oh, bless my gay heart, aren't you pretty." Julian grinned, and as the dark-haired lady made her way over to me, the other two followed.

She held out her hand and beamed. "Hi, I'm Zara. I was wondering if we could have a chat?"

I looked from one smiling face to another and then nodded, gesturing to the table where Helen was still sitting. Julian pulled up a chair from another table, and Dee sat on one side, while Zara, who was just as gorgeous as Dee, sat on the other side of me.

"So, is there a problem you have with my café?"

"No," Zara answered and then introduced herself to Helen.

"Hi, I'm Helen, Ivy's best friend."

"I'm Deanna, but most call me Dee."

"Or Hell Mouth, slutguts, hooker, sponge cake...oh, I could go on and on." Julian smiled and then shook Helen's offered hand. "I'm Julian. I just came along for the ride with these two interfering crazies."

"Whatever, gay man." Dee snorted. "You love this shit just as much as us."

I cleared my throat. "And what is *this*?" I questioned.

"You just had a date with Killer right?" Zara asked.

"Killer?"

"Sorry, I mean Fox."

"How is it that you know all their first names and I don't?" Dee asked Zara.

"Because I have a heart and I care."

Dee shrugged and rolled her eyes. "I have a heart...now."

Zara patted her hand and said, "You do, honey, you do, and I'm so happy for you."

Oh, my God. What in the hell is going on? Who were these nice freaks?

"What in the hell is going on?" I asked.

"Sorry," Zara said, "you see, we just wanted to make sure you were okay after the date with Killer or as you know him Fox."

My heart started tap dancing. "Shouldn't I be?" I squeaked.

"Yes, no, um...Yes," Zara stuttered, "the thing is, Fox lost a bet with his biker brothers—"

"He's a biker?" I gasped.

"Well, yes, but a nice one...sort of. Anyway, what I was saying was that after he lost the bet, he was dared to join this dating site and go on at least one date and you were it. I just wanted to make sure he treated you right. Sometimes he can be a bit...broody and abrupt or not talk at all."

Julian and Deanna nodded along with Zara.

"He, um, he was fine?" I said, making it sound like a question.

Helen scoffed. "She was more than fine. At first glance when I arrived, he'd already left, but when I spotted Ivy here, she was off in la-la land. I think she fell already and hard."

"Hoo-boy." Julian clapped.

"Awesome." Dee smiled.

"What happened?" Zara asked.

"That's what I want to know," Helen said.

"Well..." I fidgeted in my seat. "You see, he really didn't get a chance to say much." I bit my lip and then spewed once again. "I get nervous around good-looking people, not that you all aren't good looking because you are, and if I was I'd be checking you out more. Anyway, I have a tendency to ramble when I'm nervous, which is what I did with Fox and I ended up telling him my plan—"

"Oh, God," Helen moaned in sympathy. She knew all about my ramblings.

"I mentioned to him that I just really needed a date for my bitchy cousin's wedding and something about not having sex in a long time. Though I did say I didn't go to the site to just have sex, it was all because I need to find a date for the wedding." I took a breath and looked at their wide eyes. "Then, he said he had to go. But that he was going to be here at five to take me to dinner where we will talk about why he was on the site, my cousin's wedding and... um, intercourse."

"Holy sex on wheels, I wish I was there to hear that. I mean Killer is smoking hot," Julian said.

Deanna and Zara shared a look, a look that caused them to smile. That look and smile had me on edge.

"What?" I asked. "What's that look about?" I pointed from one woman to another.

"Nothin'," Dee smirked.

"Should I be worried about this?" I squawked. "I mean, he's a biker. Aren't bikers bad guys? Oh, my God, did he get his name from being a killer? Do I need to run and hide?"

Zara placed her hand over mine. "Honey, no to all of the above. You have nothing to fear from this man. Sure he *is* broody and snappy, but it's obvious you have caught his attention and honestly," —she looked to Dee and then back— "we're glad. He's a nice guy, Ivy, and yes he may be a biker, but the Hawks MC Club members are good men. I should know, I married their president."

My eye widened. "You did?"

"Yes and he's wonderful, sweet, kind, but bossy and all alpha male. Deanna has just gotten engaged to another biker too."

"You are?"

"Hell yes, they're hot." She grinned.

I turned to Julian and asked, "What about you?"

"Oh no, lovey, I'm not married, engaged or doing any bikers. My partner is Zara's brother, and he runs in his own kind of hotness. Though, I do have to say...not many bikers would put up with my," he waved his hands over himself "whole greatness, but these men do, and it just proves how special these women's snatches are. These bikers love and devote their time and lives to their women. If I weren't with Mattie, I'd try and snag me one, because then I'd know I'd be safe and loved for the rest of my gay life. Not that I won't be with Mattie. He is possessive and manly hot," he sighed, smiling.

Wow. These men sounded wonderful.

"Are you going to go on this date with Fox?" Helen asked me.

They all waited with baited breath for my answer. I already knew I would, even after I found out he was a broody biker. However, these three awesome people had sold me on Fox.

Smiling, I said, "Yes."

Helen smiled back at me.

Julian squealed. Deanna yelled, "Fuck yeah." And Zara quietly said, "Yay," with a big smile upon her face.

CHAPTER THREE

MY AFTERNOON WAS VERY BIZARRE. I left Justine and Manny in charge while I went home to find something to wear.

I wasn't alone though.

No, Helen and my three new friends all followed me the block to my house. While Julian, with Trixie, my dog, at his side, riffled through my wardrobe looking for something for me to wear, I sat at the kitchen table with Zara standing in front of me as she applied my makeup. Helen was sitting opposite us gabbing with Deanna.

How was it possible that we had only met these three people hours ago, yet it already felt like we'd known them for years?

"Okay, I'm nearly done. It's not too much, so you don't look like a..."

"Hooker," Deanna supplied for Zara.

"Yes." Zara nodded. She picked up my makeup mirror from the table and held it out in front of me. "What do you think?" she asked.

"Oh, my," I sighed. She had done a wonderful job. It was delicate and subtle. Just perfect. "I love it, thank you."

She beamed down at me. "My pleasure. Julian," she called down the hall. Trixie came running. When we had walked through my front door, and Julian started cooing over Trixie, she hadn't left his side.

"What, cabbage breath?" Julian answered.

"We'd better get going soon, get your skinny butt out here." She helped me tidy the makeup as she explained, "I can't leave the twins with Talon for too long, and it's already been an hour."

"You have twins?" I gushed.

"Sure do..." she paused to grin, "and Maya who's seven and Cody who's thirteen, one big, happy family."

"That sounds wonderful. What about you, Deanna, do you have any children?" I asked.

She smiled a warm smile, her eyes softening. "Yes, my man has a two-year-old. Her name is Swan."

We heard Julian's shoes clip-clopping down the wooden hallway floor when he said, "And don't forget you're trying for your own little demon. God knows I'd never get out of bed if I was trying to get knocked up with Griz's kid." He laughed as he walked around the corner carrying a red and white sundress.

I gulped. "Really?"

"Shit, yes," Deanna said.

"Killer will love that on you," Zara added.

"And maybe you'll get more than a sentence out of him." Julian grinned.

"You'll look smoking hot in that, Ivy." Helen smiled.

I ARRIVED BACK at work in the red-and-white sunflower dress. My hair was loose and wavy, my makeup minimal and pretty. I teamed my outfit with black ballet slippers. In case the night grew cold, I also brought along a black jacket. As soon as I was through the door, Manny wolf-whistled, and Justine clapped and said, "You look hot, Ivy."

Blushing, I replied, "Um, thanks. Is everything nearly ready for lock-up?"

"Sure is, Miss M. But I doubt you'll be checking everything twice before *you* leave."

"Why do you say that?"

Manny gestured with his chin just as the bell jingled as the door opened. I turned to find Fox standing in the doorway. His body had stilled, except for his eyes. No, they ran along my body and finally landed on my face. "You ready?" he asked.

My body sagged. I was a little deflated from his reaction. I guess that maybe he wasn't happy with what he saw.

Justine must have seen this, and I was thankful that no one else, besides Manny, was in the store when she hissed, "Don't be a jerk. You just eye fucked her, now tell her how much you like what you see."

"Justine—" I started.

"Justine," Manny warned. He grabbed her hand and pulled until she stood behind him. I was wondering why he'd done that until I saw Fox's face. It looked like he was about to verbally rip shreds through Justine. His lip was raised, his brows drawn together and a growl rumbled from within his chest.

"Fuck," he snapped. "This is why I don't do this datin' shit." He took a step forward, wrapped an arm around my waist and pulled me close. His mouth met mine. It was hard and possessive, and when his tongue ran over my bottom lip, I gasped. He took the chance to force his tongue into my mouth, which I liked, a lot. Coming out of my shocked state, I wrapped my arms around his neck and gripped him tightly to me.

He growled from deep within. I moaned and then a throat cleared behind us. Fox pulled away and I whimpered. He ignored our audience, and with our faces close, he uttered, "You look edible. In fact, you taste like cupcakes, and I want fuckin' more."

I whimpered again.

"Wow, oh wow, oh wow." I heard Justine say behind me.

"Now, are you ready?" Fox asked.

"Um... yes?" I said and made it sound like a question because honestly, I wasn't sure I was ready for Fox Kilpatrick.

He smirked for a second and then it disappeared. He looked behind me and said, "Later." He took my hand and turned back to the door.

I looked over my shoulder to a worried Manny and a smiling Justine and said, "You'll both be okay?"

"Oh, we'll be fine, Ivy. Have fun," Justine sang.

I managed a nod before we were out the door and in front of his black Jeep.

He opened the passenger door for me and nodded to it. "In," he stated.

Biting my bottom lip to hide my smile, I thought of what Zara, Deanna, and Julian had said. They were right. Fox was a man of minimal words. Climbing in, he shut the door, and I got to admire the view of Fox in black jeans and a white tee as he walked around the front of his car and then climbed in.

"Um," I started, "where are we going?"

There's a seafood joint a few blocks away. Hell, do you even like seafood?" he asked. Worry marred his face with drawn brows.

"Yes, I do. It sounds nice."

He looked at me and then back to the road. "Good."

It didn't take us long to get there. Soon enough, we were seated opposite each other with a menu in front of us. I knew *I* was studying the menu, but I could feel Fox's gaze on me.

Looking up, I asked, "Do you know what you want?"

"Yes," he growled.

My eyes widened. The heated stare told me that I was what he wanted.

"Ah... okay, I mean, um. What do you want to eat?" I blushed when he smirked. "On the menu... in front of you," I clarified.

"Because the seafood basket for two looks good. Would you share at all? You don't have to, you're a big guy, and...so you probably like to eat a lot. I don't know if that will be enough for you... ah, is it?"

"Sounds good." He gestured with his head to the waiter. Once he came over, Fox ordered for us. He also ordered us both a beer to drink, which I liked. I wasn't a wine or champagne drinker. After the waiter disappeared, Fox said, "Let's talk about why I was on the site."

Playing with the napkin in my lap, I informed him, "Oh, I already know."

"How?" he growled.

I bit my inner cheek and told him, "I met Zara, Deanna, and Julian this afternoon. They told me all about the bet you made before Zara gave birth. I would have done the same and guessed both boys," I mumbled.

He closed his eyes and uttered, "Fuck."

Clearing my throat, he opened his eyes to glare. I continue when I saw his jaw clenched with anger, "No, it's okay. They, ah, they're really nice people. I like them, and they obviously care about you and... um, all the men in your group."

He rolled his eyes. "They like to stick their noses where they shouldn't."

"Well, at least I spoke to them, because, um, now I'm not so nervous about you being in your group and... I, you seem nice, and you're very good looking. I know I've said that and I... you must get a lot of attention from women... I don't know where I was going with that statement," I admitted.

He studied me with a small smile upon his face. "I like it when you get all flustered."

My eyes widened. "You do?"

"Yes," he said with a nod. "So I guess I won't be tearing through the three musketeers for interfering if it means you're here because of whatever they said."

I licked my lips. "Yes, I mean, I'm glad I met them, and yes, they helped me be here, but...."

"But?" he asked.

"I knew I was going to come as soon as you asked me, no matter what."

His eyes flared with surprise. I had shocked him.

"I'm glad then, cupcake," he whispered.

Had he just called me cupcake?

"Cupcake?" I asked

"Yeah, cupcake because you make 'em, because you smell like 'em, and because you taste like 'em. You're fuckin' lucky we're out in public, or I'd be demanding more of a taste from you."

That was intense and so damned hot in a scary, stomach-fluttering, happy way. I didn't know if that made sense, but right then I didn't care.

"Okay," I whispered.

"Okay to what?"

"Um...." I looked around the restaurant and then back to Fox's heated gaze. "Okay to everything."

"Good." He smiled, and this time, for the first time, it did reach his eyes. "Now, let's talk about your bitch cousin and her wedding. Then we can move onto the subject of sex."

My cheeks blushed. Immediately, I wanted to hide under the table. But then hiding under the table made me think of the fact that Fox's crotch would be down there, and then that made me think of his penis and me undoing his zipper, taking his cock into my mouth.

"Oh, God, is it hot in here?" I asked before I took a big gulp of water from my glass.

"No," he chuckled.

Nodding, I put the glass back on the table and looked to my side as the waiter placed the seafood platter for two in front of us. As we both started to munch, I began to talk... not a good sign.

"So, um... as you know I have my cousin's wedding to go to and its next weekend. But you see, I don't reeeeally want to go. Though, if I don't turn up, my mum will publicly be congratulating me about my sex change on Facebook." He coughed on his mouthful. "Yes, she can be evil. She's like the rest of them; they all think their shit don't stink." I sighed and took a bite of a prawn while thinking. "I love them, of course I do; they're my family. But they annoy the hell out of me and can be... um, cruel in ways." I looked up from my plate with wide eyes. "Oh God, have I just scared you away from the whole thing? Of course, it's totally up to you if you want to go or not. Or, even, I mean...you might not want anything to do with me after this first date... shit, I have to stop talking. I talk too much. It's your fault." I waved my hand that held a shrimp stick at him. "You're too... everything. Sorry," I mumbled and turned my gaze away.

"Finished?" Fox asked.

I glance back, then away again and asked, "Do you mean eating or talking?" I looked back at the platter in front of us. "I could do with more food." I picked up a scallop in some sauce and sucked it back.

"I meant talking, even though it turns me the fuck on listening to your voice."

"Oh," I whispered.

"Ivy, finally, I'm fuckin' pleased that my brothers made me go through with a bet or else I wouldn't have met you, and from what I see, I like you, a lot. So much so, I'm willin' to put up with your family at this goddamn wedding."

Grinning widely, I asked, "Really?"

He watched my mouth, and in turn, his own lips formed another smile for me before he said, "Hell yes."

With fisted hands in front of me, I did a little jig and uttered, "Yay."

He chuckled. "Christ, you're cute. Now let's finish this meal."

While we ate we chatted, okay, I mainly did all the talking, but at least when I asked questions, Fox answered them. So I ended up finding out that he was in construction. He was part owner of his company with another member from the Hawks MC club named Stoke. He also, when he could, worked in the mechanic business at the bikers' compound. He lived on his own on some land in the suburb of Nerrina; he had no other family members besides his biker brothers. He joined Hawks after meeting Talon five years ago and learned that Talon ran things differently than other biker clubs. Fox wanted to be a part of the cleaner, safer living. He said he wouldn't have it any other way because what he had before he met Talon was shit.

That made me sad.

I think he saw this because after the waiter had cleared away our plates, he stated, "I want in you tonight. What are your thoughts on that?"

So of course, all sadness from that moment fled, and instead, I clenched my legs together so I wouldn't come.

He... Fox Kilpatrick, a.k.a Killer, wanted in me tonight.

He meant sex, right?

That he wanted to stick his hotdog in my bun? Right?

"Cupcake, I can see that I've shocked you." Fox smirked.

"Um...." I leaned over the table. He leaned in as well and then I whispered, "I just want to clarify what you mean. Is it... sex? You want to have sex with me tonight?"

"Yes," he growled as he reached a hand out to tuck my hair behind my ear.

As Fox kept my stare with his wild, heated one, I uttered, "Yes."

He grinned. "Good. Let's get the hell outta here before I spread your legs over this table and fuck you hard."

Leaning back, I nodded. "Ah, that's a good idea...I think." He chuckled and stood from the table. "Wait," I shouted, causing people to look at us. I took hold of Fox's wrist and pulled him around to me, where I was still sitting. Tugging him down so our noses near touched, I told him, "I... um, I don't *usually* sleep with a man on the first date. I just wanted you to know that. But, you, um, you seem to have some effect on my body... and mind," I admitted, which made me blush like a virgin on her wedding night.

"Shit, woman, I never thought I could get harder from watching you for the past two hours, but I am. *I know* you're not like that, but I'm goddamn happy that you'll be tonight, just for me." With that, he shook off my hold, took my hand and led me from the restaurant, after paying of course.

CHAPTER FOUR

Fox TOLD me his place was too far away and he couldn't wait that long to be inside me. That was why I was unlocking my front door with Fox standing at my back. Trixie came barrelling down the hallway from, no doubt, my bedroom. Usually, she'd growl or bark if I had someone new with me as she had with Deanna, Zara, and Julian. Only with Fox, she took one sniff of him, wagged her tail and whimpered up at him for a pat.

Yeah, girl, I would do the same.

"She likes you," I said as I led the way down my hall and into my kitchen. I looked behind me for Fox, only he wasn't there. I went back to the hall and glanced down it. I found him just inside the door, crouching down, patting and comforting Trixie.

My heart melted.

He looked up and said in his deep, strip-worthy, voice, "Good because I like her owner." Then he stood and stalked toward me. "You want me, Ivy?" he growled his question.

I backed up into the kitchen where my back hit the bench.

"Ivy, I asked you a question. Answer me," he ordered as he kept coming.

"Yes," I panted. Because I sure did want him in any way I could have him.

At my words, he stopped a few steps away from me.

"Show me your bedroom, Ivy," he hissed through clenched teeth.

Studying him, with his hands clenched into tight fists, I asked, "Why did you stop, Fox?"

He closed his eyes for a moment. When he opened them, they were wild once again, this time filled with lust. "Because, cupcake, if I come at you right now, in your kitchen, I won't be able to control myself. I will be between your sweet legs fuckin' you rough, crazy and fast. I at least want you comfortable while I do it." He smirked. "Go to your room, Ivy, and I will follow, but look out when I do."

Licking my lips, I nodded. As I made my way down the hall towards the bedroom, my heart beat rapidly, and my chest rose and fell quickly. Though, on the way, I had a wicked thought. I gripped the bottom of my dress and pulled it up and over my head, dropping it to the floor, leaving me in my matching red lacy bra and panties.

I heard a hiss, growl and thump behind me. I glanced over my shoulder to see that Fox had hit the wall with an open palm. "Fuck, you just had to, didn't you!" It wasn't a question, so I said nothing. He took two long strides toward me. In the next second, I was over his shoulder and he was rushing into my room. He threw me to my bed. I bounced up and down and stared at him with wide eyes as his own eyes raked my body.

"You're so goddamn beautiful. I've never had a piece like you," he growled. He whipped his tee up over his head and threw it to the floor. His tattooed chest, stomach, and arms were the sexiest thing I had ever seen.

Rubbing my legs together, I said, "And I've never had anyone as hot as you, Fox Kilpatrick."

"Christ," he swore as he undid the button on his jeans, sliding down his zipper. "Tell me you're wet and ready for me, cupcake. Tell me?" he asked as he removed his jeans and boxers. He stood, and I watched his big, hard cock spring up.

Oh, hang on, eyes off the candy. It was hard, so very hard—pun intended—but he was waiting for an answer, so I gave him one, "I'm more than ready for you, handsome."

He nodded, kneeling on the end of the bed, only to rethink it and stood back up. Instead, he grabbed both my ankles. I let out a squeak as he pulled me down the bed toward him. He let go of my legs, and his hands went to my underwear at the crotch, where he ripped them apart and plunged two fingers inside of me. My back arched and I moaned, "God, yes."

"Damn, woman, fuckin' beautiful and wet, so tight too." He leaned over me, his hand landed on the bed beside my head as he used his other hand to fuck me. "Yeah, gorgeous, take my fingers." And I did. He ran his thumb over my clit causing me to cry out.

But then his fingers disappeared, and I watched with hooded eyes as he sucked them dry. Then I felt him lining his cock up at my entrance.

"After this, after I come inside you. No one else is allowed. You get me, Ivy?" he asked as he rubbed his cock up and down my slick lips.

"Um?" I said, because I truly wasn't focused, all I wanted was his cock inside of me.

"Ivy," he growled. I looked up at him; he seemed strained, holding back control until he got what he wanted out of me. "You take no other but me inside of you. Yes?"

"Yes," I agreed.

"Good, you on the pill?" he asked.

"Yes, babe, now fuck me already," I snapped, only to groan as he thrust forward so all of him was embedded inside of me.

"Fuck," he swore. "You okay?"

"Oh, yeah," I sighed.

"Good," he hissed against my cheek and then he moved back out to thrust back in. "Beautiful pussy, fuckin' glorious," he growled as his pace picked up and he fucked me hard and fast, just like he said he would. His lips met mine. I wrapped my arms around his neck and melded my body, as tightly as I could against his, kissing him back.

"Dammit," he hissed against my lips, and then he pulled all the way out and away from me.

"Fox?" I whined.

"You nearly had me coming already. I'm not used to that, and I don't want to blow my load just yet," he explained and then knelt on the floor between my legs. His lips, teeth, and tongue were at my center, running up and down, driving me insane.

"F-fox," my breath hitched as my orgasm built inside of me.

"That's it, gorgeous. Come for me," he ordered as he inserted two fingers inside of me and I came around them.

"Hell," I cried as I kept coming. "Yes, yes." Fox removed his fingers only to have his cock deep in me once more. As he pumped into me over and over, I mewed as I ran my hands over his smooth, built body.

"Shit, cupcake, shit. I'm gonna come. Fuck," he swore as I felt his hot seed fill me. Still, he kept pumping and then grunted. Once he stopped moving, with his hands on the bed on either side of my head, he looked down at me and growled, "No fuckin' one but me." I nodded. "Good," he stated and then pulled out of me only to place two fingers inside of me once again.

"W-what are you doing?" I asked.

"You only came once. I want another one out of you before we sleep. I'd do just about anything to you, but I won't eat my own cum, so you get my fingers again until your pussy is clamping around them," he said as he continued to drive his fingers in and out of me.

"Um...o-okay," I gasped. He leaned over me and his lips latched onto my nipple where he bit down as he ran this thumb over and over my clit.

The orgasm ripped through me. I grabbed his arm with both hands and yelled through it.

As he slipped his fingers from me, I caught him smiling down at me. I was spent. All I wanted to do was curl up and sleep.

"Cupcake, let's clean up to sleep."

"Mm-kay," I mumbled, but didn't move, then I heard his chuckle.

"Ivy, come wash up, and then we can sleep," he said, and I just knew there was a smile in his voice. I was sure he was smug because he had worn me out.

"In a sec," I answered and then snail crawled up to the end of the bed where my pillow was.

"Fuck, cute and sweet." I heard Fox laugh. Then mumbled to himself, "Never had that before."

He must have left for a while because I had drifted off until the bed was dipping and Fox said, "Lift up, cupcake, and I'll get the blanket over you." I lifted. He shifted, and then I was brought back into his arms. He curled his front around my back, and before I drifted off again, I heard, "I fuckin' love the fact you don't give a shit you're sleeping with my seed in you. Fuckin' beautiful."

My alarm woke me at seven am. I'd forgotten to turn it off last night and couldn't help but be annoyed that I was awake so early on my only day off. Until, that was, I remembered the night before. Smiling, I reached out to the spot next to me, only to find it vacant and cold. I sat up quickly, turning. Fox was gone. He must have disappeared early hours for there to be no warmth next to me.

It felt like he had taken the warmth from my body.

How stupid was I? To think that a hot, sexy tattooed man would stick around. He obviously got what he was after last night.

Slumping back on my bed, I screamed into the pillow next to me. Only it smelt like him, so I threw it across the room.

Tears prickled my eyes. No! There was no way I would be crying over my own stupidity. I threw the covers from my naked body and went for a shower with a sad Trixie at my side; she was just upset as I was that Fox had left. As I showered Fox from my body, I thought about what I was going to do regarding the wedding, *and* regarding the longing I felt for a certain Foxy man.

How could he have weaved his way into my system so quickly? I didn't have an answer for the last, but the first I knew; I was going to attend my cousin's wedding on my own. Which somehow, I didn't know how, reminded me of cancelling my date with Jim, the doctor. I was in no mood to deal with another member of the male species.

After the shower and dressing in jean shorts and an old tee—it was house cleaning day after all—I went into the kitchen and fed Trixie some dry food. She barked at me happily. At least she was easily over her mood with the thought of food. *Yeah, that's an idea. I need a good breakfast of chocolate.*

Instead, I booted up my laptop and then turned to start the coffee maker. That was when I found a piece of paper.

Mornin' Cupcake
    Had to run, shit to do. Be back to pick you up at eleven. You're coming to a lunch thing.
    Fox

MY HANDS SHOOK. My heart beat rapidly, and I smiled so wide my jaw hurt. Fox still wanted to see me. He still wanted... me. Okay, so my mind had pegged him as a bad-boy biker type. I'd never had one before, so of course I was shocked that he wanted more than just one night from me.

Gripping the paper to my chest, I did a jig in the kitchen like some giddy little schoolgirl. Only to stop and look at the clock above the sink. It was ten am. I had taken too long in the shower. I raced from the kitchen with Trixie at my heels, only to run back to bring up the dating site on my laptop and send a quick apology message to Jim. Trixie and I then raced back to my room to get dressed.

It was ten-to-eleven by the time I was dressed. I had changed so many times, I was sure I had whiplash. In between wardrobe changes, I remembered I'd forgotten to check my letterbox on Friday. As I walked back into the house, I found another weird letter. That one stated, again, that I was disgusting and I'd be soon paying for my behaviour. I seriously had an effed-up family. Someone—probably a certain cousin who didn't want me at her wedding so my mum would be pissed at me—was playing stupid tricks on me and I was becoming unbelievably annoyed by it. With a sigh, I threw it in the bin and grabbed something quick to eat. After I put Trixie out in the backyard for the day, I was walking toward my room for my purse when the front doorbell rang. Squealing under my breath, I couldn't have Fox hearing I was too eager I ran-walked to the front door, dressed in jeans and a white-and-blue checked cowgirl blouse.

As soon as I had the door opened, I was encased in strong tattooed arms. "Fuck, what in the hell have you done to me?" Fox growled into my hair above my ear.

"Huh?" I questioned.

He placed his forehead against mine, his hooded eyes bore into mine. "It was damn hard to leave this mornin'. All I could think about was getting' back to you. I don't do this feelin' shit. Well, I hadn't for a fuckin' long time until you." He closed his eyes. "Or this talkin' shit," he chuckled.

There went my heart again. It swooned big time for this man in front of me. This scary biker man holding me tenderly.

"I'm glad then because you have turned me upside down and inside out with feelings." I wrapped my arms around his neck and gently, slowly pulled his face closer to mine and whispered, "I like the way you make me feel, Fox Kilpatrick, a lot." Then I kissed him on my front porch for anyone to see.

He moved a step away and snapped, "Jesus, woman. Go get your shit so we can go or I'll be draggin' you inside to fuck you."

Turning my head on the side, I asked, "And that would be a problem how?"

He smirked, shook his head and said, "Nope, I told my brothers I'd be bringin' someone. They think I'm lying." He ran a finger from my temple down and across my bottom lip. "I need to prove the fuckers wrong. Let's go, cupcake."

I gulped, bit my lip and then uttered, "Y-your brothers, as in, you're biker brothers from your group."

He snorted and then chuckled, bringing me back into his arms. "Yeah, precious, my biker brothers, but it's called a club, not a group. You don't hav'ta worry about anythin' though. Nothin' will happen to you. I won't let it," My body warmed, not from just his touch, but from his protectiveness. "Besides," he continued, "Hell Mouth, Wildcat and the gay dude will be there."

The gay dude I understood. I pulled back to ask, "Hell Mouth? Wildcat?"

"Shit, that's what the brothers' call 'em. I'm talking about Deanna, she's Hell Mouth, and Zara, the boss's misses, is Wildcat."

Giggling, I said, "I can understand Hell Mouth, but Zara as Wildcat?"

"There's a story behind it, but Wildcat can explain it to you. We hav'ta get movin'."

"I'll grab my purse. Meet you at the car," I said quickly and took off to do just that. Excitement blossomed in my chest; I was getting to see Fox in his group—sorry, club situation.

As I climbed into his truck, I asked, "So do I get a nickname? I mean, will everyone call me cupcake there too?"

"Christ, no. Well, they better not. That's my name for you. I'm sure the brothers will think of somethin' else."

I beamed at him and uttered, "Cool."

He chuckled. "Fuck me, you are too cute."

CHAPTER FIVE

I HAD the time of my life. To start with, I'd been scared shitless when I walked into what they called a compound. It was where all biker business and meetings were attended to. The dimly lit hallway kind of freaked me out, but then we came to a large room that held a bar, couches, tables, chairs, and games. It was filled with people standing around shooting the breeze.

What also freaked me out was when we entered; Fox was in front, dragging me behind him with his hand in mine. I came to a stop beside him. If it weren't for the music playing, I would have heard cricket's chirping. The laughter and talking stopped; they all turned to take in Fox and me.

I was just about to take a step back and flee when Fox's arm came around my shoulders, He leaned his head in and whispered against my temple, "It ain't you they're starin' at. Okay, they are, but it's 'cause I don't bring women here. Never have, never thought I would," he pulled away and looked into my eyes, "until you."

Smiling up at him, I reached my hand out, forgetting that we had a large audience and cupped his face. I said, "You keep being nice to me, you won't get rid of me."

He winked and said, "Good."

It was then someone boomed, "Well, fuck me." A guy around Fox's age came up to us. Damn it to hell. He was good looking. He held out his hand, and as I shook it, he said, "Good to fuckin' meet *you*, the killer charmer. I'm Stoke." He beamed, then let go of my hand when Fox glared at him, causing him to chuckle.

Before I could respond to the biker, three other men walked up, and shit a brick, all of them were good-looking, tattooed, biker men. "Hey, Ivy, Zara's told me all 'bout you. I'm Talon, her man. This is Griz, Deanna's man, and Blue," spunky Talon said. Again, I didn't get to reply because Talon turned to Fox and said, "Never thought I'd see the fuckin' day." He gave a chin lift and added, "It's good, brother."

Stoke cleared his throat and asked me, "What in the hell are you doin' with this ugly fucker? Baby, I could treat you better."

I knew he was teasing, but that didn't stop me, especially because they were all good-looking, which made me nervous. I said the first thing that popped into my head and then, once again, I continued spewing words, "Because he gave me multiple orgasms last night," I gasped. My hand flew to my mouth. Talon, who was sipping his beer, choked on it. Griz guffawed, Blue burst out laughing, Stoke beamed a mega-watt smile at me and Fox's arm, around my shoulders, squeezed me.

"Holy shit. I'm so sorry. That was rude and private. I shouldn't have said it, but you see, I get nervous around good-looking people, and you're all...." I waved my hand at them, "good-looking, though...." I paused and leaned in, bringing Fox with me because his arm was still around my shoulders. Noticing they didn't lean in toward me, I went on and whispered, "I'm sorry to say this, but Fox is way better." Standing up straight, I added, "Still, I get nervous and I can't help it. I've always been like that. To make it up to you for saying that you're not as good looking as Fox, you can all come to my café. I'll give you some cupcakes." I nodded and smiled.

"Fuck me, I missed out again," Blue grumbled and walked off.

Glancing at the other three men, who looked like they all wanted to laugh, I turned to look up at an amused Fox and asked, "Did I say something wrong? I mean besides the orgasm part, but something to upset him?"

"No, cupcake," he smiled.

"He's just jealous Killer got a woman before him," Stoke answered.

"Oh, well, I have a friend—"

Stoke stepped forward and growled, "Do not tell him that. Let's keep it between you and me for now. I'd love to fuckin' meet her," he smiled. I couldn't help but laugh.

"Hey, woman, good to see you here," Deanna said as she came up beside Griz and placed her arm around his waist. His arm automatically went around her shoulders, where he brought her in closer.

"Hi, Hell Mouth," I smiled.

She glared at me and then Killer, but turned back to me and ordered, "Ivy, I ain't Hell Mouth to you—"

"No, but she'll answer to slutguts, wench, hooker, sin eater... haven't we been through this? Anyway, she'll answer to just about anything else really." Julian smiled at me as he walked up to our group with a very sexy man beside him. "This is Mattie, my partner, and Zara's brother."

"Hi." I smiled and held out my hand to shake. He shook it and said, "It's nice to meet you."

Julian clapped with glee and announced, "We need a nickname for you." He then went on pondering it.

"Bitchface?" Deanna offered. I glared at her, but it was Fox who hissed, "You better fuckin' not."

Deanna smiled. "Relax, killer, I was just jesting."

"Chatter," Talon said.

"Ooooh, good one, Hawk-eye," Julian said.

"Definitely suits her," Griz laughed.

A blush finally rose to my cheeks from my earlier comments.

"Come on, Chatter. Let's go see what Zara's doing with the tribe of kids. You can meet her and Mattie's parents too." Julian grinned a cheeky I-know-something-you-don't grin. I looked to Fox who grimaced. Were Zara and Mattie's parent that bad?

"Fox?" I asked.

"Brace yourself, cupcake, brace. You think the three you met yesterday were in any way crazy... wait till you meet Wildcat's mum."

"She isn't that bad," Mattie offered.

Julian turned to his man, took both of his hands and said gently, "My sweet, sexy man, you are a part of her loins, so maybe you don't see it so much. But your dear mother is cray-cray, in a sweet, want to choke her way."

Mattie shuddered. "Please never talk of her loins again."

"I second that." Talon glared.

"But," Julian added, "alas, we love her. We truly do because she made two beautiful children. Isn't that right, Cap'," Julian asked Talon.

I giggled at him. Julian had been right. These bikers were scary, but once you were in their fold, you could see the love they had for their partners... or else there was no way in hell Julian would get away with anything he said or did.

I smiled up at Fox, who was grinning back down at me. *Does that mean I'm a part of this fold because of this man? Yes, it does. I'm not ashamed to admit I really like that.* Fox just touched his mouth to mine when Julian said, "Oh no, once you two start, I'll have to pry you both apart with a crowbar." He tugged me away from Fox's arms. I laughed when I saw the deathly glare Fox was sending Julian, who ignored it, saying to me, "I know it's all new and sweet, my little rose petal, but he has to know he's got to share you with us. It's what we do, and besides, I'm sure, by the way he watches you take everything in, you'll be getting more action between the sheets tonight."

I sure hope so.

With Deanna and Mattie following, Julian led me by my hand to the backyard. That was where I met the loud, funny, quirky, hot-man crazed Nancy, and the sweet, mild-mannered, caring Richard. I also got to meet Cody, Maya, Drake and Ruby, all of them cute in their own way. Cody being the oldest took his role seriously. He watched the twins like an eagle, while he also played cards with Maya. Then I met Swan, Deanna and Griz's gorgeous little girl, who had a white head of hair. She came up with a young girl named Josie. I found out later Josie's ordeal. It was no wonder she was quiet. I was happy to hear that Zara's parents had adopted her.

The men came outside to start cooking and drinking... well, more than they were inside. Often I felt eyes on me, and every time I searched, I saw Fox watching me with a small smile upon his sexy face. If I was butter, I would have melted into a puddle.

We ate at the picnic benches outside in the warm sun. I had the best day getting to know everyone, even the other bikers seemed less and less scary to me by the end of the day. In the end, I was becoming more comfortable with them all and only had a few slip-ups of talking too much around good looking people. What was the best though was the fact that they thought nothing of it. They all accepted me as I came and I think that had a lot to do with the man I was with. I could sense that they all wanted Fox to be happy, and for some reason, they thought I was the one who was capable of doing it. I found out later, just before Fox and I left, why.

Stoke came up to me while I waited for Fox to finish talking to Talon off to the side. He stood beside me, his face serious and said, "I never thought I'd see my brother smiling again." He turned to look at me. "Keep doin' what your doin'. Be sweet, just like you are. We can all see it. We all wish we had it, but I'm fuckin' glad that it was Killer who got it. That got you. Best fuckin' bet I ever made. Making him go through it was hard, but now that he has and I see the outcome...fuck, it makes me so fuckin' happy. He's had shit in his past, which was why he was a man who didn't talk, who didn't give a shit about a lot of things. It's different now." He took my shaking hand. I hated the thought of Fox having anything shit in his life. "I just want to thank you. You've brought him back to us. If you need anything, ever, just ask. We're more than willing to help."

Tears filled my eyes. "Thank you," I whispered. "But, um...what kind of shit do you mean...for his life?" I asked.

He shook his head. "Just normal stuff. Parents were arseholes, girlfriend died. That shit, but it's up to Killer to tell you it all."

"Okay," I uttered.

He squeezed my hands and said, "Okay." Then he smiled and let go of my hand just as Fox came up beside us.

"Everything all right, brother?" Fox asked.

"Sure, sure." Stoke grinned. "Just askin' your old woman if she wanted to dump your arse."

Fox arched an eyebrow, shook his head and looked to me.

"I said I wouldn't." I smiled and added quietly, "Ever."

Fox's eyes warmed. He stepped up to me and draped his arm around my shoulders. Walking off, arm still around me, Fox said over his shoulder to Stoke, "Later, brother."

Stoke chuckled and replied with, "Later, you lucky fucker."

Fox drove us back to my house where he got out of his car with a bag in his hand and walked me inside.

In my house, I alternated between chewing on my bottom lip and biting my fingernails as I walked into the kitchen. Fox went to the back door and let a very happy Trixie into the house.

Yes... swoon.

After giving Trixie a rubdown, he stood and looked at me. I caught the heated look as my eyes flittered from the floor to his bag, to him and back all over again. My mind was busy pondering... feelings, thoughts that worried me.

"You mind if I stay the night?"

I looked over at him, standing there with Trixie at his parted feet; he had his hands on his hips and a scowl now upon his face. Was he worried I was going to say no? There was no way I could, and to be honest, that was one thought that was scaring me a little.

"Does it worry you that this is weird?" I asked, though I didn't wait for an answer. I went on while looking at the floor. "And I mean weird because we've just met each other and I don't like the thought of not being around you. Oh, God, that sounds scary. I'm not crazy. I'm not going to be calling you all the time, questioning you. I promise, but it... all this is kind of scary. I've had boyfriends in the past," I thought I heard a growl, "but I felt nothing for them like what I feel for you, even after one day and it's scary. We hardly know each other. Shouldn't I be putting distance between us? Playing hard to get? But I've already slept with you, and hell, it was the best sex I've ever had, like ever. Dammit, I'm sorry my mouth flies off on its own. I have to learn to shut-up. I like your friends by the way. I really like them... not as much as I like you of course." I giggled. "That's just silly. They're so nice, and you all care for one another... it's good to see—"

"Ivy," Fox growled low in his throat.

I stood straight and turned to him. I looked at his throat, afraid I had just bumbled my way out of this... whatever this was with my stupid words.

"Look at me," he ordered. I did. His eyes were intense, only I couldn't work out exactly what the intensity meant. "First, I fuckin' love your ramblings. If you didn't do it, I wouldn't know how you're feeling about this shit between us, and second, you seem to tell the truth every damn time. Never stop and never make excuses for it. Third, yes it scares me how I feel about you because I hate the thought of having you out of my sight. It's serious, but it's good. And Four and fuckin' final because I want in between those sweet legs of yours... I'm glad you like my brothers and their women and families because if you didn't, it wouldn't have worked between us. This is who I am. Those are my people, and I can't change that."

"I would never ask you to," I said.

"Good," he clipped, and then he came at me.

Talking time was over.

CHAPTER SIX

Picking me up, I wrapped my arms and legs around him. His mouth met mine and we kissed, hard, heavy and heated while he carried me down the hall to my bedroom. With his hands on my butt, he ground his jean-clad, hard cock against my core. I arched, threw my head back and moaned.

"Fox, I need you inside me," I demanded.

He let my legs fall to the floor, his hands on my arms steadying me. After he knew I wouldn't collapse in a puddle of turned-on goo, he moved his hands to rip my cowgirl shirt from my body. In return, I pulled off his top. Our breaths were heavy with desire. I would never get enough of this beautiful specimen in front of me.

Fox reached out again and undid my jeans. He pulled them roughly from my body. Not that I minded in the slightest because I was just as rough getting his jeans off him. Though, as I was kneeling down, helping him get his feet out of his jeans I came face to face with his sausage, which looked ready to be eaten. I wound my hand around his large length. He hissed through clenched teeth. I smiled up at him as I slowly took his cock in my mouth.

"Fuck," he growled. "Damn, I love your mouth." He watched me with hooded eyes as I bobbed up and down, running my tongue all around his cock. The way he was watching me had me reaching with my other hand between my legs. A shiver ran over my body as I touched my clit. I spread my pussy lips wider and dipped two fingers into my drenched center, moaning around Fox's dick. He gripped my hair tightly; the small amount of pain turned me on even more. I'd never had a lover do that before, never felt pain while being intimate. I decided, right then, it was something I was more than willing to explore.

"That's it, precious. Fuck your pussy with your fingers," he said.

I hummed around his cock, causing him to groan. His enthusiasm sent me into a frenzy, and I drove my fingers in and out of myself faster. I brought my thumb up and rubbed my clit, ripping my mouth from Fox's dick I cried out through my orgasm.

While I was coming down, Fox picked me up, sat on the edge of the bed and brought me straight down on his erection. I gasped as he hissed, "Ride me, cupcake. Ride my cock." And I did. With his hands squeezing my hips, I gripped his shoulders and rode myself up and down his length.

"Yeah, precious, that's it. Fuck, I love your mouth, but I love your pussy even more, so tight and wet." One of his hands let go of my hips and he wound his fingers through my hair, tugging my head down so our lips touched. We devoured each other. While our mouths tasted and teased, Fox slowed my rhythm down so I was rocking slightly up and down on him.

He tore his mouth away from mine. I whimpered, but when I met his eyes, I didn't mind that he'd slowed the pace because what I saw within his eyes was so much better. He was feeling everything I was. While our bodies bonded, our hearts were mirroring the connection.

I hadn't realised I had closed my eyes until Fox ordered, "Open your eyes, cupcake. I want you to see what you do to me while I come inside your sweet pussy." Opening them, Fox's fingers reached my clit, and with a flick, I was coming again. "Open, precious." The pressure of my orgasm had me closing my eyes, but I opened them as he told me. In response, I watched his eyes soften, his brow tighten, his mouth part as he groaned through his own orgasm. His seed pumped into me and I moaned in contentment, loving every second of it.

Later in the middle of the night, I rolled in bed, still half asleep. Moments later, I felt an arm wrap around my waist and I was pulled back against a hard chest.

Warm breath tickled my neck where I felt a delicate kiss. "I like you near," Fox whispered through the room. I smiled to myself and thanked, for once in my life, my bitch-cousin, because if it weren't for her, I wouldn't be spooned by a scary, sweet, and beautiful biker man. With that smile upon my face, I fell back asleep.

As I sat in my office at my café, I thought back to my morning. Fox woke me in the early hours, even before I was due to get up, by spreading my legs and saying, "I need inside you before I have to get to work. I wanna remember your pussy milking my cock all day." He then continued to fuck me, sweet and slow, and yes, my pussy did end up milking his orgasm out of him. He then kissed me gently, but it soon turned rough before he got out of my bed naked. As I watched him walk to my bathroom, I felt like singing 'Zip-a-de-doo-dah, zip-a-dee-day, what a wonderful feeling, what a wonderful day.'

After his shower, he came back to the bed, kissed me again and told me he'd see me later. With a smack on my butt, he walked out of the room, only to come back to inform me that he was going to feed Trixie and let her out the back.

If a man treated an animal right, you just knew he would treat you right.

Finding a man in life who made you feel different in so many nice ways was hard. What was harder was finding out that your heart already knew what it wanted even before your brain acknowledged it. Because it was right then that my mind caught up to my heart and it told me Fox Kilpatrick was the one for me.

I dozed for another hour before my alarm rang, which scared the crap out of me. Getting ready for work, I didn't even try to ignore the new spring in my step after getting me more than a little something-something all weekend long.

Later at work, I brought up the dating site for the last time as I sat at my desk with a stupid grin on my face. As I was about to delete my account, I noticed I had a message. Opening it, my heart sank to my arse.

Ivy

I thought you were different, but you aren't. You're just like the rest of them. I watched you fawn over that delinquent man like some slut, and then you go on a date with him and **then** fuck him. You chose the wrong man, Ivy. You are going to regret it. I'll make sure of it.

Jim

No. No. What was I supposed to do with a message like that? Jim had seen me with Fox? Here in *my* café. He'd been watching us? He followed us. My stomach clenched at the thought of it. My heart was beating out of control. I pushed my chair back and bent over with my head between my legs, trying to steady my heart, breath, and shaky body.

I gasped… he was the one! The one who sent me those notes.

This was serious. *He* was serious.

What was he going to do?

Was he out there watching me?

What did he mean by pay for it?

Oh, my God. What do I do?

My office door opened and I heard Justine ask, "Ivy, are you okay?"

All I could do was shake my head and continue shaking it because I wasn't okay. There was no way I was okay... would I ever be again? Tears formed in my eyes and then spilled over. I was in no state of mind to stop them or my body from shaking with shock and fright.

"Ivy, what's wrong?" She sounded frantic as she tried to pull me up, but I shook her off and closed my arms around my legs as tightly as I could. I then rested my head sideways on my knees. "Manny?" Justine yelled.

"What? What is it?" he asked as he ran into the room.

"I don't know. Something is wrong with Ivy. She won't talk to me."

I closed my eyes to try to stop the tears. My stomach tightened. I closed my mouth, my lips thinning, trying to get my breath under control so I didn't lose the contents of my stomach all over the floor.

Shit, what does he mean I'm going to pay? Why me? Why this now? Fuck, he'd been to my house. He knew where I lived, where I worked.

"Miss M, what's happening? Come on, Miss M," Manny pleaded. I shook my head, and with my eyes closed, I started humming. I hated hearing their concern. It worried me and I had enough to worry about. "Get me her mobile," Manny ordered. "I'm going out front. You stay with her." Over my humming, I heard shuffling and then I felt an arm come over my back. It was small in frame so I knew it was Justine's.

"It's going to be okay. Whatever it is, it'll be fine," she assured me.

I was doubtful. No one had ever threatened me. I had no idea what to do.

Please, please...what do I do?

Sometime later, the door to my office banged open—Manny must have shut it. I jumped, but I didn't bother looking to see who it was.

"Ivy?" Fox's voice broke through it all. I opened my eyes to watch him kneel beside me so he could meet my gaze from where my head still rested on my knees. He reached out a hand and gently pushed my hair away from my face. "Cupcake, what's wrong?" His voice was gentle. I had never heard it that gentle. He was handling me with care. My scary biker man was beautiful.

"She's been like this for a while. She won't say anything. I don't know what's going on," Justine explained, her tone filled with concern.

"Ivy, please fuckin' tell me what set this off?" Fox asked.

Still, I watched him blinking. I wasn't ready to talk. I wanted to. I wanted to tell Fox everything. But I didn't. I couldn't when my own mind couldn't comprehend what was happening. I just wanted to fade...fade away so nothing could happen. Though, my heart knew it wanted to take Fox with it.

I fought with my body to keep from reaching out to Fox. I had to tell it and my heart that it wouldn't be safe for him. I needed to protect him.

But I was weak. How could I fight this... man on my own?

Fox had said he wanted to protect me....

I didn't know what to do. Everything was too hard.

Even my thoughts.

"Ivy, I need to know how to fix it, precious, please." He got nothing back from me. "Fuck," he hissed. "Fuck," he yelled.

"Brother," someone snapped, "let me try."

Fox moved out of the way, and Stoke came to his knees in front of me. He smiled. "Woman, you need to come out of this. You need to tell us what the fuck happened, because if you don't, my brother, your old man, will tear everything and everyone apart to find out what it is. He'll go fuckin' crazy doin' it too. Don't let that happen, Ivy. For him, get the fuck up and tell us what we need to know."

Oh, my God. He was right. I couldn't do that to Fox. Not after I'd only found out his brothers just got him back. I was hurting him by trying to keep him out of this. I was hurting my man by what I was doing. I blinked long and hard and then stood on shaky legs.

"That'a girl," Stoke said.

"Fox," I uttered. He turned from holding onto the door frame to me. I was in his arms in the next second. He even shoved Stoke out of the way to get to me.

"Precious, Jesus, cupcake. What the hell?" He leaned back to look at me. I placed a hand on his cheek and said, "I'm sorry for worrying you. All of you," I added as I looked at Justine.

Stoke cleared his throat and told Justine, "Give me a minute, sweetheart."

"I ain't your sweetheart," she glared, "but I'll give you a minute. Someone has to keep an eye on Manny," she said and left the office, closing the door behind her.

"Ivy?" Fox said, and my eyes went straight to him. "What happened? I left you all sweet this mornin', but then I get a phone call from the dude out front sayin' you're in a damn state. I need to know why, cupcake?"

Licking my lips, I nodded. I looked into his hard, intense gaze. He was panicked and worried about me. He wanted to help, and I knew then that I really needed it. Not only that, I needed him. I couldn't let this step between Fox and me.

I raised my hand, and with one finger, I pointed to my computer. The screen had gone blank, in rest mode, but Stoke shook the mouse. He paused to read the message and whispered, "*Fuuuck.* Brother, you need to see this." Fox let go of me. I wrapped my arms around my waist trying to keep his heat on my body, but it fled.

"What the fuck?" Fox hissed. "What the fuck?" he yelled. "Shit," he said, shaking his head. He hit the deck with his fist before he turned back to me and I was pulled into his arms. "Whatever he means, it ain't gonna happen. He won't touch you. Fuck, he should never have threatened you." He looked over my shoulder to Stoke. "Make a meet with Talon. This guy is gonna go down. You get me, brother?"

"I get you. Fuck, do I get you."

"Make the call then," Fox growled. Stoke gave a stiff nod and disappeared out of the office. "No one will touch you. I will not lose you too, cupcake." His voice held a softer emotion, and it had me thinking that his thoughts were lying in the past... only, I wish I knew how he lost his first girlfriend.

It also made me think that I needed to be stronger. Not only for my sanity but also for the man with his arms around me.

"Fox..." I started.

He took a deep breath and said, "I heard Stoke telling you I had a shit past. I did. Some of it was my own fault. I don't give a shit about losing my parents. They're dead, and they're better off dead. But I had a woman once. Yeah, we were young, but I knew I loved her. We'd surrounded ourselves with the wrong people, and it caught up with us. Fuck... promise me you will not hate me for this?" He pulled me away from his chest to meet my stare. I nodded. I doubted anything could make me hate this man. "I need words, Ivy."

"Fox," I said softly, "I promise I won't hate you."

He nodded and led me over to sit in my office chair again. Kneeling in front of me, he took my hands in his. He didn't look at me. Instead, his eyes were on our hands.

"We'd partied hard, like most nights, but one night...I lost sight of her. In the end, she got raped and stabbed by two, what I fuckin' thought at the time, friends." I gasped and gripped his hands tighter. "It was my fault. I trusted the people around us, but I should have known better. My last name is *Kil*patrick, but I got my nickname Killer for how I dealt the payback. I hunted them and killed them both," he uttered.

If the tables were turned... if anything happened to Fox like that, I would have done the same. I would have found the people responsible and exacted justice. It may be crazy talk since I'd only known the man for a couple of days. Although, by the way he made my heart shimmer with love, I knew I would go beyond anything to help him. At least I wasn't crazy enough to voice it. That *could* scare my man away. I wasn't ready to risk that.

I pulled my hands from his and watched him nod his head. He thought I was rejecting him. That caused my body to react in sadness. My eyes filled with tears, my stomach tightened, and a pain in my chest appeared.

I pushed my chair back and knelt in front of him. His head came up, his eyes wide. I took his face in my hands and smiled at him. "You're a wonderful man, Fox Kilpatrick. Nothing you just told me could ever have me hating you, so get that thought out of your head. I'm scared, worried and... really, really scared. But I know, I know you will protect me with everything you have, from whatever this psycho will do, as long as you know I will do the same for you. I'll do anything to keep you safe, Fox. We've only just started this. There is no way I am willing to lose this or you."

I took a deep breath. On a roll, I kept going and felt Fox's warm eyes sink into my soul, suffusing me in heat and warmth. "Be that, I'm not ready to move in with each other or anything. We're still testing the waters. You never know, one day you could get sick of my jibber jabbering. Until then, we'll take each day as it comes... that is, after we deal with this weirdo." I stood and started pacing.

"Which I don't get. Why take a fascination in me... and how dare he call me a slut. Slut, Fox. I'm no slut. You're the first man I've slept with in... God, two years I think." Spinning toward him, I finally felt it. Anger. "This guy will ruin everything. Finally, freaking finally, I find a man, you, who will put up with me and my word spewing." I stomped my foot. "No. That guy, that loser, idiot, cocksucker will not, and I mean, will NOT ruin this. Right?" I asked with my hands on my hips, glaring down at Fox, who was smiling up at me with an amused expression.

Standing, he swooped me up into his arms and placed me on my desk. "Fuck me. How did I get so lucky? One second you're breaking, the next you're consoling me, and then you're as angry as a crazy woman. Christ, you're mental, cute and feisty."

I glared at him as he stepped closer between my legs. "You're bloody lucky I like you, Fox... like a lot, or you'd be kicked out for that crazy comment. And yes, I'm a little highly strung, and my moods can change from one to another in seconds. Are you still willing to put up with *that*?"

"Hell yes." He grinned. Even though I saw a glimmer of worry within his eyes, he still made sure I'd see the warmer emotions he had for me, right before he kissed me. I wrapped my arms and legs around him and kissed him back with just as much gusto.

A knock on the office door interrupted us.

"In," Fox barked.

The door opened, and Stoke walked in with a smile on his face. "Damn, I thought you'd have her naked by now," he complained and then chuckled when Fox picked up my stapler and threw it at him. He dodged, and with his hands in front of him, he added, "I come bearing news. Talon said no meeting required. You want protection from the brothers for your woman, it's there. Anything you need will be there if you want it. Just call and organise it."

I witnessed Fox bow his head. It was clear the loyalty of his club really meant something to him. His brothers were willing to fight at his side for me...for his woman. It also meant something to me, which was why I shouted, "Free coffee and cupcakes all round."

Later that afternoon, I dragged Fox back into my office and told him about the notes I had received. I'd completely forgotten about them after the more recent, scarier events. I explained that I had thought it was my cousin playing pranks on me. I mentioned that we should call the police. He pulled me close and gripped me tightly. As he rested his forehead against mine, he whispered, "Do you trust me, Ivy?" I nodded. "No cops just yet. If something doesn't happen soon, we'll call them. Until then, let me and my brothers deal with it. Can you do that for me?"

Everything, but my heart, told me that this was wrong. That the police should have been called as soon as it happened. But, and that but had a huge capital b, my man, the man I wanted in my life for a very long time, he followed a path of what someone could call, different laws. The question was, now that I was with this man, was I prepared to live *my* life like his when it came to something like this?

Licking my dry lips, I answered, "Yes, but, Fox…if it doesn't work out, if you and your brothers can't find him, we will call the police, right?"

"Yeah, cupcake. Two weeks, that's all I'm asking for."

I smiled. "I can do that."

CHAPTER SEVEN

As THE WEEK PASSED, my mood and days were similar to a vomit-inducing roller coaster. One second I'd be smiling, and that, of course, was because I was thinking of Fox and my new found friends. That was until I'd remember that I was being followed by some weirdo, and then my mood would fall into the despair. Not only because I was worried for my safety, but because of everything Fox was doing to keep me safe, not only him either, but his biker brothers and also their women. If Fox couldn't be with me, one of his brothers were, even overnight. Though, I noticed it was either a brother who was married or in a relationship.

Fox arranged for his brothers to install a security system in my house and workplace. He told me there was no way in hell this fuckhead would drive me off from the places I called home. Relief had filled me when he'd made that statement. Glad didn't even begin to cover it, so instead, I showed him by giving him the best head-job I had ever given.

Despite my week of anxiety, time didn't stand still, and Friday soon arrived, the day before the wedding. Fox had pretty much demanded that we shouldn't attend it. I told him that I had to or hell would rain down upon us. He said he could take it, but I highly doubted it, not when the hell would come from my mother. In the end, he gave in... okay, it was only after I got him all sweet when I jumped his bones and he came hard.

I learned that sex did wonders for my biker man and helped me get what I wanted. Even though I was more than happy to please him in bed, the getting my own way made it that much sweeter. Plus the multiple orgasms from both parties helped. The funny thing was, he knew exactly what my motive was, and he played along with it, smirking at me. I was also learning that I couldn't fool my man.

Helen came in Monday afternoon and yelled at me, asking why I hadn't called her to inform her of *everything*. I told her I was a little distracted and occupied, but that my man and his men were dealing with it all. She sighed and mumbled with a blush to her cheeks that she knew. Stoke had taken it upon himself to go to her work and introduce himself. He'd then filled her in on everything that happened. Yes, even the part that Fox and I have had sex. Then he asked her out. She agreed. I laughed. She glared. We cried, yelled and then we got over it together. From then on, she also called in every day and rang every night. I never felt more suffocated in my life, but I didn't mind. In fact, it all warmed my heart.

MY CAFÉ HAD GAINED MORE customers over the week. Apparently, Stoke had spread the word that one of their brothers' misses owned a café that they'd get discounted food and drinks. I did try to give it to them for free, but none of them accepted that. They paid.

My lunch times were always busy. Not only from the biker brothers but also from my new friends. Deanna, Zara, Julian, Mattie, even Zara's parents and all the children came in. It could have been a ruse to keep my mind busy; most of the time it worked. No matter what though, I loved having them come in.

The only strange thing that happened for the week—well, besides when I blundered through conversations with the good-looking bikers—was that I hadn't heard from Stupid Jim. No other email, phone call, visit or anything. Fox told me not to let my guard down. Just because he hadn't made more contact didn't mean he wasn't out there watching. I was happy that he hadn't made another move, but it also annoyed me. I wanted him out of my life for good, so I could move on with it and finally stop the daily worry.

Friday lunchtime, I was sitting at a table in my café across from a large built man. He was similar to a lumberjack wearing his blue jeans and checked shirt. His name was Butch, and he worked for a PI agency. Zara had called his company and asked for help since Fox, and the bikers were unable to find Jim. He had asked questions, and I answered them, even showing him the dating site and Jim's profile. After he took notes, smiling, laughing and making me comfortable through it all, he laid his hand over mine and his sobered, hard gaze met mine. Then he said, "We'll find the bastard." His was so sincere, the way he switched from a sweet man to a gruff looking, scary one told me that he was ready to do anything to find Jim. It also had me wondering from his sever change of moods that something could have happened in his past, something that made him aggressive to any type of abuse on a woman, a little like Fox. To reassure Butch, I smiled and nodded.

Hearing hard footfalls heading our way, we both turned. Fox, with a killer look upon his face, stalked toward us.

Ignoring Butch, he asked me, "Who's this fucker?"

I gasped and glared. "Fox, that is no way to talk. And this is Butch. He works for a PI place."

Fox turned to Butch and glared. "Talon's sister's?"

Butch glared back and said, "Yeah."

Oh, wow, bad-arse, biker boss Talon had a sister in the PI business. I felt like giggling for some reason.

Fox's eyes moved from Butch to his hand that, I then noticed, still covered mine. "So I shouldn't kill him for touchin' what's mine?" he asked as he looked from our hands to me.

I moved my hand from under Butch's and stood, curling my

arms around his waist. "No, handsome, but we could talk about your possessive ways."

He smirked down at me. "Not up for discussion."

Rolling my eyes, I uttered, "Thought so." I looked down at Butch, who now seemed amused by the interaction between Fox and myself. Ignoring Butch's smirk, I added, "Sorry about him. He gets a little carried away."

Butch shook his head, stood up and said, "You bikers have all the fuckin' luck. Ivy, you rest easy. We'll find him."

"If you do, you hand him over to Hawks," Fox ordered.

Butch clenched his jaw. "Vi's already told me."

Fox smiled. "Good."

Butch gave a chin lift to both of us and left.

Fox turned me, so my front pressed against his chest. He leaned his head down so our foreheads touched and he growled, "Go to your office, Ivy. I need to fuck you. No one touches you but me. I need to fuck the thought of his touch outta my system."

My body hummed. His possessiveness was a pain sometimes, though, most of the time, it got me all hot and bothered. That was why I whispered, "Um...okay."

He took my hand and walked my dazed-self to my office. Justine gave me a knowing wink, and I watched her laugh, I smiled shyly and shrugged, though I didn't stop. Once we reached the office, Fox threw the door open. He pulled me inside, slammed the door shut and pushed me up against it as his mouth assaulted mine. His hands went to my jeans, and he popped the button. Just as I was running my hands under his tee and Fox was slowly unzipping my jeans, someone cleared their throat from behind us.

I squeaked. Fox spun fast, had a gun drawn from somewhere and pointed it at his friend's head.

Stoke laughed and said, "I guess you worked out what that dude was doing here and touching her for. Did you forget you sent me in here to wait?"

"Fuck," Fox hissed. Which told me he had forgotten.

I couldn't help but laugh. I never thought I'd see the day that Fox forgot something as his passion took over. Fox shook his head and turned back to me. "Don't you fuckin' laugh," he said with a smile, which made me giggle even more. "Goddamn, you keep up the cuteness I'll just fuck you in front of him."

My eyes widened and my lips clamped shut. But what surprised me was the tingle of lust, from the thought of someone watching us, sent me to my core. I rubbed my legs together and Fox, being so close, noticed my reaction.

"Hey, be my guest. I wouldn't mind the show," Stoke teased.

He leaned closer and whispered so Stoke wouldn't hear, "You want him to watch me take you, cupcake? Does that turn you on?"

"M-maybe…." I said and bit my bottom lip.

"Christ, it does. I don't mind having my brother watch. You're fuckin' perfect when you come. But he will not touch you. Hear me?"

"Yes," I whispered. "As long as you're sure?" I asked.

"Jesus, yes." Fox pulled my hips forward and slanted his lips across mine. He kissed me fiercely as my hands groped anywhere they could on his body.

"Ah… do you want me to leave?" Stoke asked from behind Fox. He sounded confused.

Instead of answering, Fox turned and pulled me over to the front of the desk. As I breathed heavily, he placed my hands on the desk where Stoke sat on the other side in my office chair.

Stoke licked his lips. His eyes were hooded. I gasped when my jeans were pulled roughly down my legs. "Fuck me," Stoke hissed.

"Step outta them, cupcake." I did as I was told and I was rewarded with Fox's hands running up my legs to my butt. I felt his chin on my shoulder. I just knew he was looking at Stoke because as I watched, Stoke turned to look back at Fox. "You look. You watch, but you never fuckin' touch. She's mine. You get me?" Fox asked.

Stoke licked his lips again, and for once, he refrained from any wise cracks. His eyes were serious and held desire as he nodded slowly.

My heart rate took off. Oh, my God, this was thrilling, sexy and hot all at the same time. Never in my life had I thought it would be that wild to have someone watch as another man, who I adored, take me.

"You wet already, precious?" Fox asked. He didn't wait for an answer. Instead, he slid two fingers inside of me. "Fuck, you're drenched. You like to be watched, cupcake. That's damn hot." He got in closer to me, so his body leaned over mine as his fingers pushed in and out of me. "Stoke, her pussy is so ready for me. Should I take her?"

Stoke cleared his throat and uttered, "Yes."

Fox removed his fingers. I felt his hand working to undo his jeans. I moaned, my head thrusting back, as he slid his erection inside me slowly.

"Shit," Stoke whispered. I looked back down at him; his chest was rising up and down fast. Fox gripped my hips and started to move faster, pounding into me, sounds of our flesh slapping against each other echoed around the room.

"Isn't she fuckin' beautiful?" Fox asked. His arms came around my chest, and he pulled me up more. Then one hand slid down to my waist and glided over my bare stomach. My tee must have come up, Fox pushed it up further with his hand and cupped my breast, squeezing.

"Damn exquisite," Stoke answered. I opened my eyes and moved my head from Fox's shoulder to look down at Stoke. The feel of his eyes on me and Fox's cock in me was wonderful. I watched as Stoke pushed back in the chair a bit and started to rub his dick through his jeans. "Brother?" he asked.

What the question was I didn't know, but when Fox barked, "Yes," Stoke then undid his jeans and pulled his cock free of his boxers. He began to stroke himself in front of me.

"*My* Ivy likes that, Stoke. She just got wetter," Fox growled, and he was right. Fox took his hand off my breast and ran it down my body to between my legs where he rubbed my clit.

"Yes, God, yes," I moaned. I wanted to close my eyes, but I didn't. Instead, I watched as Stoke moved his hand faster and faster over his dick.

"Precious, come for me while he watches you," Fox ordered. His finger on my clit rubbed that little bit harder, driving me closer and closer to my orgasm.

"Please, God, please, harder," I begged.

Fox rubbed and slammed his cock into me harder. It was building and it was going to be big. I leaned forward and gripped the desk with my hands to brace, and then it hit me. I cried out and bit my bottom lip, humming through it as my walls milked Fox's cock. When I heard a groan come from Stoke, I looked to see him lift his tee higher as his cum shot out, landing on his stomach. I felt Fox's hot seed fill me as he swore through his orgasm.

CHAPTER EIGHT

AFTER STOKE CLEANED HIMSELF OFF, he stood and mumbled something about getting takeaway for their lunch, and he'd meet Fox out the front. His parting words were, "Lucky, lucky fucker." Which caused Fox to laugh.

Even though I was embarrassed by what we just did in front of him, I still yelled after him, "Bye Stoke." As I put my jeans back on.

His reply was "Later, sweetheart."

Then I turned to Fox ready to ask him some questions and tell him my worries, but he got there first. Pulling me to his chest, he shared, "Stoke and I have been mates since I joined Hawks. He was the only one I talked to. He's the only one, *the only fuckin' one*, I'd let see you half naked with my cock inside you. You like people watchin' us, I'll take you to a nightclub where we can do that, but no one touches you. If you fancy my brother watchin' us again, I can deal with that." He grinned. "I like showin' what I have off, makes me fuckin' happy that they know I get to have you when they can't. Whatever you want, whenever you want it, we'll deal, yeah?"

I licked my lips and nodded. "Okay... um, as long as no one touches you too. I wouldn't like that," I admitted. For someone to watch what we had together was a big turn on, but that was it. I wouldn't want anyone to join in or touch what was mine either. So I totally got what Fox was saying and I was all for it.

"Good, no one would ever touch me but you." His lips pressed against mine gently. "I gotta shoot off. See you tonight."

"Ah, Fox?"

"Yeah, precious?"

"The wedding's tomorrow."

"I know that, cupcake. What of it?"

"Um, do you have a suit?"

He threw his head back and laughed. I liked seeing that a whole heap. When he calmed down, he kissed me quickly and said, "Ivy, there is no way in hell I'd be caught dead in a suit, even when I'm dead. I'm a jeans man, precious, and your family will just have to deal, yeah?"

"Okay." I smiled. I could handle that. After all, he was willing to put up with my family.

"I gotta go, cupcake. Stay in the shop. Griz should be here soon."

"Yeah, handsome," I murmured against his lips, and then kissed him long, deep and hard, pulling a groan from him.

He shifted back and ran a hand down my cheek. "How is it that we've just fucked, good and proper, but I'm already hard to go again?"

"Um?" Was all I could say because right then I really wanted to go again as well.

"Shit, Christ." He kissed me one last time and took two steps to the office door. "I'll take care of you again tonight." He smiled over his shoulder.

I clapped and uttered, "Yippee." Shaking his head, he laughed before he disappeared.

I walked around my desk and slumped down in my chair, sighing, but smiling. I really could not believe that just happened.

Oh. My. I had awesome, wonderful sex in front of Stoke and I liked it, a lot… not as much as I loved my alone time with Fox, but still, at least I discovered a new turn on for me.

After I tidied up, I walked back out to the front of my café and found Griz sitting in the corner booth so he was facing the whole store. As I made my way to the counter, I smiled and waved at him. He sent me a chin lift. I gestured with my hand up to my mouth, sipping an invisible coffee, and then with my other hand, I pretended I was munching on something. I could see his chest moving; he was chuckling at me. He gave me a wink, and I took that as a yes, so I went ahead and got him some lunch.

I was getting the hang of being a biker's woman. Now all I had to do was work out what the grunts and some of the chin lifts meant, and I'd be set—because let's face it, those men communicated in their own secret way with chin lifts.

SATURDAY MORNING, I'd woken late, and now I was running around like a mad woman or like a chicken with its head cut off. All this while Fox calmly sat at the kitchen table with his feet up on another chair sipping his coffee with an amused smile upon his lips.

"Cupcake, calm the fuck down. We have three damn hours," he said as I was going through my kitchen drawers looking for some extra bobby pins. I turned my head to glare at him and saw Trixie wander in, trot over to Fox and lay at his feet. He put his feet on the ground and bent to give her some attention.

I shook my head and went back to the dilemma. "Fox!" I screeched. "Three hours isn't going to be enough. I still have to shower, dress, and put makeup on; have breakfast because God only knows why my stupid cousin would have a wedding right at lunchtime." I turned fully to Fox with my hands on my hips. "I mean, who does that, handsome? A wedding right at lunchtime. She knows people will be starving. Why would she do that? Does she want everyone cranky?" I threw my hands up in the air. "She probably does, which means we need to feed you up before we go. I can't have you getting cranky, even though you'll get cranky having to be around my family, but I mean even crank*ier*. You'll end up killing everyone and then we'd have to go on the run... after we come back and pack and get Trixie—hmmm, maybe we should pack before we go? No, no, no, I'll just feed you up real good and calm your beast." I turned to the pantry. "Now what do you want to eat? Steak, bacon, stir-fry?"

"Cupcake?" Fox said, his voice had me looking over my shoulder to him straight away. Yes, he was laughing his arse off. "Before you have a panic attack, go and start to get ready, I'll make us something for breakfast and I'm sure as fuck ain't having steak or stir-fuckin'-fry for breakfast." He stood, came at me and pried my hands away from the cupboard doors. "Move your arse, woman, or I'll smack it."

I bit my fingernail and pondered the smacking. Would we have time? That was the question.

"Christ, woman, you keep looking at me like that, we won't make it to the fuckin' wedding. Get your arse in the shower before I change my mind about even attending your dipshit cousin's wedding."

He was serious. I could tell. Kissing him quickly, I jogged from the kitchen. Usually, Trixie would be at my heels, but she stayed with her new master. I couldn't blame her. He certainly was my master in bed.

"Don't forget to feed your beast, we need to tame him," I yelled down the hall. I knew I couldn't get an answer, so I went for my shower.

I showered and dressed in a long, shoestring strapped, black dress. I was just applying the final touches to my light make-up, just like Zara had done for me, when Fox called from the kitchen, "Cupcake, you better fuckin' come eat before we have to go or you'll be the one killing your family 'cause you're so hungry."

I smiled and made my way down the hall. Upon entering the kitchen, I heard Fox hiss, "Fuck." My eyes met his warm ones as they raked over my body. "It's gonna be the shortest wedding in damn history. We'll give 'em two hours and then I want you here on your back with my cock inside you *while* you wear that dress."

I giggled. "I guess you like the dress."

"Christ, woman, I love it. Eat so we can go and get home quicker," he ordered.

I MADE sure we sat at the back of the church for the ceremony so no one would notice us, which they didn't. It helped as I also had us in the corner. I told Fox I wanted to show him off, but I wasn't ready just yet for the questions and... evilness. He chuckled, no doubt thinking I was being over the top, but he didn't know. Once he found out, I was ready to tell him 'I told you so.'

Outside the reception room, at a ridiculously expensive hotel, I stopped Fox with a hand on his chest. He looked down at it and then to my eyes. "Um, I ah, I left out one part of information."

He closed his eyes and sighed, "What?"

"I said your name was Max and that you're a cop," I said quickly.

He opened his eyes wide, but then they turned slanty. He glared at me. *Uh oh.* "I was under pressure when I was making you up. By the way, we've been dating for two years," I added and pouted.

"Fuck me," he growled. "No, cupcake. No, we ain't fuckin' lyin', especially when I will be around for a fuckin' long time."

"Fox," I whined. "Oh, my God, please just go with it; otherwise, what am I going to tell them?"

"We'll wing it," he smiled.

"Wing it?" I yelled.

"Yeah, precious," he said, taking my hand in his while I was in shock. Opening the doors, we walked into the room.

Like the vultures they were, we were surrounded in seconds by my mother, father, Aunt Lisa—Leanne's mother, bitch-cousin herself and her new husband.

"Brace yourself, handsome, brace," I uttered out the side of my mouth, throwing his words back at him. His eyes were hard, but he grinned for me and placed his arm around my waist.

"Ivy-lee, I see you finally made it," Mum sneered. "You should have seen the ceremony. It was beautiful."

Fox looked down at me and mouthed, 'Ivy-lee.' I shrugged. It was just my mum's way to make my name sound more elegant. I thought it sucked. Throughout my whole life, Mum always thought she was better than anyone. Even her children. To her we were a burden, she brushed us off to the cooks and cleaners, in the house I was brought up in. I think it had something to do with the fact that her parents were the same to her. My mum grew up with money and was taught at a young age not to care about anyone else but herself. She was mean and vindictive, even toward her own husband.

Dad and Mum met at a young age when she wasn't so uptight. A very long time ago, he used to be fun and caring, but she drew that out of him. Now, he was a man with no backbone. He lived his life quietly and worked long hours to get away from his wife.

Really, I was surprised that my sister, brother and I turned out half-normal when we had no love in the house as children.

"I was there, Mum. We were sitting in the back. You just didn't see me."

"Oh, I saw you." Aunt Lisa smiled, eyeing Fox. She then continued to lick her lips. I glanced at Leanna to see she was also eyeing Fox.

"Why didn't you say anything, Lisa?" Mum questioned her sister, who ignored her.

"So this is your mystery man, Max?" Dad asked.

"Um...." I began.

"No. I'm Fox *Kil*patrick. I'm your daughter's new man. We've been dating for nearly two weeks now."

"Really and what happened to Max?" Mum asked, the look on her face told me she never believed my lie in the first place. Her next words backed that look up. "You may as well come clean. I knew no one would date you for two years. You're too annoying, even as a child." My cousin laughed. Dad sighed and walked off to the bar while my Aunt still eye-fucked my fella.

"It's true," Leanne added. "You never could keep down a boyfriend. They only wanted you for one thing. God knows why," she looked me up and down, "and once they got that, they took off. Pitiful really."

"Oh, come now. Let's not forget Lester," Aunt Lisa said. They all laughed.

I groaned. Lester was our neighbour when I was fourteen. I had a major crush on him, and he pretended to like me because my mum and Aunt paid him to.

"So let me guess, dear," Mum started. "This here…." she gestured to Fox with her hand and a gleam in her eye. Even she liked the way Fox looked. "….is a friend of a friend helping my poor child out, so she didn't look like a fool in front of her family. She has always been the lost soul of the family. The black sheep that no one could handle being around for too long." She moved to Fox's side and took his arm, leaning into his side. "That is so sweet of you," she cooed. "Let me know if you need anything. I'm more than willing to help."

Fox raised his top lip at her and shook her off. He stepped back bringing me with him. He looked down at me and glared.

"Sorry," I uttered because I was so very sorry. Being there was all a mistake. I should never have put him up to this, made him put up with my family. No one, none of my friends liked them; hell, I didn't even like them.

"Cupcake," he growled.

"Did he just call *her* cupcake?" Leanne gasped. "More like a mountain cake. Her arse looks like she eats a whole heap of them. Why did you even make me invite her?" she whined, no doubt to her mother.

"Because we had to show that we can understand when it came to people like her."

"Fuckin' enough," Fox barked.

"Fox," I started.

"No, precious, you don't put up with that. My woman doesn't put up with that, even if they are fuckin' family."

"Keep your voice down, young man," Mum warned.

"No." He let go of me and stepped up to Mum with Aunt Lisa and Leanne beside her. "You do not talk to my woman like that. From now on, you will be sweet and charming to her. I don't give a fuck if you're her mother or not. If I see or feel her body tense once more because of words you, any of you, have spoken to her, then I will make you pay. My woman, Christ, *your* daughter, is the best thing to happen to my life. You don't even deserve to be in her presence. But she's too kind for her own good and came to this shit, over-the-fuckin'-top wedding." Fox took a step back and held my hand. "You threaten her again into something like this, you'll be hearing from me," he warned. All of them were frozen in shocked states. The room was quiet. There were several eyes on us, and then, from the bar, came clapping.

I turned wide-eyed to my father, who was smiling big and clapping. "Here, here," he said.

I tugged on Fox's hand. He looked down at me and said, "Your mum's a bitch. Your Aunt's a bitch, and so's your cousin. Fuck, precious, next time I'll take your warning. You wanna get out of here?" he asked, turning us, so we faced each other.

Grinning huge, I laughed and shook my head. "You have made my day."

"Good," he grunted.

"And I'm sure you'll make my night even better."

His eyes warmed instantly. "Fuck yeah."

"So I'll need food for energy. Let's eat their food and drink their booze, then we'll get out of here."

He chuckled and said, "Sounds like a plan."

THE PLAN HAD BEEN GOOD. We ate. We laughed, and even my father came to talk to us. He told me he was proud I'd found a man who was willing to take care of me and protect me from anyone, even our family. He then told me he was going to file for a divorce. I gasped in surprise and gripped Fox's hand hard. I never thought I would see the day my father grew some balls. I was glad to witness it. He said he couldn't take her attitude any longer and that he wished he had stood up for my siblings and me as my man did, a long time ago. He hated himself for it and asked for my forgiveness. He also told me he hoped I was willing to spend more time with him. He looked to Fox after asking that.

Fox, who was leaning back in his chair with his arm along the back of my chair, said, "It's up to Ivy."

Dad looked back at me. I smiled and said, "I would really like that."

"Thank you," he answered, emotion in his voice. He hugged me and disappeared from the reception.

The plan that we had went to shit when I told Fox I was running to the loo before we left. They were inside the reception room so I guess we both thought everything would be fine, and really, I had been lulled into a sense of safeness being around Fox and hearing nothing from Jim.

I was wrong.

Opening the door to the bathroom, someone shoved me from behind. I went flying. Thankfully, the sink was in front of me and I managed to grab it before I sprawled on the floor.

"What the—" I began.

"Shut the fuck up, you stupid slut." I turned to find the man I once saw from his profile picture online. Jim was standing there with a knife held out, pointed at me.

CHAPTER NINE

KILLER

I WAS WAITING for Ivy by the doors so we could get the fuck outta this fucked-up reception. I wanted to get back to her place and pound into her. I was already hard just thinkin' about it. Shit, let's face it; my dick was hard as soon as she walked outta her room in that goddamn dress.

My thoughts soon changed. I had been waiting on a call all night to see if Vi, Talon's sister, had any more luck finding the cockhead antagonisin' my woman. She said she had a lead. Obviously, that didn't pan out, which pissed me off. I just wished her shit would be over. I wanted someone to find the fucker who threatened her, so I could beat the hell outta him for scaring her.

She was right though. There was no way in hell this prick would ruin what we had goin' on. It had been fuckin' years, *years* since my dead heart woke from its doze. Now that it had, because of Ivy, I was ready to protect it and her in every fuckin' way. Which meant I was willing to do anything to get this fucker out of her life so we could move the fuck on and *then* I'd tell her I was movin' in permanently.

From past experiences, there was no time worth wastin'. When you saw what you wanted, you went for it, and I had. I wanted it around me all the damn time. I wanted Ivy around me as much as I could, and that meant one of us was shiftin' places, likely me.

My phone rang from my pocket. I fished it out and flipped it open, "Yeah?"

"Where in the fuck are you? Tell me, brother, that Ivy is at your side?" Stoke growled over the noise of a movin' vehicle.

"She went to the bathroom. What in the hell, Stoke?" Drawing my hand into a fist, my brows drew down. I was annoyed by his question. He knew where we were, yet a panic settled deep with my gut.

"Find her. Get her, Killer. He's there. The fucker is there. Billy just called. He was knocked out outside the fuckin; reception place. He's there, man."

"Christ," I yelled. The people in the room paused to watch me. I didn't give a shit. I ran for the ladies' room and ripped the door open. "FUCK!" I bellowed. "He's got her. The window's open. They're outside on the move. I'm heading out." I punched my fist into the wall. Pulling away my hand, dust and shit flew every-where from the hole I'd left behind. No sooner had I done it, I was on the move again. I had to get to her. I had to find her...I just had to.

"We're a minute away. Billy should be out there. Go, brother, go."

I threw the front doors open and bolted around the side on the gravel road in the car park and suddenly came to an abrupt halt.

"*What the fuck?*" I whispered.

The dick with my woman spun toward me, away from Billy, who was holding a gun to the wanker. But as he spun, the knife at Ivy's throat cut into her, causing her to cry out. I watched as blood dripped down her neck.

"Move away. Back off now or I'll kill her."

"What in the world?"

Christ. Ivy's whore of a mother walked up beside me, others

gathered around. Jim moved their bodies so he could see both Billy and me.

"*You* need to back the fuck up and take your hands off my woman."

"H-handsome," Ivy started. I watched her swallow. "There's no use talking any sense into him. I've tried."

"Shut up you slut," Jim screamed, shaking her.

"Dammit, that hurt," Ivy complained. "And I'm not a slut. I never was and never have been. I hadn't even had sex for two years before I met Fox. Two years, Jim."

I rolled my eyes. Bloody hell my woman could talk at any inappropriate time. I pulled my gun from the back of my jeans and pointed it at him. "I won't say it again. Let her go and we won't kill you."

"Can someone please tell me what is going on?" Ivy's mum snapped.

"Shut it, woman," I hissed.

She put her hand on her hips and said, "I will not shut it. A man has a knife to my daughter's throat." She looked toward Jim. "Who are you and what are you doing? I can't believe you brought this trouble here Ivy-lee. It's disgusting."

Fuck. Just that statement had me wanting to punch the bitch out. Too damn bad I didn't hit women. I was seriously thinkin' about changing that for a second. For once, I wished Hell Mouth was around. She could have done it for me.

"Really, Mum?" Ivy glared. She tugged at Jim's arm at her throat.

"You all need to shut the fuck up, or I *will* kill her," Jim screamed.

A van came barrelling around the corner and stopped. I smiled. My brothers were here. The door to the van opened, and Griz got out, Talon came around from the other side, and from the back of the van, came Stoke, Blue, and Pick. All had their guns out and aimed at Jim.

Jim looked about ready to piss himself. I could see sweat beads on his brow. His hand now shook at Ivy's throat.

"Oooooh, someone's going to get it," Ivy sang.

"Jesus, precious. How about you don't tease the fucker while you have a knife at your throat."

She looked like she was pondering the damn thought and then she said, "Good idea."

"W-who are you all?" Jim stuttered.

"You played with the wrong woman, Jim," Talon started. "She belongs to us. She's Hawks."

Jim actually squeaked like a little girl, causing my brothers to laugh. There was no way I would laugh until my woman was outta harm's way.

"Blue?" I called.

"Yeah, brother?"

"Can you and Pick get these people out of here?" I asked. If something was gonna go down, we didn't need the witnesses.

"Everyone clear the fuck out. Now," Blue yelled.

Most moved all except Ivy's damned mother.

"I'm not going anywhere," she said.

"Fine," I barked.

Just then another car came around the corner, a sleek Mercedes. As soon as it stopped, out hopped Vi, her man, Travis, and Butch.

Vi walked up and stood to the front of the bikers. She pulled her gun out and pointed it at Jim and my woman.

"Jim Coben, you are under arrest for the murder of three women. Come in quietly or not," she shrugged. "My brother and his crew will take care of you."

"Y-you can't do that. Cops can't threaten people."

Vi smiled. "I'm not a cop. I'm just a PI."

"You are the shit." Ivy smiled. My brothers once again chuckled around me. "We so have to have coffee one day. I want to hear all about your PI days. Oh, hey, Butch." She waved. She fuckin' waved like nothin' was really going down. Like she didn't have a goddamn knife at her throat.

"Ivy," I growled.

"Yeah, yeah. Right, I'll stay quiet now while this dick has me. But can we hurry this along? I was on a happy high earlier, but it's fading."

"Holy shit," I heard Billy utter. I was thinkin' that same fuckin' thing. Could my woman never shut the hell up?

"Dammit, Ivy," I snapped.

"Don't you snap at me, Fox Kilpatrick," she barked back. "Sorry, sorry just a little tense here, right..." She made a zipping motion across her lips.

"Hang on." We all groaned when she started up again. Jim yelled for her to shut up. She told him no.

"I think I like her." Vi grinned.

"What do you mean, Vi, by Jim is under arrest for murder?"

"The cops have been looking for him for the last three months. He's done this to three other girls from that dating site."

"You met on a dating site," Ivy's mum screeched.

"T-three other women?" Ivy stuttered. "Three?" She moved her head slightly, making the blade dig in.

"Cupcake, please," I asked.

"You've hurt three other women." Her tone was low, a mix of sadness and a hint of anger.

"And they deserved everything they got. Stupid sluts."

Ivy looked back at me. She had tears in her eyes for women she never knew.

"Ivy," I warned.

"Handsome, he can't keep doing this."

"And we'll take care of it," I said. I just knew she was forming some sort of plan in her head.

"Fox, you know that isn't going to work until I'm out of the way."

"Ivy, whatever you're thinkin', fuckin' don't," Talon ordered.

Ivy closed her eyes, and when she opened them, they looked so sad it hurt me to my core. "Don't," I uttered.

She didn't listen. She pulled her head down causing the knife to slice her throat more, and then brought her head back hard, hitting

Jim in the nose. He dropped her, gripping his nose. As my brothers jumped him, I went for Ivy, who had fallen to the ground.

Laying my gun on the ground, I reached for her arms and rolled her over. Blood flowed from her neck. Ripping off my tee, I held it against it.

"Get her to the car, Killer. The car," Vi yelled beside me. I picked her up and ran to the car where Travis was already waiting in the driver's side.

I climbed in the back with Ivy on my lap. She looked up at me and smiled. She went to talk, but I shushed her. "No, precious, don't. I'll tell you how fuckin' foolish you were later, and then you can tell me how sorry you are." *Fuck, fuck, fuck.* My tee was soaked with her blood. I applied more pressure, trying not to hurt her. She reached her hand up and touched my cheek. She was in pain and bleeding, yet she was still trying to comfort me.

Christ.

"I'm movin' into your place, cupcake. After this, I'm movin' in, and you will not say anything about it." I told her as her eyes started to close. "No, no, no, Ivy, precious, keep your eyes open for me. Fuck, please, keep them open for me." I blinked and blinked, but the stupid tears wouldn't go away. I turned my head to wipe them on my shoulder. "That's it, cupcake. Keep your eyes on me. Good girl."

"We're here. I'll get someone to help," Travis said and then vanished.

"When this is over, I'm gonna tan your arse," I promised at her temple. "You have my heart to take care of, Ivy Morrison. I need you, so don't go gettin' any ideas, woman. I need you because you're my other half. You stay with me," I croaked as the passenger door opened and emergency staff pulled her from my arms. It was then I realised she was unconscious.

EPILOGUE

FOX DIDN'T LIE. After I got out of the hospital, with my neck bandaged up hiding eleven stitches, he moved in. The earlier days in the hospital were still a blur because I was that doped up on drugs for the pain. Still, Fox Kilpatrick, my biker man never left my side, unless it was to shower. He even had his biker brothers bring food for us because he said the hospital food was shit. I told them not to bother, but they also said that they wanted to come and visit me anyway. I thought that was sweet.

My mum had come to visit me. I woke to find Fox standing in the doorway growling at her saying she wasn't welcome. It was only hours before I fell asleep that Fox, yet again, told me my mum was a bitch. At the incident, she showed no concern for me at all. Blue mentioned to Fox that he watched her turn up her nose and stalk back into the reception to continue the night as nothing happened. Like her daughter hadn't been rushed to the hospital.

So there were a few things I wanted to say to her, which was why I said, "Handsome, let her come in."

Fox looked over his shoulder to me. Once I gave him a thumbs up, he moved aside and Mum glided into the room like the blood-sucking vampire she was.

"Ivy-lee, I'm really not happy with your choice in a man. Did you know he was in a biker club? A biker club for God's sake. I understand you tie yourself to anyone who shows a bit of interest in you, but really, you need to find someone mentally stable." She took my hand in hers, leaned in and whispered, "I'm sorry I didn't get here any sooner. I had things to do. But now I'm here, you can tell that hooligan to clear out and that you never want to see him again." She stood and nodded at me.

I removed my hand from hers and wiped it on the sheet. I glanced over at Fox and smiled. Right there, standing in his usual jeans and tight tee that showed his beautiful body, was my future. There was no way I would ever want to get rid of him.

I looked back to Mum. My voice clear and strong, I said, "No, Mum."

She gasped and then snapped, "What do you mean *no?*"

"I mean no. I'm not getting rid of the man who cares for me. He may be a biker man, but I love that about him. I love his friends, his family, his possessiveness, his crankiness and I love that he can communicate what he wants without words. All I have to do is look at him." Tears pooled in my eyes. "I love that man, Mum. He's my future and I'm sorry to say, you're my past, a past I can do without in my life."

"What?" she screeched, her face contorting.

Fox took a step forward, but I waved him off and continued, "Mum, it's been four days and you haven't seen me. You didn't even come to the hospital after what happened. Dad did. He came, but you didn't. You don't really care. What you do care about is what other people think. You care that I embarrassed you." I licked my lips, feeling tired again. I wanted to sleep, but I needed to finish this. "Do you know what, Mum? My man hasn't left my side. He was even pushed to shower and change clothes because he was worried I'd wake and he wouldn't be here. Do you know how I know this? Because his friends told me. They've all been here. Not only them but their women as well. They have shown me more love and warmth in the last week than I've ever felt in my life," I sighed. "I love you, Mum, of course I do. But I can't be around you. I'm sorry." Even though sadness filled me, I couldn't help but feel like a heavy weight had been lifted from my shoulders.

"You were always a self-centered little shit, Ivy. I'll be glad to have you out of my life."

"You fuckin' bitch," Fox barked. "Get out! Get the fuck out now before I remove you myself." Stepping toward her, she dodged around him and left.

Fox came to my side, sat down on the seat and took my hand. "Your mum's a bitch, precious."

I laughed, but it hurt. My hand went to my throat. "I know, handsome. I know."

"So... you love me?" He smiled.

"You weren't supposed to hear that. It's too soon." I grinned. He got up and leaned over, so our noses touched. Before he could say anything, I continued, "But of course I love the man who told me I held his heart and that I was his other half."

"You heard that?"

"Yes," I uttered.

His eyes were soft, softer than I had ever seen. "Good," he stated. "Because I meant every word. You're crazy, but I wouldn't be without you. I fuckin' love you, too, cupcake." A sob caught in my throat. Tears broke, and my man kissed them away before his lips gently touched mine.

On the fourth day in hospital, I woke to find Fox at my side sitting in a chair. He said I could be getting a visit from the police soon. He'd held them at bay until I was more myself, and hadn't mentioned anything earlier, wanting me to recover. No sooner had he told me that, there was a knock at my door. The police had arrived. I never asked Fox what was done with Jim. But when they asked me to identify the man who attacked me, I was shocked. I mumbled a yes, and they brought forward a picture. It was of Jim, battered and bruised. I looked at Fox. He smirked and winked. The proof was right in front of me. They did hand him over to the authorities, and I was glad. I wanted him judged for what he did to the other women. Though, from the picture, it looked like Fox had time for a little payback himself. I was amazed I wasn't repulsed by my man beating another. I hated violence. This confirmed I was absolutely at peace with Fox and the way he worked through situations. I was at peace because I knew deep down that Jim deserved it for what he did. Not only to me but for taking the lives of three women.

When I got out of the hospital, Fox took me home. I walked in to find a very happy Trixie. She bounced around and barked. Once I gave her enough attention, she settled. I left Fox in the kitchen to go and have a lay down on my bed. That was when I discovered Fox had moved in. I went to dump my bag in my closet and found his clothing hanging. I bit my bottom lip to keep myself from squealing with glee. I walked out of the closet to see him leaning against the doorframe.

"Do not say one word. It's happenin'. Get over it," Fox said.

I shrugged, took off my tee, removed my jeans and then lay on the bed. "I'm tired, handsome, so you're going to have to do all the work."

"Christ," he barked. I smiled over at him. Desire raced through my body as he removed his clothes quickly. He got on the bed and hovered over me. "You good then? You don't care I moved in?"

"No, I don't mind at all. Now get to work, Mr Kilpatrick."

"I'm on it," he grinned. I arched so he could unhook my bra. He slowly bought it down my arms and flung it somewhere in the room. Intense eyes stared down at me. Then with one hand, he cupped my breast. I sighed. He smiled as he lowered his mouth to my nipple and sucked it in, swirling his tongue around it.

"Yes, handsome, that feels good."

"You'll feel even better soon," he growled.

"Promises, promises."

"Don't get cheeky on me, woman. I still owe you a tanning." I didn't get to reply. Instead, his mouth met mine, and he kissed me hard, only to gentle it by running his tongue along my lips as his hand made its way down my stomach to in-between my legs. He pulled my panties aside and ran a finger over my lower lips, separating them. Our kiss turned urgent as soon as he entered two fingers inside of me. I moved one hand from his shoulder down to grip him through his boxers. He groaned. I panted around his lips as he drove his fingers faster in and out of me.

"Fox," I mumbled against his lips. He moved back. "I want you inside of me when I come."

"Fuck, yes." He was too eager even to remove his boxers. I supposed it had been a week since we'd had sex, so I couldn't help but giggle when he ripped my panties from me and shoved his boxers down, without removing them completely. He spread my legs further, and he glided inside of me. I sighed content.

"Jesus, cupcake, I love seein' that look upon your face as you take my cock. Fuckin' beautiful," he said as he slowly pushed and withdrew from my wet pussy.

"Handsome, I need it hard and fast," I moaned as he pushed deep and hit my G-spot.

"No. I might hurt you."

I opened my eyes and glared up at my man. "If you don't fuck me hard and fast, it'll be another two weeks before you get any."

"Bullshit, you love this."

"I do, Fox. I do." He kept going slowly and gently. "Okay, handsome, let me say this then. Fuck me hard and fast, Fox Kilpatrick or I'll have Julian here for dinner every night for a week."

"Christ, woman, you play dirty."

"That's because I like it dirty," I said.

He smirked. "All right, precious. Brace." I did. I moved my arm above my head and held onto the headboard. He lifted my hips by his hand, placing it on my butt and slammed into me. His thrusts were wild and crazy. I fucking loved it.

"God, yes, Fox, yes. Like that," I moaned.

"Play with your pussy, Ivy. Touch yourself," he ordered.

I opened my eyes and took in his hooded eyes as he watched my hand slid down my body to my clit. I rubbed it and cried out. Fox groaned.

"I'm close, so close," I panted, but there was no way I was taking my eyes off my man. I wanted to witness him come and lose himself. His eyes were on my slicked finger as it ran over my clit faster. Raising his eyes, he smiled a smile that lit up his face.

"Mine," he growled, sending me over the edge. I forced my eyes to stay open as my walls clenched around his cock. I whimpered through it. "Fuck, you're gorgeous," he whispered. He let go of my legs and leaned down over me so he could touch his lips to mine. I was about to deepen the kiss, but he pulled back. Our eyes met, and he bit out, "I'm gonna come, precious."

"Yes," I uttered.

He kept my stare as I felt his seed flow into me. Fox grunted and pumped fast four times. As he slowed, he said, "Fuckin' love you."

"You too, handsome," I smiled.

THE ONE THING that surprised me, after the hiccup with Jim, was that I didn't have nightmares. I thought I would. People told me I would, but they never showed. I still woke in the middle of the night, but for a different reason, and it had a lot to do with Fox. Not only because he was curled tightly around me every night, but when I did wake, it was from words of love sweeping through my mind, chasing away any bad thoughts or dreams...*You have my heart to take care of, Ivy Morrison. I need you, so don't go gettin' any ideas, woman. I need you because you're my other half. You stay with me.*

You see, even in my dreams, my biker man protected me.

SNEAK PEEK — BLACK OUT

HAWKS MC BALLARAT CHARTER #3

CHAPTER ONE

CLARINDA

Three weeks of hearing his voice and I was addicted. While my sister was busy doing whatever she had to do every Saturday for the past three weeks for her realty work, she dropped me off at a café so I wouldn't get in her way and annoy her.

So for those three Saturdays, I had my ears glued to the door of that café, waiting for him to walk in and order his tall cappuccino. His voice was deep, rough and warming. His scent filled the room and made me want to wear leather and drink the men's cologne Joop, so that I could have it surrounding me all the time.

Sex.

That word never really crossed my mind. Mainly because my first and *only* time was not worth remembering. I had been eighteen when I met *the unnameable,* and he had swooned his way into my life. I thought he was the one. He showered me with gifts and sweet words.

Until I gave him my virginity.

As soon as he'd donned the condom, stuck it in me—and Jesus, it had hurt so much, I was ready to punch the uncaring idiot in the throat— he'd thrust three times and grunted in my ear. The next day when I rang him, he said he didn't want to hang, that I was a lousy lay.

So anyone could understand why sex, lust or making love never crossed my mind.

Until him, the stranger in the café.

It sounded strange; I knew it did. I wasn't usually a stalker type of person, but it was a small enjoyment in my troubled life, and it wasn't harming anyone in return.

So yet another Saturday, and I found myself sitting in that café drinking a coffee and nibbling on a blueberry muffin, while I waited to get my pleasure for the day of hearing his voice.

The bell over the café door rang, heavy footsteps coming in and walking toward the front counter. I knew this with relative ease because every time I walked in, I'd counted the number of steps it took me to get to the counter to make my order. I'd also counted them to my usual table, the table my sister had shown me to on the very first time I had come here. She knew my counting game, so at least she knew from then on, I could make it in and to my seat without embarrassing myself.

I was sitting off to the left of the front counter, taking in a deep breath, and his manly scent soon filled my senses once again. I had to take my fill before he walked out like he always did.

What was funny was I'd never felt the need to do it with any other customer. I hadn't cared to. Still, when he walked in that first time, there was something about the way he walked, the way he talked and the way the room had quieted and people took notice of him.

It left me wanting to know him.

However, that was something I'd never have a chance of obtaining, especially when no one took notice of me these days.

My appearance was less than to be desired. My clothes were baggy and big, while my red hair was a mess, and I wore no makeup, and sunglasses sat on my nose.

His order was called. I heard him say a rumble of a 'Thank you' and then I waited for his retreating footsteps, back to the front door.

Only, for the first time, he didn't.

He wasn't walking out of the café; he was staying. I could tell when I heard his pounding footsteps coming my way. I smiled a little because I knew I'd appreciate taking in his wonderful masculine scent a little longer.

"Hey, sugar, mind if I sit here?" he asked.

My lips pulled between my teeth. Was he talking to me? Was the place that full we'd have to share a table?

I tipped my head in his direction and said quietly, in case he wasn't talking to me, and I was about to make a fool out of myself, "I don't mind."

It's days like this I wish I could see. But I couldn't. My eyesight had been perfect until five years before, four days after my nineteenth birthday. After one tragic night—the night my older sister and I lost our parents.

On that horrid night, I ended up in a coma for a month, and when I woke, I could no longer see properly. My sister explained to me, once released from the hospital that my visual impairment was caused by carbon monoxide poisoning from being in the fire. That and the loss was a result of emotional trauma from witnessing my parents burn to death. They'd been stuck behind a locked door and couldn't escape.

The pain from the loss of my parents hurt more than any side effect or injury. Five years, and I was still feeling that loss deep inside.

It was lucky my sister hadn't been there that dreadful night, or she also would be waking every night from the same nightmares still haunting me.

The chair opposite me grated across the floor as he pulled it out and set something on the table in front of him.

Sounds were my best friend these days.

"Three weeks," he stated.

"I'm sorry?" I uttered.

"Three weeks, baby. Three weeks I've been coming here every Saturday, waiting for you to come to me to make a move. But you never have, so I thought I would."

My eyes widened behind my glasses, my mouth ajar. He had shocked me to silence as my heart went haywire behind my loose tee.

"I s'pose I should be the one to introduce myself, now that I'm finally fuckin' here in front of you."

Quickly closing my gaping mouth, I brought my bottom lip between my teeth and bit down once again. I couldn't answer; so instead, I nodded.

"Name's Blue Skies."

A small smile tugged at my lips as I held back the inappropriate giggle. What were his parents thinking at the time they named him? I cleared my throat and whispered like it was a secret, "I'm Clarinda."

"Clarinda... Clary. I like it." I could hear the smile in his voice, and for some reason, it had me blushing. "Seems it's our first date, so I guess we should tell each other about us."

My head went back a little, again, shocked at his statement. So shocked, in fact, I laughed. "Are you sure you have the right person?" I asked after I controlled my laughter.

"Yes."

Puzzled, I asked, "How?"

"Because I have had my eyes on you for three damn Saturdays, waiting to catch your eye, waiting for you to get the courage to come talk to me, but you haven't. So now, we do this my way."

"Your way?" I asked in a whisper.

"Yeah, sugar," he said softly, "my way."

Licking my suddenly dry lips, I then said, "You sure are..."

"Cocky? Great with words? Smart? Handsome?"

Smiling, I shook my head. "I wouldn't know. I can't see," I told him and removed my sunglasses, blinking in his direction.

He hissed, "Your eyes are damn beautiful like that."

My eyes widened, *yet again*. This man in front of me sure knew how to make an impression. I wasn't sure if I liked it. All right, I did. I guess I was more confused over why the man was saying those words to me.

Three weeks. His words rippled through my mind again.

Three weeks I've been coming here every Saturday, waiting for you to come to me to make your move.

How was it...*he* possible? Was I dreaming?

Light footsteps approached our table, and a woman cleared her throat. "Hey, handsome."

Blue interrupted her to say to me, "See? I told you." I giggled. "What can I do for you, sweetheart?"

I snorted. Oh, God, he was a charmer to every lady.

"I have to go, but I just wanted to give you this," the woman said.

This was embarrassing; I just knew she was passing him her number. Even a strange woman could see it was weird Blue was sitting with me.

Actually, that was reality, and it just smacked me in the face.

I stood up and said, "I'm leaving, as well. Why don't you take my seat?"

"No," Blue growled. "Sugar, sit your arse down. We're talking. And woman, you need to go. I don't want your number...ever." He sounded disgusted; I was surprised.

Quietly feeling my way back into my seat, I sat across from him. The woman huffed and puffed, and then I listened to her retreating footsteps.

I wondered if he got that a lot. If many women picked him up wherever he went. It also made me want to know what he looked like, especially if that sort of thing *did* happen a lot.

"Stupid woman," Blue grumbled.

"I'm sure you could still chase her," I giggled.

"You, shut it," he said with a smile in his voice. "Now, tell me about Clary."

I shrugged; it was the weirdest situation I had ever been in. No man had ever approached me before. "There isn't much to say."

"What do you like to do?" he asked.

"Read—I mean, listen to audiobooks." I smiled. "What do *you* like to do, Blue?"

"I'd fuckin' love to know—" His phone rang, cutting him off. "Christ," he swore and answered it with a gruff, "What? Shit. Yeah, all right, I'm comin'." I heard him shut his phone and slam it to the table. "I have to go."

"That's okay."

"No, it ain't."

Without thinking, I uttered, "You're right. It isn't."

He groaned. "Shit, now I don't wanna leave, but if I don't, we won't get this car out, and the dick fucked it up even more." His chair was shifted back, meaning he stood. A finger trailed down my cheek. "Will you be here next Saturday?"

"I think so."

"I'll see you then, sugar."

The following Saturday, my sister dropped me off. When I walked to the counter, the guy behind it said, "I have a message for you. Blue's sorry he can't make it, but he hopes you'll try to come back Monday and he'll be here." I smiled wide and nodded my thanks.

Since I was at the café, I still had to sit and wait for my sister, so I ordered an iced coffee and blueberry muffin.

Even though I knew he wasn't coming, my heart still thumped

hard every time the front door opened. Once my sister turned up, I was relieved; my poor heart needed the break. She led me out to the car and told me to get in.

"How was your day?" I asked Amy.

"Fine. Look, I'm not in the mood to chit-chat, just…zip it, okay?"

Sighing quietly so she wouldn't get upset by it, I nodded. I sat back in my seat, thought of a certain man and contemplated how I was going to make it there on Monday.

I waited until the next day before I spoke to my sister. Amy was sitting in the living room.

I made my way from my room down the hall, with my hands on the walls to guide me. In the living room, I counted the five steps to the couch; only I didn't get there.

Instead, I tripped and fell to the carpeted floor on my hands and knees.

"What are you doing?" Amy yelled.

"Sorry, I um… tripped." I felt around on the floor to see what had been laying there to trip me, but my hands ran over nothing but the carpet.

"There's nothing there. Get up," Amy snapped. I did, and I reached out to the couch and climbed from my knees to sit on it. "Was there something you wanted? Usually, you stay in your room."

Nodding, I asked, "I was hoping you could take me to the café on Monday."

"Why?" she huffed.

"I… um, I have to meet someone there."

"I'll see, okay? I have a lot to do to keep us fed and a roof over our heads."

She'd said that to me many times. I'd questioned her about it on a few occasions because I was sure our parents would have helped provide for us after their deaths. Not that I would want it, but since I was disabled, we needed it even more. Our parents were well off, so every time Amy would hiss back, 'They never left enough for all *your* hospital bills,' I never could understand that.

I knew I was a burden to her, so I nodded and said, "Okay, Amy," even though everything inside me told me to fight with her, to demand she take me because God knew I didn't ask for much. Still, I said no more, knowing one day, I would have to get out from under my sister and learn to live again.

Monday came and went. Amy said she was too busy to take me, and when I suggested a taxi, she yelled at me for wanting to waste our money on something so unnecessary. I felt terrible that I couldn't inform Blue I wouldn't be there like he had me. We didn't have a home phone; the only phone we had was Amy's mobile, and she had taken that with her.

If I had a friend, I would have called one, but they all soon disappeared after the accident.

I could only hope he would be there on Saturday and would understand my situation.

Wednesday night, Amy came home from work and told me to get on a warmer coat because she needed to go food shopping. She only liked me to come so I could push the trolley. She hated doing it and laughed if I crashed into anything.

At the supermarket, I trolled along slowly while Amy took off ahead. Thankfully, the place was lit bright enough for me to see her shadowed, blurred form in front of me.

"Rinda, stay there. I'm just going to grab some stuff. You're going too slowly. I'll be quicker on my own." There was no point saying anything; her footsteps were already departing the aisle.

I felt awkward just standing there, so I turned to the shelves and pretended to look at what was in front of me. I didn't know how long I had been standing there, but suddenly, there was heat at my back and a whisper in my ear, "Why are you searching the condoms, sugar?"

No, God no. Blue was right behind me, and apparently, I was looking at condoms.

"Um," was all I could say.

"Were you thinkin' of buying them for me?"

Oh, my God!

Again, my reply was, "Um,"

He chuckled deeply.

"I'm only teasin', baby," he uttered against my neck, and I swear he drew in a deep breath.

With his hands on my hips, he turned me. I looked up his blurred form toward his head and smiled shyly, knowing there was heat in my cheeks.

"Where were you Monday, Clary?" he asked, his hands still on my hips, making it hard for me to concentrate.

"Um, I-I'm sorry, Blue. I couldn't make it, and I had no way of telling you."

"Sugar, I'm gonna tell you straight up. I wanna see more of you. You willin' for that to happen?"

"Yes," I responded immediately. Hell, did that sound too keen?

"Best fuckin' word. What's your number? I gotta jet, but I need your number, baby."

I rattled off my sister's mobile and then added, "It was nice seeing you."

"You, too. Fuck, you, too. Take care, sugar, and we'll talk soon, yeah?"

"Yes." I smiled.

Later that night, I ended up telling my sister all about Blue. I think she could tell how excited I was when I talked about him, but I got nothing from her other than, "We'll see if he rings. Not many men would want such a burden in their life, Rinda. I hope you know that."

Deflated, I went back to my room, hoping Blue would prove my sister wrong.

Chapter Two

ONE MONTH LATER

CLARINDA

I was sitting in the passenger seat of the car, waiting for my sister while she ran an errand. It was a month after I saw Blue at the supermarket. He hadn't called, so I guessed my sister had been right. He hadn't even shown the times I went to the café again. Why did he act as though he liked me enough to call? Had I said something that night in the supermarket to change it? No, I couldn't have; he was the one who asked me for my number. I shook my head, attempting to shake the thoughts away.

The sun was shining brightly in the car that late afternoon, so I wound down my window to let the breeze through. The sounds of the outside world grew louder with vehicles driving near our parking spot at the side of the road. People walked up and down the pathway beside the car. I only wished I could see it. Unfortunately, like always, my eyes only managed a shadowy outline of things.

I tilted my head toward the breeze more and saw an outline of a building. What that building was, I had no clue.

Soon, I found myself blinking away tears as I thought of my most recent doctor's appointment, which I had just the day before. Even though I had been seeing that doctor for nearly four years, I still felt uncomfortable around him. His touch left me feeling dirty for some reason. Though, my sister swore he was the best in town and was the perfect doctor to try and help us fix my eyes.

Three years later, and I was still waiting for the right answer.

His words from yesterday ran through my mind. *You're coming along fine, Clarinda. Just give it time.*

Time was all I had.

Amy still refused to let me work, to let me do anything, really. If I tried, we ended up in an argument. I was born an independent yet shy woman, and I was sick of relying on my sister for help. I was twenty-four, for god's sake.

I shifted in my seat, so my head was closer to the window and wondered why my sister was taking so long. She said she'd only be a moment.

"What the fuck are you looking at?" I heard yelled in a harsh voice from somewhere close.

Ignoring it, I went back to blinking at nothing until a dark form loomed in front of me. I jumped, hitting my head on the car roof.

"I said, what the fuck are you looking at, bitch?" A shadow of a manly-shaped hand reached in and gripped my hair, pulling my head toward the window.

"Please, please," I begged. "I wasn't staring at anything."

"You wanna be up in my business, watching what went down? I'll give you a better taste of it, slut." He shook my head roughly with the hand still in my hair.

I reached up with both hands and grabbed his wrist, trying to pull free. "I didn't see anything. I *can't* see anything. Please, I'm blind. You've got it wrong."

"Bullshit. I don't give a fuck either way." He jerked my head again, and it banged into the top of the window frame. His stinking, hot breath blew against my face as he leaned closer. "You are a looker. I think a lesson needs to be learned."

"No!" I yelled. "Please." My body shook with fright.

My hands sweated and my heart leaped from the thought of what could happen. *Amy, please hurry, please!*

"Shut the fuck up," he hissed. Suddenly, my hair was freed, and I flopped back ungracefully. My hands felt for the seat as I straightened myself.

What now? Dread filled my stomach. I didn't know what was going on, why all of a sudden he was silent, but then came the sound of my door being opened, causing me to jump. I threw my arms out in front of me, waving them around.

"No, please!" I cried.

A hand clamped around my thigh, his grip painful. "Come on, bitch. Take off your pants and spread 'em." He tugged on my sweatpants. My hands fought his hold.

"Stop, no. Stop. Amy!" I yelled.

He kept swatting my hands away and grumbling about something under his breath.

Then I heard another manly call, and then a thumping sound. The hands which were on me fell away.

"Leave her alone, Henry," the new person growled.

"Fuck off, Blue. This is none of your business."

Blue?

"I think it is. The lady doesn't want to be touched. If you don't back the hell off, I'll make you."

"Shit, she wasn't worth it anyway," the first man grumbled.

Silence, and then retreating footsteps. With shaking hands, I felt for the door to close it, but my hands came against a hard, warm wall. Bouncing back in my seat, I retracted them quickly.

"You all right, sugar?" my saviour asked.

Blue. Oh, God, it *was* Blue.

I nodded. Clenching my trembling hands, I whispered, "Yes." I was still tense, unsure if I was completely safe.

The thump of my door closing had me jumping once again. "He won't bother you again. You waitin' on someone?"

"My sister," I whispered.

Does he not remember me?

My heart plummeted. Maybe he didn't want to recognise me. That could be why he didn't call. I never left a good enough impression on him for him to care.

"Why didn't you call me?" I bravely asked through the silence.

"I did, Clarinda. I was told you didn't want anything to do with me."

499

My eyes widened. "No… I-I'd never say that, Blue."

"Fuck. Your sister…."

My heart pounded into my throat as the driver's side door opened beside me. I turned to it as my sister spat, "What have you done now, Clarinda?"

Tears pooled in my eyes. The adrenaline rush I had started to wear off. "Nothing, Amy. This…." I gestured with my hand in the general direction of the man I had thought of so frequently, "….is Blue. Um, I've talked about him. He, ah, just now helped me. Someone tried to attack me."

She snorted. "You probably brought it on yourself."

"She didn't," Blue clipped. My heart warmed.

"Whatever," Amy responded and started the car.

"You going to be okay?" he asked.

I nodded and looked toward the window. "I think so." I reached my hand out. He must have sensed I was having trouble finding him, so he placed his hand in mine. I squeezed it, my heart beat faster from the warmth and thrill of touching him. "Thank you," I whispered. "Can… would you meet me at the café? I'll be there next Saturday."

"I'll be there, sugar. Count on it." I could hear the smile in his voice. It had my cheeks heating and an urgent need to actually see him. I desperately wished to know what he looked like, what he felt like under my touch. I'd lay awake countless nights debating the colour of his eyes, not knowing if they were light or dark. While I'd heard his smile when he spoke, I was eager to see it and half-expected to find a dimple. Regardless of what he would look like to the outside world, none of it really mattered. His voice alone held me captive. As long as a man was kind to his woman like my father was to my mother, nothing else mattered.

"Hand in the car. We've got to go," Amy said.

I hadn't realised I was still gripping Blue's hand, but once I let go, I felt the warmth from his hold disappear. The reality of what happened slipped into my mind, and the smile fell from my face.

Before I could say any more to Blue, Amy put the car into drive and took off.

I wanted her to turn the car around so I could find that warmth again, find the safety I felt around a man I hardly knew. I curled my arms around my waist, leaned my head back and closed my eyes thinking of the sweet yet hard, delicious tone of Blue's voice and found some comfort from it.

"What were you thinking, talking to a stranger?"

Sighing, I turned my head toward my sister. "He's not a stranger, Amy. He did help me." I shuddered at the thought of that dirty man touching me. "A man was attacking me."

"Well, what did you do for that to happen?"

"Nothing," I uttered.

"See, this is why you need me around all the time. You keep getting into trouble, and in the end, *I* keep having to save you."

Only that time, it wasn't her.

However, she was right. Over the past six months, I'd had many little accidents, and Amy had always been there for me. I had to admit—if Blue hadn't shown up, at least I knew my sister would have. She was always there.

Though, the accident which had just occurred was the worst I'd ever had... if I could call it an accident. The others before that were small incidents—a trip, a burn, stubbing my toe—and I'd been abused verbally many times on the street.

Still, it all gave me enough pause to think about how I would be lost without Amy. It actually made me sick to my stomach at the thought of fending for myself while in my condition. Yes, we annoyed each other, and yes, she could be downright mean, but she changed her ways to fit me into her life when I was nineteen and she was twenty-two. Without her, I wouldn't have had much of a life at all.

Okay, that wasn't entirely true.

People who were completely blind and saw nothing but blackness still coped. They used their other senses or had the help of guide dogs. There were many possibilities. I'd even suggested all those things to my sister at the start, told her I wanted to live on my own and learn to live with my disability. She wouldn't have it.

After what happened a few moments before, I wasn't sure I was ready to do any of that anymore.

I was scared something like that could happen again.

What would I do if I was on my own, walking down the street, and I didn't know someone was following me? I could turn a wrong corner and be trapped. I could witness something I never knew I was observing and be in a mess like I was earlier. So many things could happen. It was hard being with my sister all the time, but the thought of being without her scared me more.

At least I had my daily outings to the library while Amy worked. Those I really enjoyed, especially since I hardly sat on my own anymore. Not that it bothered me to sit on my own; at least I was able to listen to so many wonderful stories. Until, that was, Julian decided he had to know me. That had been about four months before. From that day forward, I would get several visits in the library from him.

He made me laugh, he made me smile, and the world seemed that much brighter with him around in it.

I also met his friend, Deanna, who works there. That had only been in the past two months, and still, we hadn't encouraged each other to talk openly. I was slowly warming up to her, but it was hard because of how snappy and annoyed she seemed to be all the time. The customers usually got a reprieve from her mouth, but if she came over to the table to grumble about something, look out. I had never in my twenty-four years heard a woman swear so much in my life. What was comical about it, though, was when Julian would bait her, she'd get frustrated and tell him where to go…explicitly. Julian didn't care. I loved to hear their interactions. Anyone could tell the 'family love' they had for each other.

At least I have someone *who's happy to see me.*

I turned my head toward Amy as she drove. Knowing my sister, her brows would be drawn, her jaw would be clenched, and her hands would be tight around the steering wheel. She was annoyed by me, for the attention I received but didn't want. I was her embarrassment.

Why had she told Blue I didn't want anything to do with him when he called? Was she jealous? Or maybe she just didn't want to see me hurt?

I wasn't sure, and I didn't want to ask. It would just end in a fight.

Everything was so confusing. One moment, I wanted to be independent and try to make Amy see I could do things for myself, and then the next, I found myself scared of what it would be like without her.

Confusion didn't accurately describe the chaos of my emotions.

I wanted to fight back and have my independence, and I wanted my sister to treat me with respect instead of a piece of poo under her shoe...then again, I was scared of so many things, which was why I clammed up so many times and said nothing, even though I regretted it every time.

However, what I *was* confident about was that Amy wasn't simply annoyed at me; rather, she truly hated me.

That hurt more than what the foul-breathed man tried to do to me.

My sister, my own family, hated me because I was useless. At least, that was how I felt.

ALSO BY LILA ROSE

Hawks MC: Ballarat Charter

Holding Out (FREE) Zara and Talon

Climbing Out: Griz and Deanna

Finding Out (novella) Killer and Ivy

Black Out: Blue and Clarinda

No Way Out: Stoke and Malinda

Coming Out (novella) Mattie and Julia

Hawks MC: Caroline Springs Charter

The Secret's Out: Pick, Billy and Josie

Hiding Out: Dodge and Willow

Down and Out: Dive and Mena

Living Without: Vicious and Nary

Walkout (novella) Dallas and Melissa

Hear Me Out: Beast and Knife

Breakout (novella) Handle and Della

Fallout: Fang and Poppy

Standalones related to the Hawks MC

Out of the Blue (Lan, Easton, and Parker's story)

Romantic comedies

Making Changes

Making Sense

Fumbled Love

Trinity Love Series

Left to Chance

Love of Liberty (novella)

Paranormal

Death (with Justine Littleton)

In The Dark

CONNECT WITH THE AUTHOR

Webpage: www.lilarosebooks.com
Facebook: http://bit.ly/2du0taO
Instagram: www.instagram.com/lilarose78/
Goodreads:
www.goodreads.com/author/show/7236200.Lila_Rose

CPSIA information can be obtained
at www.ICGtesting.com
Printed in the USA
LVHW050833200122
708837LV00011B/812

9 780648 481621